THE FACE

MARY ELIZABETH BRADDON

THE FACE IN THE GLASS

AND OTHER GOTHIC TALES

MARY ELIZABETH BRADDON

THE BRITISH LIBRARY

This collection first published in 2014 by
The British Library
96 Euston Road
London NW1 2DB

Cataloguing in publication data
A catalogue record for this book is available from the British Library

ISBN 978 0 7123 5751 7

Typeset by IDSUK (DataConnection) Ltd
Printed in England by TJ International

CONTENTS

Introduction

If you have heard of Mary Elizabeth Braddon (1835–1915) then the chances are you know her as the author of *Lady Audley's Secret* (1862), one of the first and best of the 'sensation novels' so popular with the Victorian reading public during the 1860s. With its blonde, blue-eyed, seemingly angelic but (in reality) utterly scheming anti-heroine, Lucy Graham, and its labyrinthine plot involving bigamy, deception and attempted murder, *Lady Audley's Secret* combined the criminal with the domestic, and deservedly joined Wilkie Collins's *The Woman in White* (1859–60) and Ellen Wood's *East Lynne* (1861) as one of the three most influential novels in the emerging genre of sensation fiction.

Undeniably excellent though *Lady Audley's Secret* is, the novel's enduring popularity has undoubtedly overshadowed the rest of Braddon's considerable output, especially for a modern audience. While some of her other books have begun to creep back into print—*Aurora Floyd* (1863) for example, complete with its notorious scene in which the heroine whips a stableman with considerable passion and vigour—the vast majority of Braddon's work remains in the shadows. In particular, her tales of the macabre and the supernatural have been neglected for far too long—a situation which, given the popularity of the Victorian ghost story and Braddon's excellence as a storyteller, is surprising. The Victorian era witnessed the ghost story reach new heights of invention. Gaslight, séances, spirit photography, the ghostly taps from telegraph machines and the birth of psychoanalysis in which the 'ghosts' lurked within the mind, rather than in the external world, all contributed to the Victorian fascination with the supernatural. Authors such as Charles Dickens, Elizabeth Gaskell, Henry James and Oscar Wilde produced fine tales of the uncanny but, even in such a distinguished field, Braddon's ghost stories stand out as brilliant examples of sustained atmosphere and unease.

Mary Elizabeth Braddon's life was defined by creativity and industry tinged with scandal. She wrote some eighty novels and edited several magazines and periodicals. In 1861, however, she became romantically involved with the publisher John Maxwell, and notoriety ensued. Maxwell was already married, with five children, and his wife Mary Ann Crowley Maxwell was still very much alive, although confined to an asylum in Dublin. The difficulties of Braddon's real-life situation—living openly with a man already married to someone else—found expression in her fiction. In particular, her free-spirited heroines take some of their feistiness and passion from her own experiences as a woman running against convention. Braddon's fiction, including many of the supernatural tales reprinted here, featured women railing against the strictures of Victorian (and distinctly male) opinion by following their own desires regardless of the cost. Braddon was at the forefront not only of the sensation genre, but also at the heart of critiquing Victorian gender and social stereotypes.

The selection of stories presented here provides a taste of Braddon's brilliance with the supernatural tale. The stories run through a terrific range and variety. Some feature visitations from beyond the grave in the pursuit of either love or revenge. There are haunted houses and mirrors that reflect something other than a straightforward representation of reality. There is a mysterious island seemingly populated by the dead, and a story featuring a vampire with a clinically scientific method of drawing the blood from her victims. There is a strange story of a lion tamer, untroubled by his performing lions but profoundly disturbed by a particular visitor to his acts; and a morality tale in which the spirit of a selfish man initially flies towards Heaven, only to be cast back towards a very different destination.

Braddon, as these tales show, had a gift for evoking atmosphere; a knack for creating engaging characters; and an ability to induce that delicious sensation of something being 'not quite right'.

On occasion Braddon's stories also contain eerie echoes of other Gothic tales. 'My Wife's Promise' (1868) with its Arctic setting is reminiscent of certain snow-bound passages in Mary Shelley's *Frankenstein* (1818), while 'Herself' (1894), with its evocation of warmth, sun-drenched olive trees and cypresses, is similar to the setting of Robert Louis Stevenson's vampire tale 'Olalla' (1885). The secret contained in the chill room hidden from the sun in 'Herself' is in some ways similar to the secret hidden in

Dorian Gray's attic from Oscar Wilde's famous novel, although arguably even more disturbing. 'The Cold Embrace' (1860), meanwhile, with its portrayal of a love that will not lie still in its grave, is so disturbing that it sounds like something by Edgar Allan Poe.

All of the stories in this collection show Braddon's gift for crafting haunting atmospheres. Some of the tales have been almost completely lost from sight, and I am particularly grateful to Dr Janine Hatter, Honorary Research Associate at the University of Hull, for bringing two of the tales republished here—'Three Times' and 'The Higher Life'—to my attention. Presented in chronological order, the stories also highlight Braddon's development as a writer, ranging from the youthful vitality of, for example, 'Eveline's Visitant' (1867) to the melancholy 'Her Last Appearance' (1876)—a tale which draws heavily upon Braddon's own career on the stage—through to the measured, complex horrors of 'Herself'. By turns disturbing, dramatic, unexpected and inventive, Mary Elizabeth Braddon's Gothic tales and supernatural chillers deserve to find a new audience and a place back in the limelight they so richly deserve.

Greg Buzwell
Curator, Printed Literary Sources, British Library

The Cold Embrace

HE WAS AN artist—such things as happened to him happen sometimes to artists.

He was a German—such things as happened to him happen sometimes to Germans.

He was young, handsome, studious, enthusiastic, metaphysical, reckless, unbelieving, heartless.

And being young, handsome, and eloquent, he was beloved.

He was an orphan, under the guardianship of his dead father's brother, his uncle Wilhelm, in whose house he had been brought up from a little child; and she who loved him was his cousin—his cousin Gertrude, whom he swore he loved in return.

Did he love her? Yes, when he first swore it. It soon wore out, this passionate love; how threadbare and wretched a sentiment it became at last in the selfish heart of the student! But in its first golden dawn, when he was only nineteen, and had just returned from his apprenticeship to a great painter at Antwerp, and they wandered together in the most romantic outskirts of the city at rosy sunset, by holy moonlight, or bright and joyous morning, how beautiful a dream!

They keep it a secret from Wilhelm, as he has the father's ambition of a wealthy suitor for his only child—a cold and dreary vision beside the lover's dream.

So they are betrothed; and standing side by side when the dying sun and the pale rising moon divide the heavens, he puts the betrothal ring upon her finger, the white and taper finger whose slender shape he knows so well. This ring is a peculiar one, a massive golden serpent, its tail in its mouth, the symbol of eternity; it had been his mother's, and he would know it amongst a thousand. If he were to become blind tomorrow, he could select it from amongst a thousand by the touch alone.

He places it on her finger, and they swear to be true to each other for ever and ever—through trouble and danger—sorrow and change—in wealth or poverty. Her father must needs be won to consent to their union by-and-by, for they were now betrothed, and death alone could part them.

But the young student, the scoffer at revelation, yet the enthusiastic adorer of the mystical asks:

'Can death part us? I would return to you from the grave, Gertrude. My soul would come back to be near my love. And you—you, if you died before me—the cold earth would not hold you from me; if you loved me, you would return, and again these fair arms would be clasped round my neck as they are now.'

But she told him, with a holier light in her deep-blue eyes than had ever shone in his—she told him that the dead who die at peace with God are happy in heaven, and cannot return to the troubled earth; and that it is only the suicide—the lost wretch on whom sorrowful angels shut the door of paradise—whose unholy spirit haunts the footsteps of the living.

* * * * *

The first year of their betrothal is passed, and she is alone, for he has gone to Italy, on a commission for some rich man, to copy Raphaels, Titians, Guidos, in a gallery at Florence. He has gone to win fame, perhaps; but it is not the less bitter—he is gone!

Of course her father misses his young nephew, who has been as a son to him; and he thinks his daughter's sadness no more than a cousin should feel for a cousin's absence.

In the meantime, the weeks and months pass. The lover writes—often at first, then seldom—at last, not at all.

How many excuses she invents for him! How many times she goes to the distant little post-office, to which he is to address his letters! How many times she hopes, only to be disappointed! How many times she despairs, only to hope again!

But real despair comes at last, and will not be put off any more. The rich suitor appears on the scene, and her father is determined. She is to marry at once. The wedding-day is fixed—the fifteenth of June.

The date seems burnt into her brain.

The date, written in fire, dances for ever before her eyes.

The date, shrieked by the Furies, sounds continually in her ears.

But there is time yet—it is the middle of May—there is time for a letter to reach him at Florence; there is time for him to come to Brunswick, to take her away and marry her, in spite of her father—in spite of the whole world.

But the days and weeks fly by, and he does not write—he does not come. This is indeed despair which usurps her heart, and will not be put away.

It is the fourteenth of June. For the last time she goes to the little post-office; for the last time she asks the old question, and they give her for the last time the dreary answer, 'No, no letter.'

For the last time—for tomorrow is the day appointed for her bridal. Her father will hear no entreaties; her rich suitor will not listen to her prayers. They will not be put off a day—an hour, tonight alone is hers—this night, which she may employ as she will.

She takes another path than that which leads home; she hurries through some by-streets of the city, out on to a lonely bridge, where he and she had stood so often in the sunset, watching the rose-coloured light glow, fade, and die upon the river.

*   *   *   *   *

He returns from Florence. He had received her letter. That letter, blotted with tears, entreating, despairing—he had received it, but he loved her no longer. A young Florentine, who has sat to him for a model, had bewitched his fancy—that fancy which with him stood in place of a heart—and Gertrude had been half-forgotten. If she had a rich suitor, good; let her marry him; better for her, better far for himself. He had no wish to fetter himself with a wife. Had he not his art always?—his eternal bride, his unchanging mistress.

Thus he thought it wiser to delay his journey to Brunswick, so that he should arrive when the wedding was over—arrive in time to salute the bride.

And the vows—the mystical fancies—the belief in his return, even after death, to the embrace of his beloved? O, gone out of his life; melted away for ever, those foolish dreams of his boyhood.

So on the fifteenth of June he enters Brunswick, by that very bridge on which she stood, the stars looking down on her, the night before. He strolls across the bridge and down by the water's edge, a great rough dog at his heels, and the smoke from his short meerschaum pipe curling in blue wreaths fantastically in the pure morning air. He has his sketch-book under his arm, and attracted now and then by some object that catches his artist's eye, stops to draw: a few weeds and pebbles on the river's brink—a crag on the opposite shore—a group of pollard willows in the distance. When he has done, he admires his drawing, shuts his sketch-book, empties the ashes from his pipe, refills from his tobacco-pouch, sings the refrain of a gay drinking song, calls to his dog, smokes again, and walks on. Suddenly he opens his sketch-book again; this time that which attracts him is a group of figures: but what is it?

It is not a funeral, for there are no mourners.

It is not a funeral, but a corpse lying on a rough bier, covered with an old sail, carried between two bearers.

It is not a funeral, for the bearers are fishermen—fishermen in their everyday garb.

About a hundred yards from him they rest their burden on a bank—one stands at the head of the bier, the other throws himself down at the foot of it.

And thus they form a perfect group; he walks back two or three paces, selects his point of sight, and begins to sketch a hurried outline. He has finished it before they move; he hears their voices, though he cannot hear their words, and wonders what they can be talking of. Presently he walks on and joins them.

'You have a corpse there, my friends?' he says.

'Yes; a corpse washed ashore an hour ago.'

'Drowned?'

'Yes, drowned. A young girl, very handsome.'

'Suicides are always handsome,' says the painter, and then he stands for a little while idly smoking and meditating, looking at the sharp outline of the corpse and the stiff folds of the rough canvas covering.

Life is such a golden holiday for him—young, ambitious, clever—that it seems as though sorrow and death could have no part in his destiny.

At last he says that, as this poor suicide is so handsome, he should like to make a sketch of her.

He gives the fishermen some money, and they offer to remove the sail-cloth that covers her features.

No; he will do it himself. He lifts the rough, coarse, wet canvas from her face. What face?

The face that shone on the dreams of his foolish boyhood; the face which once was the light of his uncle's home. His cousin Gertrude—his betrothed!

He sees, as in one glance, while he draws one breath, the rigid features—the marble arms—the hands crossed on the cold bosom; and, on the third finger of the left hand, the ring which had been his mother's—the golden serpent; the ring which, if he were to become blind, he could select from a thousand others by the touch alone.

But he is a genius and a metaphysician—grief, true grief, is not for such as he. His first thought is flight—flight anywhere out of that accursed city—anywhere far from the brink of that hideous river—anywhere away from remorse—anywhere to forget.

*   *   *   *   *

He is miles on the road that leads away from Brunswick before he knows that he has walked a step.

It is only when his dog lies down panting at his feet that he feels how exhausted he is himself, and sits down upon a bank to rest. How the landscape spins round and round before his dazzled eyes, while his morning's sketch of the two fishermen and the canvas-covered bier glares redly at him out of the twilight!

At last, after sitting a long time by the roadside, idly playing with his dog, idly smoking, idly lounging, looking as any idle, light-hearted travelling student might look, yet all the while acting over that morning's scene in his burning brain a hundred times a minute; at last he grows a little more composed, and tries presently to think of himself as he is, apart from his cousin's suicide. Apart from that, he was no worse off than he was yesterday. His genius was not gone; the money he had earned at Florence still lined his pocket-book; he was his own master, free to go whither he would.

And while he sits on the roadside, trying to separate himself from the scene of that morning—trying to put away the image of the corpse covered with the damp canvas sail—trying to think of what he should do next, where he should go, to be farthest away from Brunswick and remorse, the old diligence comes rumbling and jingling along. He remembers it; it goes from Brunswick to Aix-la-Chapelle.

He whistles to his dog, shouts to the postilion to stop, and springs into the *coupé*.

During the whole evening, through the long night, though he does not once close his eyes, he never speaks a word; but when morning dawns, and the other passengers awake and begin to talk to each other, he joins in the conversation. He tells them that he is an artist, that he is going to Cologne and to Antwerp to copy Rubenses, and the great picture by Quentin Matsys, in the museum. He remembered afterwards that he talked and laughed boisterously, and that when he was talking and laughing loudest, a passenger, older and graver than the rest, opened the window near him, and told him to put his head out. He remembered the fresh air blowing in his face, the singing of the birds in his ears, and the flat fields and roadside reeling before his eyes. He remembered this, and then falling in a lifeless heap on the floor of the diligence.

It is a fever that keeps him for six long weeks on a bed at a hotel in Aix-la-Chapelle.

He gets well, and, accompanied by his dog, starts on foot for Cologne. By this time he is his former self once more. Again the blue smoke from his short meerschaum curls upwards in the morning air—again he sings some old university drinking-song—again stops here and there, meditating and sketching.

He is happy, and has forgotten his cousin—and so on to Cologne.

It is by the great cathedral he is standing, with his dog at his side. It is night, the bells have just chimed the hour, and the clocks are striking eleven; the moonlight shines full upon the magnificent pile, over which the artist's eye wanders, absorbed in the beauty of form.

He is not thinking of his drowned cousin, for he has forgotten her and is happy.

Suddenly some one, something from behind him, puts two cold arms round his neck, and clasps its hands on his breast.

And yet there is no one behind him, for on the flags bathed in the broad moonlight there are only two shadows, his own and his dog's. He turns quickly round—there is no one—nothing to be seen in the broad square but himself and his dog; and though he feels, he cannot see the cold arms clasped round his neck.

It is not ghostly, this embrace, for it is palpable to the touch—it cannot be real, for it is invisible.

He tries to throw off the cold caress. He clasps the hands in his own to tear them asunder, and to cast them off his neck. He can feel the long delicate fingers cold and wet beneath his touch, and on the third finger of the left hand he can feel the ring which was his mother's—the golden serpent—the ring which he has always said he would know among a thousand by the touch alone. He knows it now!

His dead cousin's cold arms are round his neck—his dead cousin's wet hands are clasped upon his breast. He asks himself if he is mad. 'Up, Leo!' he shouts. 'Up, up, boy!' and the Newfoundland leaps to his shoulders—the dog's paws are on the dead hands, and the animal utters a terrific howl, and springs away from his master.

The student stands in the moonlight, the dead arms around his neck, and the dog at a little distance moaning piteously.

Presently a watchman, alarmed by the howling of the dog, comes into the square to see what is wrong.

In a breath the cold arms are gone.

He takes the watchman home to the hotel with him and gives him money; in his gratitude he could have given that man half his little fortune.

Will it ever come to him again, this embrace of the dead?

He tries never to be alone; he makes a hundred acquaintances, and shares the chamber of another student. He starts up if he is left by himself in the public room at the inn where he is staying, and runs into the street. People notice his strange actions, and begin to think that he is mad.

But, in spite of all, he is alone once more; for one night the public room being empty for a moment, when on some idle pretence he strolls into the street, the street is empty too, and for the second time he feels the cold arms round his neck, and for the second time, when he calls his dog, the animal slinks away from him with a piteous howl.

After this he leaves Cologne, still travelling on foot—of necessity now, for his money is getting low. He joins travelling hawkers, he walks side by side with labourers, he talks to every foot-passenger he falls in with, and tries from morning till night to get company on the road.

At night he sleeps by the fire in the kitchen of the inn at which he stops; but do what he will, he is often alone, and it is now a common thing for him to feel the cold arms around his neck.

Many months have passed since his cousin's death—autumn, winter, early spring. His money is nearly gone, his health is utterly broken, he is the shadow of his former self, and he is getting near to Paris. He will reach that city at the time of the Carnival. To this he looks forward. In Paris, in Carnival time, he need never, surely, be alone, never feel that deadly caress; he may even recover his lost gaiety, his lost health, once more resume his profession, once more earn fame and money by his art.

How hard he tries to get over the distance that divides him from Paris, while day by day he grows weaker, and his step slower and more heavy!

But there is an end at last; the long dreary roads are passed. This is Paris, which he enters for the first time—Paris, of which he has dreamt so much—Paris, whose million voices are to exorcise his phantom.

To him tonight Paris seems one vast chaos of lights, music, and confusion—lights which dance before his eyes and will not be still—music that rings in his ears and deafens him—confusion which makes his head whirl round and round.

But, in spite of all, he finds the opera-house, where there is a masked ball. He has enough money left to buy a ticket of admission, and to hire a domino to throw over his shabby dress. It seems only a moment after his entering the gates of Paris that he is in the very midst of all the wild gaiety of the opera-house ball.

No more darkness, no more loneliness, but a mad crowd, shouting and dancing, and a lovely Débardeuse hanging on his arm.

The boisterous gaiety he feels surely is his old light-heartedness come back. He hears the people round him talking of the outrageous conduct of some drunken student, and it is to him they point when they say this—to him, who has not moistened his lips since yesterday at noon, for even now he will not drink; though his lips are parched, and his throat burning, he cannot drink. His voice is thick and hoarse, and his utterance indistinct; but still this must be his old light-heartedness come back that makes him so wildly gay.

The little Débardeuse is wearied out—her arm rests on his shoulder heavier than lead—the other dancers one by one drop off.

The lights in the chandeliers one by one die out.

The decorations look pale and shadowy in that dim light which is neither night nor day.

A faint glimmer from the dying lamps, a pale streak of cold grey light from the new-born day, creeping in through half-opened shutters.

And by this light the bright-eyed Débardeuse fades sadly. He looks her in the face. How the brightness of her eyes dies out! Again he looks her in the face. How white that face has grown! Again—and now it is the shadow of a face alone that looks in his.

Again—and they are gone—the bright eyes, the face, the shadow of the face. He is alone; alone in that vast saloon.

Alone, and, in the terrible silence, he hears the echoes of his own footsteps in that dismal dance which has no music.

No music but the beating of his breast. For the cold arms are round his neck—they whirl him round, they will not be flung off, or cast away; he can no more escape from their icy grasp than he can escape from death. He looks behind him—there is nothing but himself in the great empty *salle*; but he can feel—cold, deathlike, but O, how palpable!—the long slender fingers, and the ring which was his mother's.

He tries to shout, but he has no power in his burning throat. The silence of the place is only broken by the echoes of his own footsteps in the dance from which he cannot extricate himself. Who says he has no partner? The cold hands are clasped on his breast, and now he does not shun their caress. No! One more polka, if he drops down dead.

The lights are all out, and, half an hour after, the *gendarmes* come in with a lantern to see that the house is empty; they are followed by a great dog that they have found seated howling on the steps of the theatre. Near the principal entrance they stumble over——

The body of a student, who has died from want of food, exhaustion, and the breaking of a blood-vessel.

Eveline's Visitant

IT WAS AT a masked ball at the Palais Royal that my fatal quarrel with my first cousin André de Brissac began. The quarrel was about a woman. The women who followed the footsteps of Philip of Orleans were the causes of many such disputes; and there was scarcely one fair head in all that glittering throng which, to a man versed in social histories and mysteries, might not have seemed bedabbled with blood.

I shall not record the name of her for love of whom André de Brissac and I crossed one of the bridges, in the dim August dawn on our way to the waste ground beyond the church of Saint-Germain des Près.

There were many beautiful vipers in those days, and she was one of them. I can feel the chill breath of that August morning blowing in my face, as I sit in my dismal chamber at my château of Puy Verdun tonight, alone in the stillness, writing the strange story of my life. I can see the white mist rising from the river, the grim outline of the Châtelet, and the square towers of Notre Dame black against the pale-grey sky. Even more vividly can I recall André's fair young face, as he stood opposite to me with his two friends—scoundrels both, and alike eager for that unnatural fray. We were a strange group to be seen in a summer sunrise, all of us fresh from the heat and clamour of the Regent's saloons—André in a quaint hunting-dress copied from a family portrait at Puy Verdun, I costumed as one of Law's Mississippi Indians; the other men in like garish frippery, adorned with broideries and jewels that looked wan in the pale light of dawn.

Our quarrel had been a fierce one—a quarrel which could have but one result, and that the direst. I had struck him; and the welt raised by my open hand was crimson upon his fair, womanish face as he stood opposite to me. The eastern sun shone on the face presently, and dyed the cruel mark with a deeper red; but the sting of my own wrongs was fresh, and I had not yet learnt to despise myself for that brutal outrage. To André de Brissac such an insult was most terrible. He was the favourite of Fortune, the favourite of women; and I was nothing—a rough soldier who had done my country good service, but in the boudoir of a Parabère a mannerless boor.

We fought, and I wounded him mortally. Life had been very sweet for him; and I think that a frenzy of despair took possession of him when he felt the life-blood ebbing away. He beckoned me to him as he lay on the ground. I went, and knelt at his side.

'Forgive me, André!' I murmured.

He took no more heed of my words than if that piteous entreaty had been the idle ripple of the river near at hand.

'Listen to me, Hector de Brissac,' he said. 'I am not one who believes that a man has done with earth because his eyes glaze and his jaw stiffens. They will bury me in the old vault at Puy Verdun; and you will be master of the château. Ah, I know how lightly they take things in these days, and how Dubois will laugh when he hears that *Ca* has been killed in a duel. They will bury me, and sing masses for my soul; but you and I have not finished our affair yet, my cousin. I will be with you when you least look to see me—I, with this ugly scar upon the face that women have praised and loved. I will come to you when your life seems brightest. I will come between you and all that you hold fairest and dearest. My ghostly hand shall drop a poison in your cup of joy. My shadowy form shall shut the sunlight from your life. Men with such iron will as mine can do what they please, Hector de Brissac. It is my will to haunt you when I am dead.'

All this in short broken sentences he whispered into my ear. I had need to bend my ear close to his dying lips; but the iron will of André de Brissac was strong enough to do battle with Death, and I believe he said all he wished to say before his head fell back upon the velvet cloak they had spread beneath him, never to be lifted again.

As he lay there, you would have fancied him a fragile stripling, too fair and frail for the struggle called life; but there are those who remember the brief manhood of André de Brissac, and who can bear witness to the terrible force of that proud nature.

I stood looking down at the young face with that foul mark upon it, and God knows I was sorry for what I had done.

Of those blasphemous threats which he had whispered in my ear I took no heed. I was a soldier, and a believer. There was nothing absolutely dreadful to me in the thought that I had killed this man. I had killed many men on the battlefield; and this one had done me cruel wrong.

My friends would have had me cross the frontier to escape the consequences of my act; but I was ready to face those consequences, and I remained in France. I kept aloof from the court, and received a hint that I had best confine myself to my own province. Many masses were chanted in the little chapel of Puy Verdun for the soul of my dead cousin, and his coffin filled a niche in the vault of our ancestors.

His death had made me a rich man; and the thought that it was so made my newly acquired wealth very hateful to me. I lived a lonely existence in the old château, where I rarely held converse with any but the servants of the household, all of whom had served my cousin, and none of whom liked me.

It was a hard and bitter life. It galled me, when I rode through the village, to see the peasant children shrink away from me. I have seen old women cross themselves stealthily as I passed them by. Strange reports had gone forth about me; and there were those who whispered that I had given my soul to the Evil One as the price of my cousin's heritage. From my boyhood I had been dark of visage and stern of manner; and hence, perhaps, no woman's love had ever been mine. I remembered my mother's face in all its changes of expression; but I can remember no look of affection that ever shone on me. That other woman, beneath whose feet I laid my heart, was pleased to accept my homage, but she never loved me; and the end was treachery.

I had grown hateful to myself, and had well-nigh begun to hate my fellow-creatures, when a feverish desire seized upon me, and I pined to be back in the press and throng of the busy world once again. I went back to Paris, where I kept myself aloof from the court, and where an angel took compassion upon me.

She was the daughter of an old comrade, a man whose merits had been neglected, whose achievements had been ignored, and who sulked in his shabby lodging like a rat in a hole, while all Paris went mad with the Scotch Financier, and gentlemen and lackeys were trampling one another to death in the Rue Quincampoix. The only child of this little cross-grained old captain of dragoons was an incarnate sunbeam, whose mortal name was Eveline Duchalet.

She loved me. The richest blessings of our lives are often those which cost us least. I wasted the best years of my youth in the worship of a wicked woman, who jilted and cheated me at last. I gave this meek angel but a few courteous words—a little fraternal tenderness—and lo, she loved me. The life which had been so dark and desolate grew bright beneath her influence; and I went back to Puy Verdun with a fair young bride for my companion.

Ah, how sweet a change there was in my life and in my home! The village children no longer shrank appalled as the dark horseman rode by, the village crones no longer crossed themselves; for a woman rode by his side—a woman whose charities had won the love of all those ignorant creatures, and whose companionship had transformed the gloomy lord of the château into a loving husband and a gentle master. The old retainers forgot the untimely fate of my cousin, and served me with cordial willingness, for love of their young mistress.

There are no words which can tell the pure and perfect happiness of that time. I felt like a traveller who had traversed the frozen seas of an arctic region, remote from human love or human companionship, to find himself on a sudden in the bosom of a verdant valley, in the sweet atmosphere of home. The change seemed too bright to be real; and I strove in vain to put away from my mind the vague suspicion that my new life was but some fantastic dream.

So brief were those halcyon hours, that, looking back on them now, it is scarcely strange if I am still half inclined to fancy the first days of my married life could have been no more than a dream.

Neither in my days of gloom nor in my days of happiness had I been troubled by the recollection of André's blasphemous oath. The words which with his last breath he had whispered in my ear were vain and meaningless to me. He had vented his rage in those idle threats, as he might have vented it in idle execrations. That he will haunt the footsteps of his enemy after death is the one revenge which a dying man can promise himself; and if men had power thus to avenge themselves the earth would be peopled with phantoms.

I had lived for three years at Puy Verdun; sitting alone in the solemn midnight by the hearth where he had sat, pacing the corridors that had echoed his footfall; and in all that time my fancy had never so played me false as to shape the shadow of the dead. Is it strange, then, if I had forgotten André's horrible promise?

* * * * *

There was no portrait of my cousin at Puy Verdun. It was the age of boudoir art, and a miniature set in the lid of a gold *bonbonnière*, or hidden artfully in a massive bracelet, was more fashionable than a clumsy life-size image, fit only to hang on the gloomy walls of a provincial château rarely visited by its owner. My cousin's fair face had adorned more than one *bonbonnière*, and had been concealed in more than one bracelet; but it was not among the faces that looked down from the panelled walls of Puy Verdun.

In the library I found a picture which awoke painful associations. It was the portrait of a de Brissac, who had flourished in the time of Francis the First; and it was from this picture that my cousin André had copied the quaint hunting-dress he wore at the Regent's ball. The library was a room in which I spent a good deal of my life; and I ordered a curtain to be hung before this picture.

* * * * *

We had been married three months, when Eveline one day asked: 'Who is the lord of the château nearest to this?'

I looked at her in astonishment.

'My dearest,' I answered, 'do you not know that there is no other château within forty miles of Puy Verdun?'

'Indeed!' she said. 'That is strange.'

I asked her why the fact seemed strange to her; and after much entreaty I obtained from her the reason of her surprise.

In her walks about the park and woods during the last month she had met a man who, by his dress and bearing, was obviously of noble rank. She had imagined that he occupied some château near at hand, and that his estate adjoined ours. I was at a loss to imagine who this stranger could be; for my estate of Puy Verdun lay in the heart of a desolate region, and unless when some traveller's coach went lumbering and jingling through the village, one had little more chance of encountering a gentleman than of meeting a demigod.

'Have you seen this man often, Eveline?' I asked.

She answered, in a tone which had a touch of sadness: 'I see him every day.'

'Where, dearest?'

'Sometimes in the park, sometimes in the wood. You know the little cascade, Hector, where there is some old neglected rock-work that forms a kind of cavern. I have taken a fancy to that spot, and have spent many mornings there reading. Of late I have seen the stranger there every morning.'

'He has never dared to address you?'

'Never. I have looked up from my book, and have seen him standing at a little distance, watching me silently. I have continued reading; and when I have raised my eyes again I have found him gone. He must approach and depart with a stealthy tread, for I never hear his footfall. Sometimes I have almost wished that he would speak to me. It is so terrible to see him standing silently there.'

'He is some insolent peasant who seeks to frighten you.'

My wife shook her head.

'He is no peasant,' she answered. 'It is not by his dress alone I judge, for that is strange to me. He has an air of nobility which it is impossible to mistake.'

'Is he young or old?'

'He is young and handsome.'

I was much disturbed by the idea of this stranger's intrusion on my wife's solitude; and I went straight to the village to enquire if any stranger had been seen there. I could hear of no one. I questioned the servants closely, but without result. Then I determined to accompany my wife in her walks, and to judge for myself of the rank of the stranger.

For a week I devoted all my mornings to rustic rambles with Eveline in the park and woods; and in all that week we saw no one but an occasional peasant in *sabos*, or one of our own household returning from a neighbouring farm.

I was a man of studious habits, and those summer rambles disturbed the even current of my life. My wife perceived this, and entreated me to trouble myself no further.

'I will spend my mornings in the pleasaunce, Hector,' she said; 'the stranger cannot intrude upon me there.'

'I begin to think the stranger is only a phantasm of your own romantic brain,' I replied, smiling at the earnest face lifted to mine. 'A châtelaine who is always reading romances may well meet handsome cavaliers in the woodlands. I dare say I have Mademoiselle Scuderi to thank for this noble stranger, and that he is only the great Cyrus in modern costume.'

'Ah, that is the point which mystifies me, Hector,' she said. 'The stranger's costume is not modern. He looks as an old picture might look if it could descend from its frame.'

Her words pained me, for they reminded me of that hidden picture in the library, and the quaint hunting costume of orange and purple, which André de Brissac wore at the Regent's ball.

After this my wife confined her walks to the pleasaunce; and for many weeks I heard no more of the nameless stranger. I dismissed all thought of him from my mind, for a graver and heavier care had come upon me. My wife's health began to droop. The change in her was so gradual as to be almost imperceptible to those who watched her day by day. It was only when she put on a rich gala dress which she had not worn for months that I saw how wasted the form must be on which the embroidered bodice hung so loosely, and how wan and dim were the eyes which had once been brilliant as the jewels she wore in her hair.

I sent a messenger to Paris to summon one of the court physicians; but I knew that many days must needs elapse before he could arrive at Puy Verdun. In the interval I watched my wife with unutterable fear.

It was not her health only that had declined. The change was more painful to behold than any physical alteration. The bright and sunny spirit had vanished, and in the place of my joyous young bride I beheld a woman weighed down by rooted melancholy. In vain I sought to fathom the cause of my darling's sadness. She assured me that she had no reason for sorrow or discontent, and that if she seemed sad without a motive, I must forgive her sadness, and consider it as a misfortune rather than a fault.

I told her that the court physician would speedily find some cure for her despondency, which must needs arise from physical causes, since she had no real ground for sorrow. But although she said nothing, I could see she had no hope or belief in the healing powers of medicine.

*   *   *   *   *

One day, when I wished to beguile her from that pensive silence in which she was wont to sit an hour at a time, I told her, laughing, that she appeared to have forgotten her mysterious cavalier of the wood, and it seemed also as if he had forgotten her.

To my wonderment, her pale face became a sudden crimson; and from crimson changed to pale again in a breath.

'You have never seen him since you deserted your woodland grotto?' I said.

She turned to me with a heart-rending look.

'Hector,' she cried, 'I see him every day; and it is that which is killing me.'

She burst into a passion of tears when she had said this. I took her in my arms as if she had been a frightened child, and tried to comfort her.

'My darling, this is madness,' I said. 'You know that no stranger can come to you in the pleasaunce. The moat is ten feet wide and always full of water, and the gates are kept locked day and night by old Massou. The châtelaine of a medieval fortress need fear no intruder in her antique garden.'

My wife shook her head sadly. 'I see him every day,' she said.

On this I believed that my wife was mad. I shrank from questioning her more closely concerning her mysterious visitant. It would be ill, I thought, to give a form and substance to the shadow that tormented her by too close inquiry about its looks and manner, its coming and going.

I took care to assure myself that no stranger to the household could by any possibility penetrate to the pleasaunce. Having done this, I was fain to await the coming of the physician.

*　*　*　*　*

He came at last. I revealed to him the conviction which was my misery. I told him that I believed my wife to be mad. He saw her—spent an hour alone with her, and then came to me. To my unspeakable relief he assured me of her sanity.

'It is just possible that she may be affected by one delusion,' he said; 'but she is so reasonable upon all other points that I can scarcely bring myself to believe her the subject of a monomania. I am rather inclined to think that she really sees the person of whom she speaks. She described him to me with a perfect minuteness. The descriptions of scenes or individuals given by patients afflicted with monomania are always more or less disjointed; but your wife spoke to me as clearly and calmly as I am now speaking to you. Are you sure there is no one who can approach her in that garden where she walks?'

'I am quite sure.'

'Is there any kinsman of your steward, or hanger-on of your household—a young man with a fair, womanish face, very pale and rendered remarkable by a crimson scar, which looks like the mark of a blow?'

'My God!' I cried, as the light broke in upon me all at once. 'And the dress—the strange, old-fashioned dress?'

'The man wears a hunting costume of purple and orange,' answered the doctor.

I knew then that André de Brissac had kept his word, and that in the hour when my life was brightest his shadow had come between me and happiness.

* * * * *

I showed my wife the picture in the library, for I would fain assure myself that there was some error in my fancy about my cousin. She shook like a leaf when she beheld it, and clung to me convulsively.

'This is witchcraft, Hector,' she said. 'The dress in that picture is the dress of the man I see in the pleasaunce; but the face is not his.'

Then she described to me the face of the stranger, and it was my cousin's face line for line—André de Brissac, whom she had never seen in the flesh. Most vividly of all did she describe the cruel mark upon his face, the trace of a fierce blow from an open hand.

* * * * *

After this I carried my wife away from Puy Verdun. We wandered far—through the southern provinces, and into the very heart of Switzerland. I thought to distance the ghastly phantom, and I fondly hoped that change of scene would bring peace to my wife.

It was not so. Go where we would, the ghost of André de Brissac followed us. To my eyes that fatal shadow never revealed itself. *That* would have been too poor a vengeance. It was my wife's innocent heart which André made the instrument of his revenge. The unholy presence destroyed her life. My constant companionship could not shield her from the horrible intruder. In vain did I watch her, in vain did I strive to comfort her.

'He will not let me be at peace,' she said. 'He comes between us, Hector. He is standing between us now. I can see his face with the red mark upon it plainer than I see yours.'

*　*　*　*　*

One fair moonlight night, when we were together in a mountain village in the Tyrol, my wife cast herself at my feet, and told me she was the worst and vilest of women. 'I have confessed all to my Director,' she said; 'from the first I have not hidden my sin from heaven. But I feel that death is near me; and before I die I would fain reveal my sin to you.'

'What sin, my sweet one?'

'When first the stranger came to me in the forest, his presence bewildered and distressed me, and I shrank from him as from something strange and terrible. He came again and again; by and by I found myself thinking of him, and watching for his coming. His image haunted me perpetually; I strove in vain to shut his face out of my mind. Then followed an interval in which I did not see him; and, to my shame and anguish, I found that life seemed dreary and desolate without him. After that came the time in which he haunted the pleasaunce; and—oh, Hector, kill me if you will, for I deserve no mercy at your hands!—I grew in those days to count the hours that must elapse before his coming, to take no pleasure save in the sight of that pale face with the red brand upon it. He plucked all old familiar joys out of my heart, and left in it but one weird, unholy pleasure—the delight of his presence. For a year I have lived but to see him. And now curse me, Hector; for this is my sin. Whether it comes of the baseness of my own heart, or is the work of witchcraft, I know not; but I know that I have striven against this wickedness in vain.'

*　*　*　*　*

I took my wife to my breast, and forgave her. In sooth, what had I to forgive? Was the fatality that overshadowed us any work of hers? On the next night she died, with her hand in mine; and at the very last she told me, sobbing and affrighted, that *he* was by her side.

My Wife's Promise

It WAS MY fate at an early period of my life to abandon myself to the perilous delights of a career which of all others exercises the most potent fascination over the mind of him who pursues it. As a youth I joined a band of brave adventurers in an Arctic expedition, and from the hour in which I first saw the deep cold blue of the northern sea, and felt the subtle influence of the rarefied polar air, I was for all common purposes and objects of life a lost man. The expedition was unfortunate, though its leader was a wise and scientific navigator—his subordinates picked men. The result was bitter disappointment and more bitter loss—loss of valuable lives as well as of considerable funds. I came back from my cruise in the *Weatherwise*, to the western world, rejoiced beyond measure at the idea of being once more at home, and determined never again to face the horrors of that perilous region which had lost me so many dear companions.

I, Richard Dunrayne, was the elder son of a wealthy house, my father, a man of some influence in the political world, and there were few positions which need have been impossible for me had I aspired to the ordinary career affected by British youth. I had been indulged in my early passion for the sea, in my later rage for Arctic exploration; and it was hoped that, having satisfied these boyish fancies, I should now settle down to a pursuit more consonant with the views and wishes of my people. My mother wept over her restored treasure, and confessed how terrible had been her fears during my absence; my father congratulated me upon having ridden my hobby, and alighted therefrom without a broken neck; and my family anxiously awaited my choice of a profession.

Such a choice I found impossible. If I had bartered myself body and soul, by the most explicit formula, to some demon of the icebergs, or incarnate spirit of the frozen sea, I could not have been more completely bound than I was. From the Christmas hearth round which dear friends were gathered, from my low seat at my mother's knee, from worldly wealth and worldly pleasure, the genius of the polar ocean beckoned me away, and all the blessings of my life, all the natural affections of my heart, were too weak to hold me. In my dreams, again and again, with maddening repetition, I trod the old paths, and saw, ghastly white against the intense purple of that northern sky, the walls of ice that had blocked our passage. It seemed to me that if I could but find myself again in that dread solitude, success would be a certainty. It seemed to me as if we had held the magic clue to that awful labyrinth between our fingers, and had, in very folly, suffered it to escape us. 'A new expedition, aided by the knowledge of the past, *must* succeed,' I said to myself; and when I could no longer fight against the prepossession that held me, I consulted the survivors of our unfortunate voyage, and found in their opinions the actual echo of my own convictions.

We met many times, and our meetings resulted in the organisation of a new expedition. Money was poured into our little treasury like water, so poor a dross did it seem to us compared with the jewel we went to seek. Our preparations had begun before I dared tell those who loved me that I had pledged myself to a second expedition. But at last, one bright spring evening, I went home and announced my decision. I look back now and wonder at my own heartlessness, and yet I was *not* indifferent to their grief. The cry that my mother gave when she knew the truth rings in my ears as I write this. No; I was not indifferent. I was possessed.

My second voyage resulted in little actual success, but was to me one prolonged scene of enjoyment. I was a skilled seaman and navigator, no indifferent sportsman, and having acquired some slight reputation during the previous voyage, now ranked high among the junior officers on board the *Ptarmigan*. We wintered at Repulse Bay, with a short stock of fuel, and a shorter supply of provisions; but we managed with a minimum of the former luxury, and supplied all deficiency of the latter by the aid of our guns. Never was a merrier banquet eaten than our Christmas dinner of reindeer steaks and currant dumplings, though the thermometer had sunk 79° below freezing point, and our jerseys and trousers sparkled with hoar-frost.

The brief summer of that northern latitude brought us some small triumphs. We spent a second winter in snow houses, which resembled gigantic bee-hives, and were the snuggest possible habitations, and in the second summer turned our course homeward, in excellent health and spirits, but my gladness was to be sorely dashed on landing in England.

I returned to find my mother's grave bright with familiar autumnal flowers in a suburban cemetery, and to know that the tender arms which had clung about me in the hour of parting would never encircle me again. The blow was a severe one, and for some time to come I thought with aversion of that strange northern world which had cost me, and which was yet to cost me, so much.

Time passed, and I remained in England, at twenty-five years of age a broken man. With the men I met I had no point of sympathy. Their pursuits bored me, their paltry ambitions disgusted me. The pleasures of civilised life had not the faintest charm for me. A polar bear would have been as much at home as I was in a West End ballroom, and would have been as interested in the conversation of a genteel dinner-table. Away from my old comrades of the *Weatherwise* and the *Ptarmigan*, I had not a friend for whom I really cared; and as the civilised world grew day by day more distasteful to me, the old longing revived—the old dreams haunted my sleep. In my father's handsome drawing-rooms I yearned for the rough stone cabin of Repulse Bay, or the snow-hives of Cape Crozier. Another expedition was afloat, and letters from my old messmates announced anticipated triumphs, and warned me of the remorse which I should suffer when the hardy victors returned to reproach the idler who preferred to live at home at ease, while old friends were drifting among the ice-floes, and bearding the grisly tyrant of the north.

I let them go without me, at what sacrifice was only known to myself. My father's health had been declining from the hour of my mother's death, and I was determined not to leave him. *This* duty at least I would not abnegate. This last sad privilege of attending a father's death-bed I would not barter to the all-exacting demon of the frozen seas. For three empty, patient years I remained at home. My hands reverently closed the eyes that had never looked upon me but with affection, and I alone watched the last quiet sleep. This being done, I was free once more, and the old infatuation held me close as ever. My father's death left me wealthy, and to my mind wealth had but one use. All the old yearnings were intensified by tenfold, for the saddest reason. The *Ptarmigan* had never been heard of since the hour she left Baffin's Bay, and the fate of those familiar comrades with whom I had lived in the closest communion for two happy years was a dark enigma, only to be solved by patient labour. The expedition had not been of sufficient importance to attract much attention from the scientific world; there had been too much of a volunteer and amateur character in the business; but when the fact of the *Ptarmigan's* disappearance became known, a meeting of the Royal Society gave all due consideration to the case, and promised help to a party of investigation.

My ample fortune enabled me to contribute largely to the expenses of the new voyage, while volunteers and voluntary contributions poured in from every quarter. I had difficulty in selecting officers and crew from so large a number of hardy adventurers; but I was prudent enough to engage the crew of a battered old whaler for the staple of my men. We were away in all six years, wintering sometimes in South America—once in New York, and getting our supplies as best we might. We made some discoveries, which the Royal Society received with civil approval; but of those we went to seek we found no trace; and I began to think that the fate of my old friends was a mystery never to be solved below the stars.

I came back to England at thirty-four years of age, a hardy wanderer, with a long brown beard that seemed lightly powdered with the northern snow, and with the strength of a sea-lion. For the best years of my life I had lived in snow-hives and stone-cabins, or slept at night amidst the wilderness of ice, in a boat which my stalwart shoulders had helped to carry during the day. Heavens! what a rough, unlicked cub, what a grim sea-monster I must have been; and yet Isabel Lawson loved me! Yes, I came back to England to find a fairer enchantress than the spirit of the frozen deep, and to barter my liberty to a new mistress. One of my sisters had married during my absence, and it was at her country house I took up my abode. The young sister of her husband, Captain Lawson, was here on a visit, and thus I met my fate.

I will not attempt to describe her; the innocent face, so lovely to my eyes, was perhaps less perfect than I thought it; but if perfection wears another shape, it is one that has no charm for me. Isabel was my junior by sixteen years, and for a considerable period of our acquaintance regarded me as a newly acquired elder brother, whose age gave something of a paternal character to the relationship. For a long time I looked upon her as a beautiful picture, an incarnate presentment of all that is tender and divine in womanhood, and as far away from me as the stars which I pointed out to her in our summer evening rambles by the seashore near our country home.

How I grew to love her I will not ask myself. She was a creature whom to know was to love. How she grew to love me is a mystery I have often tried to solve; and when I have asked her, with fear and wondering, why I was so blessed, she told me it was because I was brave and frank and true, and worthy of a woman's love. God help my darling, the glamour of the frozen north was upon me, and the mere story of the wondrous world I knew had magic enough to win me the heart of this angel. She was never tired of hearing me describe that wild region I loved so well. Again and again I told her the histories of my several voyages, and the record seemed always to have a new charm for her.

'I think I know every channel in Davis's Strait and Baffin's Bay,' she said to me a day or two before our wedding; 'and the icebound coast, from Repulse Bay to Cape Crozier, and the ice-packs over which you carried your boats, and the shoals of seals and clouds of ducks, and the colony of white whales, and the dear little snow-houses in which you lived so snugly. Don't you think we ought to spend our honeymoon at Cape Crozier, Richard?'

'My precious one, God forbid that I should ever see you in that wild place.'

'Be sure, Richard, if you went there, I should follow you.'

And she kept her word.

*   *   *   *   *

Dreamlike, and oh, how mournful seems the bright scene of my bridal day, as I recall it tonight beside a lonely hearth in the house of a stranger. My Isabel looked like a spirit in her white gown and veil; and I, to whom the memories of the North were ever present, could well-nigh have fancied she was clad in a snow-cloud. I asked her if she were content to have given her young beauty to a battered veteran like me; and she told me yes, a thousand times more than content—inexpressibly happy.

'But you will never leave me, Richard?' she said, looking up at me with divine love in her deep-blue eyes; and I promised again, as I had promised many times before, that the North should never draw me away from my beloved.

'You shall be my pole-star, dearest, and I will forget that earth has any wilder region than the woods and hills around our happy home.'

My darling loved the country, and I loved all that was dear to her: so I bought a small estate in North Devon—a grange and park in the heart of such a landscape as can only be found in that western shire. I was rich, and it was my pride and delight to make our home as beautiful as money and care could make it. The restoration of the house, which was as old as the Tudors, and the improvement of the park, employed me for more than a year—a happy year of home joys with as sweet a wife as heaven ever gave to man since Adam saw Eve smiling on him among the flowers of paradise—and during the whole of that time I had scarcely thought of the North. With the beginning our second year of happy union, I had even less inclination to think of my old life; for God had blessed us with a son, pure and blooming and beautiful as the region in which he was born.

Upon this period of my life I dare not linger. For nearly two years we held our treasure; and if anything could have drawn us nearer to each other than our love had made us long ago, it would have been our affection for this child. He was taken from us. 'The Lord gave, and the Lord taketh away; blessed be the name of the Lord.' We repeated the holy sentences of resignation; but it was not resignation, it was despair that subdued the violence of our grief. I laid my darling in his grave under the midsummer sky, while a skylark was singing high up in the heaven, where I tried to picture him, among the band of such child-angels; and I knew that life could never again be to me what it had been. People told me I should perhaps have other children as dear as this.

'If God would give this one back to me, He could not blot from my memory his suffering and his death,' I answered impiously.

For some time my sorrow was a kind of stupor—a dull dead heaviness of the soul, from which nothing could raise me. Isabel's grief was no less intense, no less bitter; but it was more natural and more unselfish. She grew alarmed by my state of mind, and entreated me to try change of scene.

'Let us go to London, Richard,' she said; 'I shall be glad to leave this place, beautiful and dear as it is.'

Her pale face warned me that she had sad need of change; and for her sake, rather than my own, I took her to London, where we hired a furnished house in a western square.

Being in town, and an idle man, with no London tastes and no friends, it is scarcely strange that I should attend the meetings of the Royal Society. The fate of Franklin was yet unknown, and the debates upon this subject were at fever-heat. A new expedition was just being fitted out by the Government, and there could be no better opportunity for a volunteer band, which might follow in the track of the Government vessel.

In the rooms of the Society I encountered an old comrade who had served with me in my first voyage on board the *Weatherwise*, and he exerted his utmost powers of persuasion to induce me to join himself and others in a northward cruise, to search for Franklin and for our lost companions of the *Ptarmigan*. I was known to be an old hand, well provided with the sinews of war, adventurous and patient, hardened by many a polar winter, and my friend and his party wanted me for their leader. The proposal flattered me more than I can describe, and caused me the first thrill of pleasure I had known since my son's death. But I remembered my promise.

'No, Martyn,' I answered; 'the thing is impossible. I am a married man, and have given my word to the dearest wife in Christendom that I will never go out yonder again.'

Frank Martyn took no pains to conceal his disappointment at my decision, nor his contempt for my motives.

It was my habit to tell my wife everything; and I told her of the debates of the Royal Society, and of this meeting with an old comrade.

'But you will keep your promise, Richard?' she asked, with a sudden look of fear.

'Until the end of life, my darling, unless you should release me from it.'

'Oh, Richard, that is not likely; I am not capable of such a sacrifice.'

I went again and again to the Royal Society: and I dined at a club, with my friend Martyn, who made me known to his friends, those eager volunteers who panted for the icy winds of the Arctic zone, and languished to tread the frozen labyrinth of polar seas. I listened to them, I talked with them, and the demon of the North resumed his hold upon me. My wife saw that some new influence was at work, that my home life was no longer all in all to me.

One day, after much anxious questioning, she beguiled me of my secret. The old yearning was upon me. I told her how every impulse of my mind— every longing of my heart—urged me to join the new enterprise; and how, for her dear sake, I was determined to forego the certainty of pleasure, and the chances of distinction. She thanked me with a sigh.

'I stand between you and the purpose of your life, Richard,' she said; 'how selfish I must seem to you!'

'No, darling, only tender and womanly.'

Upon my persistent refusal to command the expedition, my friend Martyn was unanimously elected captain. A wealthy brewer of an adventurous turn provided the larger part of the funds, to which I gladly contributed my quota.

'I know Dunrayne will go with us,' said Frank Martyn. 'He'll turn up at the last moment, and beg leave to join. But remember, Dick,' he added, turning to me, 'if it is the last moment you'll be welcome, and I shall be proud to resign the command to a fellow who knows the Arctic zone as well as a Cockney knows the Strand.'

The preparations for the voyage lasted longer than had been anticipated. Months went by, and I still lingered in town, though I knew that Isabel would have preferred to return to Devonshire. I could not tear myself away while the *Forlorn Hope*, the vessel chartered by the brewer, was still in dock. I saw the adventurers almost daily, assisted in their preparations, pored over the chart with them, and travelled over every inch of the old ground with a pencil for their edification.

It was within a week of the departure, and the fever and excitement of preparation was stronger upon me than on any one of the intending voyagers, when my wife came to me suddenly one morning, and threw herself, sobbing, into my arms.

'My dear Isabel, what is this?' I asked in alarm.

'O Richard, you must go,' she sobbed; 'I cannot hold you from your destiny. My selfish fears are killing you. I can see it in your face. You *must* go to that wild, awful world, where heaven has guided you in safety before, and will guard and guide you again. Yes, darling, I release you from your promise. Is God less powerful to protect you yonder than here? He made that world of eternal ice and snow; and where He is there is safety. No, Richard;

I will not despair. I will not stand between you and fame. I heard you talking in your sleep last night, as you have talked many nights, of that distant solitude: and I know that your heart is there. Shall I keep my husband prisoner when his heart has fled from me? No, Richard, you shall go.'

She kissed me, and fell fainting at my feet. I was blinded by my own selfish folly, and did not perceive how much of her fortitude was the courage of despair. I thought only of her generosity, and my release. It was not too late for me to accept the command of the *Forlorn Hope*. I thanked my wife with a hundred kisses as her sweet eyes opened upon me once more.

'My darling, I shall never forget this,' I cried; 'and it shall be the last journey, the very last. I swear it, by all that is most sacred to me. There is no danger, believe me, none, for a man who has learnt prudence as I have done—in the school of hardship.'

There was only a week for leave-taking.

'I can bear it better so,' said my wife: 'such a blow cannot be too sudden.'

'But, my darling, it is no more than any other absence; and, remember, it is to be the last time.'

'No, Richard, do not tell me that. I think I know you better than you know yourself. A man cannot serve two masters. Your master is *there*. He beckons you away from me.'

'But for the last time, Isabel.'

'Well, yes,' she answered, with a profound sigh, 'I think that when you and I say goodbye next week, we shall part for the last time.'

The sadness of her tone seemed natural to the occasion; nor did I remark the melancholy significance of her words, though they often recurred to my mind in the time to come.

'I will make you a flag, Richard,' she said to me next day. 'If you should discover any new spot of land out yonder, you will like to raise the British standard there, and I should like to think that my hands are to be associated with your triumph.'

She set to work upon the fabrication of a Union Jack. I remembered a melancholy incident in the life of Sir John Franklin, and I hardly cared to see her thus employed; but I could not sadden her with the story, and she worked on, with a happier air than I could have believed possible to her.

Alas! I little knew that this gaiety was but an heroic assumption sustained to save me pain.

My darling insisted upon examining my charts, and made me show her every step of our projected journey—the point where we hoped to winter—the land which we intended to explore on sledges—the spots where we should erect cairns to mark our progress. She dwelt on every detail of the journey with an interest intense as my own.

'I think I know that distant world as well as you, Richard,' she said to me on the last day of all. 'In my dreams I shall follow you—yes, I *know* that I shall dream of you every night, and that my dreams will be true. There must be some magnetic chain between two beings so closely united as we are, and I am sure that sleep will show you to me as you are—safe or in danger, triumphant or despondent. And in my waking dreams, too, dear, I shall be on your track. My life will be a double one—the dull, commonplace existence at home, where my body must needs be, and the mystic life yonder, where my spirit will follow you. And, dear husband,' she continued, clinging to me and looking up with a new light in her eyes, 'if I should die before you return——'

'Isabel!'

'Of course that is not likely, you know; but if I should be taken from you, dearest, you will know it directly. Yes, dear, at the death-hour my spirit will fly to you for the last fond parting look upon earth, as surely as I hope it will await you in heaven!'

I tried to chide her for her old-world Scottish superstition; but this speech of hers, and the looks that accompanied it, shook me more than I cared to confess to myself; and if it had been possible to recede with honour, I think I should have resigned the command of the *Forlorn Hope* and stayed with my wife. O God, that I had done so, at any cost of honour, at any sacrifice of friendship!

But my fate drew me northward, and I went. We started in July, and reached the point that we had chosen for our winter harbour at the end of August. Here we walled our vessel round with snow, and roofed her over; and in this grim solitude prepared to await the opening seas of summer. To me the winter seemed unutterably long and dreary. I was no longer the careless bachelor who found amusement in the rough sports of the sailors, and delight in an occasional raid upon the reindeer of the ice-bound coast. I had indeed tried to serve two masters; and the memory of her I had left behind was ever with me, a reproachful shadow. If, now, I could have recalled the past, and found myself once more by that hearth beside which I had languished for the old life of adventure, how gladly would I have made the exchange!

The long, inactive winter that was so dreary to me seemed pleasant enough to my companions. We had plenty of stores, and all were hopeful as to the exploits of the coming summer. We should find the crew of the *Ptarmigan*, perhaps, hardy dwellers in some inaccessible region, patiently awaiting succour and release. With such hopeful dreams my comrades beguiled the wasted days; but I had lost my old power of dreaming, and a sense of duty alone sustained my spirits. My friend Frank told me that I was a changed man—cold and stern as the veriest martinet.

'But all the better man for your post,' he added; 'the sailors love you as much as they fear you, for they know that they would find you as steadfast as a rock in the hour of peril.'

*   *   *   *   *

The summer came, the massive ice-packs were loosened with sounds as of thunder, and drifted away before a southern breeze. But our freedom brought us nothing save disappointment. No traces of our friends of the *Ptarmigan* gladdened our eyes: no discovery rewarded our patience. Scurvy had cost us four of our best men, and the crew was short-handed. Before the summer was ended we had more deaths, and when the next winter began, Martyn and I faced it drearily, with the prospect of scant stores and scanter fuel, and with a sickly and disheartened crew. We had reason to thank God that the poor fellows were faithful to us under conditions so hopeless.

Before the coldest season set in, we left our vessel in tolerably safe harbour, and started on a land expedition, still bent on our search for traces of the missing *Ptarmigan*. We had a couple of sledges and a pack of Esquimaux dogs, faithful, hardy creatures, who thrived on the roughest fare, and were invaluable to us in this toilsome journey. No words can paint the desolation of this wild region—no mind can imagine that horror of perpetual snow, illimitable as eternal.

Martyn and I worked hard to keep up the flagging spirits of our men. One poor fellow had lost his foot from a frostbite, and but for our surgeon's clever amputation of the disabled member, must have surely perished. He was of course no small drag upon us in this time of trial, but his own patient endurance taught us fortitude. We had hoped to fall in with a tribe of Esquimaux, but saw none after those from whom we bought our dogs.

So we toiled on, appalled by the grim change in each other's forms and faces, as short rations and fatigue did their work. The dead winter found us again reduced in number. We built ourselves a roomy snow-house, with a cabin for the dogs; and here my friend Frank Martyn lay sick with three other invalids throughout our hopeless Christmas. My own health held out wonderfully. My spirits rose with the extremity of trial, and I faced the darkening future boldly, beguiling myself with dream-pictures of my return home, and my wife's glad face when she looked up from her lonely hearth and saw me standing on the threshold of the door.

It was Christmas-day. We had dined on pemmican—a peculiar kind of preserved meat—biscuit, and rice. Spirit we had none, save a little carefully stored in case of urgent need. After our scant repast the able men went out in a body in search of sport for their guns, but with little hope of finding anything. The invalids slept, and I sat by the fire of dried moss which served to light our hut, with the aid of a glimmer of cold, dull daylight that came to us through a window of transparent ice in the roof.

I was thinking of England and my wife—what else did I ever think of now?—when one of the men rushed suddenly into the hut, and fell on the snow-bank that served for a bench. He was white to the lips, and shivering as no man shivers from cold alone.

'Good God, Hanley, what is the matter?' I cried, alarmed by the man's terror.

'I went away from the others, Captain,' he began, in rapid, gasping accents, 'thinking I saw the traces of a bear upon the snow; and I had parted from them about half-an-hour when I saw——' His voice died away suddenly, and he sat before me, with lips that moved but made no sound.

'What? For pity's sake speak out, man.'

'A woman!'

'Yes; and of an Esquimaux tribe, no doubt. Why didn't you hail her, and bring her back to us? Why, you must be mad, Hanley. You know how we have been wishing to fall in with some of those people, and you see one, and let her slip through your fingers, and come back scared, as if you'd seen a ghost.'

'That's it, your honour,' the man answered hoarsely. 'What I saw was a ghost.'

'Nonsense, man!'

'But I say yes, Captain, and will stand by my word. She was before me, moving slowly over the snow; you could scarce call it walking, 'twas such a smooth gliding motion. She was dressed in white—no common dress—but one that turns the heart cold only to think of. While I stood, too scared to move hand or foot, she turned and beckoned to me, and I saw her face as plain as I see yours at this moment, a sweet face, with blue eyes, and long fair hair falling loosely round it.'

I was on my feet in a moment, and rushing towards the door.

'Great God of heaven!' I cried, 'my wife!'

The conviction that possessed me was supreme. From the moment in which the sailor described the figure he had seen, there was no shadow of doubt in my mind. It was Isabel, and she only. The wife who had promised that her spirit should follow me step by step upon my desolate journey was near me now. For one moment only I considered the possibility or impossibility of her presence, and pondered whether some northern-bound vessel might have brought her to an Esquimaux station near at hand that we knew not of; for one instant only, and then I was hurrying across the snow in the direction to which the sailor pointed as he stood at the door of our hut.

The brief winter day was closing in, and there was only a long line of faint yellow light in the west. Eastwards the moon was rising, pale and cold like that region of eternal snow. I had left our hut some two hundred yards behind me, when I saw a white-robed figure moving towards the low western light; a figure at once so dear, so familiar, and yet in that place so awful, that an icy shiver shook me from head to heel as I looked upon it.

The figure turned and beckoned. The sweet face looked at me, awfully distinct in that clear cold light. I followed, and it drew me on, far across a patch of snowy waste that I had left unexplored, or had no memory of traversing until now. I tried to overtake the familiar form, but though its strange gliding movement seemed slow, it eluded my pursuit, follow swiftly as I might. In this manner we crossed the wide bleak waste, and as the last glimmer of the western light died out, and the moon shone brighter on the frozen plain, we came to a spot where the snow lay in mounds—seven separate mounds ranged in the form of a cross beneath that wild northern sky.

A glance told me that civilised hands had done this work. The Christian emblem told me more. But though I saw the snow-mounds at my feet, my eyes seemed never to leave the face of my wife—O God, how pale in the moonlight!

She pointed with extended finger to one of the mounds, and I saw that it was headed by a rough wooden board, almost buried in snow. To snatch a knife from my belt, and throw myself on my knees, and begin to scrape the coating of mingled ice and snow from this board, was the work of a few moments. Though it was of *her* I thought only, yet it was as if an irresistible force compelled me to stop, and to obey the command of that pointing hand. When I looked up I was alone beneath the wintry sky. My wife was gone. I *knew* then what I had *felt* from the first—that it was her shadow I had followed over that wintry waste, and that on earth she and I would never look upon each other again.

She had kept her promise as truly as I had broken mine. The gentle spirit had followed me to that desolate world in the very moment it was liberated from its earthly prison.

It was late that night when Hanley and his messmates found me lying senseless on the snow-mound, with the open knife beside my stiffening hand.

They brought me back to life somehow, and by the light of the lanterns they carried, we examined the board at the head of the mound. An inscription roughly cut upon it told us we had found the lost crew of the *Ptarmigan*.

Here lies the body of Morris Haynes, commander of the Ptarmigan, who died in this unknown region, Jan. 30th, 1829, aged 35.

The other mounds also had headboards bearing inscriptions, which we dug out from the snow on the following day, and carefully transcribed. After this we found a cairn containing empty provision-tins, in one of which was a book that had evidently been used for a journal; but rust and snow had done their work, and of this journal nothing was decipherable but the name of the writer, Morris Haynes.

These investigations were not made by me. The new year found me laid low with rheumatic fever, and Frank Martyn had to take his turn as sick-nurse beside the snow-bank where I lay. Our provisions held out better than we had expected, thanks to the game our men shot, and the patience with which they endured privation. The spring came, and with it release. We contrived to make our way to Baffin's Bay—a consummation I scarcely thought possible in my dreary reveries of midwinter—and a Greenland whaler brought us safely home.

I went straight to my brother-in-law's house at the West End of London. He was at home, and came without delay to the library where I had been ushered, and where I sat awaiting him with a gloomy face.

Yes; as I expected: he was in mourning: and behind him came my sister, with a pale face, on which there was no smile of greeting.

Lawson held out both his hands to me.

'Richard,' he began in a faltering voice, 'God knows I never thought it possible I could be otherwise than glad of your coming home—but——'

'That will do,' I said; 'you need tell me no more. My wife is dead.'

He bent his head solemnly.

'She died on the twenty-fifth of last December, at four o'clock in the afternoon.'

'You have been told, then,' cried my sister, 'you have seen someone?'

'Yes,' I answered, 'I have seen *her!*'

At Chrighton Abbey

THE CHRIGHTONS WERE very great people in that part of the country where my childhood and youth were spent. To speak of Squire Chrighton was to speak of a power in that remote western region of England. Chrighton Abbey had belonged to the family ever since the reign of Stephen, and there was a curious old wing and a cloistered quadrangle still remaining of the original edifice, and in excellent preservation. The rooms at this end of the house were low, and somewhat darksome and gloomy, it is true; but, though rarely used, they were perfectly habitable, and were of service on great occasions when the Abbey was crowded with guests.

The central portion of the Abbey had been rebuilt in the reign of Elizabeth, and was of noble and palatial proportions. The southern wing, and a long music-room with eight tall narrow windows added on to it, were as modern as the time of Anne. Altogether, the Abbey was a very splendid mansion, and one of the chief glories of our county.

All the land in Chrighton parish, and for a long way beyond its boundaries, belonged to the great Squire. The parish church was within the park walls, and the living in the Squire's gift—not a very valuable benefice, but a useful thing to bestow upon a younger son's younger son, once in a way, or sometimes on a tutor or dependent of the wealthy house.

I was a Chrighton, and my father, a distant cousin of the reigning Squire, had been rector of Chrighton parish. His death left me utterly unprovided for, and I was fain to go out into the bleak unknown world, and earn my living in a position of dependence—a dreadful thing for a Chrighton to be obliged to do.

Out of respect for the traditions and prejudices of my race, I made it my business to seek employment abroad, where the degradation of one solitary Chrighton was not so likely to inflict shame upon the ancient house to which I belonged. Happily for myself, I had been carefully educated, and had industriously cultivated the usual modern accomplishments in the calm retirement of the vicarage. I was so fortunate as to obtain a situation at Vienna, in a German family of high rank; and here I remained seven years, laying aside year by year a considerable portion of my liberal salary. When my pupils had grown up, my kind mistress procured me a still more profitable position at St Petersburg, where I remained five more years, at the end of which time I yielded to a yearning that had been long growing upon me—an ardent desire to see my dear old country home once more.

I had no very near relations in England. My mother had died some years before my father; my only brother was far away, in the Indian Civil Service; sister I had none. But I was a Chrighton, and I loved the soil from which I had sprung. I was sure, moreover, of a warm welcome from friends who had loved and honoured my father and mother, and I was still further encouraged to treat myself to this holiday by the very cordial letters I had from time to time received from the Squire's wife, a noble warm-hearted woman, who fully approved the independent course I had taken, and who had ever shown herself my friend.

In all her letters for some time past Mrs Chrighton begged that, whenever I felt myself justified in coming home, I would pay a long visit to the Abbey.

'I wish you could come at Christmas,' she wrote, in the autumn of the year of which I am speaking. 'We shall be very gay, and I expect all kinds of pleasant people at the Abbey. Edward is to be married early in the spring—much to his father's satisfaction, for the match is a good and appropriate one. His fiancée is to be among our guests. She is a very beautiful girl; perhaps I should say handsome rather than beautiful. Julia Tremaine, one of the Tremaines of Old Court, near Hayswell—a very old family, as I daresay you remember. She has several brothers and sisters, and will have little, perhaps nothing, from her father; but she has a considerable fortune left her by an aunt, and is thought quite an heiress in the county—not, of course, that this latter fact had any influence with Edward. He fell in love with her at an assize ball in his usual impulsive fashion, and proposed to her in something less than a fortnight. It is, I hope and believe, a thorough love-match on both sides.'

After this followed a cordial repetition of the invitation to myself. I was to go straight to the Abbey when I went to England, and was to take up my abode there as long as ever I pleased.

This letter decided me. The wish to look on the dear scenes of my happy childhood had grown almost into a pain. I was free to take a holiday, without detriment to my prospects. So, early in December, regardless of the bleak dreary weather, I turned my face homewards, and made the long journey from St Petersburg to London, under the kind escort of Major Manson, a Queen's Messenger, who was a friend of my late employer, the Baron Fruydorff, and whose courtesy had been enlisted for me by that gentleman.

I was three-and-thirty years of age. Youth was quite gone; beauty I had never possessed; and I was content to think of myself as a confirmed old maid, a quiet spectator of life's great drama, disturbed by no feverish desire for an active part in the play. I had a disposition to which this kind of passive existence is easy. There was no wasting fire in my veins. Simple duties, rare and simple pleasures, filled up my sum of life. The dear ones who had given a special charm and brightness to my existence were gone. Nothing could recall *them*, and without them actual happiness seemed impossible to me. Everything had a subdued and neutral tint; life at its best was calm and colourless, like a grey sunless day in early autumn, serene but joyless.

The old Abbey was in its glory when I arrived there, at about nine o'clock on a clear starlit night. A light frost whitened the broad sweep of grass that stretched away from the long stone terrace in front of the house to a semicircle of grand old oaks and beeches. From the music-room at the end of the southern wing, to the heavily framed Gothic windows of the old rooms on the north, there shone one blaze of light. The scene reminded me of some weird palace in a German legend; and I half expected to see the lights fade out all in a moment, and the long stone façade wrapped in sudden darkness.

The old butler, whom I remembered from my very infancy, and who did not seem to have grown a day older during my twelve years' exile, came out of the dining-room as the footman opened the hall-door for me, and gave me cordial welcome, nay insisted upon helping to bring in my portmanteau with his own hands, an act of unusual condescension, the full force of which was felt by his subordinates.

'It's a real treat to see your pleasant face once more, Miss Sarah,' said this faithful retainer, as he assisted me to take off my travelling-cloak, and took my dressing-bag from my hand. 'You look a trifle older than when you used to live at the vicarage twelve year ago, but you're looking uncommon well for all that; and, Lord love your heart, miss, how pleased they all will be to see you! Missus told me with her own lips about your coming. You'd like to take off your bonnet before you go to the drawing-room, I daresay. The house is full of company. Call Mrs Marjorum, James, will you?'

The footman disappeared into the back regions, and presently reappeared with Mrs Marjorum, a portly dame, who, like Truefold the butler, had been a fixture at the Abbey in the time of the present Squire's father. From her I received the same cordial greeting, and by her I was led off up staircases and along corridors, till I wondered where I was being taken.

We arrived at last at a very comfortable room—a square tapestried chamber, with a low ceiling supported by a great oaken beam. The room looked cheery enough, with a bright fire roaring in the wide chimney; but it had a somewhat ancient aspect, which the superstitiously inclined might have associated with possible ghosts.

I was fortunately of a matter-of-fact disposition, utterly sceptical upon the ghost subject; and the old-fashioned appearance of the room took my fancy.

'We are in King Stephen's wing, are we not, Mrs Marjorum?' I asked; 'this room seems quite strange to me. I doubt if I have ever been in it before.'

'Very likely not, miss. Yes, this is the old wing. Your window looks out into the old stable-yard, where the kennel used to be in the time of our Squire's grandfather, when the Abbey was even a finer place than it is now, I've heard say. We are so full of company this winter, you see, miss, that we are obliged to make use of all these rooms. You'll have no need to feel lonesome. There's Captain and Mrs Cranwick in the next room to this, and the two Miss Newports in the blue room opposite.'

'My dear good Marjorum, I like my quarters excessively; and I quite enjoy the idea of sleeping in a room that was extant in the time of Stephen, when the Abbey really was an abbey. I daresay some grave old monk has worn these boards with his devout knees.'

The old woman stared dubiously, with the air of a person who had small sympathy with monkish times, and begged to be excused for leaving me, she had so much on her hands just now.

There was coffee to be sent in; and she doubted if the still-room maid would manage matters properly, if she, Mrs Marjorum, were not at hand to see that things were right.

'You've only to ring your bell, miss, and Susan will attend to you. She's used to help waiting on our young ladies sometimes, and she's very handy. Missus has given particular orders that she should be always at your service.'

'Mrs Chrighton is very kind; but I assure you, Marjorum, I don't require the help of a maid once in a month. I am accustomed to do everything for myself. There, run along, Mrs Marjorum, and see after your coffee; and I'll be down in the drawing-room in ten minutes. Are there many people there, by the bye?'

'A good many. There's Miss Tremaine, and her mamma and younger sister; of course you've heard all about the marriage—such a handsome young lady—rather too proud for my liking; but the Tremaines always were a proud family, and this one's an heiress. Mr Edward is so fond of her—thinks the ground is scarcely good enough for her to walk upon, I do believe; and somehow I can't help wishing he'd chosen someone else—someone who would have thought more of him, and who would not take all his attentions in such a cool off-hand way. But of course it isn't my business to say such things, and I wouldn't venture upon it to any one but you, Miss Sarah.'

She told me that I would find dinner ready for me in the breakfast-room, and then bustled off, leaving me to my toilet.

This ceremony I performed as rapidly as I could, admiring the perfect comfort of my chamber as I dressed. Every modern appliance had been added to the sombre and ponderous furniture of an age gone by, and the combination produced a very pleasant effect. Perfume-bottles of ruby-coloured Bohemian glass, china brush-trays and ring-stands brightened the massive oak dressing-table; a low luxurious chintz-covered easy-chair of the Victorian era stood before the hearth; a dear little writing-table of polished maple was placed conveniently near it; and in the background the tapestried walls loomed duskily, as they had done hundreds of years before my time.

I had no leisure for dreamy musings on the past, however, provocative though the chamber might be of such thoughts. I arranged my hair in its usual simple fashion, and put on a dark-grey silk dress, trimmed with some fine old black lace that had been given to me by the Baroness—an unobtrusive demi-toilette, adapted to any occasion. I tied a massive gold cross, an ornament that had belonged to my dear mother, round my neck with a scarlet ribbon; and my costume was complete. One glance at the looking-glass convinced me that there was nothing dowdy in my appearance; and then I hurried along the corridor and down the staircase to the hall, where Truefold received me and conducted me to the breakfast-room, in which an excellent dinner awaited me.

I did not waste much time over this repast, although I had eaten nothing all day; for I was anxious to make my way to the drawing-room. Just as I had finished, the door opened, and Mrs Chrighton sailed in, looking superb in a dark-green velvet dress richly trimmed with old point lace. She had been a beauty in her youth, and, as a matron, was still remarkably handsome. She had, above all, a charm of expression which to me was rarer and more delightful than her beauty of feature and complexion.

She put her arms round me, and kissed me affectionately.

'I have only this moment been told of your arrival, my dear Sarah,' she said; 'and I find you have been in the house half an hour. What must you have thought of me!'

'What can I think of you, except that you are all goodness, my dear Fanny? I did not expect you to leave your guests to receive me, and am really sorry that you have done so. I need no ceremony to convince me of your kindness.'

'But, my dear child, it is not a question of ceremony. I have been looking forward so anxiously to your coming, and I should not have liked to see you for the first time before all those people. Give me another kiss, that's a darling. Welcome to Chrighton. Remember, Sarah, this house is always to be your home, whenever you have need of one.'

'My dear kind cousin! And you are not ashamed of me, who have eaten the bread of strangers?'

'Ashamed of you! No, my love; I admire your industry and spirit. And now come to the drawing-room. The girls will be so pleased to see you.'

'And I to see them. They were quite little things when I went away, romping in the hay-fields in their short white frocks; and now, I suppose, they are handsome young women.'

'They are very nice-looking; not as handsome as their brother. Edward is really a magnificent young man. I do not think my maternal pride is guilty of any gross exaggeration when I say that.'

'And Miss Tremaine?' I said. 'I am very curious to see her.'

I fancied a faint shadow came over my cousin's face as I mentioned this name.

'Miss Tremaine—yes—you cannot fail to admire her,' she said, rather thoughtfully.

She drew my hand through her arm and led me to the drawing-room: a very large room, with a fireplace at each end, brilliantly lighted tonight, and containing about twenty people, scattered about in little groups, and all seeming to be talking and laughing merrily. Mrs Chrighton took me straight to one of the fireplaces, beside which two girls were sitting on a low sofa, while a young man of something more than six feet high stood near them, with his arm resting on the broad marble slab of the mantel-piece. A glance told me that this young man with the dark eyes and crisp waving brown hair was Edward Chrighton. His likeness to his mother was in itself enough to tell me who he was; but I remembered the boyish face and bright eyes which had so often looked up to mine in the days when the heir of the Abbey was one of the most juvenile scholars at Eton.

The lady seated nearest Edward Chrighton attracted my chief atten-tion; for I felt sure that this lady was Miss Tremaine. She was tall and slim, and carried her head and neck with a stately air, which struck me more than anything in that first glance. Yes, she was handsome, undeniably handsome; and my cousin had been right when she said I could not fail to admire her; but to me the dazzlingly fair face with its perfect features, the marked aquiline nose, the short upper lip expressive of unmitigated pride, the full cold blue eyes, pencilled brows, and aureole of pale golden hair, were the very reverse of sympathetic. That Miss Tremaine must needs be universally admired, it was impossible to doubt; but I could not under-stand how any man could fall in love with such a woman.

She was dressed in white muslin, and her only ornament was a superb diamond locket, heart-shaped, tied round her long white throat with a broad black ribbon. Her hair, of which she seemed to have a great quantity, was arranged in a massive coronet of plaits, which surmounted the small head as proudly as an imperial crown.

To this young lady Mrs Chrighton introduced me.

'I have another cousin to present to you, Julia,' she said smiling—'Miss Sarah Chrighton, just arrived from St Petersburg.'

'From St Petersburg? What an awful journey! How do you do, Miss Chrighton? It was really very courageous of you to come so far. Did you travel alone?'

'No; I had a companion as far as London, and a very kind one. I came on to the Abbey by myself.'

The young lady had given me her hand with rather a languid air, I thought. I saw the cold blue eyes surveying me curiously from head to foot, and it seemed to me as if I could read the condemnatory summing-up—'A frump, and a poor relation'—in Miss Tremaine's face.

I had not much time to think about her just now; for Edward Chrighton suddenly seized both my hands, and gave me so hearty and loving a welcome, that he almost brought the tears 'up from my heart into my eyes'.

Two pretty girls in blue crape came running forward from different parts of the room, and gaily saluted me as 'Cousin Sarah'; and the three surrounded me in a little cluster, and assailed me with a string of questions—whether I remembered this, and whether I had forgotten that, the battle in the hayfield, the charity-school tea-party in the vicarage orchard, our picnics in Hawsley Combe, our botanical and entomological excursions on Chorwell-common, and all the simple pleasures of their childhood and my youth. While this catechism was going on, Miss Tremaine watched us with a disdainful expression, which she evidently did not care to hide.

'I should not have thought you capable of such Arcadian simplicity, Mr Chrighton,' she said at last. 'Pray continue your recollections. These juvenile experiences are most interesting.'

'I don't expect you to be interested in them, Julia,' Edward answered, with a tone that sounded rather too bitter for a lover. 'I know what a contempt you have for trifling rustic pleasures. Were you ever a child yourself, I wonder, by the way? I don't believe you ever ran after a butterfly in your life.'

Her speech put an end to our talk of the past, somehow. I saw that Edward was vexed, and that all the pleasant memories of his boyhood had fled before that cold scornful face. A young lady in pink, who had been sitting next Julia Tremaine, vacated the sofa, and Edward slipped into her place, and devoted himself for the rest of the evening to his betrothed. I glanced at his bright expressive face now and then as he talked to her, and could not help wondering what charm he could discover in one who seemed to me so unworthy of him.

It was midnight when I went back to my room in the north wing, thoroughly happy in the cordial welcome that had been given me. I rose early next morning—for early rising had long been habitual to me—and, drawing back the damask-curtain that sheltered my window, looked out at the scene below.

I saw a stable-yard, a spacious quadrangle, surrounded by the closed doors of stables and dog-kennels: low massive buildings of grey stone, with the ivy creeping over them here and there, and with an ancient moss-grown look, that gave them a weird kind of interest in my eyes. This range of stabling must have been disused for a long time, I fancied. The stables now in use were a pile of handsome red-brick buildings at the other extremity of the house, to the rear of the music-room, and forming a striking feature in the back view of the Abbey.

I had often heard how the present Squire's grandfather had kept a pack of hounds, which had been sold immediately after his death; and I knew that my cousin, the present Mr Chrighton, had been more than once requested to follow his ancestor's good example; for there were no hounds now within twenty miles of the Abbey, though it was a fine country for fox-hunting.

George Chrighton, however—the reigning lord of the Abbey—was not a hunting man. He had, indeed, a secret horror of the sport; for more than one scion of the house had perished untimely in the hunting-field. The family had not been altogether a lucky one, in spite of its wealth and prosperity. It was not often that the goodly heritage had descended to the eldest son. Death in some form or other—on too many occasions a violent death—had come between the heir and his inheritance. And when I pondered on the dark pages in the story of the house, I used to wonder whether my cousin Fanny was ever troubled by morbid forebodings about her only and fondly loved son.

Was there a ghost at Chrighton—that spectral visitant without which the state and splendour of a grand old house seem scarcely complete? Yes, I had heard vague hints of some shadowy presence that had been seen on rare occasions within the precincts of the Abbey; but I had never been able to ascertain what shape it bore.

Those whom I questioned were prompt to assure me that they had seen nothing. They had heard stories of the past—foolish legends, most likely, not worth listening to. Once, when I had spoken of the subject to my cousin George, he told me angrily never again to let him hear any allusion to *that* folly from my lips.

That December passed merrily. The old house was full of really pleasant people, and the brief winter days were spent in one unbroken round of amusement and gaiety. To me the old familiar English country-house life was a perpetual delight—to feel myself amongst kindred an unceasing pleasure. I could not have believed myself capable of being so completely happy.

I saw a great deal of my cousin Edward, and I think he contrived to make Miss Tremaine understand that, to please him, she must be gracious to me. She certainly took some pains to make herself agreeable to me; and I discovered that, in spite of that proud disdainful temper, which she so rarely took the trouble to conceal, she was really anxious to gratify her lover.

Their courtship was not altogether a halcyon period. They had frequent quarrels, the details of which Edward's sisters Sophy and Agnes delighted to discuss with me. It was the struggle of two proud spirits for mastery; but my cousin Edward's pride was of the nobler kind—the lofty scorn of all things mean—a pride that does not ill-become a generous nature. To me he seemed all that was admirable, and I was never tired of hearing his mother praise him. I think my cousin Fanny knew this, and that she used to confide in me as fully as if I had been her sister.

'I daresay you can see I am not quite so fond as I should wish to be of Julia Tremaine,' she said to me one day; 'but I am very glad that my son is going to marry. My husband's has not been a fortunate family, you know, Sarah. The eldest sons have been wild and unlucky for generations past; and when Edward was a boy I used to have many a bitter hour, dreading what the future might bring forth. Thank God he has been, and is, all that I can wish. He has never given me an hour's anxiety by any act of his. Yet I am not the less glad of his marriage. The heirs of Chrighton who have come to an untimely end have all died unmarried. There was Hugh Chrighton, in the reign of George the Second, who was killed in a duel; John, who broke his back in the hunting-field thirty years later; Theodore, shot accidentally by a schoolfellow at Eton; Jasper, whose yacht went down in the Mediterranean forty years ago. An awful list, is it not, Sarah? I shall feel as if my son were safer somehow when he is married. It will seem as if he has escaped the ban that has fallen on so many of our house. He will have greater reason to be careful of his life when he is a married man.'

I agreed with Mrs Chrighton; but could not help wishing that Edward had chosen any other woman than the cold handsome Julia. I could not fancy his future life happy with such a mate.

Christmas came by-and-by—a real old English Christmas—frost and snow without, warmth and revelry within; skating on the great pond in the park, and sledging on the ice-bound high-roads, by day; private theatricals, charades, and amateur concerts, by night. I was surprised to find that Miss Tremaine refused to take any active part in these evening amusements. She preferred to sit among the elders as a spectator, and had the air and bearing of a princess for whose diversion all our entertainments had been planned. She seemed to think that she fulfilled her mission by sitting still and looking handsome. No desire to show off appeared to enter her mind. Her intense pride left no room for vanity. Yet I knew that she could have distinguished herself as a musician if she had chosen to do so; for I had heard her sing and play in Mrs Chrighton's morning-room, when only Edward, his sisters, and myself were present; and I knew that both as a vocalist and a pianist she excelled all our guests.

The two girls and I had many a happy morning and afternoon, going from cottage to cottage in a pony-carriage laden with Mrs Chrighton's gifts to the poor of her parish. There was no public formal distribution of blanketing and coals, but the wants of all were amply provided for in a quiet friendly way. Agnes and Sophy, aided by an indefatigable maid, the Rector's daughter, and one or two other young ladies, had been at work for the last three months making smart warm frocks and useful under-garments for the children of the cottagers; so that on Christmas morning every child in the parish was arrayed in a complete set of new garments. Mrs Chrighton had an admirable faculty of knowing precisely what was most wanted in every household; and our pony-carriage used to convey a varied collection of goods, every parcel directed in the firm free hand of the châtelaine of the Abbey.

Edward used sometimes to drive us on these expeditions, and I found that he was eminently popular among the poor of Chrighton parish. He had such an airy pleasant way of talking to them, a manner which set them at their ease at once. He never forgot their names or relationships, or wants or ailments; had a packet of exactly the kind of tobacco each man liked best always ready in his coat-pockets; and was full of jokes, which may not have been particularly witty, but which used to make the small low-roofed chambers ring with hearty laughter.

Miss Tremaine coolly declined any share in these pleasant duties.

'I don't like poor people,' she said. 'I daresay it sounds very dreadful, but it's just as well to confess my iniquity at once. I never can get on with them, or they with me. I am not *simpatica*, I suppose. And then I cannot endure their stifling rooms. The close faint odour of their houses gives me a fever. And again, what is the use of visiting them? It is only an inducement to them to become hypocrites. Surely it is better to arrange on a sheet of paper what it is just and fair for them to have—blankets, and coals, and groceries, and money, and wine, and so on—and let them receive the things from some trustworthy servant. In that case, there need be no cringing on one side, and no endurance on the other.'

'But, you see, Julia, there are some kinds of people to whom that sort of thing is not a question of endurance,' Edward answered, his face flushing indignantly. 'People who like to share in the pleasure they give—who like to see the poor careworn faces lighted up with sudden joy—who like to make these sons of the soil feel that there is some friendly link between themselves and their masters—some point of union between the cottage and the great house. There is my mother, for instance: all these duties which you think so tiresome are to her an unfailing delight. There will be a change, I'm afraid, Julia, when you are mistress of the Abbey.'

'You have not made me that yet,' she answered; 'and there is plenty of time for you to change your mind, if you do not think me suited for the position. I do not pretend to be like your mother. It is better that I should not affect any feminine virtues which I do not possess.'

After this Edward insisted on driving our pony-carriage almost every day, leaving Miss Tremaine to find her own amusement; and I think this conversation was the beginning of an estrangement between them, which became more serious than any of their previous quarrels had been.

Miss Tremaine did not care for sledging, or skating, or billiard-playing. She had none of the 'fast' tendencies which have become so common lately. She used to sit in one particular bow-window of the drawing-room all the morning, working a screen in Berlin-wool and beads, assisted and attended by her younger sister Laura, who was a kind of slave to her—a very colourless young lady in mind, capable of no such thing as an original opinion, and in person a pale replica of her sister.

Had there been less company in the house, the breach between Edward Chrighton and his betrothed must have become notorious; but with a house so full of people, all bent on enjoying themselves, I doubt if it was noticed. On all public occasions my cousin showed himself attentive and apparently devoted to Miss Tremaine. It was only I and his sisters who knew the real state of affairs.

I was surprised, after the young lady's total repudiation of all benevolent sentiments, when she beckoned me aside one morning, and slipped a little purse of gold—twenty sovereigns—into my hand.

'I shall be very much obliged if you will distribute that among your cottagers today, Miss Chrighton,' she said. 'Of course I should like to give them something; it's only the trouble of talking to them that I shrink from; and you are just the person for an almoner. Don't mention my little commission to any one, please.'

'Of course I may tell Edward,' I said; for I was anxious that he should know his betrothed was not as hard-hearted as she had appeared.

'To him least of all,' she answered eagerly. 'You know that our ideas vary on that point. He would think I gave the money to please him. Not a word; pray, Miss Chrighton.' I submitted, and distributed my sovereigns quietly, with the most careful exercise of my judgement.

So Christmas came and passed. It was the day after the great anniversary—a very quiet day for the guests and family at the Abbey, but a grand occasion for the servants, who were to have their annual ball in the evening—a ball to which all the humbler class of tenantry were invited. The frost had broken up suddenly, and it was a thorough wet day—a depressing kind of day for any one whose spirits are liable to be affected by the weather, as mine are. I felt out of spirits for the first time since my arrival at the Abbey.

No one else appeared to feel the same influence. The elder ladies sat in a wide semicircle round one of the fireplaces in the drawing-room; a group of merry girls and dashing young men chatted gaily before the other. From the billiard-room there came the frequent clash of balls, and cheery peals of stentorian laughter. I sat in one of the deep windows, half hidden by the curtains, reading a novel—one of a boxful that came from town every month.

If the picture within was bright and cheerful, the prospect was dreary enough without. The fairy forest of snow-wreathed trees, the white valleys and undulating banks of snow, had vanished, and the rain dripped slowly and sullenly upon a darksome expanse of sodden grass, and a dismal background of leafless timber. The merry sound of the sledge-bells no longer enlivened the air; all was silence and gloom.

Edward Chrighton was not amongst the billiard-players; he was pacing the drawing-room to and fro from end to end, with an air that was at once moody and restless.

'Thank heaven, the frost has broken up at last!' he exclaimed, stopping in front of the window where I sat.

He had spoken to himself, quite unaware of my close neighbourhood. Unpromising as his aspect was just then, I ventured to accost him.

'What bad taste, to prefer such weather as this to frost and snow!' I answered. 'The park looked enchanting yesterday—a real scene from fairyland. And only look at it today!'

'O yes, of course, from an artistic point of view, the snow was better. The place does look something like the great dismal swamp today; but I am thinking of hunting, and that confounded frost made a day's sport impossible. We are in for a spell of mild weather now, I think.'

'But you are not going to hunt, are you, Edward?'

'Indeed I am, my gentle cousin, in spite of that frightened look in your amiable countenance.'

'I thought there were no hounds hereabouts.'

'Nor are there; but there is as fine a pack as any in the country—the Daleborough hounds—five-and-twenty miles away.'

'And you are going five-and-twenty miles for the sake of a day's run?'

'I would travel forty, fifty, a hundred miles for that same diversion. But I am not going for a single day this time; I am going over to Sir Francis Wycherly's place—young Frank Wycherly and I were sworn chums at Christchurch—for three or four days. I am due today, but I scarcely cared to travel by cross-country roads in such rain as this. However, if the flood-gates of the sky are loosened for a new deluge, I must go tomorrow.'

'What a headstrong young man!' I exclaimed. 'And what will Miss Tremaine say to this desertion?' I asked in a lower voice.

'Miss Tremaine can say whatever she pleases. She had it in her power to make me forget the pleasures of the chase, if she had chosen, though we had been in the heart of the shires, and the welkin ringing with the baying of the hounds.'

'O, I begin to understand. This hunting engagement is not of long standing.'

'No; I began to find myself bored here a few days ago, and wrote to Frank to offer myself for two or three days at Wycherly. I received a most cordial answer by return, and am booked till the end of this week.'

'You have not forgotten the ball on the first?'

'O, no; to do that would be to vex my mother, and to offer a slight to our guests. I shall be here for the first, come what may.'

Come what may! so lightly spoken. The time came when I had bitter occasion to remember those words.

'I'm afraid you will vex your mother by going at all,' I said. 'You know what a horror both she and your father have of hunting.'

'A most un-country-gentleman-like aversion on my father's part. But he is a dear old book-worm, seldom happy out of his library. Yes, I admit they both have a dislike to hunting in the abstract; but they know I am a pretty good rider, and that it would need a bigger country than I shall find about Wycherly to floor me. You need not feel nervous, my dear Sarah; I am not going to give papa and mamma the smallest ground for uneasiness.'

'You will take your own horses, I suppose?'

'That goes without saying. No man who has cattle of his own cares to mount another man's horses. I shall take Pepperbox and the Druid.'

'Pepperbox has a queer temper, I have heard your sisters say.'

'My sisters expect a horse to be a kind of overgrown baa-lamb. Everything splendid in horseflesh and womankind is prone to that slight defect, an ugly temper. There is Miss Tremaine, for instance.'

'I shall take Miss Tremaine's part. I believe it is you who are in the wrong in the matter of this estrangement, Edward.'

'Do you? Well, wrong or right, my cousin, until the fair Julia comes to me with sweet looks and gentle words, we can never be what we have been.'

'You will return from your hunting expedition in a softer mood,' I answered; 'that is to say, if you persist in going. But I hope and believe you will change your mind.'

'Such a change is not within the limits of possibility, Sarah. I am fixed as Fate.'

He strolled away, humming some gay hunting-song as he went. I was alone with Mrs Chrighton later in the afternoon, and she spoke to me about this intended visit to Wycherly.

'Edward has set his heart upon it evidently,' she said regretfully, 'and his father and I have always made a point of avoiding anything that could seem like domestic tyranny. Our dear boy is such a good son, that it would be very hard if we came between him and his pleasures. You know what a morbid horror my husband has of the dangers of the hunting-field, and perhaps I am almost as weak-minded. But in spite of this we have never interfered with Edward's enjoyment of a sport which he is passionately fond of; and hitherto, thank God! he has escaped without a scratch. Yet I have had many a bitter hour, I can assure you, my dear, when my son has been away in Leicestershire hunting four days a week.'

'He rides well, I suppose.'

'Superbly. He has a great reputation among the sportsmen of our neighbourhood. I daresay when he is master of the Abbey he will start a pack of hounds, and revive the old days of his great-grandfather, Meredith Chrighton.'

'I fancy the hounds were kennelled in the stable-yard below my bedroom window in those days, were they not, Fanny?'

'Yes,' Mrs Chrighton answered gravely; and I wondered at the sudden shadow that fell upon her face.

I went up to my room earlier than usual that afternoon, and I had a clear hour to spare before it would be time to dress for the seven o'clock dinner. This leisure hour I intended to devote to letter-writing; but on arriving in my room I found myself in a very idle frame of mind, and instead of opening my desk, I seated myself in the low easy-chair before the fire, and fell into a reverie.

How long I had been sitting there I scarcely know; I had been half meditating, half dozing, mixing broken snatches of thought with brief glimpses of dreaming, when I was startled into wakefulness by a sound that was strange to me.

It was a huntsman's horn—a few low plaintive notes on a huntsman's horn—notes which had a strange far-away sound, that was more unearthly than anything my ears had ever heard. I thought of the music in *Der Freischutz*; but the weirdest snatch of melody Weber ever wrote had not so ghastly a sound as these few simple notes conveyed to my ear.

I stood transfixed, listening to that awful music. It had grown dusk, my fire was almost out, and the room in shadow. As I listened, a light flashed suddenly on the wall before me. The light was as unearthly as the sound— a light that never shone from earth or sky.

I ran to the window; for this ghastly shimmer flashed through the window upon the opposite wall. The great gates of the stable-yard were open, and men in scarlet coats were riding in, a pack of hounds crowding in before them, obedient to the huntsman's whip. The whole scene was dimly visible by the declining light of the winter evening and the weird gleams of a lantern carried by one of the men. It was this lantern which had shone upon the tapestried wall. I saw the stable-doors opened one after another; gentlemen and grooms alighting from their horses; the dogs driven into their kennel; the helpers hurrying to and fro; and that strange wan lantern-light glimmering here and there in the gathering dusk. But there was no sound of horse's hoof or of human voices—not one yelp or cry from the hounds. Since those faint far-away sounds of the horn had died out in the distance, the ghastly silence had been unbroken.

I stood at my window quite calmly, and watched while the group of men and animals in the yard below noiselessly dispersed. There was nothing supernatural in the manner of their disappearance. The figures did not vanish or melt into empty air. One by one I saw the horses led into their separate quarters; one by one the redcoats strolled out of the gates, and the grooms departed, some one way, some another. The scene, but for its noiselessness, was natural enough; and had I been a stranger in the house, I might have fancied that those figures were real—those stables in full occupation.

But I knew that stable-yard and all its range of building to have been disused for more than half a century. Could I believe that, without an hour's warning, the long-deserted quadrangle could be filled—the empty stalls tenanted?

Had some hunting-party from the neighbourhood sought shelter here, glad to escape the pitiless rain? That was not impossible, I thought. I was an utter unbeliever in all ghostly things—ready to credit any possibility rather than suppose that I had been looking upon shadows. And yet the noiselessness, the awful sound of that horn—the strange unearthly gleam of that lantern! Little superstitious as I might be, a cold sweat stood out upon my forehead, and I trembled in every limb.

For some minutes I stood by the window, statue-like, staring blankly into the empty quadrangle. Then I roused myself suddenly, and ran softly downstairs by a back staircase leading to the servants' quarters, determined to solve the mystery somehow or other. The way to Mrs Marjorum's room was familiar to me from old experience, and it was thither that I bent my steps, determined to ask the housekeeper the meaning of what I had seen. I had a lurking conviction that it would be well for me not to mention that scene to any member of the family till I had taken counsel with someone who knew the secrets of Chrighton Abbey.

I heard the sound of merry voices and laughter as I passed the kitchen and servants' hall. Men and maids were all busy in the pleasant labour of decorating their rooms for the evening's festival. They were putting the last touches to garlands of holly and laurel, ivy and fir, as I passed the open doors; and in both rooms I saw tables laid for a substantial tea. The house-keeper's room was in a retired nook at the end of a long passage—a charming old room, panelled with dark oak, and full of capacious cupboards, which in my childhood I had looked upon as storehouses of inexhaustible treasures in the way of preserves and other confectionery. It was a shady old room, with a wide old-fashioned fireplace, cool in summer, when the hearth was adorned with a great jar of roses and lavender; and warm in winter, when the logs burnt merrily all day long.

I opened the door softly, and went in. Mrs Marjorum was dozing in a high-back armchair by the glowing hearth, dressed in her state gown of grey watered silk, and with a cap that was a perfect garden of roses. She opened her eyes as I approached her, and stared at me with a puzzled look for the first moment or so.

'Why, is that you, Miss Sarah?' she exclaimed; 'and looking as pale as a ghost, I can see, even by this firelight! Let me just light a candle, and then I'll get you some sal volatile. Sit down in my armchair, miss; why, I declare you're all of a tremble!'

She put me into her easy-chair before I could resist, and lighted the two candles which stood ready upon her table, while I was trying to speak. My lips were dry, and it seemed at first as if my voice was gone.

'Never mind the sal volatile, Marjorum,' I said at last. 'I am not ill; I've been startled, that's all; and I've come to ask you for an explanation of the business that frightened me.'

'What business, Miss Sarah?'

'You must have heard something of it yourself, surely. Didn't you hear a horn just now, a huntsman's horn?

'A horn! Lord no, Miss Sarah. What ever could have put such a fancy into your head?'

I saw that Mrs Majorum's ruddy cheeks had suddenly lost their colour, that she was now almost as pale as I could have been myself.

'It was no fancy,' I said; 'I heard the sound, and saw the people. A hunting-party has just taken shelter in the north quadrangle. Dogs and horses, and gentlemen and servants.'

'What were they like, Miss Sarah?' the housekeeper asked in a strange voice.

'I can hardly tell you that. I could see that they wore red coats; and I could scarcely see more than that. Yes, I did get a glimpse of one of the gentlemen by the light of the lantern. A tall man, with grey hair and whiskers, and a stoop in his shoulders. I noticed that he wore a short-waisted coat with a very high collar—a coat that looked a hundred years old.'

'The old Squire!' muttered Mrs Marjorum under her breath; and then turning to me, she said with a cheery resolute air, 'You've been dreaming, Miss Sarah, that's just what it is. You've dropped off in your chair before the fire, and had a dream, that's it.'

'No, Marjorum, it was no dream. The horn woke me, and I stood at my window and saw the dogs and huntsmen come in.'

'Do you know, Miss Sarah, that the gates of the north quadrangle have been locked and barred for the last forty years, and that no one ever goes in there except through the house?'

'The gates may have been opened this evening to give shelter to strangers,' I said.

'Not when the only keys that will open them hang yonder in my cupboard, miss,' said the housekeeper, pointing to a corner of the room.

'But I tell you, Marjorum, these people came into the quadrangle; the horses and dogs are in the stables and kennels at this moment. I'll go and ask Mr Chrighton, or my cousin Fanny, or Edward, all about it, since you won't tell me the truth.'

I said this with a purpose, and it answered. Mrs Marjorum caught me eagerly by the wrist.

'No, miss, don't do that; for pity's sake don't do that; don't breathe a word to missus or master.'

'But why not?'

'Because you've seen that which always brings misfortune and sorrow to this house, Miss Sarah. You've seen the dead.'

'What do you mean?' I gasped, awed in spite of myself.

'I daresay you've heard say that there's been *something* seen at times at the Abbey—many years apart, thank God; for it never came that trouble didn't come after it.'

'Yes,' I answered hurriedly; 'but I could never get any one to tell me what it was that haunted this place.'

'No, miss. Those that know have kept the secret. But you have seen it all tonight. There's no use in trying to hide it from you any longer. You have seen the old Squire, Meredith Chrighton, whose eldest son was killed by a fall in the hunting-field, brought home dead one December night, an hour after his father and the rest of the party had come safe home to the Abbey. The old gentleman had missed his son in the field, but had thought nothing of that, fancying that master John had had enough of the day's sport, and had turned his horse's head homewards. He was found by a labouring-man, poor lad, lying in a ditch with his back broken, and his horse beside him staked. The old Squire never held his head up after that day, and never rode to hounds again, though he was passionately fond of hunting. Dogs and horses were sold, and the north quadrangle has been empty from that day.'

'How long is it since this kind of thing has been seen?'

'A long time, miss. I was a slip of a girl when it last happened. It was in the winter-time—this very night—the night Squire Meredith's son was killed; and the house was full of company, just as it is now. There was a wild young Oxford gentleman sleeping in your room at that time, and he saw the hunting-party come into the quadrangle; and what did he do but throw his window wide open, and give them the view-hallo as loud as ever he could. He had only arrived the day before, and knew nothing about the neighbourhood; so at dinner he began to ask where were his friends the sportsmen, and to hope he should be allowed to have a run with the Abbey hounds next day. It was in the time of our master's father; and his lady at the head of the table turned as white as a sheet when she heard this talk. She had good reason, poor soul. Before the week was out her husband was lying dead. He was struck with a fit of apoplexy, and never spoke or knew anyone afterwards.'

'An awful coincidence,' I said; 'but it may have been only a coincidence.'

'I've heard other stories, miss—heard them from those that wouldn't deceive—all proving the same thing: that the appearance of the old Squire and his pack is a warning of death to this house.'

'I cannot believe these things,' I exclaimed; 'I *cannot* believe them. Does Mr Edward know anything about this?'

'No, miss. His father and mother have been most careful that it should be kept from him.'

'I think he is too strong-minded to be much affected by the fact,' I said.

'And you'll not say anything about what you've seen to my master or my mistress, will you, Miss Sarah?' pleaded the faithful old servant. 'The knowledge of it would be sure to make them nervous and unhappy. And if evil is to come upon this house, it isn't in human power to prevent it coming.'

'God forbid that there is any evil at hand!' I answered. 'I am no believer in visions or omens. After all, I would sooner fancy that I was dreaming— dreaming with my eyes open as I stood at the window—than that I beheld the shadows of the dead.'

Mrs Marjorum sighed, and said nothing. I could see that she believed firmly in the phantom hunt.

I went back to my room to dress for dinner. However rationally I might try to think of what I had seen, its effect upon my mind and nerves was not the less powerful. I could think of nothing else; and a strange morbid dread of coming misery weighted me down like an actual burden.

There was a very cheerful party in the drawing-room when I went downstairs, and at dinner the talk and laughter were unceasing; but I could see that my cousin Fanny's face was a little graver than usual, and I had no doubt she was thinking of her son's intended visit to Wycherly.

At the thought of this a sudden terror flashed upon me. How if the shadows I had seen that evening were ominous of danger to him—to Edward, the heir and only son of the house? My heart grew cold as I thought of this, and yet in the next moment I despised myself for such weakness.

'It is natural enough for an old servant to believe in such things,' I said to myself; 'but for me—an educated woman of the world—preposterous folly.'

And yet from that moment I began to puzzle myself in the endeavour to devise some means by which Edward's journey might be prevented. Of my own influence I knew that I was powerless to hinder his departure by so much as an hour; but I fancied that Julia Tremaine could persuade him to any sacrifice of his inclination, if she could only humble her pride so far as to entreat it. I determined to appeal to her in the course of the evening.

We were very merry all that evening. The servants and their guests danced in the great hall, while we sat in the gallery above, and in little groups upon the staircase, watching their diversions. I think this arrangement afforded excellent opportunities for flirtation, and that the younger members of our party made good use of their chances—with one exception: Edward Chrighton and his affianced contrived to keep far away from each other all the evening.

While all was going on noisily in the hall below, I managed to get Miss Tremaine apart from the others in the embrasure of a painted window on the stairs, where there was a wide oaken seat. Seated here side by side, I described to her, under a promise of secrecy, the scene which I had witnessed that afternoon, and my conversation with Mrs Marjorum.

'But, good gracious me, Miss Chrighton!' the young lady exclaimed, lifting her pencilled eyebrows with unconcealed disdain, 'you don't mean to tell me that you believe in such nonsense—ghosts and omens, and old woman's folly like that!'

'I assure you, Miss Tremaine, it is most difficult for me to believe in the supernatural,' I answered earnestly; 'but that which I saw this evening was something more than human. The thought of it has made me very unhappy; and I cannot help connecting it somehow with my cousin Edward's visit to Wycherly. If I had the power to prevent his going, I would do it at any cost; but I have not. You alone have influence enough for that. For heaven's sake use it! do anything to hinder his hunting with the Daleborough hounds.'

'You would have me humiliate myself by asking him to forgo his pleasure, and that after his conduct to me during the last week?'

'I confess that he has done much to offend you. But you love him, Miss Tremaine, though you are too proud to let your love be seen: I am certain that you do love him. For pity's sake speak to him; do not let him hazard his life, when a few words from you may prevent the danger.'

'I don't believe he would give up this visit to please me,' she answered; 'and I shall certainly not put it in his power to humiliate me by a refusal. Besides, all this fear of yours is such utter nonsense. As if nobody had ever hunted before. My brothers hunt four times a week every winter, and not one of them has ever been the worse for it yet.'

I did not give up the attempt lightly. I pleaded with this proud obstinate girl for a long time, as long as I could induce her to listen to me; but it was all in vain. She stuck to her text—no one should persuade her to degrade herself by asking a favour of Edward Chrighton. He had chosen to hold

himself aloof from her, and she would show him that she could live without him. When she left Chrighton Abbey, they would part as strangers.

So the night closed, and at breakfast next morning I heard that Edward
had started for Wycherly soon after daybreak. His absence made, for me at
least, a sad blank in our circle. For one other also, I think; for Miss Tremaine's
fair proud face was very pale, though she tried to seem gayer than usual, and
exerted herself in quite an unaccustomed manner in her endeavour to be
agreeable to everyone.

The days passed slowly for me after my cousin's departure. There was a
weight upon my mind, a vague anxiety, which I struggled in vain to shake
off. The house, full as it was of pleasant people, seemed to me to have
become dull and dreary now that Edward was gone. The place where he had
sat appeared always vacant to my eyes, though another filled it, and there
was no gap on either side of the long dinner-table. Light-hearted young
men still made the billiard-room resonant with their laughter; merry girls
flirted as gaily as ever, undisturbed in the smallest degree by the absence
of the heir of the house. Yet for me all was changed. A morbid fancy had
taken complete possession of me. I found myself continually brooding over
the housekeeper's words; those words which had told me that the shadows
I had seen boded death and sorrow to the house of Chrighton.

My cousins, Sophy and Agnes, were no more concerned about their
brother's welfare than were their guests. They were full of excitement
about the New Year's ball, which was to be a very grand affair. Every one of
importance within fifty miles was to be present, every nook and corner of
the Abbey would be filled with visitors coming from a great distance, while
others were to be billeted upon the better class of tenantry round about.
Altogether the organisation of this affair was no small business; and Mrs
Chrighton's mornings were broken by discussions with the housekeeper,
messages from the cook, interviews with the head-gardener on the subject of floral decorations, and other details, which all alike demanded the
attention of the châtelaine herself. With these duties, and with the claims
of her numerous guests, my cousin Fanny's time was so fully occupied, that
she had little leisure to indulge in anxious feelings about her son, whatever
secret uneasiness may have been lurking in her maternal heart. As for the
master of the Abbey, he spent so much of his time in the library, where,

under the pretext of business with his bailiff, he read Greek, that it was not easy for anyone to discover what he did feel. Once, and once only, I heard him speak of his son, in a tone that betrayed an intense eagerness for his return.

The girls were to have new dresses from a French milliner in Wigmore Street; and as the great event drew near, bulky packages of millinery were continually arriving, and feminine consultations and expositions of finery were being held all day long in bedrooms and dressing-rooms with closed doors. Thus, with a mind always troubled by the same dark shapeless foreboding, I was perpetually being called upon to give an opinion about pink tulle and lilies of the valley, or maize silk and apple-blossoms.

New Year's morning came at last, after an interval of abnormal length, as it seemed to me. It was a bright clear day, an almost spring-like sunshine lighting up the leafless landscape. The great dining-room was noisy with congratulations and good wishes as we assembled for breakfast on this first morning of a new year, after having seen the old one out cheerily the night before; but Edward had not yet returned, and I missed him sadly. Some touch of sympathy drew me to the side of Julia Tremaine on this particular morning. I had watched her very often during the last few days, and I had seen that her cheek grew paler every day. Today her eyes had the dull heavy look that betokens a sleepless night. Yes, I was sure that she was unhappy— that the proud relentless nature suffered bitterly.

'He must be home today,' I said to her in a low voice, as she sat in stately silence before an untasted breakfast.

'Who must?' she answered, turning towards me with a cold distant look.

'My cousin Edward. You know he promised to be back in time for the ball.'

'I know nothing of Mr Chrighton's intended movements,' she said in her haughtiest tone; 'but of course it is only natural that he should be here tonight. He would scarcely care to insult half the county by his absence, however little he may value those now staying in his father's house.'

'But you know that there is one here whom he does value better than any one else in the world, Miss Tremaine,' I answered, anxious to soothe this proud girl.

'I know nothing of the kind. But why do you speak so solemnly about his return? He will come, of course. There is no reason he should not come.'

She spoke in a rapid manner that was strange to her, and looked at me with a sharp enquiring glance, that touched me somehow, it was so unlike herself—it revealed to me so keen an anxiety.

'No, there is no reasonable cause for anything like uneasiness,' I said; 'but you remember what I told you the other night. That has preyed upon my mind, and it will be an unspeakable relief to me when I see my cousin safe at home.'

'I am sorry that you should indulge in such weakness, Miss Chrighton.'

That was all she said; but when I saw her in the drawing-room after breakfast, she had established herself in a window that commanded a view of the long winding drive leading to the front of the Abbey. From this point she could not fail to see anyone approaching the house. She sat there all day; everyone else was more or less busy with arrangements for the evening, or at any rate occupied with an appearance of business; but Julia Tremaine kept her place by the window, pleading a headache as an excuse for sitting still, with a book in her hand, all day, yet obstinately refusing to go to her room and lie down, when her mother entreated her to do so.

'You will be fit for nothing tonight, Julia,' Mrs Tremaine said, almost angrily; 'you have been looking ill for ever so long, and today you are as pale as a ghost.'

I knew that she was watching for *him*; and I pitied her with all my heart, as the day wore itself out, and he did not come.

We dined earlier than usual, played a game or two of billiards after dinner, made a tour of inspection through the bright rooms, lit with wax-candles only, and odorous with exotics; and then came a long interregnum devoted to the arts and mysteries of the toilet; while maids flitted to and fro laden with frilled muslin petticoats from the laundry, and a faint smell of singed hair pervaded the corridors. At ten o'clock the band were tuning their violins, and pretty girls and elegant-looking men were coming slowly down the broad oak staircase, as the roll of fast-coming wheels sounded louder without, and stentorian voices announced the best people in the county.

I have no need to dwell long upon the details of that evening's festival. It was very much like other balls—a brilliant success, a night of splendour and enchantment for those whose hearts were light and happy, and who could abandon themselves utterly to the pleasure of the moment; a far-away picture of fair faces and bright-hued dresses, a wearisome kaleido-scopic procession of form and colour for those whose minds were weighed down with the burden of a hidden care.

For me the music had no melody, the dazzling scene no charm. Hour after hour went by; supper was over, and the waltzers were enjoying those latest dances which always seem the most delightful, and yet Edward Chrighton had not appeared amongst us.

There had been innumerable enquiries about him, and Mrs Chrighton had apologised for his absence as best she might. Poor soul, I well knew that his non-return was now a source of poignant anxiety to her, although she greeted all her guests with the same gracious smile, and was able to talk gaily and well upon every subject. Once, when she was sitting alone for a few minutes, watching the dancers, I saw the smile fade from her face, and a look of anguish come over it. I ventured to approach her at this moment, and never shall I forget the look which she turned towards me.

'My son, Sarah!' she said in a low voice—'something has happened to my son!'

I did my best to comfort her; but my own heart was growing heavier and heavier, and my attempt was a very poor one.

Julia Tremaine had danced a little at the beginning of the evening, to keep up appearances, I believe, in order that no one might suppose that she was distressed by her lover's absence; but after the first two or three dances she pronounced herself tired, and withdrew to a seat amongst the matrons. She was looking very lovely in spite of her extreme pallor, dressed in white tulle, a perfect cloud of airy puffings, and with a wreath of ivy-leaves and diamonds crowning her pale golden hair.

The night waned, the dancers were revolving in the last waltz, when I happened to look towards the doorway at the end of the room. I was star-tled by seeing a man standing there, with his hat in his hand, not in evening costume; a man with a pale anxious-looking face, peering cautiously into the room. My first thought was of evil; but in the next moment the man had disappeared, and I saw no more of him.

I lingered by my cousin Fanny's side till the rooms were empty. Even Sophy and Aggy had gone off to their own apartments, their airy dresses sadly dilapidated by a night's vigorous dancing. There were only Mr and Mrs Chrighton and myself in the long suite of rooms, where the flowers were drooping and the wax-lights dying out one by one in the silver sconces against the walls.

'I think the evening went off very well,' Fanny said, looking rather anxiously at her husband, who was stretching himself and yawning with an air of intense relief.

'Yes, the affair went off well enough. But Edward has committed a terrible breach of manners by not being here. Upon my word, the young men of the present day think of nothing but their own pleasures. I suppose that something especially attractive was going on at Wycherly today, and he couldn't tear himself away.'

'It is so unlike him to break his word,' Mrs Chrighton answered. 'You are not alarmed, Frederick? You don't think that anything has happened— any accident?'

'What should happen? Ned is one of the best riders in the county. I don't think there's any fear of his coming to grief.'

'He might be ill.'

'Not he. He's a young Hercules. And if it were possible for him to be ill—which it is not—we should have had a message from Wycherly.'

The words were scarcely spoken when Truefold the old butler stood by his master's side, with a solemn anxious face.

'There is a—a person who wishes to see you, sir,' he said in a low voice, 'alone.'

Low as the words were, both Fanny and myself heard them.

'Someone from Wycherly?' she exclaimed. 'Let him come here.'

'But, madam, the person most particularly wished to see master alone. Shall I show him into the library, sir? The lights are not out there.'

'Then it *is* someone from Wycherly,' said my cousin, seizing my wrist with a hand that was icy cold. 'Didn't I tell you so, Sarah? Something has happened to my son. Let the person come here, Truefold, here; I insist upon it.'

The tone of command was quite strange in wife who was always deferential to her husband, in a mistress who was ever gentle to her servants.

'Let it be so, Truefold,' said Mr Chrighton. 'Whatever ill news has come to us we will hear together.'

He put his arm round his wife's waist. Both were pale as marble, both stood in stony stillness waiting for the blow that was to fall upon them.

The stranger, the man I had seen in the doorway, came in. He was curate of Wycherly church, and chaplain to Sir Francis Wycherly; a grave middle-aged man. He told what he had to tell with all kindness, with all the usual forms of consolation which Christianity and an experience of sorrow could suggest. Vain words, wasted trouble. The blow must fall, and earthly consolation was unable to lighten it by a feather's weight.

There had been a steeplechase at Wycherly—an amateur affair with gentlemen riders—on that bright New Year's day, and Edward Chrighton had been persuaded to ride his favourite hunter Pepperbox. There would be plenty of time for him to return to Chrighton after the races. He had consented; and his horse was winning easily, when, at the last fence, a double one, with water beyond, Pepperbox baulked his leap, and went over head-foremost, flinging his rider over a hedge into a field close beside the course, where there was a heavy stone roller. Upon this stone roller Edward Chrighton had fallen, his head receiving the full force of the concussion. All was told. It was while the curate was relating the fatal catastrophe that I looked round suddenly, and saw Julia Tremaine standing a little way behind the speaker. She had heard all; she uttered no cry, she showed no signs of fainting, but stood calm and motionless, waiting for the end.

I know not how that night ended: there seemed an awful calm upon us all. A carriage was got ready, and Mr and Mrs Chrighton started for Wycherly to look upon their dead son. He had died while they were carrying him from the course to Sir Francis's house. I went with Julia Tremaine to her room, and sat with her while the winter morning dawned slowly upon us—a bitter dawning.

*   *   *   *   *

I have little more to tell. Life goes on, though hearts are broken. Upon Chrighton Abbey there came a dreary time of desolation. The master of the house lived in his library, shut from the outer world, buried almost as completely as a hermit in his cell. I have heard that Julia Tremaine was never known to smile after that day. She is still unmarried, and lives entirely at her father's country house; proud and reserved in her conduct to her equals, but a very angel of mercy and compassion amongst the poor of the neighbourhood. Yes; this haughty girl, who once declared herself unable to endure the hovels of the poor, is now a Sister of Charity in all but the robe. So does a great sorrow change the current of a woman's life.

I have seen my cousin Fanny many times since that awful New Year's night; for I have always the same welcome at the Abbey. I have seen her calm and cheerful, doing her duty, smiling upon her daughter's children, the honoured mistress of a great household; but I know that the main-spring of life is broken, that for her there hath passed a glory from the earth, and that upon all the pleasures and joys of this world she looks with the solemn calm of one for whom all things are dark with the shadow of a great sorrow.

Three Times

CHAPTER I.
THE FIRST TIME.

'POSITIVELY the last night of Herr Rudolph Prusinowski and the performing lions! Positively the last night! For the benefit of Herr Rudolph Prusinowski. Under the distinguished patronage of their Majesties Queen Victoria, the Emperor of China, the Cham of Tartary, his Serene Highness the Grand Duke of Baden, Simeon Muddlebrain, Esq. M.P., the Mayor and Corporation of Spindlecum, and other august personages too numerous to mention. Come early. Positively the last time. Come and see the lions. Herr Rudolph Prusinowski, the favourite of crowned heads and the élite of Europe. Take notice! The great Prusinowski has had the honour of performing before the Mikado of Japan. The world-renowned Prusinowski has been decorated with the order of Rouge et Noir by the Grand Duchess of Selzerwasserburg. Don't miss the lions!'

The above sentences, and many others of the same character—in which a picturesque fancy, aided by the experience of a public career, trifled with the sobrieties of fact and tripped lightly across the borderland of fiction—appeared in gigantic black letters upon a yellow poster on the side wall of the Queen's Theatre, Spindlecum, and in the streets and market-place, upon the quays, and in the back slums of the same town. Spindlecum was a large manufacturing town—a town that did a good deal of business in the export way, and had much commerce by land and sea; and Spindlecum could boast of two theatres: the Royal, an elegantly appointed edifice in a side-street off the quay, with a stone portico surmounted by a bust of Shakespeare; a house about which elderly inhabitants of Spindlecum cherished traditions of Edmund Kean, and where Macready and Harley were remembered as stock actors, but a house which had never paid a manager within the memory of man: and the Queen's, a vast barn-like building, with a lofty roof supported by iron girders, three tiers of boxes, and Alpine heights in the way of galleries, which, contemplated from the broad valley of the pit, seemed inaccessible to the foot of man. The Queen's was making a fortune for its managers. There was a sixpenny pit, and there was a threepenny gallery, whereby the house was never empty, and on Mondays and Saturdays overflowed with noisy human life. The audience at the Queen's was critical, but on the whole good-natured; requiring plenty of life and movement in the pieces, and what may be called showy action in the performers. The Queen's liked stars, and was tolerably universal in its appreciation of these luminaries: this week clamorous in their applause of some stalwart Othello or loud-voiced Hamlet, next week gaping entranced upon the contortions of a family of acrobats; now crowding to see Mr Reginald Montmorency and his celebrated mare Black Bess in the grand spectacular drama of *Dick Turpin, or the Ride to York*, anon rushing to behold Signor Poloni and his striped Zebra of the Prairie.

A man with a pale sallow face, blue chin, and close-cut hair sat in a lounging attitude upon a low wall opposite the stage-door of the Queen's, smoking a meditative pipe, and contemplating the big yellow poster with a dreamy fondness. He had a little group of satellites about him, also close-cropped, blue-chinned, and tobacco-consuming; minor lights in the dramatic heaven, the stock company of the Queen's, who were thrown a little into the background by the lions, shuffling through a preliminary melodrama nightly, before an audience who beheld them with impatience, and heard them sometimes with derision, eager for the grand business of the evening.

'I think that ought to hit 'em up,' said the Herr thoughtfully (he spoke excellent English for a foreigner, but seemed scarcely to have acquired the language in the most aristocratic or æsthetic circles). 'The Mikado looks well, doesn't he?'

'First rate,' replied Mr de la Zouche, the walking gentleman. 'Was he a nice kind of chap, the Mikado?'

Herr Prusinowski turned his contemplative eyes upon the inquirer with a look of placid scorn.

'You ain't so jolly green as to suppose I ever set eyes upon him,' he said, knocking the ashes out of his pipe. 'I was never in Japan in my life; never nearer than a japan candlestick. The Mikado is a safe card, he is; who's to ask any questions about *him?* And so's the Cham of Tartary; I always bring out them two for the last night. Queen Victoria's legitimate business. I did perform once before the royal servants, and got a fiver from the royal seckitary. That *is* immediate patronage.'

'I expect you'll have a clipping house, cully,' remarked Mr Tiddikins, the low comedian, a small man with a falsetto voice.

'I look forward to it, Tiddikins; and if it goes over eighty, I'll stand a supper, mind that.'

There was a subdued murmur of applause.

'Hot or cold?' inquired Mr de la Zouche.

'Hot,' replied the lion-tamer. 'None of your cold fowls and 'am, your pastry and rubbish, for me. A sirloin of beef at top, and a prime goose at bottom, a veal pie and a stewed steak at the sides, and plenty of smoking hot vegetables; a prime old stilton and a bowl of salad to wind up with, and as much champagne as you can swallow, with brandy-and-water to settle it on your stomachs. That's what I'll do, at the Lion and Lamb, if the house goes over eighty when the half price to the boxes is in.'

This time the applause was louder.

'I always said you were a jolly good fellow, Bill,' said Mr Tiddikins, 'and I don't mind how often I say it again.'

It is to be observed that Mr Tiddikins addressed the distinguished Rudolph by the simpler cognomen Bill, one of the playful licenses of friendship, no doubt.

'It's wonderful how those animals draw,' said Mr de la Zouche thoughtfully, as if he were contemplating the feasibility of setting-up on his own account as a lion-tamer. 'You've been here three seasons, Prusinowski, and, egad, the people ain't tired of 'em yet. They seem as eager as ever. One would suppose they liked to see a poor beggar hazard his life every night.'

'There's something in that,' replied the Herr. 'If it wasn't for the danger, the wild-beast business would be as flat as ditch-water.'

'Were you ever frightened?' asked the walking gentleman. 'I know what a plucky fellow you are, and that you handle those three brutes as if they were so many tabby cats; but still sometimes, you know, a man's nerve must fail. Come, now, Prusinowski, were you never frightened?'

'Never but once,' answered the lion-tamer, 'and then I thought it was all over with me.'

He grew suddenly grave, gloomy even, at the mere recollection waked by the walking gentleman's inquiry.

'Never but once,' he repeated, 'and God grant I never may be so again! When a man in my trade loses his head, it's all up with him.'

'How did it happen, old fellow?' asked Mr Tiddikins.

Herr Prusinowski stopped to fill his pipe before answering the question. It was four o'clock upon a blazing July afternoon, rehearsal was over, her Majesty's servants of the Queen's Theatre, Spindlecum, had dined in the intervals of the day's work at their several lodgings, and had nothing particular to do with themselves until tea-time. An actor of this class has generally a rooted aversion to going home.

'Well, you see,' the lion-tamer began in a leisurely way, stopping to take a few preliminary whiffs after those three words of prelude, 'I was at Manchester nigh upon five years ago, and it was my last night and my "ben," as it might be tonight.' A pause and a few more puffs. 'We was doing first-rate business, fizzing, and I don't think I was ever in such high spirits in my life. My pockets were stuffed with money that I'd been taking about the town for tickets, and I hadn't a place to let in my dress-circle.

'"Why, Bill," says my little woman, when I kept running in and out of our lodgings between whiles at rehearsal—we was close agen the slum—taking her in a handful of money every time, "you seem as if you was bewitched; I don't like to see you like that. I had a Scotch friend once as said it was a bad sign—a sign of something going to happen."

'"Lord love your little foolish heart," I answered, "it's a sign of nothing except that I'm going to have a screaming house tonight. I don't suppose there'll be a corner you can screw yourself into if you want to see me." For she's a rare one for going in front of a night, you know, is the missus.'

Mr de la Zouche and Mr Tiddikins murmured their acquaintance with this domestic fact. Herr Prusinowski smoked his pipe for a minute or so, and then went on:

'"Why, there's the family box!" she said.

'That's a large private box on the opposite prompt, that don't often let, unless there's Italian Opera, or Charles Mathews, or something out of the common.

' "No, there ain't," I answered, laughing.

' "What!" cried the missus, "is that let too?"

' "Let this morning," said I, "and there's the money—three pound three—thirty-one-and-six of which comes to us."

'For I had a half share clear of expenses, same as here. Lizzie—that's my wife, you know—was quite proud to think I was going to have such a good box audience, for it isn't every box audience as will take to wild beasts. You may get schools and pious people, that object to the drama, but consider a man putting his head into a lion's mouth improving—there's quite a run upon lions in the Scriptures—but as a rule, your boxes are shady. So my Liz was proud of my dress-circle that night.

' "I wonder whether it's the mayor and his family," she said, speculating about that big private box.

' "No," I told her, "it's a gentleman and a stranger, no name."

'Well, the night came, a sweltering hot summer evening, such as it will be tonight. The performances began with one of your talkee-talkee genteel comedies, and the house was so full and noisy the actors couldn't hear themselves speak. They got through it somehow, there was a short overture, and then the curtain went up for my performance. The three lions discovered in a forest, to slow music, which gets a round for *them*, and gives me my entrance and reception.

'You know the beasts, they were the same three I've got now—Brown, Jones, and Robinson. Old Brown's a harmless old chap enough, not a sound tooth in his head, and no more harm in him than in an elderly jackass; Jones is a deep old dodger, but there isn't *much* harm in him; but Robinson's a nasty-tempered beast, a brute you never can be sure of, an animal that will lick your hand one minute, and be ready to snap your head off the next.

'Well, I got a first-rate reception; I thought the gallery would have never left off applauding; and the sight of the house, crammed to the ceiling, made me almost giddy. Perhaps it was the heat of the place, which was like an oven; perhaps, as I'd been standing treat or being stood for off and on pretty well all day, I may have taken a little more than was good for me; anyhow, I felt the house spinning round me, just as if I'd been some duffer of a novice, instead of the old stager I am.

'I looked at the family box O.P., curious to see who'd taken it. There was only one gentleman there, a man of fifty or thereabouts, with a cadaverous lantern-jawed face, and light reddish hair, very straight, combed neatly on each side of his forehead. He was dressed in black, regular evening dress, white choker and all complete, and, do you know, the instant I set eyes upon that man, he gave me a turn.'

'That was a queer fancy,' said Mr de la Zouche, helping himself to tobacco from the Herr's guttapercha pouch, which lay open on the wall.

'Perhaps it was; but if that night was to come over again, I should have the fancy over again,' replied Prusinowski. 'It was partly his own looks, I think, partly the way he looked at me; not like the rest of the audience, all good nature, expecting to be amused, but with a steadfast ravenous kind of look, that made my blood run cold. "That's a man who'd like to see something happen to me," I said to myself.

'I didn't give way to the fancy all at once. I began the performance; but I stole a glance at my sandy-haired pale-faced gentleman now and then, and always found him looking at me in the same way. He had large light-gray eyes, very light, and very prominent. I can see them now, and they followed every move I made, like a cat's following a mouse. He never moved his eyes from me, he never smiled, he never applauded; he sat in a half-crouching attitude, leaning over the front of the box, watching me, and he made me feel as if I had a ton weight tied to each of my legs. Everything went well for some time, though I felt I'd never done things worse. Brown and Jones behaved beautifully; but just towards the last, when I had to put my head into Robinson's mouth to bring down the curtain, I saw that the brute was in one of his nasty tempers. I suppose the heat had put him out—I know the perspiration was pouring down my face—or perhaps *he* didn't like the look of that cadaverous gentleman in the private box. Anyhow, he turned nasty, and when I wanted to collar him bounced away from me.

'The house turned as still as death all in a moment, and I could see the audience was frightened. I gave a look at my gentleman in the box. He was leaning a little farther over the cushion, with something like a smile on his face. Such a smile; I could fancy any one going to see a man hung smiling like that.

' "Bray to not pe vrighened, laties and shentlemens," I said in my broken English (old Sauerkraut, the ophecleid at the Lane, taught me that dodge), "id is nozing. Te peast vill to all I veesh;" and then I gave Robinson a pretty smart cuff, and began to drag his jaws open.

'The brute snarled, turned upon me, and in the next instant would have had his teeth in my shoulder, if I hadn't given the signal for the curtain. Half-a-dozen carpenters rushed upon the stage and helped me to tackle him. We had him safe in less than a minute; but just at that one moment, before the curtain dropped, it was as near as a toucher.

'There was a good deal of applause; not that I'd done anything to deserve it, for the business of putting my head in the brute's mouth was in the bill, and the audience had been swindled out of that; but they evidently knew I'd been in danger, and they called me before the curtain. I looked up at that white-faced devil in the private box. He was standing up, rubbing his hands in a satisfied kind of way, as if he had seen what he wanted to see; and as I passed just under him he said in a slow measured voice that gave me the shivers:

"A narrow escape, Herr. Very well done indeed! I congratulate you."

'I gave him a look, which he ought to have understood if he didn't, made my bow to the house, and went off the stage. Robinson was quiet enough by this time. My man Joe Purdy had walked him off to his box, and there he was growling over his shin-bones, as mild a lion as you'd wish to see. "Only let me get you safe back to London, my friend," says I, "and I'll take you down to Jamrack's and swop you for something better tempered. Talent is all very well; but temper's worth all the talent in the world." However, that's five years ago, and there's Robinson still performing with me. The brute has such a wonderful gift for his profession! and his heart and soul's in it too. Take that animal in the middle of the day, when he ain't particular hungry, and he's a decent fellow enough; but come between him and his business, and you'll find out what a lion is. He's the vainest beast out, and cuts up rough if he don't get a round of applause for every trick he does. But, Lord bless you, there's no such thing as genius without vanity. He's been a fortune to me first and last, has that animal. Brown and Jones are nothing more than supers to him.'

'You didn't see any more of your friend in the box?' inquired Mr de la Zouche, who was not particularly interested in these praises of the gifted Robinson.

'Curse him, no! By the time I'd changed my clothes he had left the house. I went round to the box-office to see if the box-keepers could tell me anything about him. No; he was a stranger. He had taken his box that morning, finding there was no stall to be had, and paid his three guineas without a question.

'Now I daresay you'll think me an out-and-out fool when I tell you I couldn't sleep that night, nor many nights after, for thinking of that man. I couldn't get his pale cheeks and lank jaws and light gray eyes, with that horrid gloating look in them, out of my mind. "That's a fellow who'd go to see a man hung," I said to myself. "That's a man who'd stand by to see his fellow-creatures hung, drawn, and quartered, and enjoy it—especially the drawing." I hadn't a doubt in my mind that he was on the look-out for an accident all the evening; I hadn't a doubt in my mind that it was through him I made a mess of it at the end.'

'Did you never see him again?' asked the low comedian.

'Never; God forbid I ever should, for I've a notion that if I did, it would be the death of me. I'm not a nervous man in a general way, nor superstitious either; but I'd give up the biggest haul I ever made by a benefit rather than act before that man.'

'A queer notion,' said the humorous Tiddikins.

'A very queer notion,' echoed the gentlemanly De la Zouche.

He was not a fine actor, the walking gentleman, belonging rather to that class of performer who is contemptuously likened to a stick, and his dramatic path had been by no means strewn with roses; yet he was fain to congratulate himself that it had not been beset by lions. He had been somewhat inclined to envy Rudolph Prusinowski the distinction and prosperity of his career; but just now it occurred to him that there were two sides to the picture. He rubbed his shoulder thoughtfully, and was glad to think that he was exposed to the assaults of no fiercer animals than those rampant tragedians who snubbed him when he played Horatio, and made light of him in Cassio, but who melted a little on their benefit nights, and treated him to beer.

CHAPTER II.
THE SECOND TIME.

THE Spindlecum people showed their appreciation of the British drama as represented by lion-taming by giving Herr Prusinowski a bumper. Whether it was the influence of the Cham of Tartary, or the Mikado, the Grand Duchess of Selzerwasserburg, or the local member, or the simple merits of the performance, is a moot question; but the Spindlecumians assembled in full force; and before the Herr had left the family tea-table to repair to the theatre, he received the pleasing intelligence that the crowd at the pit and gallery doors was half-way across the street.

'If we only go on like this for another year or so, Liz, I'll cut the profession,' exclaimed Herr Prusinowski cheerily, 'and start a theatrical public, somewhere on the Surrey side. It's a trying life is the wild-beast business.'

'And a dangerous life too, William,' said the little woman, with a sigh.

(The renowned Rudolph's name in private life was William.)

'Not much of that, old girl. I'm more than a match for Robinson by this time. There isn't a move he's up to that I'm not down upon; and he's the cunningest beast that ever picked a bone. You're going into the front tonight, eh, Liz?'

'O yes, I shall get a seat at the back of the boxes. Mrs. Prodger's going with me. She's took her ticket, and paid for it, you know, William, like a lady.'

Mrs Prodger was the Prusinowskis' landlady, a ponderous matron of fifty, who had let lodgings to 'theatricals' for the last twenty years.

'Ta-ta, Liz, then; I'm off.'

'It's early, William. There's the *Miller and his Men*—that'll last an hour and a half, surely.'

'I don't believe it'll play an hour. You ought to know what my benefit audiences are—all agog for the lions. I want to have a look at the beasts before I begin, and I'm always a little nervous on my ben. Good-bye.'

This was a mere conjugal excuse. The theatre to a man bred at the side-scenes is his club. The Herr preferred smoking his pipe in the free-and-easy atmosphere of the dressing-room at the Queen's to the tamer delights of the domestic tea-table. He had very little anxiety about his beasts. Joe Purdy, his factotum, a keeper who had served his apprenticeship with the great Wombwell, had the custody of them.

* * * * *

The house was an excellent one. The boxes were not so well filled as on that memorable night at Manchester, which Herr Prusinowski had described to his friends; but the pit was a seething caldron of humanity, the gallery looked like a wall of eager faces piled one upon the other up to the iron roof. The *Miller and his Men* was performed almost in dumb show, or seemed so to be, though the leading tragedian retained on the establishment was roaring himself hoarse in the character of Grindoff, with a faint hope of snatching a stray leaf from the crown of wild olive which would be cast at the feet of the lion-tamer by and by.

Grindoff did not bate a syllable of his part or the minutest detail of his stage business; not a stamp of his russet boot, or a scowl of his heavily corked eyebrows; but the rest of the company, less enthusiastic, scamped their work to the best of their abilities, and the drama was raced through in one hour ten minutes and seven seconds by the prompter's chronograph.

Then came a stirring overture—the 'Bronze Horse'—during which the audience cracked nuts and became momentarily more excited; and then the act-drop rose to slow music of a soul-appalling character, and revealed Brown, Jones, and Robinson picturesquely grouped in the stock primeval forest.

There was a pause. The house applauded vociferously. There was something stirring in the notion that these three unfettered beasts might leap into the pit at any moment. It was quite a pleasant sensation—especially for the gallery. Brown, who was elderly and decrepit, yawned and stretched himself out as if for slumber, with the air of having been untimely disturbed from his after-dinner nap. Jones, who was of a lively temperament, whisked his tail, and snapped at an imaginary fly. Robinson stared full at the audience, as if he really did understand and appreciate their plaudits.

The music quickened, broke into a stirring march, and then, at a fortissimo chord from the full orchestra, the lion-tamer bounded on to the stage—a striking figure, broad-shouldered and muscular, in close-fitting flesh-coloured raiment, a scarlet girdle round his waist, and a leopard's skin over his shoulder.

There was a good strong Sheffield knife in his belt, but he had no appearance of being armed.

His reception was tremendous. He stood bowing and moving his lips in vague murmurs, with an air of being quite overcome by his feelings, for nearly five minutes before he could begin his performance. His eyes wandered all round the house with the gaze of calculation, till they grew suddenly fixed, glaring at the stalls.

Now the stalls at the Queen's Theatre, Spindlecum, were a delusion and a snare. Spindlecum at its best was not an aristocratic town, and the Queen's was not the aristocratic theatre of Spindlecum. Except on a mayor's bespeak or under masonic patronage, the stalls were rarely tenanted. But there they were, two long rows of partitioned seats, covered with dusty red cloth.

Tonight there were three people in all the length and breadth of them—two faded-looking elderly women in opera-cloaks at one end, and in the middle, in a position that commanded every inch of the stage, a middle-aged man, with a cadaverous face, prominent light-gray eyes, and lank reddish hair, carefully dressed in full evening costume.

He sat in an attitude of extreme attention, with his arms folded on the back of the seat in front of him—he was in the back row—and his eyes fixed upon the lion-tamer. For the moment the sight of him seemed to turn Rudolph Prusinowski to stone. It was the man he had been talking of that day.

The cold sweat broke out upon his forehead; but he stamped his foot savagely, angry with himself for this folly, muttered an oath, and began his business with the lions—standing upon their backs, riding round the stage upon all three at once, leading them through a kind of dance movement, described in the bills as a set of quadrilles, with garlands of paper roses, and otherwise disporting himself with them, the red-haired man in the stalls watching his every movement and every movement of the animals breathlessly, and never stirring by a hair's-breadth from his attentive attitude, or turning his eyes away from the stage.

Then came the feature of the evening—a single combat between Herr Prusinowski and Robinson—who was described in the bills, by the way, as 'Moloch, the royal brindled lion, presented to Herr Prusinowski by one of the native princes of the Punjaub'—at the end of which the Herr dragged asunder the animal's jaws, and put his head into the red-hot-looking mouth.

Tonight, in spite of that deadly terror which had come upon the Herr at the sight of that one detested spectator, everything went smoothly enough. Robinson, otherwise Moloch, kept his temper, suffered his jaws to be opened to their widest extent, and the tamer's head to repose upon his tongue as on a pillow for half-a-dozen seconds or so, and the curtain came down to vociferous applause; but when the *bénéficiaire* was called for, there was no response. The prompter found him leaning against one of the wings, white to the lips.

'Did you ever see a man tremble?' he asked, in a voice that shook so much as to be scarcely intelligible. 'If you want to see one, look at me.'

He was shaking in every limb, like a man stricken with ague.

'Why, what's the matter, cully?' asked the prompter, with more friendliness of tone than elegance of diction. 'They're calling for you like mad. You'd better go on.'

'I'm going as soon as I can steady myself. I never neglect my business; but I've had a turn. I never thought I should come off the stage alive tonight.'

'Why, the animals were quiet enough.'

'Yes, as mild as lambs; but there's a man in front that's my evil genius. I never felt superstitious about anything else before—none of your ghosts or that kind of rot—but I've got my fancy about that man. He'd like to see me killed, and—he'll contrive to see it.'

'Prusinowski,' said the prompter, 'I couldn't have believed it of you. I thought you was a man of sense.'

But the prompter felt uncomfortable nevertheless. The human mind is especially open to uncomfortable sensations of this kind.

'Come, my boy,' he exclaimed, 'they're losing temper.' This in allusion to the audience, who were clamouring hoarsely for their favourite. 'You'd better go on.'

Prusinowski wiped his damp forehead, pulled himself together, as it were.

'All right,' he said, and followed the prompter to the first entrance, and went through the narrow opening which that functionary made for him by pulling the heavy drop-scene a little on one side. He went on, made his accustomed mechanical bow, and crossed the stage, to disappear with renewed bowings on the opposite side. He was looking at the stalls all the time. The man was gone.

'Curse him!' muttered the lion-tamer. 'If he'd given me time to change my clothes, I'd have been in front of the house in time to see him come out. I want to know who he is; I want to know what he means.'

He dressed hurriedly, tearing off his close-fitting garb, and shuffling on the costume of everyday life anyhow, and then went back to the prompt entrance before the curtain had risen for the farce, and took another survey of the stalls, thinking it just possible that his evil genius had returned. But the man's place was empty. There were only the two dreary women, waiting meekly for one of the stalest inanest farces known to dramatic literature, and fanning themselves with their pocket-handkerchiefs.

Herr Prusinowski went round to the public doors of the theatre, and hung about there, with a vague idea that the man might be lingering also. There was a large tavern just opposite the Queen's, where the audience were wont to refresh themselves—even the stalls and boxes—with brandy-and-soda. The Herr crossed the road by and by, went into the crowded bar, still looking for his man, and looking vainly.

While he was staring about him a friendly hand tapped him on the shoulder.

'It was well over eighty, my boy,' said the voice of De la Zouche, upon whose youthful cheek still lingered some trace of the vermilion it had worn in the *Miller and his Men*, and whose upper lip was still stiff with the glue that had secured his horsehair moustache. 'Nearer ninety, Tiddikins tells me, and he knows how to reckon up a house with any man in the profession. I wish you joy.'

'Thank you, old fellow,' replied the lion-tamer vaguely. 'Yes, I think it's a good house.'

'Think! There's no room for thinking. The perspiration was running down their faces in the pit all through the *Miller*. The house was like a furnace; and uncommonly thirsty that kind of thing makes a man. The pongelow you sent in was very acceptable. I thought Fitz Raymond would never have taken his head out of the pewter. He's awful coally on his Grindoff—goes in a perisher, even when he can't hear himself speak for the noise in front. But I say, Prusi, how about the little supper you talked of?' This in an insinuating tone.

Prusinowski stared at him blankly for a moment, and then said carelessly:

'The supper—O, to be sure. I'd forgotten all about it.' The noble countenance of De la Zouche fell, and his open brow was overshadowed by a sudden gloom. 'But it's all right,' continued the *bénéficiaire*. 'It's ordered for twelve o'clock sharp. I ordered it on spec. I thought I should have a good house.'

'Prusinowski, you are a gentleman!' exclaimed the actor. 'You are one of Nature's nobility, sir, and daily contact with the brute creation has not degraded your lofty mind. At twelve sharp. I'll go home and put on a clean collar. I think you mentioned a goose?'

'Roast beef at the top, roast goose at the bottom,' said the Herr absently.

'It is a bird which, on the supper-table, I appreciate above any of the feathered tribe,' replied the walking gentleman. '*Au reservoir.*'

He departed, wondering at the silence and gravity of a man who could draw an eighty-pound house.

Herr Prusinowski left the tavern and strolled listlessly along the street. It was not quite eleven. He had a clear hour before him, in which he could do what he pleased with himself. Under ordinary circumstances he might have gone home, to have a few words with his 'little woman,' and make some amendment in his toilet; but tonight he hardly cared to face his wife. She would see that something was wrong, and question him. The impression that man's appearance had made upon him was a subject he did not want to talk about, not even with her. He turned out of the busy thoroughfare in which the Queen's Theatre was situated presently into a broad, quiet, old-fashioned-looking street leading down to the quay— a street of broad square red-brick houses of the Georgian era, grim and respectable, with a shop only here and there, and then a superior class of shop. It was a very quiet street at this time of night. The summer moon was shining full upon the broad pavement and empty road, and there was just a glimpse of moonlit water at the end of the street where it opened on the quay.

There was only one shop open at this hour, a tobacconist's at a corner. Prusinowski felt in his coat-pocket with a dim recollection of having allowed Mr Fitz Raymond to empty his tobacco-pouch that evening, and then strolled across the road towards the tobacconist's shop. While he was in the act of crossing, a man came out of the shop and walked slowly away towards the quay. The lion-tamer recognised him at a glance, and darted after him. It was the occupant of the stalls, a tall angular figure in the moonlight, with more or less the air of a gentleman.

It was an unjustifiable thing to do, of course; but Rudolph Prusinowski did not stop to consider the etiquette of the situation. He was resolved to accost this man. He would have done the same wherever he had met him.

'I beg your pardon,' he said, at the stranger's shoulder, 'I believe you were in front tonight in the stalls at the Queen's?'

The man turned and faced him. It was not a prepossessing countenance by any means, that long cadaverous visage, with the pale prominent eyes and lank sandy hair. The moonlight made it look more than usually cadaverous.

'Yes,' he said, 'I have been at the Queen's Theatre this evening. Dear me! you are the lion-tamer, I believe. This is really curious!'

He spoke in a formal deliberate way that was strangely irritating to Herr Prusinowski's nerves. These artists—even professors of the lowest arts— are apt to be sensitive.

'You have some kind of business with me, Herr Prusinowski?' the stranger said interrogatively, the lion-tamer standing for the moment staring at him like a newly awakened sleep-walker, utterly lost and helpless.

'I—I wanted to ask you a question,' he said abruptly, rousing himself with an effort. 'This isn't the first time I've seen you. You took a private box at Manchester five years ago for my benefit.'

'I did,' replied the stranger. 'I congratulate you on the possession of an excellent memory, Mr Prusinowski. You had a narrow escape that night at Manchester, I imagine. One of your animals turned restive.'

'Yes,' said the lion-tamer moodily, 'that brute Robinson cut up rough. I lost my nerve, and he saw it. It *was* a narrow escape—a disappointment for you, wasn't it?'

'Excuse me, I hardly catch your meaning.'

'You thought it was all over with me, didn't you? Come now, I want to know your motive for coming to see me that time—I want to know your motive for coming to see me tonight.'

'Motive?' repeated the stranger. 'I should suppose the motive must be sufficiently obvious. People generally attend that sort of entertainment, and every sort of entertainment, in search of amusement.'

'Other people, perhaps—not you. I know what a man's face means, and I watched yours, as close—well, almost as close as you watched me. It wasn't the face of a man that came to be amused.'

'You seem to have a peculiar way of looking at things, Mr Prusinowski,' replied the stranger, rubbing his bony close-shaven chin thoughtfully. 'However, to be candid with you, I am somewhat interested in lion-taming. I am an idle man, you see. My means enable me to live pretty much as I please and where I please, and a man without occupation is in a manner compelled to create an interest for himself in things outside his own life. I am an amateur of wild-beast shows. There was a man called Green—you may have heard of him, perhaps. I saw that man Green perform seventeen consecutive times. I was peculiarly interested in him.'

'Yes,' said Prusinowski, 'I know all about Green. He was killed—killed by a tiger that he'd made a good deal of money out of.'

'He was,' answered the stranger; 'I saw it.'

Herr Prusinowski shuddered.

'I thought so,' he said; 'I thought as much. You've tasted blood.'

'Upon my honour, that is a very unpleasant way of putting it,' replied the stranger. 'I look at these things entirely from an artistic point of view. I have heard it asserted that men of your profession always do meet with some fatal accident sooner or later. Since you push me so closely, I am bound to admit that has formed one element of interest for me in this kind of performance. I can understand the delight of the Roman people, from the emperor down to the humblest freedman, in their gladiatorial shows. I have a somewhat classical turn of mind, perhaps, and am proud to acknowledge a taste which connects me with a classic age.'

'I don't understand half that palaver,' said Herr Prusinowski rudely; 'but I trust in God I may never see your face again.'

'Really, now! but why?'

'Because you are a cold-blooded scoundrel, and you would like to see me killed.'

'My dear Mr Prusinowski, that is a style of language which, if I were an ill-tempered man, I might resent. Happily I am not an ill-tempered man, so let it pass. You have no right to remark that I should like to see you killed by one of those brutes of yours. But if you *are* destined to meet your death in that manner, which it is to be hoped you are not, I freely admit that I should wish to be a spectator of the catastrophe. It would not make the smallest difference to you, and it would be highly interesting to me. Is this your way? No? In that case, goodnight.'

He lifted his hat ceremoniously, and departed towards the patch of moonlit water at the end of the street, leaving the lion-tamer standing on the pavement, transfixed and brooding.

It was just as he had imagined—the man was an amateur of sudden death.

*   *   *   *   *

The supper at the Lion and Lamb public-house—a snug little hostelry five doors from the theatre, and much affected by the actors—was a gastro-nomic success, but not a social one. The fare was excellent. The giver of the feast ordered liquors on a liberal scale, and eatables and drinkables disappeared with a celerity cheering to witness. Yet the banquet was not a cheerful one. Nothing could rouse Prusinowski from the gloom that had fallen upon him. The actors did their utmost to beguile him into gaiety, with boisterous talk and laughter, racy anecdotes, and an unlimited amount of that humorous converse commonly known as 'chaff,' to which the theatrical mind is especially prone; but all their efforts failed. Once or twice he did make some faint show of rallying—gave a smart answer or two, threw a lobster-claw at the tragic and dignified Fitz Raymond when that great artist was engaged in argument, and pushed a stick of celery down the coat-collar of the absentminded De la Zouche. But these were the feeblest spurts of gaiety, and by degrees the talk fell flat, and the revels, which under happier auspices would have lasted far into the summer dawning, broke up abruptly at a quarter past two.

Mr Warbeck the prompter walked home with Tiddikins and De la Zouche, and told them what had happened after the fall of the curtain.

'Prusinowski's as good a fellow as ever breathed,' he said in conclusion, being thoroughly warmed through with gin-and-water. 'If he was my own brother, I could not like him better than I do. But I'm afraid there's something queer hereabouts.'

He tapped his forehead significantly.

'A loose slate,' said Mr Tiddikins.

'A bee in his bonnet,' said Mr de la Zouche.

CHAPTER III.
THE THIRD TIME.

IT was three years later in the life of the lion-tamer, and he was performing for three nights only at a seacoast town in the north of England, a dreary little place enough, whither he had strayed from the rich manufacturing districts where his harvests were wont to be so plenteous—a dismal little town, beside which the sea seemed to howl more dolefully than by other shores; a stony High-street, a damp windy fish-market, a beach of great loose pebbles, and a long wooden jetty stretching out to sea, and slippery always with slime and weed, dead fish, and other refuse of the great ocean.

Three years!—and yet on his benefit night at Spindlecum Herr Prusinowski had talked about retiring on his laurels in a year. He had not been doing badly either; prosperity had followed all his wanderings; but the human mind is elastic in its estimate of money, and Herr Prusinowski's notions of the fortune he ought to retire upon had widened with the passage of time.

'Another six months, little woman,' he said, 'and I'll sell the beasts by auction, and take a public-house,' which was his notion of peace and retirement.

'I wish it was to be tomorrow, William,' the little woman answered sadly. 'I shall never know a happy moment till you've done with those animals.'

The first two nights at Lowshore, this obscure northern seaport, had been tolerably successful. The theatre was the mouldiest old barn perhaps that had ever been dedicated to public entertainment, and was opened about once in two years for a week or so of transient splendour, when some wandering star of the dramatic firmament, more wildly speculative than his brethren, essayed his fortunes at Lowshore, and informed the nobility and gentry of the district that he was about to appear for six nights only in a round of favourite characters. Rarely as the doors of the temple were open, the denizens of Lowshore were not wont to rush with remarkable unanimity to the shrine. It would have seemed, indeed, as if the drama were a dead letter in the seaport, the audience which came to be subdued by pity and terror being generally restricted to some two or three dozen seafaring men smelling strongly of fish, a sprinkling of boys, and a dash of brightness and colour in the shape of young women in service, or fishermen's wives and daughters.

But what the drama, whether legitimate or illegitimate, failed to do, the lions succeeded in doing. They drew very fair houses—not the nobility and gentry, as represented by one elderly peer, whose estates bordered Lowshore, but who was rarely known to inhabit his great stone castle, preferring a little box at Richmond, stuffed with rare old silver and costly curios; and the vicar; but the shopkeepers and their young men and maidens; the few visitors and the lodging-house proprietors; all the seafaring men and their families; the maids-of-all-work and fisher-boys; the policeman off duty, and a sprinkling of farmers from inland farms. It was late in October, the very dreariest time of the year, and Herr Prusinowski had come to Lowshore in a speculative humour, just to fill up a blank week in his winter programme.

The house was nearly full the first night, a trifle less well attended the second, and on the third a considerable falling-off was apparent. Still it was a very fair house for Lowshore. There was a cheerful sprinkling in the pit, a very good gallery. The boxes alone had a cavernous and dismal aspect. The box audience—the upper middle-class of Lowshore, tradespeople and lodging-letters—had exhausted itself. Herr Prusinowski had brought a dramatic company of three with him to support the lions, and to eke out the evening's entertainment with a couple of farces or comediettas. This company consisted of a light comedian, a low comedian, and a comedy lady. The light comedian was the aspiring De la Zouche, who had blossomed from a walking gentleman into the popular provincial Charles Mathews— white hat, patent-leather boots, light-green trousers, cane, and rapid utterance. The performances began with *Delicate Ground*, and were to conclude with the *Secret*, a farce of an ancient and respectable character.

The lion-tamer, who was a spoilt child of fortune, had a supreme contempt for bad houses, and with a flagrant injustice was wont to wreak upon the innocent few who did come to see him that wrath inspired by the guilty many who stopped away. That is to say, he punished the scanty but admiring audience by scamping his performance, and depriving them of their just due. The dramatic company were accustomed to empty benches and a barren dress-circle.

The weather was against Herr Prusinowski on this particular evening. The north winds came howling across the German Ocean as if they were intent upon sweeping Lowshore from the face of the earth, driving a salt-flavoured sleet before them, which well-nigh blinded the adventurous pedestrian. The Herr expressed himself very forcibly about the weather, as he took leave of his family before setting out for the theatre. The comedietta was just over as he went in at the stage-door, and he had to dress in a hurry, struggling into his close-fitting raiment, and girding himself with scarlet and gold, while a feeble little orchestra of four—clarionet, flute, and two fiddles—played some old-fashioned country-dance tunes, what time the audience regaled themselves with prawns and porter. The three lions looked tremendously big on the small stage, awfully real against the background of faded scenery. Robinson was out of sorts. He was sensitive upon the subject of weather, and had an especial aversion to high winds;

perhaps some hereditary yearning for Libyan sands or Asia's burning sky—personally he could know nothing about either, having been born in Whitechapel—may have affected him at such times; at any rate the fact remained, cold or blusterous weather disturbed his leonine mind.

The feeble little orchestra made a great struggle to produce a soul-inspiring chord, and came out superbly, the second violin a trifle in the rear. Herr Prusinowski bounded on to the stage from a rocky set piece, and began his work rather languidly, handling Robinson with a certain amount of caution.

He had got through half his performance, and was leading the three lions round the stage on their hind feet, to the stirring music of the march in 'Blue Beard'—stirring even from those poor feeble players—when he heard the opening and shutting of a door at the back of the boxes. He looked up quickly. A gentleman in evening dress was seating himself deliberately in the centre place, a pale-complexioned man, with straight reddish hair. The lion-tamer's heart turned cold. It was the man he had seen at Manchester and Spindlecum, the man whose presence, by some morbid fancy, he associated with the idea of peril to himself. During the last three years he had been always more or less on the look-out for this man, and had never seen him—had begun to congratulate himself upon the probability that he would finish his public career without ever performing before him again; and here he was, in this remote seaport town, watching him with the same eager eyes and hungry face, watching as men watched the gladiators in old time, greedy for their blood.

If he could have brought the entertainment to an abrupt conclusion that instant, he would have done so. He would have willingly returned the people their money, and sacrificed the night's profits to escape performing before that man. He was half inclined to plead sudden illness, bring down the curtain with an apology; but to do that would be to confess himself afraid of that man.

'D—n him!' he muttered to himself, 'he sha'n't see that I'm afraid of him. Faster!' he called out to the orchestra, 'faster and louder!' and as the music quickened, he urged the animals with his whip.

Robinson, *alias* Moloch, resented the impertinence with a suppressed roar, and from that moment Rudolph Prusinowski lost his presence of mind and lost his temper. He was determined to bate not one of his tricks, to demonstrate to that cold-blooded wretch in the boxes that he was not afraid of him. He made the animals do more work than usual, looking defiantly at that watchful face in the boxes all the while. The little theatre shook with applause, the pit rose to him, as the good old actors were wont to say; the gallery rang with bravoes.

All in a moment, at the last, in the crowning feat which was to conclude the performance, the bravoes changed to an awful shout of horror. No one could say how it happened, the brute's movements were too rapid for human eyes to follow. Herr Prusinowski was lying on the stage mawled and torn, the lion crouching upon him.

The keeper and a couple of brawny scene-shifters rushed upon the stage; they dragged him from under the infuriated beast insensible and covered with blood, and carried him off to the dressing-room, where the two rival surgeons of Lowshore came rushing in to him five minutes afterwards. Surgery could do nothing; his ribs were crushed to powder, and there was a perforation of the lung and hæmorrhage. He breathed stertorously for about half an hour, and then died, without one ray of returning consciousness.

'Strange,' the red-haired gentleman used to say afterwards, when he told the story as a pleasant kind of thing after dinner, and in some manner reflecting distinction upon himself; 'the poor devil was the second of his trade I saw killed, and I had come across him three times at long intervals in the course of my travels in the north. I take a considerable interest in that sort of thing; there's more excitement about it than there is in the drama. Prusinowski was a very respectable fellow; had saved money, I believe; and left his wife and children comfortably provided for.'

Her Last Appearance

Chapter I
Her Temptation

'HE IS A SCOUNDREL,' said the gentleman.

'He is my husband,' answered the lady.

Not much in either sentence, yet both came from bursting hearts and lips passion-pale.

'Is that your answer, Barbara?'

'The only answer God and man will suffer me to give you.'

'And he is to break your heart, and squander your earnings on his low vices—keep you shut up in this shabby lodging, while all the town is raving about your beauty and your genius—and you are to have no redress, no escape?'

'Yes,' she answered, with a look that thrilled him, 'I shall escape him—in my coffin. My wrongs will have redress—at the day of judgement.'

'Barbara, he is killing you.'

'Don't you think that may be the greatest kindness he has ever shown me?'

The gentleman began to pace the room distractedly. The lady turned to the tall narrow glass over the chimney-piece, with a curious look, half mournful, half scornful.

She was contemplating the beauty which was said to have set the town raving.

What did that tarnished mirror show her? A small pale face, wan and wasted by studious nights and a heavy burden of care, dark shadows about dark eyes. But such eyes! They seemed, in this cold light of day, too black and large and brilliant for the small white face; but at night, in the lamplit theatre, with a patch of rouge under them, and the fire of genius burning in them, they were the most dazzling, soul-ensnaring eyes man had ever seen; or so said the cognoscenti, Horace Walpole among them; and Mrs Barbara Stowell was the last fashion at Covent Garden Theatre.

It was only her second season on those famous boards, and her beauty and talent still wore the bloom of novelty. The town had never seen her by daylight. She never drove in the Ring, or appeared at a fashionable auction, or mystified her admirers at a masquerade in the Pantheon, or drank whey in St James's Park—in a word, she went nowhere—and the town had invented twenty stories to account for this secluded existence. Yet no one had guessed the truth, which was sadder than the most dismal fiction that had floated down the idle stream of London gossip. Barbara Stowell kept aloof from the world for three reasons—first, because her husband was a tyrant and a ruffian, and left her without a sixpence; secondly, because her heart was broken; thirdly, because she was dying.

This last reason was only known to herself. No stethoscope had sounded that aching breast—no stately physician, with eye-glass and gold-headed cane, and chariot and footman, had been called in to testify in scientific language to the progress of the destroyer; but Barbara Stowell knew very well that her days were numbered, and that her span of life was of the briefest.

She was not in the first freshness of her youth. Three years ago she had been a country parson's daughter, leading the peacefullest, happiest, obscurest life in a Hertfordshire village—when, as ill luck would have it, she came to London to visit an aunt who was in business there as a milliner, and at this lady's house met Jack Stowell, an actor of small parts at Covent Garden—a cold-hearted rascal with a fine person, a kind of surface cleverness which had a vast effect upon simple people, and ineffable conceit. He had the usual idea of the unsuccessful actor, that his manager was his only enemy, and that the town was languishing to see him play Romeo, and Douglas, and the whole string of youthful heroes. His subordinate position soured him; and he sought consolation from drink and play, and was about as profligate a specimen of his particular genus as could be found in the purlieus of Bow Street. But he knew how to make himself agreeable in society, and passed for a 'mighty pretty fellow'. He had the art of being sentimental too on occasion, could cast up his eyes to heaven and affect a mind all aglow with honour and manly feeling.

Upon this whitened sepulchre Barbara wasted the freshness of her young life. He was caught by her somewhat singular beauty, which was rather that of an old Italian picture than of a rustic Englishwoman. Beauty so striking and peculiar would make its mark, he thought. With such a Juliet he could not fail as Romeo. He loved her as much as his staled and withered heart was capable of loving, and he foresaw his own advantage in marrying her. So, with a little persuasion, and a great many sweet speeches stolen from the British Drama, he broke down the barriers of duty, and wrung from the tearful, blushing girl a hasty consent to a Fleet marriage, which was solemnised before she had time to repent that weak moment of concession.

The milliner was angry, for she had believed Mr Stowell her own admirer, and although too wise to think of him as a husband, wished to retain him as a suitor. The Hertfordshire parson was furious, and told his daughter she had taken the first stage to everlasting destruction without his knowledge, and might go the rest of the way without his interference. She had a step-mother who was very well disposed to widen the breach, and she saw little hope of reconciliation with a father who had never erred on the side of fondness. So she began the world at twenty years of age, with Jack Stowell for her husband and only friend. In the first flush and glamour of a girlish and romantic love, it seemed to her sweet to have him only, to have all her world of love and hope bound up in this one volume.

This fond and foolish dream lasted less than a month. Before that moon which had shone a pale crescent in the summer sky of her wedding night had waxed and waned, Barbara knew that she was married to a drunkard and a gambler, a brute who was savage in his cups, a profligate who had lived amongst degraded women until he knew not what womanly purity meant, a wretch who existed only for self-gratification, and whose love for her had been little more than the fancy of an hour.

He lost no time in teaching her all he knew of his art. She had real genius, was fond of study, and soon discovered that he knew very little. She had her own ideas about all those heroines of which he only knew the merest conventionalities and traditions. She sat late into the night study-ing, while he was drinking and punting in some low tavern. Her sorrows, her disappointments, her disgusts drove her to the study of the drama for consolation, and temporary forgetfulness. These heroines of tragedy, who were all miserable, seemed to sympathise with her own misery. She became passionately fond of her art before ever she had trodden the stage.

Jack Stowell took his wife to Rich, and asked for an engagement. Had Barbara been an ordinary woman, the manager would have given her a subordinate place in his troupe, and a pittance of twenty shillings a week. But her exceptional beauty struck the managerial eye. He had half a dozen geniuses in his company, but their good looks were on the wane. This young face, these Italian eyes, might attract the town—and the town had been leaning a little towards the rival house lately.

'I'll tell you what, Stowell,' said the manager, 'I should like to give your wife a chance. But to take any hold upon the public she must appear in a leading part. I couldn't trust her till she has learnt the A B C of her profession. She must try her wings in the provinces.'

They were standing at noontide on the great stage at Covent Garden. The house was almost in darkness, and the vast circle of boxes shrouded in linen wrappings had a ghostly look that chilled Barbara's soul. What a little creature she seemed to herself in that mighty arena! Could she ever stand there and pour out her soul in the sorrows of Juliet, or the Duchess of Malfi, or Isabella, as she had done so often before the looking-glass in her dingy lodging?

'Jack,' she said, as they were walking home—he had been unusually kind to her this morning—'I can't tell you what an awful feeling that great, dark, cold theatre gave me. I felt as if I were standing in my tomb.'

'That shows what a little goose you are,' retorted Jack, contemptuously; 'do you think anybody is going to give you such a big tomb as that?'

Mrs Stowell appeared at the Theatre Royal, Bath, and tried her wings, as the manager called it, with marked success. There could be no doubt that she had the divine fire, a genius and bent so decided that her lack of experience went for nothing; and then she worked like a slave, and threw her soul, mind, heart—her whole being—into this new business of her life. She lived only to act. What else had she to live for, with a husband who came home tipsy three or four nights out of the seven, and whose infidelities were notorious?

She came to London the following winter, and took the town by storm. Her genius, her beauty, her youth, her purity, were on every tongue. She received almost as many letters as a prime minister in that first season of success; but it was found out in due time that she was inaccessible to flattery, and the fops and fribbles of her day ceased their persecutions.

Among so many who admired her, and so many who were eager to pursue, there was only one who discovered her need of pity and pitied her.

This was Sir Philip Hazlemere, a young man of fashion and fortune—neither fop nor fribble, but a man of cultivated mind and intense feeling.

He saw, admired, and, ere long, adored the new actress; but he did not approach her, as the others did, with fulsome letters which insulted her understanding, or costly gifts which offended her honour. He held himself aloof, and loved in silence—for the instinct of his heart told him that she was virtuous. But he was human, and his sense of honour could not altogether stifle hope. He found out where she lived, bought over the lodging-house keeper to his interest, and contrived to learn a great deal more than the well-informed world knew about Barbara Stowell.

He was told that her husband was a wretch, and ill-used her, that this brilliant beauty, who shone and sparkled by night like a star, was by daylight a wan and faded woman, haggard with sorrow and tears. If he had loved her before, when the history of her life was unknown to him, he loved her doubly now, and, taking hope from all that made her life hopeless, flung honour to the winds and determined to win her.

Could she be worse off, he asked himself, than she was now—the slave of a low-born profligate—the darling of an idle, gaping crowd—scorned and neglected at home, where a woman should be paramount? He was rich and his own master—there was all the bright glad world before them. He would take her to Italy, and live and die there for her sake, content and happy in the blessing of her sweet companionship. He had never touched her hand, never spoken to her, but he had lived for the last six months only to see and hear her, and it seemed to him that he knew every thought of her mind, every impulse of her heart. Had he not seen those lovely eyes answer his fond looks sometimes, as he hung over the stage box, and the business of the scene brought her near him, with a tender intelligence that told him he was understood?

If John Stowell should petition for a divorce, so much the better, thought Philip. He could then make his beloved Lady Hazlemere, and let the world see the crowning glory of his life. He was so deeply in love that he thought it would be everlasting renown to have won Barbara. He would go down to posterity famous as the husband of the loveliest woman of his time; like that Duke of Devonshire, of whom the world knows so little except that he had a beautiful duchess.

One day Sir Philip Hazlemere took courage—emboldened by some new tale of Jack Stowell's brutality—and got himself introduced to the presence of his beloved. She was shocked at first, and very angry; but his deep respect melted her wrath, and for the first time in her life Barbara learnt how reverential, how humble, real love is. It was no bold seducer who had forced himself into her presence, but a man who pitied and honoured her, and who would have deemed it a small thing to shed his blood for her sake.

He was no stranger to her, though she had never heard his voice till today. She had seen him in the theatre—night after night, and had divined that it was some stronger feeling than love of the drama which held him riveted to the same spot, listening to the same play, however often it might be repeated in the shifting repertoire of those days.

She knew that he loved her, and that earnest look of his had touched her deeply. What was it now for her, who had never known a good man's love, to hear him offer the devotion of a lifetime, and sue humbly for permission to carry her away from a life which was most abject misery!

Her heart thrilled as she heard him. Yes, this was true love—this was the glory and grace of life which she had missed. She could measure the greatness of her loss now that it was too late. She saw what pitiful tinsel she had mistaken for purest gold. But, though every impulse of her heart drew her to this devoted lover, honour spoke louder than feeling, and made her marble. On one only point she yielded to her lover's pleading. She did not refuse him permission to see her again. He might come sometimes, but must be seldom, and the hour in which he should forget the respect due to her as a true and loyal wife would be the hour that parted them for ever.

'My life is so lonely!' she said, self-excusingly, after having accorded this permission; 'it will be a comfort to me to see you now and then for a brief half-hour, and to know that there is someone in this great busy world who pities and cares for me.'

She had one reason for granting Sir Philip's prayer, which would have well-nigh broken his heart could he have guessed it. This was her inward conviction that her life was near its close. There was hardly time for temptation between the present hour and the grave. And every day seemed to carry her further from the things and thoughts of earth. Her husband's cruelties stung less keenly than of old; his own degradation, which had been the heaviest part of her burden, seemed further away from her, as if he and she lived in different worlds. Her stage triumphs, which had once intoxicated her, now seemed unreal as the pageant of a dream. Yes, the ties that bind this weak flesh to earthly joys and sufferings were gradually loosening. The fetters were slipping off this weary clay.

Chapter II
Her Avenger

Sir Philip showed himself not undeserving Barbara's confidence. He came to the sordid London lodging—a *caravansera* which had housed wandering tribes of shabby-genteel adventurers for the last twenty years, and whose dingy panelling seemed to exhale an odour of poverty. He brought his idol hothouse flowers and fruits—the weekly papers—those thin little leaflets which amused our ancestors—a new book now and then—and the latest news of the town—that floating gossip of the clubs, which Walpole was writing to Sir Horace Mann. He came and sat beside her, as she worked at her tambour frame, and cheered her by a tenderness too reverent to alarm. In a word, he made her happy.

If she were slowly fading out of life, he did not see the change, or guess that this fair flower was soon to wither. He saw her too frequently to perceive the gradual process of decay. Her beauty was of an ethereal type, to which disease lent new charms.

One day he found her with an ugly bruise upon her forehead; she had tried to conceal it with the loose ringlets of her dark hair, but his quick eye saw the mark. When pressed hard by his solicitous questioning, she gave a somewhat lame account of the matter. She had been passing from the sitting-room to her bedchamber last night, when a gust of wind extinguished her candle, and she had fallen and wounded herself against the edge of the chest of drawers. She crimsoned and faltered as she tired to explain this accident.

'Barbara, you are deceiving me!' cried Sir Philip. 'It was a man's clenched fist left that mark. You shall not live with him another day.'

And then came the impassioned pleading which shook her soul—fond offers of a sweet glad life in a foreign land—a divorce—a new marriage—honour—station.

'But dishonour first,' said Barbara. 'Can the path of shame ever lead to honour? No, Sir Philip, I will not do evil that good may come of it.'

No eloquence of her lover's could move her from this resolve. She was firm as the Bass Rock, he passionate as the waves that beat against it. He left her at last, burning with indignation against her tyrant.

'God keep and comfort you,' he cried at parting. 'I will not see you again till you are free.'

These words startled her, and she pondered them, full of alarm. Did he mean any threat against her husband? Ought she to warn Jack Stowell of his danger?

Sir Philip Hazlemere and John Stowell had never yet crossed each other's path. The surest place in which not find the husband was his home. But now Sir Philip was seized with a certain fancy for making Mr Stowell's acquaintance—or at any rate for coming face to face with him in some of his favourite haunts. These were not difficult to discover. He played deep and he drank hard, and his chosen resort was a disreputable tavern in a narrow court out of Long Acre, where play and drink were the order of the night, and many a friendly festivity had ended in a bloody brawl.

Here on a December midnight, when the pavements about Covent Garden were greasy with a thaw, and the link-boys were reaping their harvest in a thick brown fog, Sir Philip resorted directly the play was over, taking one Captain Montagu, a friend and confidant, with him. A useful man this Montagu, who knew the theatres and most of the actors—among them, Jack Stowell.

'The best of fellows,' he assured Sir Philip, 'capital company.'

'That may be,' replied Sir Philip, 'but he beats his wife, and I mean to beat him.'

'What, Phil, are you going to turn Don Quixote and fight with windmills?'

'Never mind my business,' answered Philip; 'yours is to bring me and this Stowell together.'

They found Mr Stowell engaged at faro with his own particular friends in a private room—a small room at the back of the house, with a window opening on to the leads, which offered a handy exit if the night's enjoyment turned to peril. The mohawks of that day were almost as clever as cats at climbing a steep roof or hanging on to a gutter.

Captain Montagu sent in his card to Mr Stowell, asking permission to join him with a friend, a gentleman from the country. Jack knew that Montagu belonged to the hawk tribe, but scented a pigeon in the rural stranger, and received the pair with effusiveness. Sir Philip had disguised himself in a heavy fur-bordered coat and a flaxen periwig, but Mr Stowell scanned him somewhat suspiciously notwithstanding. His constant attendance in the stage box had made his face very familiar to the Covent Garden actors, and it was only the fumes of brandy punch which prevented Stowell's recognition of him.

The play was fast and furious. Sir Philip, in his character of country squire, ordered punch with profuse liberality, and lost his money with a noisy recklessness, vowing that he would have his revenge before the night was out. Montagu watched him curiously, wondering what it all meant.

So the night wore on, Sir Philip showing unmistakable signs of intoxication, under which influence his uproariousness degenerated by-and-by into a maudlin stupidity. He went on losing money with a sleepy placidity that threw Jack Stowell off his guard, and tempted that adventurer into a free indulgence in certain manoeuvres which under other circumstances he would have considered to the last degree dangerous.

What was his astonishment when the country squire suddenly sprang to his feet and flung half a tumbler of punch in his face!

'Gentlemen,' cried Stowell, wiping the liquor from his disconcerted countenance, 'the man is drunk, as you must perceive. I have been grossly insulted, but am too much a gentleman to take advantage of the situation. You had better get your friend away, Captain Montagu, while his legs can carry him, if they are still capable of that exertion. We have had enough play for tonight.'

'Cheat! swindler!' cried Sir Philip. 'I call my friend to witness that you have been playing with marked cards for the last hour. I saw you change the pack.'

'It's a lie!' roared Jack.

'No, it isn't,' said Montagu, 'I've had my eye on you.'

'By God! gentlemen, I'll have satisfaction for this,' cried Jack, drawing his sword a very little way out of its scabbard.

'You shall,' answered Sir Philip, 'and this instant. I shall be glad to see whether you are as good at defending your own cur's life as you are at beating your wife.'

'By heaven, I know you now!' cried Jack. 'You are the fellow that sits in the stage box night after night and hangs on my wife's looks.'

Sir Philip went to the door, locked it, and put the key in his pocket, then came back with his rapier drawn.

Montagu and the other men tried to prevent a fight, but Sir Philip was inexorably bent on settling all scores on the spot, and Stowell was savage in his cups and ready for anything. Preliminaries were hurried through—a table knocked over and a lot of glasses broken; but noise was a natural concomitant of pleasure in this tavern, and the riot awakened no curiosity in the sleepy drawer waiting below.

A space was cleared, and the two men stood opposite each other, ghastly with passion; Sir Philip's assumed intoxication thrown off with his fur-bordered coat, John Stowell considerably the worse for liquor.

The actor was a skilled swordsman, but his first thrusts were too blindly savage to be effective. Sir Philip parried them easily, and stood looking at his antagonist with a scornful smile which goaded Stowell to madness.

'I'll wager my wife and you have got up this play between you,' he said. 'I ought to have known there was mischief on foot. She's too meek and pretty-spoken not to be a——'

The word he meant to say never passed his lips, for a sudden thrust in tierce from Philip Hazlemere's sword pierced his left lung and silenced him for ever.

'When I saw the mark of your fist on your wife's forehead this morning, I swore to make her a widow tonight,' said Sir Philip, as the actor fell face downward on the sanded floor.

The tavern servants were knocking at the door presently. Jack Stowell's fall had startled even their equanimity. Tables and glasses might be smashed without remark—they only served to swell the reckoning—but the fall of a human body invited attention. Captain Montagu opened the window, and hustled his friend out upon the slippery leads below it, and, after some peril to life and limb in the hurried descent, Sir Philip Hazlemere found himself in Long Acre, where the watchman was calling 'Past four o'clock, and a rainy morning.'

Chapter III
Her Farewell Sigh

Before next evening the town knew that Jack Stowell the actor had been killed in a tavern brawl. Captain Montagu had bribed Mr Stowell's friends to keep a judicious silence. The man had been killed in fair fight, and no good could come of letting the police knew the details of his end. So when the Bow Street magistrate came to hold his interrogatory, he could only extort a confused account of the fatal event. There had been a row at faro, and Stowell and another man, whose name nobody present knew, had drawn their swords and fought. Stowell had fallen, and the stranger had escaped by a window before the tavern people came to the rescue. The tavern people had seen the stranger enter the house, a man with flaxen hair, and a dark green riding coat trimmed with grey fur, but they had not seen him leave. The magistrate drew the general conclusion that everybody had been drunk, and the examination concluded in a futile manner, which in these days would have offered a fine opening for indignation leaders in the daily papers, and letters signed 'Fiat Justitia', or 'Peckham Rye'; but which at that easy-going period provoked nobody's notice, or served at most to provide Walpole with a paragraph for one of his immortal epistles.

Sir Philip called at Mrs Stowell's, and was told that she was ill, and keeping her room. There was a change of pieces announced at Covent Garden, and the favourite was not to appear 'until tomorrow se'nnight, in consequence of a domestic affliction'.

Sir Philip sent his customary offerings of hothouse fruits and flowers to Mrs Stowell's address, but a restraining delicacy made him keep aloof while the actor's corpse lay at his lodgings, and the young widow was still oppressed with the horror of her husband's death. She might suspect his hand, perhaps, in that untimely end. Would she pity and pardon him, and understand that it was to redress her wrongs his sword had been drawn?

Upon this point Sir Philip was hopeful. The future was full of fair promises. There was only a dreary interval of doubt and severance to be endured in the present.

The thought that Barbara was confined to her room by illness did not alarm him. It was natural that her husband's death should have agitated and overwhelmed her. The sense of her release from his tyranny would soon give her hope and comfort. In the meanwhile Sir Philip counted the hours that must pass before her reappearance.

The appointed night came, and the play announced for representation was Webster's *Duchess of Malfi*, concluding with the fourth Act: 'the Duchess by Mrs Stowell'. They were fond of tragedies in those days, the gloomier the better. Covent Garden was a spacious charnel-house for the exhibition of suicide and murder.

Sir Philip was in his box before the fiddlers began to play. The house was more than half empty, despite the favourite's reappearance after her temporary retirement, despite the factitious interest attached to her as the widow of a man who had met his death under somewhat mysterious circumstances a week ago. There was dire weather out of doors—a dense brown fog. Some of the fog had crept in at the doors of Covent Garden Theatre, and hung like a pall over pit and boxes.

The fiddlers began the overture to Glucks's *Orpheus and Eurydice*. Philip Hazlemere's heart beat loud and fast. He longed for the rising of the curtain with an over-mastering impatience. It was more than a week since he had seen Barbara Stowell; and what a potent change in both their destinies had befallen since their last meeting! He could look at her now with triumphant delight. No fatal barrier rose between them. He had no doubt of her love, or of her glad consent to his prayer. In a little while—just a decent interval for the satisfaction of the world—she would be his wife. The town would see her no more under these garish lights of the theatre. She would shine as a star still, but only in the calm heaven of home.

The brightness of the picture dispelled those gloomy fancies which the half-empty theatre and its dark mantle of fog had engendered.

The curtain rose, and at last he saw her. The lovely eyes were more brilliant than ever, and blinded him to the hollowness of the wan cheek. There was a thrilling tragedy in her every look which seemed the very breath and fire of genius. The creature standing there, pouring out her story of suffering, was wronged, oppressed; the innocent, helpless victim of hard and bloody men. The strange story, the strange character, seemed natural as she interpreted it. Sir Philip listened with all his soul in his ears, as if he had never seen the gloomy play before—yet every line was familiar to him. The Duchess was one of Barbara's greatest creations.

He hung with rapt attention on every word, and devoured her pale loveliness with his eyes, yet was eager for the play to be over. He meant to lie in wait for her at the stage door, and accompany her home to her lodgings, and stay with her just long enough to speak of their happy future, and to win her promise to be his wife so soon as her weeds could be laid aside. He would respect even idle prejudice for her sake, and wait for her while she went through the ceremony of mourning for the husband who had ill-used her.

The play dragged its slow length along to the awful fourth act, with its accumulated horrors—the wild masque of madmen, the tomb-maker, the bell-man, the dirge, the executioners with coffin and cords. Barbara looked pale and shadowy as a spirit, a creature already escaped from earthly bondage, for whom death could have no terrors. Thinly as the house was occupied, the curtain fell amidst a storm of applause. Sir Philip stood looking at the dark-green blankness, as if that dying look of hers had rooted him to the spot, while the audience hurried out of the theatre, uneasy as to the possibility of hackney coaches or protecting link-boys to guide them through the gloom.

He turned suddenly at the sound of a sigh close behind him—a faint and mournful sigh, which startled and chilled him.

Barbara was standing there, in the dress she had worn in that last scene—the shroud-like drapery which had so painfully reminded him of death. She stretched out her hands to him with a sad, appealing gesture. He leaned eagerly forward, and tried to clasp them in his own, but she withdrew herself from him with a shiver, and stood, shadow-like, in the shadow of the doorway.

'Dearest!' he exclaimed, between surprise and delight, 'I was coming round to the stage door. I am most impatient to talk to you, to be assured of your love, now that you are free to make me the most blessed of men.

My love, I have a world of sweet words to say to you. I may come, may I not? I may ride home with you in your coach?'

The lights went out suddenly while he was talking to her, breathless in his eagerness. She gave one more faint sigh, half pathetic, half tender, and left him. She had not blessed him with a word, but he took this gentle silence to mean consent.

He groped his way out of the dark theatre, and went round to the stage door. He did not present himself at the entrance, but waited discreetly on the opposite side of the narrow street, till Barbara's coach should be called. He had watched for her thus, in a futile, aimless manner, on many a previous night, and was familiar with her habits.

There were a couple of hackney coaches waiting in the street under the curtain of fog. Presently a link-boy came hurriedly along with his flaring torch, followed by a breathless gentleman in a brown coat and wig of the same colour. The link-boy crossed the road, and the gentleman after him, and both vanished within the theatre.

Sir Philip wondered idly what the breathless gentleman's business could be.

He waited a long time, as it appeared to his impatience, and still there was no call for Mrs Stowell's hackney coach. A group of actors came out and walked away on the opposite pavement, talking intently. The gentleman in brown came out again, and trotted off into the fog, still under guidance of the link-boy. The stage doorkeeper appeared on the threshold, looked up and down the street, and seemed about to extinguish his dim oil lamp and close his door for the night. Sir Philip Hazlemere ran across the street just in time to stop him.

'Why are you shutting up?' he asked; 'Mrs Stowell has not left the theatre, has she?'

It seemed just possible that he had missed her in the fog.

'No, poor thing, she won't go out till tomorrow, and then she'll be carried out feet foremost.'

'Great God! what did you mean?'

'It's a sad ending for such a pretty creature,' said the doorkeeper with a sigh, 'and it was that brute's ill usage was at the bottom of it. She's been sickening of a consumption for the last three months—we all of us knew it; and when she came in at this door tonight I said she looked fitter for her coffin than for the stage. And the curtain was no sooner down than she dropped all of a heap, with one narrow streak of dark blood oozing out of her lips and trickling down her white gown. She was gone before they could carry her to her dressing-room. They sent for Dr Budd, of Henrietta Street, but it was too late; she didn't wait for the doctors to help her out of this world.'

Yes, at the moment when he had looked into that shadow face, seen those sad eyes looking into his with ineffable love and pity, Barbara's troubled soul had winged its flight skyward.

The Shadow in the Corner

WILDHEATH GRANGE STOOD a little way back from the road, with a barren stretch of heath behind it, and a few tall fir-trees, with straggling wind-tossed heads, for its only shelter. It was a lonely house on a lonely road, little better than a lane, leading across a desolate waste of sandy fields to the sea-shore; and it was a house that bore a bad name among the natives of the village of Holcroft, which was the nearest place where humanity might be found.

It was a good old house, nevertheless, substantially built in the days when there was no stint of stone and timber—a good old grey stone house with many gables, deep window-seats, and a wide staircase, long dark passages, hidden doors in queer corners, closets as large as some modern rooms, and cellars in which a company of soldiers might have lain *perdu*.

This spacious old mansion was given over to rats and mice, loneliness, echoes, and the occupation of three elderly people: Michael Bascom, whose forebears had been landowners of importance in the neighbourhood, and his two servants, Daniel Skegg and his wife, who had served the owner of that grim old house ever since he left the university, where he had lived fifteen years of life—five as student, and ten as professor of natural science.

At three-and-thirty Michael Bascom had seemed a middle-aged man; at fifty-six he looked and moved and spoke like an old man. During that interval of twenty-three years he had lived alone in Wildheath Grange, and the country people told each other that the house had made him what he was. This was a fanciful and superstitious notion on their part, doubtless, yet it would not have been difficult to have traced a certain affinity between the dull grey building and the man who lived in it. Both seemed alike remote from the common cares and interests of humanity; both had an air of settled melancholy, engendered by perpetual solitude; both had the same faded complexion, the same look of slow decay.

Yet lonely as Michael Bascom's life was at Wildheath Grange, he would not on any account have altered its tenor. He had been glad to exchange the comparative seclusion of college rooms for the unbroken solitude of Wildheath. He was a fanatic in his love of scientific research, and his quiet days were filled to the brim with labours that seldom failed to interest and satisfy him. There were periods of depression, occasional moments of doubt, when the goal towards which he strove seemed unattainable, and his spirit fainted within him. Happily such times were rare with him. He had a dogged power of continuity which ought to have carried him to the highest pinnacle of achievement, and which perhaps might ultimately have won for him a grand name and a world-wide renown, but for a catastrophe which burdened the declining years of his harmless life with an unconquerable remorse.

One autumn morning—when he had lived just three-and-twenty years at Wildheath, and had only lately begun to perceive that his faithful butler and body servant, who was middle-aged when he first employed him, was actually getting old—Mr Bascom's breakfast meditations over the latest treatise on the atomic theory were interrupted by an abrupt demand from that very Daniel Skegg. The man was accustomed to wait upon his master in the most absolute silence, and his sudden breaking out into speech was almost as startling as if the bust of Socrates above the bookcase had burst into human language.

'It's no use,' said Daniel; 'my missus must have a girl!'

'A what?' demanded Mr Bascom, without taking his eyes from the line he had been reading.

'A girl—a girl to trot about and wash up, and help the old lady. She's getting weak on her legs, poor soul. We've none of us grown younger in the last twenty years.'

'Twenty years!' echoed Michael Bascom scornfully. 'What is twenty years in the formation of a strata—what even in the growth of an oak—the cooling of a volcano!'

'Not much, perhaps, but it's apt to tell upon the bones of a human being.'

'The manganese staining to be seen upon some skulls would certainly indicate——' began the scientist dreamily.

'I wish my bones were only as free from rheumatics as they were twenty years ago,' pursued Daniel testily; 'and then, perhaps, I should make light of twenty years. Howsoever, the long and the short of it is, my missus must have a girl. She can't go on trotting up and down these everlasting passages, and standing in that stony scullery year after year, just as if she was a young woman. She must have a girl to help.'

'Let her have twenty girls,' said Mr Bascom, going back to his book.

'What's the use of talking like that, sir. Twenty girls, indeed! We shall have rare work to get one.'

'Because the neighbourhood is sparsely populated?' interrogated Mr Bascom, still reading.

'No, sir. Because this house is known to be haunted.'

Michael Bascom laid down his book, and turned a look of grave reproach upon his servant.

'Skegg,' he said in a severe voice, 'I thought you had lived long enough with me to be superior to any folly of that kind.'

'I don't say that I believe in ghosts,' answered Daniel with a semi-apologetic air, 'but the country people do. There's not a mortal among 'em that will venture across our threshold after nightfall.'

'Merely because Anthony Bascom, who led a wild life in London, and lost his money and land, came home here broken-hearted, and is supposed to have destroyed himself in this house—the only remnant of property that was left him out of a fine estate.'

'Supposed to have destroyed himself!' cried Skegg, 'why the fact is as well known as the death of Queen Elizabeth, or the great fire of London. Why, wasn't he buried at the cross-roads between here and Holcroft?'

'An idle tradition, for which you could produce no substantial proof,' retorted Mr Bascom.

'I don't know about proof; but the country people believe it as firmly as they believe their Gospel.'

'If their faith in the Gospel was a little stronger they need not trouble themselves about Anthony Bascom.'

'Well,' grumbled Daniel, as he began to clear the table, 'a girl of some kind we must get, but she'll have to be a foreigner, or a girl that's hard driven for a place.'

When Daniel Skegg said a foreigner, he did not mean the native of some distant clime, but a girl who had not been born and bred at Holcroft. Daniel had been raised and reared in that insignificant hamlet, and, small and dull as it was, he considered the world beyond it only margin.

Michael Bascom was too deep in the atomic theory to give a second thought to the necessities of an old servant. Mrs Skegg was an individual with whom he rarely came in contact. She lived for the most part in a gloomy region at the north end of the house, where she ruled over the solitude of a kitchen, that looked like a cathedral, and numerous offices of the scullery, larder, and pantry class, where she carried on a perpetual warfare with spiders and beetles, and wore her old life out in the labour of sweeping and scrubbing. She was a woman of severe aspect, dogmatic piety, and a bitter tongue. She was a good plain cook, and ministered diligently to her master's wants. He was not an epicure, but liked his life to be smooth and easy, and the equilibrium of his mental power would have been disturbed by a bad dinner.

He heard no more about the proposed addition to his household for a space of ten days, when Daniel Skegg again startled him amidst his studious repose by the abrupt announcement:

'I've got a girl!'

'Oh,' said Michael Bascom; 'have you?' and he went on with his book.

This time he was reading an essay on phosphorus and its functions in relation to the human brain.

'Yes,' pursued Daniel in his usual grumbling tone; 'she was a waif and stray, or I shouldn't have got her. If she'd been a native she'd never have come to us.'

'I hope she's respectable,' said Michael.

'Respectable! That's the only fault she has, poor thing. She's too good for the place. She's never been in service before, but she says she's willing to work, and I daresay my old woman will be able to break her in. Her father was a small tradesman at Yarmouth. He died a month ago, and left this poor thing homeless. Mrs Midge, at Holcroft, is her aunt, and she said to the girl, Come and stay with me till you get a place; and the girl has been staying with Mrs Midge for the last three weeks, trying to hear of a place. When Mrs Midge heard that my missus wanted a girl to help, she thought it would be the very thing for her niece Maria. Luckily Maria had heard nothing about this house, so the poor innocent dropped me a curtsey, and said she'd be thankful to come, and would do her best to learn her duty. She'd had an easy time of it with her father, who had educated her above her station, like a fool as he was,' growled Daniel.

'By your own account I'm afraid you've made a bad bargain,' said Michael. 'You don't want a young lady to clean kettle and pans.'

'If she was a young duchess my old woman would make her work,' retorted Skegg decisively.

'And pray where are you going to put this girl?' asked Mr Bascom, rather irritably; 'I can't have a strange young woman tramping up and down the passages outside my room. You know what a wretched sleeper I am, Skegg. A mouse behind the wainscot is enough to wake me.'

'I've thought of that,' answered the butler, with his look of ineffable wisdom. 'I'm not going to put her on your floor. She's to sleep in the attics.'

'Which room?'

'The big one at the north end of the house. That's the only ceiling that doesn't let water. She might as well sleep in a shower-bath as in any of the other attics.'

'The room at the north end,' repeated Mr Bascom thoughtfully; 'isn't that——?'

'Of course it is,' snapped Skegg; 'but she doesn't know anything about it.'

Mr Bascom went back to his books, and forgot all about the orphan from Yarmouth, until one morning on entering his study he was startled by the appearance of a strange girl, in a neat black and white cotton gown, busy dusting the volumes which were stacked in blocks upon his spacious writing-table—and doing it with such deft and careful hands that he had no inclination to be angry at this unwonted liberty. Old Mrs Skegg had religiously refrained from all such dusting, on the plea that she did not wish to interfere with the master's ways. One of the master's ways, therefore, had been to inhale a good deal of dust in the course of his studies.

The girl was a slim little thing, with a pale and somewhat old-fashioned face, flaxen hair, braided under a neat muslin cap, a very fair complexion, and light blue eyes. They were the lightest blue eyes Michael Bascom had ever seen, but there was a sweetness and gentleness in their expression which atoned for their insipid colour.

'I hope you do not object to my dusting your books, sir,' she said, dropping a curtsey.

She spoke with a quaint precision which struck Michael Bascom as a pretty thing in its way.

'No; I don't object to cleanliness, so long as my books and papers are not disturbed. If you take a volume off my desk, replace it on the spot you took it from. That's all I ask.'

'I will be very careful, sir.'

'When did you come here?'

'Only this morning, sir.'

The student seated himself at his desk, and the girl withdrew, drifting out of the room as noiselessly as a flower blown across the threshold. Michael Bascom looked after her curiously. He had seen very little of youthful womanhood in his dry-as-dust career, and he wondered at this girl as at a creature of a species hitherto unknown to him. How fairly and delicately she was fashioned; what a translucent skin; what soft and pleasing accents issued from those rose-tinted lips. A pretty thing, assuredly, this kitchen wench! A pity that in all this busy world there could be no better work found for her than the scouring of pots and pans.

Absorbed in considerations about dry bones, Mr Bascom thought no more of the pale-faced handmaiden. He saw her no more about his rooms. Whatever work she did there was done early in the morning, before the scholar's breakfast.

She had been a week in the house, when he met her one day in the hall. He was struck by the change in her appearance.

The girlish lips had lost their rose-bud hue; the pale blue eyes had a frightened look, and there were dark rings round them, as in one whose nights had been sleepless, or troubled by evil dreams.

Michael Bascom was so startled by an undefinable look in the girl's face that, reserved as he was by habit and nature, he expanded so far as to ask her what ailed her.

'There is something amiss, I am sure,' he said. 'What is it?'

'Nothing, sir,' she faltered, looking still more scared at his question. 'Indeed, it is nothing; or nothing worth troubling you about.'

'Nonsense. Do you suppose, because I live among books, I have no sympathy with my fellow-creatures? Tell me what is wrong with you, child. You have been grieving about the father you have lately lost, I suppose.'

'No, sir; it is not that. I shall never leave off being sorry for that. It is a grief which will last me all my life.'

'What, there is something else then?' asked Michael impatiently. 'I see; you are not happy here. Hard work does not suit you. I thought as much.'

'Oh, sir, please don't think that,' cried the girl, very earnestly. 'Indeed, I am glad to work—glad to be in service; it is only——'

She faltered and broke down, the tears rolling slowly from her sorrowful eyes, despite her effort to keep them back.

'Only what?' cried Michael, growing angry. 'The girl is full of secrets and mysteries. What do you mean, wench?'

'I—I know it is very foolish, sir; but I am afraid of the room where I sleep.'

'Afraid! Why?'

'Shall I tell you the truth, sir? Will you promise not to be angry?'

'I will not be angry if you will only speak plainly; but you provoke me by these hesitations and suppressions.'

'And please, sir, do not tell Mrs Skegg that I have told you. She would scold me; or perhaps even send me away.'

'Mrs Skegg shall not scold you. Go on, child.'

'You may not know the room where I sleep, sir, it is a large room at one end of the house, looking towards the sea. I can see the dark line of water from the window, and I wonder sometimes to think that it is the same ocean I used to see when I was a child at Yarmouth. It is very lonely, sir, at the top of the house. Mr and Mrs Skegg sleep in a little room near the kitchen, you know, sir, and I am quite alone on the top floor.'

'Skegg told me you had been educated in advance of your position in life, Maria. I should have thought the first effect of good education would have been to make you superior to any foolish fancies about empty rooms.'

'Oh, pray, sir, do not think it is any fault in my education. Father took such pains with me; he spared no expense in giving me as good an education as a tradesman's daughter need wish for. And he was a religious man, sir. He did not believe'—here she paused, with a suppressed shudder—'in spirits of the dead appearing to the living, since the days of miracles, when the ghost of Samuel appeared to Saul. He never put any foolish ideas into my head, sir. I hadn't a thought of fear when I first lay down to rest in the big lonely room upstairs.'

'Well, what then?'

'But on the very first night,' the girl went on breathlessly, 'I felt weighed down in my sleep as if there were some heavy burden laid upon my chest. It was not a bad dream, but it was a sense of trouble that followed me all through my sleep; and just at daybreak—it begins to be light a little after six—I woke suddenly, with the cold perspiration pouring down my face, and knew that there was something dreadful in the room.'

'What do you mean by something dreadful? Did you see anything?'

'Not much, sir, but it froze the blood in my veins, and I knew it was this that had been following me and weighing upon me all through my sleep. In the corner, between the fireplace and the wardrobe, I saw a shadow—a dim, shapeless shadow——'

'Produced by an angle of the wardrobe, I daresay.'

'No, sir; I could see the shadow of the wardrobe, distinct and sharp, as if it had been painted on the wall. This shadow was in the corner—a strange, shapeless mass; or, if it had any shape at all, it seemed——'

'What?' asked Michael eagerly.

'The shape of a dead body hanging against the wall!'

Michael Bascom grew strangely pale, yet he affected utter incredulity.

'Poor child,' he said kindly; 'you have been fretting about your father until your nerves are in a weak state, and you are full of fancies. A shadow in the corner, indeed; why, at daybreak, every corner is full of shadows. My old coat, flung upon a chair, will make you as good a ghost as you need care to see.'

'Oh, sir, I have tried to think it is my fancy. But I have had the same burden weighing me down every night. I have seen the same shadow every morning.'

'But when broad daylight comes, can you not see what stuff your shadow is made of?'

'No, sir: the shadow goes before it is broad daylight.'

'Of course, just like other shadows. Come, come, get these silly notions out of your head, or you will never do for the work-a-day world. I could easily speak to Mrs Skegg, and make her give you another room, if I wanted to encourage you in your folly. But that would be about the worst thing I could do for you. Besides, she tells me that all the other rooms on that floor are damp; and, no doubt, if she shifted you into one of them, you would discover another shadow in another corner, and get rheumatism into the bargain. No, my good girl, you must try to prove yourself the better for a superior education.'

'I will do my best, sir,' Maria answered meekly, dropping a curtsey.

Maria went back to the kitchen sorely depressed. It was a dreary life she led at Wildheath Grange—dreary by day, awful by night; for the vague burden and the shapeless shadow, which seemed so slight a matter to the elderly scholar, were unspeakably terrible to her. Nobody had told her that the house was haunted, yet she walked about those echoing passages wrapped round with a cloud of fear. She had no pity from Daniel Skegg and his wife. Those two pious souls had made up their minds that the character of the house should be upheld, so far as Maria went. To her, as a foreigner, the Grange should be maintained to be an immaculate dwelling, tainted by no sulphurous blast from the underworld. A willing, biddable girl had become a necessary element in the existence of Mrs Skegg. That girl had been found, and that girl must be kept. Any fancies of a supernatural character must be put down with a high hand.

'Ghosts, indeed!' cried the amiable Skegg. 'Read your Bible, Maria, and don't talk no more about ghosts.'

'There are ghosts in the Bible,' said Maria, with a shiver at the recollection of certain awful passages in the Scripture she knew so well.

'Ah, they was in their right place, or they wouldn't ha' been there,' retorted Mrs Skegg. 'You ain't agoin' to pick holes in your Bible, I hope, Maria, at your time of life.'

Maria sat down quietly in her comer by the kitchen fire, and turned over the leaves of her dead father's Bible till she came to the chapters they two had loved best and oftenest read together. He had been a simple-minded, straight-forward man, the Yarmouth cabinet-maker—a man full of aspirations after good, innately refined, instinctively religious. He and his motherless girl had spent their lives alone together, in the neat little home which Maria had so soon learnt to cherish and beautify; and they had loved each other with an almost romantic love. They had had the same tastes, the same ideas. Very lit-tle had sufficed to make them happy. But inexorable death parted father and daughter, in one of those sharp, sudden partings which are like the shock of an earthquake—instantaneous ruin, desolation, and despair.

Maria's fragile form had bent before the tempest. She had lived through a trouble that might have crushed a stronger nature. Her deep religious convictions, and her belief that this cruel parting would not be for ever, had sustained her. She faced life, and its cares and duties, with a gentle patience which was the noblest form of courage.

Michael Bascom told himself that the servant-girl's foolish fancy about the room that had been given her was not a matter of serious considera-tion. Yet the idea dwelt in his mind unpleasantly, and disturbed him at his labours. The exact sciences require the complete power of a man's brain, his utmost attention; and on this particular evening Michael found that he was only giving his work a part of his attention. The girl's pale face, the girl's tremulous tones, thrust themselves into the foreground of his thoughts.

He closed his book with a fretful sigh, wheeled his large armchair round to the fire, and gave himself up to contemplation. To attempt study with so disturbed a mind was useless. It was a dull grey evening, early in November; the student's reading-lamp was lighted, but the shutters were not yet shut, nor the curtains drawn. He could see the leaden sky outside his windows, the fir-tree tops tossing in the angry wind. He could hear the wintry blast whistling amidst the gables, before it rushed off seaward with a savage howl that sounded like a war-whoop.

Michael Bascom shivered, and drew nearer the fire.

'It's childish, foolish nonsense,' he said to himself; 'yet it's strange she should have that fancy about the shadow, for they say Anthony Bascom destroyed himself in that room. I remember hearing it when I was a boy, from an old servant whose mother was housekeeper at the great house in Anthony's time. I never heard how he died, poor fellow—whether he poisoned himself, or shot himself, or cut his throat; but I've been told that was the room. Old Skegg has heard it too. I could see that by his manner when he told me the girl was to sleep there.'

He sat for a long time, till the grey of evening outside his study windows changed to the black of night, and the war-whoop of the wind died away to a low complaining murmur. He sat looking into the fire, and letting his thoughts wander back to the past and the traditions he had heard in his boyhood.

That was a sad, foolish story of his great-uncle, Anthony Bascom: the pitiful story of a wasted fortune and a wasted life. A riotous collegiate career at Cambridge, a racing-stable at Newmarket, an imprudent marriage, a dissipated life in London, a runaway wife; an estate forfeited to Jew money-lenders, and then the fatal end.

Michael had often heard that dismal story: how, when Anthony Bascom's fair false wife had left him, when his credit was exhausted, and his friends had grown tired of him, and all was gone except Wildheath Grange, Anthony, the broken-down man of fashion, had come to that lonely house unexpectedly one night, and had ordered his bed to be got ready for him in the room where he used to sleep when he came to the place for the wild duck shooting, in his boyhood. His old blunderbuss was still hanging over the mantelpiece, where he had left it when he came into the property, and could afford to buy the newest thing in fowling-pieces. He had not been to Wildheath for fifteen years; nay, for a good many of those years he had almost forgotten that the dreary old house belonged to him.

The woman who had been housekeeper at Bascom Park, till house and lands had passed into the hands of the Jews, was at this time the sole occupant of Wildheath. She cooked some supper for her master, and made him as comfortable as she could in the long untenanted dining-room; but she was distressed to find, when she cleared the table after he had gone upstairs to bed, that he had eaten hardly anything.

Next morning she got his breakfast ready in the same room, which she managed to make brighter and cheerier than it had looked overnight. Brooms, dusting-brushes, and a good fire did much to improve the aspect of things. But the morning wore on to noon, and the old housekeeper listened in vain for her master's footfall on the stairs. Noon waned to late afternoon. She had made no attempt to disturb him, thinking that he had worn himself out by a tedious journey on horseback, and that he was sleeping the sleep of exhaustion. But when the brief November day clouded with the first shadows of twilight, the old woman grew seriously alarmed, and went upstairs to her master's door, where she waited in vain for any reply to her repeated calls and knockings.

The door was locked on the inside, and the housekeeper was not strong enough to break it open. She rushed downstairs again full of fear, and ran bare-headed out into the lonely road. There was no habitation nearer than the turnpike on the old coach road, from which this side road branched off to the sea. There was scanty hope of a chance passer-by. The old woman ran along the road, hardly knowing whither she was going or what she was going to do, but with a vague idea that she must get somebody to help her.

Chance favoured her. A cart, laden with sea-weed, came lumbering slowly along from the level line of sands yonder where the land melted into water. A heavy lumbering farm-labourer walked beside the cart.

'For God's sake, come in and burst open my master's door!' she entreated, seizing the man by the arm. 'He's lying dead, or in a fit, and I can't get to help him.'

'All right, missus,' answered the man, as if such an invitation were a matter of daily occurrence. 'Whoa, Dobbin; stond still, horse, and be donged to thee.'

Dobbin was glad enough to be brought to anchor on the patch of waste grass in front of the Grange garden. His master followed the housekeeper upstairs, and shattered the old-fashioned box-lock with one blow of his ponderous fist.

The old woman's worst fear was realised. Anthony Bascom was dead. But the mode and manner of his death Michael had never been able to learn. The housekeeper's daughter, who told him the story, was an old woman when he was a boy. She had only shaken her head, and looked unutterable things, when he questioned her too closely. She had never even admitted that the old squire had committed suicide. Yet the tradition of his self-destruction was rooted in the minds of the natives of Holcroft: and there was a settled belief that his ghost, at certain times and seasons, haunted Wildheath Grange.

Now Michael Bascom was a stern materialist. For him the universe, with all its inhabitants, was a great machine, governed by inexorable laws. To such a man the idea of a ghost was simply absurd—as absurd as the assertion that two and two make five, or that a circle can be formed of a straight line. Yet he had a kind of dilettante interest in the idea of a mind which could believe in ghosts. The subject offered an amusing psychological study. This poor little pale girl, now, had evidently got some supernatural terror into her head, which could only be conquered by rational treatment.

'I know what I ought to do,' Michael Bascom said to himself suddenly. 'I'll occupy that room myself tonight, and demonstrate to this foolish girl that her notion about the shadow is nothing more than a silly fancy, bred of timidity and low spirits. An ounce of proof is better than a pound of argument. If I can prove to her that I have spent a night in the room, and seen no such shadow, she will understand what an idle thing superstition is.'

Daniel came in presently to shut the shutters.

'Tell your wife to make up my bed in the room where Maria has been sleeping, and to put her into one of the rooms on the first floor for tonight, Skegg,' said Mr Bascom.

'Sir?'

Mr Bascom repeated his order.

'That silly wench has been complaining to you about her room,' Skegg exclaimed indignantly. 'She doesn't deserve to be well fed and cared for in a comfortable home. She ought to go to the workhouse.'

'Don't be angry with the poor girl, Skegg. She has taken a foolish fancy into her head, and I want to show her how silly she is,' said Mr Bascom.

'And you want to sleep in his—in that room yourself,' said the butler.

'Precisely.'

'Well,' mused Skegg, 'if he does walk—which I don't believe—he was your own flesh and blood; and I don't suppose he'll do you any hurt.'

When Daniel Skegg went back to the kitchen he railed mercilessly at poor Maria, who sat pale and silent in her corner by the hearth, darning old Mrs Skegg's grey worsted stockings, which were the roughest and harshest armour that ever human foot clothed itself withal. 'Was there ever such a whimsical, fine, lady-like miss,' demanded Daniel, 'to come into a gentleman's house, and drive him out of his own bedroom to sleep in an attic, with her nonsenses and vagaries.' If this was the result of being educated above one's station, Daniel declared that he was thankful he had never got so far in his schooling as to read words of two syllables without spelling. Education might be hanged for him, if this was all it led to.

'I am very sorry,' faltered Maria, weeping silently over her work. 'Indeed, Mr Skegg, I made no complaint. My master questioned me, and I told him the truth. That was all.'

'All!' exclaimed Mr Skegg irately; 'all, indeed! I should think it was enough.'

Poor Maria held her peace. Her mind, fluttered by Daniel's unkindness, had wandered away from that bleak big kitchen to the lost home of the past—the snug little parlour where she and her father had sat beside the cosy hearth on such a night as this; she with her smart work-box and her plain sewing, he with the newspaper he loved to read; the petted cat purring on the rug, the kettle singing on the bright brass trivet, the tea-tray pleasantly suggestive of the most comfortable meal in the day.

Oh, those happy nights, that dear companionship! Were they really gone for ever, leaving nothing behind them but unkindness and servitude?

*　*　*　*　*

Michael Bascom retired later than usual that night. He was in the habit of sitting at his books long after every other lamp but his own had been extinguished. The Skeggs had subsided into silence and darkness in their dreary ground-floor bed-chamber. Tonight his studies were of a peculiarly interesting kind, and belonged to the order of recreative reading rather than of hard work. He was deep in the history of that mysterious people who had their dwelling-place in the Swiss lakes, and was much exercised by certain speculations and theories about them.

The old eight-day clock on the stairs was striking two as Michael slowly ascended, candle in hand, to the hitherto unknown region of the attics. At the top of the staircase he found himself facing a dark narrow passage which led northwards, a passage that was in itself sufficient to strike terror to a superstitious mind, so black and uncanny did it look.

'Poor child,' mused Mr Bascom, thinking of Maria; 'this attic floor is rather dreary, and for a young mind prone to fancies——'

He had opened the door of the north room by this time, and stood looking about him.

It was a large room, with a ceiling that sloped on one side, but was fairly lofty upon the other; an old-fashioned room, full of old-fashioned furniture—big, ponderous, clumsy—associated with a day that was gone and people that were dead. A walnut-wood wardrobe stared him in the face—a wardrobe with brass handles, which gleamed out of the darkness like diabolical eyes. There was a tall four-post bedstead, which had been cut down on one side to accommodate the slope of the ceiling, and which had a misshapen and deformed aspect in consequence. There was an old mahogany bureau, that smelt of secrets. There were some heavy old chairs with rush bottoms, mouldy with age, and much worn. There was a corner washstand, with a big basin and a small jug—the odds and ends of past years. Carpet there was none, save a narrow strip beside the bed.

'It is a dismal room,' mused Michael, with the same touch of pity for Maria's weakness which he had felt on the landing just now.

To him it mattered nothing where he slept; but having let himself down to a lower level by his interest in the Swiss lake-people, he was in a manner humanised by the lightness of his evening's reading, and was even inclined to compassionate the weaknesses of a foolish girl.

He went to bed, determined to sleep his soundest. The bed was comfortable, well supplied with blankets, rather luxurious than otherwise, and the scholar had that agreeable sense of fatigue which promises profound and restful slumber.

He dropped off to sleep quickly, but woke with a start ten minutes afterwards. What was this consciousness of a burden of care that had awakened him—this sense of all-pervading trouble that weighed upon his spirits and oppressed his heart—this icy horror of some terrible crisis in life through which he must inevitably pass? To him these feelings were as novel as they were painful. His life had flowed on with smooth and sluggish tide, unbroken by so much as a ripple of sorrow. Yet tonight he felt all the pangs of unavailing remorse; the agonising memory of a life wasted; the stings of humiliation and disgrace, shame, ruin; a hideous death, which he had doomed himself to die by his own hand. These were the horrors that pressed him round and weighed him down as he lay in Anthony Bascom's room.

Yes, even he, the man who could recognise nothing in Nature, or in Nature's God, better or higher than an irresponsible and invariable machine governed by mechanical laws, was fain to admit that here he found himself face to face with a psychological mystery. This trouble, which came between him and sleep, was the trouble that had pursued Anthony Bascom on the last night of his life. So had the suicide felt as he lay in that lonely room, perhaps striving to rest his wearied brain with one last earthly sleep before he passed to the unknown intermediate land where all is darkness and slumber. And that troubled mind had haunted the room ever since. It was not the ghost of the man's body that returned to the spot where he had suffered and perished, but the ghost of his mind—his very self; no meaningless simulacrum of the clothes he wore, and the figure that filled them.

Michael Bascom was not the man to abandon his high ground of sceptical philosophy without a struggle. He tried his hardest to conquer this oppression that weighed upon mind and sense. Again and again he succeeded in composing himself to sleep, but only to wake again and again to the same torturing thoughts, the same remorse, the same despair. So the night passed in unutterable weariness; for though he told himself that the trouble was not his trouble, that there was no reality in the burden, no reason for the remorse, these vivid fancies were as painful as realities, and took as strong a hold upon him.

The first streak of light crept in at the window—dim, and cold, and grey; then came twilight, and he looked at the corner between the wardrobe and the door.

Yes; there was the shadow: not the shadow of the wardrobe only—that was clear enough, but a vague and shapeless something which darkened the dull brown wall; so faint, so shadowy, that he could form no conjecture as to its nature, or the thing it represented. He determined to watch this shadow till broad daylight; but the weariness of the night had exhausted him, and before the first dimness of dawn had passed away he had fallen fast asleep, and was tasting the blessed balm of undisturbed slumber. When he woke the winter sun was shining in at the lattice, and the room had lost its gloomy aspect. It looked old-fashioned, and grey, and brown, and shabby; but the depth of its gloom had fled with the shadows and the darkness of night.

Mr Bascom rose refreshed by a sound sleep, which had lasted nearly three hours. He remembered the wretched feelings which had gone before that renovating slumber; but he recalled his strange sensations only to despise them, and he despised himself for having attached any importance to them.

'Indigestion very likely,' he told himself; 'or perhaps mere fancy, engendered of that foolish girl's story. The wisest of us is more under the dominion of imagination than he would care to confess. Well, Maria shall not sleep in this room any more. There is no particular reason why she should, and she shall not be made unhappy to please old Skegg and his wife.'

When he had dressed himself in his usual leisurely way, Mr Bascom walked up to the corner where he had seen or imagined the shadow, and examined the spot carefully.

At first sight he could discover nothing of a mysterious character. There was no door in the papered wall, no trace of a door that had been there in the past. There was no trap-door in the worm-eaten boards. There was no dark ineradicable stain to hint at murder. There was not the faintest suggestion of a secret or a mystery.

He looked up at the ceiling. That was sound enough, save for a dirty patch here and there where the rain had blistered it.

Yes; there was something—an insignificant thing, yet with a suggestion of grimness which startled him.

About a foot below the ceiling he saw a large iron hook projecting from the wall, just above the spot where he had seen the shadow of a vaguely defined form. He mounted on a chair the better to examine this hook, and to understand, if he could, the purpose for which it had been put there.

It was old and rusty. It must have been there for many years. Who could have placed it there, and why? It was not the kind of hook upon which one would hang a picture or one's garments. It was placed in an obscure corner. Had Anthony Bascom put it there on the night he died; or did he find it there ready for a fatal use?

'If I were a superstitious man,' thought Michael, 'I should be inclined to believe that Anthony Bascom hung himself from that rusty old hook.'

*   *   *   *   *

'Sleep, well, sir?' asked Daniel, as he waited upon his master at breakfast.

'Admirably,' answered Michael, determined not to gratify the man's curiosity.

He had always resented the idea that Wildheath Grange was haunted.

'Oh, indeed, sir. You were so late that I fancied——'

'Late, yes! I slept so well that I overshot my usual hour for waking. But, by-the-way, Skegg, as that poor girl objects to the room, let her sleep somewhere else. It can't make any difference to us, and it may make some difference to her.'

'Humph!' muttered Daniel in his grumpy way; 'you didn't see anything queer up there, did you?'

'See anything? Of course not.'

'Well, then, why should she see things? It's all her silly fiddle-faddle.'

'Never mind, let her sleep in another room.'

'There ain't another room on the top floor that's dry.'

'Then let her sleep on the floor below. She creeps about quietly enough, poor little timid thing. She won't disturb me.'

Daniel grunted, and his master understood the grunt to mean obedient assent; but here Mr Bascom was unhappily mistaken. The proverbial obstinacy of the pig family is as nothing compared with the obstinacy of a cross-grained old man, whose narrow mind has never been illuminated by education. Daniel was beginning to feel jealous of his master's compassionate interest in the orphan girl. She was a sort of gentle clinging thing that might creep into an elderly bachelor's heart unawares, and make herself a comfortable nest there.

'We shall have fine carryings-on, and me and my old woman will be nowhere, if I don't put down my heel pretty strong upon this nonsense,' Daniel muttered to himself, as he carried the breakfast-tray to the pantry.

Maria met him in the passage.

'Well, Mr Skegg, what did my master say?' she asked breathlessly. 'Did he see anything strange in the room?'

'No, girl. What should she see? He said you were a fool.'

'Nothing disturbed him? And he slept there peacefully?' faltered Maria.

'Never slept better in his life. Now don't you begin to feel ashamed of yourself?'

'Yes,' she answered meekly; 'I am ashamed of being so full of fancies. I will go back to my room tonight, Mr Skegg, if you like, and I will never complain of it again.'

'I hope you won't,' snapped Skegg; 'you've given us trouble enough already.'

Maria sighed, and went about her work in saddest silence. The day wore slowly on, like all other days in that lifeless old house. The scholar sat in his study; Maria moved softly from room to room, sweeping and dusting in the cheerless solitude. The mid-day sun faded into the grey of afternoon, and evening came down like a blight upon the dull old house.

Throughout that day Maria and her master never met. Anyone who had been so far interested in the girl as to observe her appearance would have seen that she was unusually pale, and that her eyes had a resolute look, as of one who was resolved to face a painful ordeal. She ate hardly anything all day. She was curiously silent. Skegg and his wife put down both these symptoms to temper.

'She won't eat and she won't talk,' said Daniel to the partner of his joys. 'That means sulkiness, and I never allowed sulkiness to master me when I was a young man, and you tried it on as a young woman, and I'm not going to be conquered by sulkiness in my old age.'

Bedtime came, and Maria bade the Skeggs a civil goodnight, and went up to her lonely garret without a murmur.

The next morning came, and Mrs Skegg looked in vain for her patient hand-maiden, when she wanted Maria's services in preparing the breakfast.

'The wench sleeps sound enough this morning,' said the old woman. 'Go and call her, Daniel, my poor legs can't stand them stairs.'

'Your poor legs are getting uncommon useless,' muttered Daniel testily, as he went to do his wife's behest.

He knocked at the door, and called Maria—once, twice, thrice, many times; but there was no reply. He tried the door, and found it locked. He shook the door violently, cold with fear.

Then he told himself that the girl had played him a trick. She had stolen away before daybreak, and left the door locked to frighten him. But, no; this could not be, for he could see the key in the lock when he knelt down and put his eye to the keyhole. The key prevented his seeing into the room.

'She's in there, laughing in her sleeve at me,' he told himself; 'but I'll soon be even with her.'

There was a heavy bar on the staircase, which was intended to secure the shutters of the window that lighted the stairs. It was a detached bar, and always stood in a corner near the window, which it was but rarely employed to fasten. Daniel ran down to the landing, and seized upon this massive iron bar, and then ran back to the garret door.

One blow from the heavy bar shattered the old lock, which was the same lock the carter had broken with his strong fist seventy years before. The door flew open, and Daniel went into the attic which he had chosen for the stranger's bed-chamber.

Maria was hanging from the hook in the wall. She had contrived to cover her face decently with her handkerchief. She had hanged herself deliberately about an hour before Daniel found her, in the early grey of morning. The doctor, who was summoned from Holcroft, was able to declare the time at which she had slain herself, but there was no one who could say what sudden access of terror had impelled her to the desperate act, or under what slow torture of nervous apprehension her mind had given way. The coroner's jury returned the customary merciful verdict of 'Temporary insanity'.

The girl's melancholy fate darkened the rest of Michael Bascom's life. He fled from Wildheath Grange as from an accursed spot, and from the Skeggs as from the murderers of a harmless innocent girl. He ended his days at Oxford, where he found the society of congenial minds, and the books he loved. But the memory of Maria's sad face, and sadder death, was his abiding sorrow. Out of that deep shadow his soul was never lifted.

The Face in the Glass

Part I
The Warning

IN FAR-DISTANT YORKSHIRE, many years ago, stood an old manor-house—a grey, grim building surrounding an open courtyard, in the middle of which played a melancholy fountain. The house was close to the wide moors that stretch away to the city of York, and beside the village there was not another place within miles. Except for the housekeeper and the usual staff of servants the house had been uninhabited now for some time, for the late owner had been a great traveller, and had been drowned during his last voyage; close at home too, which made it all the sadder, and he was brought back to be buried in the dreary family vault one day in the spring before my story opens. Since that occurrence the housekeeper declared that, whenever there were storms out at sea, the wind used to howl and wail down the long passages like a soul in pain, and that a dreadful sound of dripping water always was to be heard in the room where the poor body was laid, in the interval before the funeral. There were also some mysterious chambers in the mansion where the doors disappeared periodically, and entrance to them was thereby prevented for months together, and when they were at last restored, the walls would be found adorned with diabolical sketches of fiends, and the furniture would be arranged in anything but an artistic manner.

However, this did not seem to weigh very heavily on the spirits of the new owners, Mr and Mrs Monroe, a high-spirited, courageous couple, who had not long been married, and were as happy as the day was long. Mrs Monroe, indeed, professed herself most anxious to see one of these wonderful ghosts; but then she was strong-minded, and actually thought nothing of going to bed alone in the dark, and she would visit the haunted chambers and walk about the passages at night until the servants almost believed she must be a ghost herself, so extremely fearless was she on the subject. Nor was her husband in any way behindhand in assisting her in her ghost hunts, but he was out a great deal hunting and shooting just then, and often came home simply to dine and fall asleep, sometimes even over the dinner-table itself, with sheer fatigue.

Mrs Monroe had been one of a large family who lived in a cheerful house in sunny Kent, and had had very little time there for the reading, writing, and walking, with which she now filled up her days in the most satisfactory manner, and she had not yet found the time hang heavily on her hands; but still she was not very sorry when the first hard frosts of the rigorous Yorkshire winter bound up the ground into an iron mass, and put a stop to the outdoor amusements which took her husband so constantly away from her side. Occasional falls of snow, too, rather spoiled his shooting, and he could only putter about the house, farm, and the little park, getting an occasional sea-bird that was driven in from the coast, and that gave him an evening's work looking it out in one of his numerous Bewick-illustrated books, for as he never could find it there, the occupation was as endless as it was enthralling. This was very well for the first fortnight or so, and Mrs Monroe could go out with him to look for the birds, and could help him with his Bewick at night; but at last the snow began to fall in earnest; and after four days of it, with scarcely a break in the chilly grey sky, when the post had never come in at all, and the one newspaper of the week had never been delivered, Mrs Monroe was beginning to wonder if it would be wicked to pray for a thaw; for she foresaw that unless something new could be contrived in the way of amusement for her lord and master, she would discover what having too much of a good thing was like; for even her company had begun to pall, and he became first fidgety, next complaining, then fractious about his dinner, and then very, very cross.

At last a bright idea struck her. 'Hugh,' she said, 'let us get Betty's keys from her this very moment, and go in for a regular ghost hunt. The evening has come on very rapidly, and the moon on the snow will make the rooms as bright as day. See,' she added, drawing apart the heavy crimson curtains that hung over the deep, small-paned windows, 'the clouds are all gone, and tomorrow you may be able to shoot again, and we may never have such a glorious opportunity for months to come, so don't let us miss it. We're both tired of sitting over the fire, and a rush through all those mysterious rooms above our bedroom floor will give us an appetite for dinner; even if we are not rewarded by the sight of the much-to-be-desired bogie.'

'It will be horribly cold,' answered Hugh, shrugging up his shoulders and stretching out his hands to the big fire that blazed up the chimney; 'and besides, if we did see a ghost, it would be the death of you; you know it's only because you didn't believe in Betty's stories that you are so courageous.'

'My dear Hugh,' said Ruth, impressively, 'I don't for one moment believe we shall see anything worse than ourselves, as old nurse used to say; but if we did, what could possibly happen to us? I have been up and about all hours of the night, especially when Betty was so ill the week before last, and really if there were anything to be seen, I should have seen it then. However, I won't go now if you don't like it.'

'Oh, we'll go,' answered Hugh. 'I was rather lazy, that's all.' And so saying, he rang the bell and ordered the keys; and after a little delay a goodly assortment of all sizes and species of key was brought them, and off started Mr and Mrs Monroe on their ghost hunt.

Hugh's spirits rose with the search, and they went upstairs and downstairs, unlocking many a cupboard and room that had not been looked at for months, and maybe years, but not a ghost was to be seen. Every now and then a most suggestive rustle was to be heard among the dusty hangings of the oak four-posters, and Hugh and Ruth held each other's hands a little tighter than usual; but on investigation it turned out to be either the wind that was beginning to rise, or a shimmer from the lamp they carried showed them a little grey mouse scuttling away under the beds; now and then, too, a dreary groan seemed to pierce the darkness as they opened some heavy door; but this, too, generally turned out to be caused by the rustiness of the hinges.

They were getting gradually in extremely high spirits, and as the hunt proceeded, and nothing was found, they were laughing and talking loudly, when suddenly they come upon a door at the very end of the passage that led down to the inhabited portion of the house, which they had not noticed before. Of course it was locked, as they discovered at once, and after trying to unlock it with every key they had, they came to the conclusion that they would have to go downstairs after one that would fit the lock; when suddenly the wind seemed to rise yet higher, and a rather strong puff came through the keyhole (through which Mrs Monroe was peeping to see if the key had been left there), extinguishing the lamp she held, and they were at once plunged in darkness. However, Mr Monroe soon lighted it again. 'The windows must all be open,' said he, 'in which case it was quite time we investigated our domain. I dare say old Betty has lost the key, and is afraid I shall scold her for her carelessness. However, if you aren't frightened, Ruth,' he added, turning to his wife, 'I'll run down and ask her about it. If she's lost it, I'll have the door broken open and those windows shut, for there's wind enough here for a ship in full sail.'

'Yes, do,' answered Mrs Monroe brightly; 'doubtless here's the sailor's ghost that makes our nights so extremely squally when the wind is high; and if we can get rid of him, perhaps I shall not be driven to have a new maid every time the wind blows from the north-west; which is beginning to be rather a trouble, especially now when the snow is so deep. I should never get one out from York.'

'Well, wait there, then,' said Mr Monroe, and he hurried off into the downstairs regions and asked the old housekeeper for the missing key. She rose from her seat by the fire, trembling, and in a hurried manner said, 'Now doant'ee, Master Hugh.'

'Doant'ee,' repeated Hugh scornfully, 'doant'ee what? if you've lost the key, what does it matter? we'll soon get a new one; but if you haven't, and it's any of your superstitious nonsense, you ought to know us better than to try on any of that with us. Be quick, too, for it's mighty cold up there. The windows are open, I think, and though the night is still, the wind seems to chill one through.'

'Master Hugh,' said Betty impressively, 'in that room has lain dead many members of the Monroe family; somehow or other every member has either died there or been carried thither in his coffin to wait for his funeral day. And tonight, Master Hugh,' she added, waxing more eloquent as her dread of his taking the key increased—'tonight is the anniversary of the day Master Charles was brought there drowned and dead from Flamborough Bay; and you know that as sure as you go into that room, so sure will you see reflected in the glass the face of any member of the family who has to die before the year is out; and on the bed, Master Hugh, you'll see the coffin, with its dreadful drip, drip, drip, from the shroud of the poor dead boy, just as it dripped ceaselessly with seawater until they buried him out of our sight.'

'What on earth are you about, Hugh?' broke in a voice from the door-way. 'I am nearly frozen to death, and I want to get into the room.'

'Give me the key, Betty,' said Hugh, 'I'll run the risk of the ghosts, coffin and all, and besides, we are ghost hunting. So, my dear,' he went on, turning to his wife, who, tired of waiting, had come down to see what he was doing, 'according to Betty we may cry Eureka, for the ghost is found;' and, laughing very much, the two young people took the key from Betty's unwilling hand, and rushing up the wide oak staircase, they were soon at the door of the ghost-chamber.

The wind seemed to have risen in their short absence, and as they rested for a moment, after their hurried race up the stairs, there seemed to come to them the regular drip, drip, drip, that old Betty had prophesied. Even their stout hearts quailed somewhat, but with an impatient 'Imagination, of course,' Hugh turned the key in the lock, and the door came open. Only a bare boarded chamber, and in the middle the bed that had held so many, many corpses: three tiny windows all close shuttered, but through the chinks came stray moonbeams, and a most tremendous rush of wind that agitated the light chintz hangings to the bed, until all sorts and shapes of figures seemed in the folds, peeping and glaring at the newcomers. Between each window was hung a looking-glass, and above the mantel-piece was another—other furniture was there none.

'A window must be broken,' said Mrs Monroe, and so saying she advanced to throw open the shutters, which she had no sooner done than she was alarmed by hearing her husband fall with a loud bang behind her, with the muttered exclamation 'My God!'

Ruth tore to the bell, and rang a tremendous peal, and before the servants came rushing up she had dragged Hugh into her arms, and regard-less of any ghosts that might be about, turned all her attention to her husband, wishing heartily that she could get at some of the water she heard so continually dripping near her. Just as the servants reached her she caught sight of a thin stream of water meandering towards them, making a line of light through the dust, and she stooped forward to dip her handkerchief into it, when Betty, who, notwithstanding her age, was the first to answer the summons she had been awaiting breathlessly ever since the key had left her hands—rushed forward, and with a 'M—m—missus, that's corpse water,' deluged Hugh and Ruth with the contents of a jug she had brought up with her, convinced that it would be required. Hugh was carried out of the room into his own, and just as Ruth turned to lock the door, she saw, or fancied she saw, in the moonlight that now flooded the room, the pale shadow of a coffin on the bed, from which proceeded the thin stream of water which she had so nearly used for her husband; and with a shudder of horror, but with a promise to herself to re-investigate the subject, she closed and locked the door, slipping the key into her pocket, and followed Hugh into his room.

By this time he had come to himself, and was beginning to wonder what on earth had been the matter; but the moment he saw his wife, the remembrance of the horror came back to him, and he nearly fainted again.

When he was all right once more, which was not until the next day, and they were seated at a late breakfast, Ruth implored him to tell her quietly and calmly all he had seen; but all she could draw from him was the assurance that no power on earth should induce him to tell her, and that he wished to forget all about it as soon as he could. 'Ghosts? oh, ghosts were nonsense, of course, but still there was no need to talk of them.'

'But Hugh,' said Ruth mysteriously, '*I* saw it too, and I didn't mind a bit. After all,' she added, alarmed at the expression on her husband's face, 'it might have been only a leak in the roof that allowed the water to come in; and moonbeams do take such curious shapes, especially when reflected from the snow, that I believe the coffin only existed in our imagination; and I shall go up again tonight, and set the matter straight once and for all. If there really should be a ghost—well, we must use all our endeavours to lay the perturbed spirit; but if there isn't, we had surely better discover that it is so, for really you look white and ready to faint at the mere idea of it.'

'You must do nothing of the kind,' answered Hugh decidedly. 'I saw neither coffin nor water, and what I did see was probably nothing of any consequence, but I cannot mention it to you of all people under the sun—at all events not until the first shock has worn off. And I must ask you to give up any idea you may have of going there again.' Before Ruth had any time to either give him the desired promise, or argue him out of his absurd superstition, as she characterised his ideas in her own mind, Hugh had caught sight of the weekly postman labouring at last through the melting mud in the avenue; and doubtless wishing to forget all about the affair of the night before, he went out to meet him.

'Very sorry, sir,' said the postman, 'to be late, but still more sorry to be the bearer of bad news: your poor brother's heart-broke. He've lost his missus, and wants to see you at once. The funeral's tomorrow, and he does hope the roads will be open enough to allow of you to come to him, for he's terribly cut up about it.'

Hugh took the letters and went in, and who shall say how thankful he was at the bad news? for he had fully believed he had seen his wife's face in the glass in the ghost room last night, and now it had turned out—so he thinks—to be that of his younger brother's wife, who was his wife's sister, and who resembled Ruth greatly. In his joy at the load lifted off his mind he almost forgot he had to tell his wife of her sister's death, and he was glad to find her absent on her household duties, where she remained until he had read his letters and felt in a more saddened frame of mind. Poor Ruth was in so much trouble, and at the same time in such a bustle to get her husband and his groom and garments off in time, that the ghost quite slipped both their minds, and it was only when he was halfway to York, and had got out on to the open moor, where the snow was rapidly melting under a warm north-west rain, that Hugh wished he had told Ruth all about it, and had asked her to give him the promise he wished for in the morning. But it was too late now, and so he jogged on until the forty-five miles of damp, cold riding were over, and he found himself entering the dark, narrow streets of York.

Part II
The Fulfilment

After the first sad questions and answers had passed between Mr Monroe and his brother Edgar, Hugh proceeded to tell how alarmed he had been in the ghost-chamber the night before by the apparition in the glass. Edgar looked up from his seat by the fire, and said, 'What time did you see it, Hugh?'

'I can't in the least tell,' answered Hugh, 'but I should say about six or a little after. But what does that matter? the warning was conveyed to me, if only I had not at once jumped to the conclusion that it must be Ruth.'

'Mary died the day before yesterday,' said Edgar; 'she was sitting there, looking to me as well as you are, and all of a sudden she fell forward, and must have died instantly. Thank God,' he added, in broken accents, 'she never suffered at all. Doctor Borcham told me that her death was instantaneous; and it's just as her father died too. It must be in the family.'

'God forbid,' exclaimed Hugh, jumping up. 'Don't for heaven's sake talk like that; Mary and Ruth are sisters, remember. Think of what you are saying.'

'I never could see why we pray against sudden death,' said Edgar, still in the same quiet tone of voice. 'Think how mercifully one glides out of all the turmoil and pain of this mortal life into perfect rest. Would I could lie down at once by Mary's side and sleep too!'

'Merciful for those who go,' said Hugh, 'but not for those that remain behind. Think of the shock! But it is getting late, and I have had a long ride. I must go to bed;' and bidding his brother goodnight, he went up the staircase into the room appointed for him.

Just across the narrow passage was that other quiet room, in which lay the body of his sister-in-law, under the doorway of which came a thin line of light and a subdued murmur of talk, that showed someone was still in the room with her. Hugh had not seen her since the day on which the two brothers and sisters had been married. He took up his candle again, and going across the passage, knocked at the door. It was opened about an inch by the old family nurse who had come to live with Mary on her marriage, and she, seeing who it was, came out, and shutting the door carefully behind her, drew Hugh back again into his own room, and shut that door too. 'Now, Mr Monroe,' said she, 'I know what you want; but listen to me, and don't ask to see poor Miss Mary again. You had far better remember her as she was the last time you saw her, a bonnie, happy bride, than take away in your mind how she looks now; and besides,' she added, 'she is so like dear Miss Ruth, that I am sure you should not look at her, it can do her no good now, poor lamb, and may give you a shock you will not easily get over—and you look white and tired enough now too.'

'All right, Povis,' answered Hugh; 'perhaps you are right, but I thought Mr Edgar might feel hurt. Anyhow, I'll leave it to you to explain matters, and as I really am almost done up, I'll take your advice. So goodnight;' and the old nurse having gone back to her melancholy task of watching by the coffin, Hugh proceeded to hurry into bed. As he was seated on the side of his bed, divesting himself of his garments, he happened to catch sight of himself in the looking-glass, and there, looking as if it were over his shoulder, was the dreadful face of the night before. This time the eyes were opened, and seemed to look in an imploring and appealing manner into his own, as if urging some action upon him. Only the face was to be seen, as if the head were cut off at the neck, or as if the head and body were enveloped in a grey fog, out of which loomed the fair appealing features of his wife—for that it was his wife Hugh never thought of doubting. He rose and hurried forward to the glass, but as he advanced the face gradually vanished; and although he stood for some time trembling and looking in all directions it did not come again. So putting it down in his own mind to imagination, he hastened to get into bed, and being dreadfully tired, soon fell fast asleep.

The morning found himself rested, and his intellect clear and alert. He rose and dressed, but when he was brushing his hair in the glass a cold wind seemed to pass over him. The brushes were poised in mid-air, and there looking again at him over his shoulders, the sad grey eyes meeting his, was the face of his wife. This time more of the figure became visible as he looked, and as he stared helplessly into the eyes before him, a hand was raised, and on one finger he saw their betrothal ring shine, the curious old ring by which all the eldest sons of the Monroe family had been betrothed since time immemorial.

'What do you wish?' asked Hugh, in a curious, hard voice that sounded weird and far off to his own ears. 'What do you want?' The pale lips opened as if to speak. No words came from them, but in the room echoed, like the strain of distant music brought from afar on a soft breeze, the words, 'Too late! Too late!' and then the vision vanished.

Utterly miserable, utterly unstrung, Hugh finished his dressing and hurried downstairs to his brother, who sat in almost the same attitude and place where he had left him last night, looking haggard and miserable in the pale light that struggled in at the closed blinds. He started up when he saw Hugh, and asked him what was the matter. Hugh told him the whole story, and ended by saying he must order his horse and go home at once.

'You cannot leave me like this,' urged Edgar, 'just for a vision or a dream, or what was most likely your own tired brain playing you a trick. You have not recovered the first shock, and then dear Mary's death harrowed you again; believe me, it is only your fancy. And what can have happened to Ruth since ten o'clock yesterday morning? I shall never get over this terrible day without you, and I do beg and implore of you to remain till tomorrow at least, when I shall be thankful to ride back with you and remain for a little time.'

Hugh still persisted in his desire to go home at once, but Edgar used so many entreaties, and at last wept in the dreadful manner that men shed tears, and so he felt obliged to give in; and what with making all arrangements, and going to and from the churchyard, and consoling and comforting his brother during the trying ceremony, the day went quickly by, and evening found them sitting again over the dining-room fire. Hugh had gone into his room several times in the course of the day, and each time had gazed with a shuddering horror at the glass; but he had never seen the face again; and he was beginning to think that, the night once over, and his ride fairly begun towards home, he could then afford to laugh at superstition and all such follies, when a low, curious sort of moan caused both brothers to look up and listen intently. Just as Edgar was going to speak, the moan grew louder and louder, until it sounded like a tremendous wind wailing through the room. Hugh started to his feet, and just at that moment the door of the room blew open violently, and there glided in a thin grey figure, that passed on silently and awfully until it reached the fireplace. The door closed after it quietly, and as Hugh and Edgar, grasping each other's hands in a clasp that was agony, advanced with slow steps towards it, a misty veil that enveloped it faded gradually and slowly away, and with a mutual shudder of horror they recognised the figure of Ruth Monroe.

The wind and moaning had gradually died away, and a dreadful silence filled the room, which felt suddenly chill and damp, as if the veil of mist had faded into the atmosphere. Ruth never stirred, never took her eyes off those of her husband, into which she gazed with the same appealing glance as she had done before. Edgar's voice trembled as he spoke, but he addressed her by her name, and implored her to speak to them. At the sound of his voice the figure raised her hand, and then moving her lips just as the face in the glass had done, words unformed and soundless seemed to pervade the room, but in such an indistinct manner that neither brother could make them out in the least; and on Hugh's darting forward to take the outstretched hand the figure slowly vanished, leaving no trace of its extraordinary visit.

'It's no use,' ejaculated Hugh; 'I shall go mad if I don't get home. Something dreadful must have happened. I shall order George and the horses, and be off at once; another night like last night or another apparition will be the death of me.' And so saying he rang the bell, and ordered his man and the horses to be ready at once. So they started, through the quiet York streets, clattering over the stones, and out into the night through Micklegate Bar. The morning was beginning to struggle through the cold thick fog that hung over the village as they drew near to the Grange, and the tired horses and men paused as they got on the bridge, and gazed at the house that stood quietly among the trees. Hugh eagerly pushed his tired horse up the avenue, and hurrying up the steps, rang the bell as if to wake the dead as well as the living.

The door was opened at the same moment by old Betty, who was in the act of letting out the doctor, who, when he saw Mr Monroe, paused in an undecided manner on the doorstep.

'For heaven's sake,' ejaculated Hugh, 'my wife——' The doctor took him by the arm and led him into the dining-room. 'My dear Mr Monroe,' he said, 'you must prepare yourself for a terrible calamity; your dear wife has received a shock that will either kill her, or result in her being out of her mind for the rest of her life. I cannot tell how or what has caused this, but Betty tells me that she was found in the death-room last night in a state of insensibility, and since then she has been calling for you in a dreadful manner. Listen,' he added; 'you can hear her now,' and opening the door Hugh heard his name called in the same weird accents as those used by the figure that had visited him in York. Shaking off the doctor's detaining hand he flew upstairs, and there, sitting up in bed, and watched by the horrified maids, was his wife, calling perpetually on his name. The moment she saw him she stopped, looked fondly at him in the same sorrowful manner that the ghost did, and then said, 'I have waited for you to say goodbye. I went three times to see you, but I wanted you at home. There *is* a ghost upstairs. I saw myself laid out on that dreadful bed, and it killed me. The doctor always said any shock would. And it nearly killed you. I am only waiting to kiss you before I go.'

Poor Hugh threw himself on his knees, and clasped her in his arms. As he did so the eyes closed, the mouth fell into lines of infinite repose, the arms crossed themselves on Ruth's breast, and she lay back dead, *and as cold as marble* in her husband's embrace.

For days and nights Hugh lay between life and death, and it was months before he could bear to be told the whole story; months before he could hear how she was found in the old room upstairs, having gone up thither to see what had so alarmed Hugh, notwithstanding the tearful prayers of old Betty and her unspoken promise to her husband; but when he did, and when he had again visited the awful room, it was only to give orders for that part of the house to be demolished, and rebuilt in such a manner that no trace whatever should remain of the death-chamber of the Monroes; and it was not until another wife and half-a-dozen noisy children had been given to him that he was known to smile again; and if ever at Christmas-time the conversation turned on that most enthralling topic, he would abruptly change the subject, and he never could be got to tell the story of the face in the glass.

The glass itself was not destroyed, and the Monroes still keep it, and regard it with superstitious reverence, for as sure as there is to be a death in the family in the ensuing year, so sure on the night of All Souls is the face of the victim to be seen in the glass—at least so tells the housekeeper, adding, with a smile on her rubicund countenance, 'No one tempts Providence now by going to look in the glass there; for the ghost can only be seen by a Monroe, and it would be very dreadful, you know, sir, if they saw their own faces looking at them out of the glass.'

His Oldest Friends

I

MAXIME DE ST VALLIER was no longer a young man when he succeeded to the family estate of St Vallier le Roi, which had belonged to his race from the time of the Fronde, when a certain Hector St Vallier commanded a regiment of light cavalry in Condé's army, and in the course of an adventurous career, including two wealthy marriages, managed to accumulate a considerable fortune, and to leave behind him the château and lands of St Vallier de Roi, adjoining the insignificant Bourg of that name, which lies ten miles from a station on the Lyons railway and in the heart of a richly wooded district. There is no more beautiful château in France of its size than this of St Vallier, with its four tall towers under steep conical roofs, its carved balconies and oriel windows, its decorated gables and floriated ironwork; a château planted on a knoll that lifts the dainty edifice just high enough above the rolling woods and fertile valley to make it a picturesque point in the landscape.

Maxime inherited the estate and a handsome fortune in stocks and shares from an eccentric bachelor to whom he was but distantly related, but who had been passionately in love with his mother before her marriage, and who had been refused by her in favour of a much poorer man. It may be that Maxime de St Vallier's early manhood would have taken a different and a better course had he known all about this good fortune which was waiting for him in the future; if he had known that at nine-and-thirty years of age he would be rich in wealth and lands, and endowed with all that weight and respectability which dignify the possessor of a fine estate.

'I should have tried to educate myself up to my fortune,' he said, 'and instead of wasting my nights in singing-cellars and dancing-gardens I should have been studying scientific agriculture and the landed interest. But the old fellow never took any notice of me, and I thought no more of him than of the Lama of Thibet or the Khan of Tartary.'

Yes, he would have shaped his life differently, and might have shaped it better had he but known. The vision of a sweet pale face and pathetic violet eyes rose before him in the first hour of his new and unexpected fortune. That lovely face had vanished for ever, as he thought, from Maxime St Vallier's adoring gaze, even years before the coming of his inheritance. He had loved the only daughter of one of Napoleon the Third's generals, had modestly offered himself and the possibilities of a journalistic career, which had been full of golden opportunities, all flung to the winds. He had enlarged upon the great things he might and would do in literature and politics if he were but urged by the noblest incentive to labour, the responsibilities of a husband who idolised his wife.

General Leroux listened to his fervid harangue with calm politeness, and smiled the bland pitying smile of age that has forgotten the sensations and dreams of youth.

'I cannot marry my daughter to possibilities, however brilliant,' he said. 'I am an old man. I should die before your efforts had begun to realise these great rewards which you say are within your power to gain. I should die harassed by the apprehension that my daughter and her offspring would starve. I am a poor man, remember. Lucie's *dot* would not do more than furnish an apartment in a respectable street. And you, sir, admit that you have saved nothing, though you tell me your earnings on the press have been considerable.'

'No, I had no motive for hoarding.'

'No more had Balzac, or Alexandre Dumas, or Gerard de Nerval, or Alfred de Musset, or a good many more whom I remember—geniuses all; and since you have lived to the age of two and thirty without having put by anything out of your earnings, you can hardly ask me to believe in your capacity for saving money in the future, when your expenses are to be increased by the maintenance of a wife and a possible family.'

'I have flung away as much money as would support a wife and a home every year of my life, since I was five-and-twenty.'

'Yes, you have had a brilliant career, I know, and you have taken life at breakneck time, as if it were a waltz at the Mabille. I admire your talents, my dear St Vallier, and I like you, in any other relation of life than as a possible husband for my daughter. Frankly, too, the question of her future has long been quietly settled between her mother and me on the one part, and a couple of old friends of ours on the other part.'

'Does Lucie know? Is Lucie content?' questioned St Vallier, with pallid lips and fast-beating heart.

No, he was sure she had been told nothing of this parental scheme, even before his question was answered. He knew that she loved him, and would marry no one else of her own free will.

'Lucie will know all in good time, and she is too dutiful to oppose the wishes of her parents,' replied the general.

He added some friendly words, he grasped the lover's cold hand, and Maxime went out into the streets of Paris, feeling as if he had a stone in his breast in the place where his heart had beaten with glad emotions when he entered General Leroux's house an hour earlier.

He knew Lucie Leroux well enough—knowing her soft pliable nature, her love of father and mother, her severely religious training at an Ursuline convent—to be very sure that she would obey her parents and marry the suitor they had chosen for her. It was hopeless to fight against his fate; the bourgeoise Nemesis called Prudence barred his path to happiness.

He went off to Algiers with one of the most brilliant imaginative writers of the day, and in the society of that gifted young man, and amidst scenes of romantic beauty, he tried to live down his love, and at least succeeded in finding life endurable, and full of inspiration for his pen.

He was still in Africa when he saw the announcement of Lucie's marriage. The bridegroom was Charles Colnet, the junior partner in Colnet & Cie., a firm of iron-founders of established position and large wealth. Looked at from the materialistic standpoint of modern Paris the match was a good one, and General Leroux and his wife were to be congratulated upon having done remarkably well for their daughter.

Maxime's business in life was to forget her. He was not able to do that all at once, but he was able to fling himself heart and soul into his literary work—embittered and hardened, but also strengthened by the one honourable passion of his life, a stronger and a better man for having loved nobly and in vain. From being known as one of the cleverest journalists of his day, he became famous as the author of a novel which struck a new string upon the seven-stringed lyre of earthly passion and heavenward-looking hope. It may have been this sudden blast of Fame's trumpet which made the childless old sybarite's eyes turn towards his distant kinsman; anyhow, his latest will was dated after the success of St Vallier's first and most remarkable story. When a man has been writing for eighteen years, and then in the maturity of his powers takes upon himself to write a book, it is probable that this first book will be better than anything he produces afterwards.

St Vallier found himself a landowner of some importance, and furnished with means which justified his taking life exactly as his own inclination suggested. He might spend the greater part of his days as a man of fashion in Paris, where he could afford to set up a bachelor establishment on the most splendid scale. He might have courted notoriety in twenty different ways in the city of pleasure; and might have won for himself that ephemeral renown which is the most brilliant and the most intoxicating of all earthly glories, while it lasts. All this he might have done, and would have done, perhaps, had fortune dropped her favours into his lap just ten years earlier. But he had lived his life, had been famous in Bohemia as the scribbler of the squib and the *entre-filet*, pungent criticisms and risky stories, famous in the great world as the writer of the cleverest book of the season. He had no vanities or ambitions which Paris could gratify. He told himself that he wanted restful days, the tranquil autumn of a life whose summer was faded and sped; so he settled quietly down in the Louis Treize château, and for the first year of his possession devoted himself to the almost impossible task of improving upon perfection. If he could not exactly improve he could at least elaborate. The old man who was gone had prided himself on his library, had deemed himself a connoisseur in books and bindings; but his taste, though excellent, had been old-fashioned, and new generations are in advance of the old. So the wonderful collection of books new and old grew under the hand of the new lord, and a taste which was simpler and yet more splendid prevailed in the new acquisitions. As in the library, so in every room in the château, in gardens and stables, in home-farm and falcon-house, the improving hand was seen, the artistic taste was at work. Maxime St Vallier made his *campagne*, as he called it, the religion of his sober middle-age. He told his friends that he only lived to expand and beautify St Vallier le Roi.

It has been said by a French classic that the greatest luxury is that which is least observable. The perfection of the Château St Vallier was a perfection in those minor details which in many splendid houses are neglected. Maxime's guests found themselves lapped in luxury, but were never oppressed with a too obvious splendour or profusion. Every desire, every need of humanity, was foreseen and provided for. An unsleeping *prévoyance* attended the guest from his arrival at the station till his departure from the same place. Not till his friends were comfortably seated in their railway carriage did Maxime's care, personal or vicarious, cease in their behalf; and were the journey long his attentions followed to the very end, in the shape of a carefully provided *pique-nique* basket, and as much light literature as the book-stall would furnish in the way of novelty. Hence it came to pass that a visit to St Vallier le Roi was among the choicest privileges of the few who yet survived of that gallant band with whom Maxime had begun life at the Sorbonne and on the 'Boul Mich'. He had not the temperament which makes new friends, and he clung with a warm affection to those he had known in the freshness of his morning hours.

Alas! they were so sorely diminished a crew. Life on the 'Boul Mich' uses itself quickly. Of Maxime's bosom-friends one had hanged himself in a blind alley; another had cut the knot of a difficulty with his razor in a miserable garret behind the church of St Sulpice; and more than one had been sacrificed to the demon absinthe. Three had been killed in the war and the siege, and pulmonary complaints had accounted for others. The list of those who had fallen by the wayside in that march of life from twenty to forty was appalling. St Vallier, who was of a thoughtful temper, had many a gloomy hour in which he pondered over the days that were gone, and the friends who were numbered with the dead. It seemed to him in these hours of despondency that fortune had come too late to be of any real value.

He might perhaps have fallen into a habit of settled melancholy but for a new and most unlooked-for happiness that came to him three years after his inheritance. Charles Colnet, of Colnet & Cie., went the way of all flesh with an awful suddenness early in the spring of that year; and in the following summer Maxime met his old sweetheart at La Bourboule, ill, nervous, and fragile as a pale March primrose—shaken and scared by the shock of an unloved husband's death, childless and despondent.

There could be but one result of such a meeting. To Maxime's eye the pensive and ailing woman was more interesting, if less lovely, than the girl he once had hoped to win. And then what exquisite delight it was for him to watch the return of the old loveliness, like the gradual glow and glory of a summer sunrise, as the widow's heart reawakened to the old love! Yes, she had loved him always, she confessed, when they parted late in September, she to return to Paris to arrange her affairs and prepare for a second wedlock, he to go back to the woods and gardens of St Vallier, and to elaborate that which he had been elaborating for the last three years. He had to prepare the apartments of the new châtelaine. Everything had been pronounced complete from garret to cellar; but nothing in existence could be good enough for the new mistress of his home and the old mistress of his heart.

The wedding was solemnised in Paris a year after Charles Colnet's death. It was a very quiet ceremonial, an arrangement in a minor key; yet the newspapers had a great deal to say about the bride and bridegroom, the wealth of the iron-foundry, the historical associations of St Vallier le Roi; but most of all about the lady's bridal gown and trousseau, her jewels and wedding gifts.

This was the beginning of a new existence for Maxime St Vallier. All things took brighter colours in the sunlight of domestic happiness. But youth that is spent is spent. No man can make himself young again, least of all the man who has taken those strong years of manhood between twenty and forty at a swinging pace. The later years of that man are like the tired hunter's return stablewards after a grand run with the hounds. The horse may have done prodigies between noon and sundown; but he has had his day, and must creep quietly home to rest. The most famous physician in Paris told St Vallier to be careful of himself.

'You have burnt the lamp of life rather too fiercely,' he said; 'there is, however, oil enough left for a good many years to come if you will only husband it.'

This was a sage warning, but it is difficult for a man who has won the fruition of his fondest hopes to remember the shadow on the dial, creeping on with slow, inevitable progress. St Vallier gave himself up to the gladness of his new life, and to the delight of his wife's society. She was charmed with her surroundings at the château, pleased at the idea of spending the greater part of every year in that tranquil home, far from the excitements and dissipations of Republican Paris. Her husband's friends were her friends; and although there was a faint flavour of the Quarter Latin and the Bal Bullier still clinging to those old comrades, they were all of them men of intellect, and some of them men of mark—poets, romancers, painters, who had made themselves famous or at least fashionable; advocates whose florid eloquence had but too often made the forger or the parricide appear rather the victim than the criminal, and had found extenuating circumstances in the darkest story of crime.

It was in the second autumn of St Vallier's wedded life that a party of these friends arrived at the château, intent upon enjoying all the sports and pleasures which St Vallier le Roi could afford—hawking, shooting, hunting, yea, even the music of village Orphéonistes, and the dances at the village fairs. Maxime's friends were all men. Lucie supplied the feminine element, and brought around her half a dozen of the most elegant women in Paris: widows, or wives on furlough, fresh from their seaside holiday, or their 'cure' in Auvergne or Savoy, Schwalbach or the Pyrenees.

Everyone was charmed with the château. Pretty women went buzzing up and down the corridors, peering into the grim seventeenth century turrets, fluttering up and down the corkscrew staircases, with much music of light laughter, and frou-frou of silk and lace.

Madame's friends were delighted with everything, but perhaps most of all to find that very audacious painter of Parisian boudoirs, Tolpâche, and that daring analyst of the female heart, Vivien the novelist, on the premises.

'There is something very awful in the idea of living for a fortnight in the same house with two such men,' said Madame Evremonde, the banker's widow; 'one feels one's principles in danger of being gradually undermined. If Vivien's conversation is anything like his books——'

'Thank heaven it isn't!' said St Vallier, 'or M. Vivien would be intolerable. Social analysis is a very good thing to dream and doze over, with a cigar between one's lips, and one's feet on the fender, but to have to listen to the analyst expounding his theories—*quelle corvée!*'

One of the first inquiries from the lady visitors was for the family ghost.

'Of course there is a ghost—some sad story of a jealous husband and a murdered lover, perhaps, or a faithless wife shut up in one of those too delicious turrets?' said Madame Belfort, who was stout and sentimental—a kindly adipose creature, who offered to the fashionable *faiseur* the problem of how to make the best of a jelly-fish.

'Unhappily, *chère dame*, there is no ghost.'

'What! in a château built in the middle of the seventeenth century—a château built when men wore long hair, and velvet doublets, and cannon sleeves, and Point d'Alençon ruffles. That cannot be! There must be a ghost. You have not hunted up the family traditions. A house without a ghost story, a family without traditions, would be hardly respectable.'

'I said there is no ghost, but I did not say there are no family traditions.'

'There are traditions, then?' asked the stout lady.

'Yes.'

'Ghostly ones?'

'There is one that savours of the supernatural; but as I never yet believed in a story of that kind when I heard it told of another man's family, I am not likely to believe in this legend because it is told of my own ancestors.'

'A legend! The very word has a fascination!' cried Madame Evremonde. 'Please let us hear it.'

'Then you own to a ghost!' exclaimed Madame Belfort, who had the density of large bodies. 'Pray show us the haunted room. I feel sure it is one of the turret-rooms, so quaint, so historical, so uncanny.'

'Again, *chère dame*, must I protest that no ghost—not the shadow of a shade—had ever been asserted to walk these corridors, or harbour in any room, garret, or cellar of this château. If you good ladies will graciously wait till after dinner, I will tell you the story of St Vallier le Roi while we take our coffee.'

'It is a long story, then?'

'Not very long, but too long to be told in this passage while your maids are running about with your luggage, and while my chef is doubtless in a fever of impatience lest the dinner should be delayed so long as to spoil his best efforts.'

His guests took the hint, and ran off to their various rooms, Madame St Vallier and her housekeeper going about with them to show them where they were lodged. Lamps were being lighted in the corridors; many wax candles were burning upon toilet tables and mantelpieces. As the great clock chimed the half-hour after six, all the windows in the château gleamed and twinkled through the October twilight. It was still early in the month. The evenings were soft and grey. The woods were still green.

The dinner was excellent. The guests were full of vivacity and light airy talk. The dining-hall, with its dark oak panelling, family portraits, gobelin tapestry, and Henri deux pottery, was a picture which delighted the eye of Adolphe Tolpâche, the painter—a background which he was likely to use in many a little pictured *tête-à-tête*, confidential, *risqué*, suggestive. On the appearance of coffee and liquers, Madame Evremonde turned to her host, by whose side she was sitting.

'Your family tradition, Monsieur,' she said. 'The moment has come.'

Maxime bowed a smiling assent.

'We'll get rid of the servants first,' he murmured in her ear. 'That will do, Robert,' to the major-domo; 'you and Jacques can put your salvers on the table yonder,' pointing to a table in a recess.

The well-trained servant understood the dismissal, and at once withdrew with his underlings. As the heavy oak door closed upon them, Maxime leant forward with his folded arms on the tablecloth.

'Now then for the ghost story,' he said. 'It is a ghost story, but, I am happy to say, the ghost has nothing to do with this house. We have no haunted room from which the too-daring guest emerges, after a self-imposed ordeal, with his hair blanched and his brain turned. Our ghosts are out-of-door ghosts. The legend of St Vallier is the legend of the phantom *char à bancs*.'

'A phantom *char à bancs*. A new manner of ghost, *par Dieu*. What does it do, this *char à bancs*?'

'Very little. It is supposed to be seen driving through the woods in the evening dusk; seen by the owner of the estate. A curious old-world carriage, a carriage belonging to a period in which coaches were a novelty, and when a Court beauty was known to barter her reputation for a gilt coach;

a beauty of rank and social status, mark you, who had resisted every other lure.'

'We know our de Grammont, *merci*,' laughed Vivien; '*revenez à votre char à bancs*.'

'It is seen in the gloaming, somewhere along that wooded road which leads to the home-farm; at least, that is the traditional place. It is seen by the owner of the estate; and in that strange antiquated vehicle he sees a strange set of passengers—the friends he cared for in his youth, the friends he valued most, the friends who have gone before.'

'*Que diable!* Your estate is well provided,' exclaimed Tolpâche. 'Not a single ghost, not the old-established family spectre, but a whole company of apparitions, a coach-load of phantoms. *Après, mon ami?* When the lord of the soil has seen the spectral *char à bancs*, what then?'

'He is forewarned of his approaching death. If the legend is to be believed, no man ever long survived the apparition of that vehicle, the passing of those noiseless wheels.'

'India-rubber tyres,' said Tolpâche; 'a carnival trick of some *roué* St Vallier's fast and furious friends. A thing done once, perhaps, in the wild days of the Regency, and exaggerated by rumour into a family custom. *Histoire de rire*. That is the way ancestral ghosts are made!'

'My dear Tolpâche, if you are a sceptic, so am I. I no more believe in my family apparition than you do; only these ladies wanted the story, and there it is for them.'

'These ladies' were charmed with the story, and were inclined to believe in the phantom *char à bancs*. Madame Belfort insisted upon being told in what direction the road lay by which the *char à bancs* was supposed to travel, in order that she might take her morning constitutional on that very road.

II

When a man has a beautiful wife and a circle of intimates, however well he may have chosen his friends, and however long he may have known them, there is always a traitor among them. There is always one man who holds no law sacred where a lovely woman's favour is, or may be, the reward of treachery. There is always one man who disbelieves in woman's chastity, and who thinks every man's wife a possible prize, if not for other men, at least for himself.

There was one such traitor in Maxime de St Vallier's circle, and that traitor was Vivien, the novelist, a writer who had painted duchesses from models picked out of the Parisian gutter, who had dissected and analysed, and poetised and bedevilled his own idea of woman, evolved out of his own very nasty inner consciousness, and who could not recognise purity when he saw it.

Hector Vivien was neither a shooting nor a hunting man, cared for neither foxhounds nor falconry. He would have bored himself to death at St Vallier le Roi if he had been without an object. Every man who lives in the country must hunt something, even if that something be only a beetle or a butterfly. Vivien hunted Lucie St Vallier. The calm, high-souled, beautiful woman was the quarry which he had chosen; and he fully believed that he should succeed in the chase.

'If not today, tomorrow.' That was his motto where women were concerned. Elated by a succession of facile conquests, he thought all conquests easy. Lucie's matronly dignity was, to his mind, only the mask worn by all well-bred women. Behind the Roman wife there was always a potential Messalina.

He pursued his accustomed arts very carefully, varying his tactics in accordance with his surroundings. He was so subtle that neither husband nor wife suspected his motives. St Vallier apologised to him for the monotony of life at the château. 'You, who care neither for hawk nor hound, must find it a very dull business,' he said.

'My dear Maxime, you forget that I have to finish my novel, and find a title for it, before the end of the year. Nothing could suit me better than the repose of this uneventful life.'

'I fear you did not make much progress with your story yesterday, Monsieur,' said Lucie, gaily; 'you were loitering about the gardens and the farm all the afternoon.'

'Dear madame, I was thinking of my title. That is the hardest work of all.'

It was to be observed that Vivien spent day after day in the same leisurely meandering between garden and farm, park and pleasaunce, or in accompanying the ladies of the party to distant ruins or rustic villages, or, indeed, in any direction that Madame de St Vallier proposed for the day's drive. He was not averse from riding, was a light weight, and rode fairly well for a literary man; so, having found a mount of St Vallier's that suited him to perfection, he took to accompanying his hostess and Madame Evremond in their morning rides, and thus familiarised himself with every path and glade in the extensive woods.

Lucie showed him the spot where the phantom *char à bancs* was said to have appeared; a point where the footpath branched off from the road, and where a giant oak spread his gnarled and withered limbs, alive and flourishing on one side, and dead on the other—fitting landmark for a haunted spot.

Vivien was very jocose about the *char à bancs*, but Lucie checked him with a sigh.

'What if the legend were true!' she said gravely; 'what if some day Maxime were to tell me he had seen the phantom carriage!'

'You would guess, dear Madame, that he had supped with the widow Cliquot overnight,' the novelist answered gaily. He was not going to encourage sentimentality about a husband.

October wore towards its close. A pack of English foxhounds had been brought over to a neighbouring quasi-royal château by an Irish nobleman, a man in whose family sport and fine riding were a tradition. The hounds afforded splendid sport, and the peer was a social success, dined at St Vallier le Roi twice in a fortnight, and made himself particularly agreeable to the ladies of the party. It was curious that, coming upon the scene as a stranger, he should have been the only visitor who saw threatened mischief in Hector Vivien's languid saunterings and close attendance upon Madame de St Vallier and her friends.

'If I were a little more intimate with St Vallier, I should try to open his eyes about that particular friend of his,' said the peer, communing with himself as he drove home after his second dinner at the château. 'A fellow who is able to sit a horse, and yet does not care for riding to hounds in such a splendid country as this, must have some darker game in view. I think I know pretty well what the Parisian novelist is aiming at.'

Maxime had been completely happy during those short autumn days. He had not been husbanding his strength, for he had ridden as hard as anybody else, yet he had felt in better health than he had enjoyed for the last ten years, full of life and vigour, and with an appetite which made him think with a pitying smile of the days when he had trifled fretfully with the choicest *entrée* at Bignon's, and disdainfully rejected the costliest *primeurs* of the season. He felt that he was rapidly acquiring the hardy vigour of the genuine *campagnard*, and that henceforth he might laugh at doctors and diagnosis.

The month was waning, and several of the visitors had left the château; but the party seemed only cosier and more lively as the circle grew smaller; 'just the right number for sitting round the fire and telling stories,' Maxime said, as they drew their chairs in a semi-circle about the wide hearth in the central hall, a hearth whereon burned huge logs of red fir, exhaling aromatic odours; just the right number to appreciate Lucie de St Vallier's low sweet voice as she sang Heine's ballads, or De Musset's passionate love-songs, in the pensive hour between daylight and darkness.

> 'Ninon, Ninon, que fais tu de la vie
>   Toi, qui n'a pas l'amour?'

'What does she do with her life, this tranquil, dignified châtelaine?' Vivien asked himself; she who seemed to know nothing of love—certainly not of love as he interpreted the passion—a transient fever, prompting to all manner of falsehood and treachery; a burning fiery furnace, from which a woman emerges scathed and seared, marked with the ineffaceable brand of infamy.

*   *   *   *   *

The meet had been more remote than usual, and the hounds had gone in a direction that led farther and farther away from St Vallier le Roi; so on this particular evening Maxime was riding home alone, having left his friends, Tolpâche the painter, and the advocate Bartrond, to take their own line. He knew that his wife would be full of anxieties and morbid fancies about him, should he not return till long after dark, and to stay with the hounds this afternoon would mean a very late home-coming. He had left the hounds at three o'clock, by which time they had lost their first fox and were drawing a wood fifteen miles from St Vallier le Roi. In all probability the fox would take them farther away from that point, and the day's sport might finish with death or disappointment thirty miles from home.

Maxime was riding a second horse, which took him homeward at the rate of seven miles an hour, and the sun was just beginning to set as he rode out of a bridle-track through a thickly planted fir wood, and came upon the carriage-road which Madame Belfort had christened the Phantom's Highway. Nothing was further from his thoughts than family traditions upon that particular evening. He was in excellent health and spirits, and was thinking how delightful it would be to get home in advance of the other men, and to enjoy a quiet hour with Lucie, *tête-à-tête*, in that quaint old turret-room which she had made her boudoir. How sweet it would be to sit beside the fire in the curious hooded chimney corner, talking confidentially, and all in all to each other, just for that one quiet hour before it was time to dress for dinner!

He rode slowly along, thinking of the woman he loved so dearly, with such a pure and placid affection; a love so strong in its unbounded faith; a love across whose brightness there had never fallen the shadow of change. He thought how blessed life had been made for him within the last three years, blest by earthly prosperity, blest how much more in this perfect and happy union, and his heart swelled with gratitude to Providence. Lucie had reawakened in his mind the devout feelings of early boyhood, the faith learnt at his mother's knees; and now he told himself he might look forward to long years of this serene and full existence—years of prosperity, social influence, and wedded love—for all those threatening signs of nervous decay, fatigued brain, wasted strength, which had scared him when he consulted the famous doctor, had gradually disappeared, and he felt as fit for the battle of life as he had felt at five-and-twenty. Full of these self-congratulations, he rode slowly along the road, towards a sharp curve where the woodland opened upon a lovely glade, sloping down to a level stretch of marshy pasture, where the cows stood breast-deep in the flowering grasses.

The sun was dipping towards this grassy expanse at the bottom of the glade, a great crimson disk. As Maxime reached the turn of the road, and saw the glade in a slanting line before him, with that red orb facing him, he was startled by the sound of a horn, curiously faint, yet seeming near. Could the hounds have been following in his direction all this time? Had the fox, as if out of sheer perversity, set his nose towards St Vallier le Roi?

While he was asking himself this question, turning in his saddle to look back and listen, a strange chill crept through his veins, colder and more sudden than the chill that comes after the sinking of the sun, and, looking straight before him, he saw a carriage approaching, and mechanically pulled his horse out of the narrow road to make way for it. The carriage was large and heavy-looking, drawn by four horses, and neither wheels nor horses' hoofs sounded on the hard gravel road.

It drove slowly past him as he stood watching it; a *char à bancs*, filled with men whose faces were all turned towards him, pallid in the grey faint light; the face of Gerard de Nerval, who hanged himself in the Rue de la Vieille Lantèrne; the face of Alfred de Musset, who wrecked his constitution by drink and dissipation; faces of men less famous than these two— all gone before. One, his oldest, dearest, trustiest friend in the long ago, stood up in the carriage, and, looking at him earnestly, pointed with solemn gesture to the setting sun. The red-gold edge of the orb dropped as he pointed, and the day was dead.

'*Ce cher Horace,*' sighed Maxime, as the carriage vanished into the shadows of the wood. 'That means a rendezvous. We are to meet soon.'

He rode homeward very slowly. He had never believed in this legend of the *char à bancs*, and yet the fact of having seen it, and the faces of his dead friends, gave him no surprise. It seemed to him, now that the thing was over, as if he had known always that he should see those familiar faces, and receive this warning of approaching death. Yet only a few minutes ago he had been rejoicing in the idea of long and happy years lying before him, a quiet leisurely journey, hand in hand with his beloved, down the hill of life. The effect of that strange vision upon him was like the effect of a blow that produces brief unconsciousness. The man who has been stunned awakens with a confused sense of time; feels as if years had gone by in those few minutes of total oblivion. Not for a moment did he try to reason away the vision, to think it a delusion of a mind prepossessed by that particular image. To him the thing was a truth, a positive indisputable fulfilment of the family legend. He was doomed shortly to die. In the midst of his calm delight in life the fateful summons had come, and he must obey. He could not misunderstand that look in his dead friend's face, the hand pointing to the sinking sun. For him, too, the sun of life was going down. He had fancied himself so much improved in health, so much stronger than of old. A fallacy born of a contented mind, perhaps. That decay which he had once dreaded was going on within the citadel of life. In brain, or heart, or lungs, somewhere there must be hidden mischief, and the finger of death had marked him.

'I'll see what science says of me,' he thought, 'and if the doctor's verdict coincides with the spectral warning, I shall know that my race is run. There is always some comfort in certainty. I will go to Paris by the Rapide tomorrow and let Bianchon overhaul me.'

Having come to this decision, he put his horse at a trot, and rode rapidly home, arriving in time for a cup of tea, which Lucie called 'le five o'clock', in the turret boudoir, and for that long cosy talk with his wife, which he had anticipated. She praised him for his devotion in leaving the hounds and coming home alone, lest she should spend uneasy hours after dark. She was gay, caressing, charming, and it was exquisite happiness to snatch this hour alone with her. Not by one word or sigh did Maxime reveal the mental shock he had experienced; yet, in the midst of their light talk and laughter, he was thinking of a day near at hand when she would be sitting lonely and widowed in that room; and he was recalling the provisions of the will which he had made directly after his marriage—a will which left his wife everything.

Before going to her boudoir he had despatched a mounted messenger with a telegram, asking Dr Bianchon to expect him at a certain hour on the following day. He would take the omnibus train from St Vallier le Roi to Dijon that night, in time to start from Dijon by the Rapide. After much happy talk, he told Lucie that he had to go to Paris on particular business, and that he meant to travel at night, both in going and returning, so that he might be absent for the shortest time possible.

'But you will fatigue yourself dreadfully by two night journeys!' said Lucie, growing sad at the prospect of even this brief separation.

'Not at all. I shall take a wagon-lit each way.'

'Be sure you do. And you will be back——'

'The day after tomorrow, much too early for breakfast.'

'I will have breakfast ready for you, however early you maybe. I shall be at the station with the carriage.'

'I beg that you will do no such thing. A long drive on a cold wintry morning might give you a dangerous chill!'

'I am too hardy a plant for that, Maxime. The life I lead in these delicious woods has made me as strong as a lioness!'

'My lioness!' he cried, smothering the fair bright face with kisses, 'Queen of my forests and of my heart!'

The gong sounded loud in the vaulted hall, signal to dress for dinner. Maxime hurried off to change his clothes, and to give orders about his departure. A carriage was to be ready at ten to take him to the station. The omnibus train left St Vallier le Roi at twenty minutes past eleven, reached Dijon in time for the Rapide, and he would be in Paris in the early morning, with two or three hours to waste before he could hope to be admitted to the great Bianchon's consulting-room.

He was full of talk and laughter at the dinner-table that evening, in the small, snug circle of seven, with the exaggerated vivacity of a man who is trying to hide a canker in his heart. Vivien, too, was unusually gay; told his best stories, flashed his brightest repartees, a shade more recklessly than usual; and it may be that if Maxime de St Vallier had not been preoccupied with his own gloomy thoughts he might have taken objection to some of the novelist's sallies. As it was he talked and rattled on, scarce hearing, certainly not heeding what was said by others, and hardly knowing what he said himself. In this feverish state he sat over the coffee and liquers till the butler announced the carriage that was to take him to the station. His servant and his valise were ready.

He took a hasty farewell of wife and friends, and was gone.

*   *   *   *   *

Dr Bianchon received M de St Vallier before any other patient, although even at nine o'clock the great man's waiting-room was crowded. He had met his patient often in society, and received him as a friend.

'My dear St Vallier, I have to congratulate you upon the improvement of your appearance. You look ten years younger since you were last in this room. In what Medea's cauldron have you been stewing?'

'My only Medea is my wife. My only medicine had been a year and a half of supreme happiness!'

'Ah, that is a kind of physic we often prescribe; but there are no chemists who make it up. And so you have come to tell me how well you are, and to get a little friendly advice that will enable you to become a centenarian,' concluded Bianchon laughingly.

A consulting physician has so often occasion to look grave that he gladly snatches any excuse for being cheerful.

'I have come to ask you to make a thorough examination, and to find out if there is any hidden mischief in my constitution.'

'Do you suspect anything?' asked the doctor, with his keen look— a look which suggested that for him the outward semblance of a man, coat and waistcoat included, was but a glass case through which he saw the inner machinery.

'No; I never felt better in my life.'

'And you deliver yourself over of your own accord to the stethoscope and the sphygmometer! Prudent man. Kindly take off your coat and waist-coat.'

Dr Bianchon made a most studious examination of his patient, sounded, rapped, and listened, and then with a smile gave him a clean bill of health.

'Your pulse is capital, so we won't trouble the sphygmometer, which I find very useful with my alcoholic patients,' said the doctor. 'I told you when you were here last that there was nothing organically wrong. I can tell you now, in all good faith, that you are as sound within as you are well-looking without—no whited sepulchre here, *mon ami*,' with a friendly tap on the patient's chest.

'And there is no fear of my dying suddenly, within the next three or four days?'

'Not unless you get yourself under the wheels of an omnibus, or by the side of some clever friend who will scrabble through a hedge with the muzzle of his gun pointed at your ribs. Death by internal disease you have no need to fear. Heart and lungs are as sound as a bell.'

'Thank God!' exclaimed Maxime, fervently.

'What put these fears into your head? You must have felt nervous about yourself, or you would hardly have come all the way from your country place to see me.'

'A foolish fancy. I am too happy in my surroundings not to fear. Goodbye; come and see me at St Vallier if ever you can find time.'

'That is just the thing I never can find; but I should like to spend a couple of days at your château when all Paris is out of town. Unfortunately, when all Paris is away, there are generally some very interesting cases at the hospitals; and I take that opportunity to go on with my education.'

Maxime and his wife possessed a *pied-à-terre* in the Rue de Varennes. It had been Lucie's house during her widowhood—a dainty little house *entre cour et jardin*—and here a couple of old servants kept all things in order while their master and mistress were in the country. Maxime had sent his servant on before him, and found a comfortable breakfast, neatly set out in the well-furnished library, which his wife had given him as his own den.

Small as the house was, and although all things in it were in perfect order, the rooms had an aspect which weighed upon Maxime's spirits. There was an atmosphere of emptiness and desolation. He was glad to put on his hat, and go out and wander aimlessly about Paris, finding his way to the Champs Elysées, and the Bois, counting the hours till the eight o'clock Rapide would take him southward.

In spite of the physician's positive assurance he was not altogether at ease. He could not feel as calm and hopeful as he should have done, under the circumstances. That vision of his old friend pointing to the setting sun, and looking at him with solemn prophetic eyes, was with him wherever he went, came between him and every cheerful thought. His mind travelled back to those old days, under the shadow of St Sulpice, fifteen years ago, when he and that dead friend had eaten the *vache enragée* together, and when in the midst of their struggles they had been hopeful and gay.

Then had come literary successes—for him who was dead, the poet's laurel wreath, that withered all too soon, and left nothing behind it but the absinthe-madness, and a premature grave in Père la Chaise.

He had engaged places in the sleeping-car for himself and his valet. He was at the terminus half an hour before the train started, tired out with his rambles about Paris, and with the wakeful night in the express; so he took off coat and boots, and laid himself down under a fur rug which his servant arranged for him, and was soon asleep.

He must have slept some hours, for it was the voice of the porters shouting, '*Tonnerre!*' that awoke him, and most of the travellers were getting out for supper. He did not care to eat or drink—felt weary in limbs and head, and composed himself to sleep again. This time sleep did not answer to his call. Two men in berths near his were gossiping in a subdued murmur, which was more exasperating to St Vallier's nerves than the loudest talking might have been.

'Know him?' said one of the speakers, 'I should think I did know him—much better than he knows the women he pretends to analyse in those sickly novels of his. I tell you he is a lump of vanities—thinks himself irresistible—thinks that where he is concerned there is no such thing as virtue or honour in a woman. A woman may have resisted every other tempter, but when he comes, he comes like Caesar, to see and to conquer.'

'I don't believe he will succeed with Madame de St Vallier, irresistible as he may consider himself,' said the other man.

'Do you know the lady?'

'I knew her when she was Madame Charles Colnet, and knew her to be a perfect wife; and yet I believe she was married to Colnet by her parents, when she was very young. He was hardly the kind of man a beautiful girl would have chosen for herself—a rough diamond, *ce cher Colnet*—but she never allowed society to see that he was not the first man in the universe for her; and if this fellow, Vivien, brags of her favours, he must be an arrant scoundrel.'

'He does not actually claim to be favoured; but he declares that he will be. You know his device: "If not today, tomorrow." I saw a letter he wrote to Julot, of the Sancho Panza, in which he vapoured as if tomorrow were near at hand.'

They talked of other things, and by-and-by the murmuring ceased; but St Vallier lay broad awake till the train steamed into Dijon, and he counted every minute that must pass before the tardy morning train would take him back, stopping at three village stations on the way, to St Vallier le Roi.

His wife was at the station to meet him with a coupé and pair, more fur rugs, and a *bouillotte*.

She was there to meet him, radiant, loving; yet his soul sickened at the thought that her fondness might be a disguise to hide a heart that was already faithless. Yet no; he would not doubt her purity, even though the tainted breath of the seducer had passed across her name.

'Is Vivien still at the château?' he asked carelessly, as they drove away from the station.

He had lost so much time on the way with that accursed omnibus train that it was already daylight, and he could see his wife's face darken suddenly at the sound of the novelist's name, and he felt the arm within his own tremble slightly.

'Yes; but he leaves this evening, by the same train by which you travelled.'

'That is rather sudden, isn't it? He talked of staying as long as we would have him, in order that he might finish his novel in the quiet of the country.'

'He may have found that his novel made very little progress, and that the air of St Vallier was not conducive to literary work.'

'Lucie! I believe that man has been guilty of some impertinence to you.'

'Not the least in the world,' his wife answered, with a little laugh, which was meant to be reassuring; 'only he has somewhat outstayed his welcome. Laure and I are of the same opinion in being tired of his company, and we ventured to let him perceive our sentiments—of course in the politest way—during your absence. Literary men are sensitive, and he was quick to understand the situation, and devise a sudden necessity to be in Paris.'

'God bless you, my dearest!' cried Maxime, clasping his wife to his heart. 'If Eve had been like you, the serpent would have crawled out of Eden baffled and humiliated.'

'Dear Maxime, I really don't know what you are thinking about,' his wife said gaily. 'The whole business was as simple as *bon jour*; and I hope you will be especially polite to M. Vivien on the last day of his visit.'

* * * * *

Maxime had not the slightest doubt that Hector Vivien had taken advantage of the husband's absence to declare himself to the wife, and that he had been repulsed with the fearless scorn of unassailable purity. He took an opportunity to question Laure Evremonde in the course of the day, and though she would tell him very little, her admissions, and even her reservations, confirmed his belief.

Vivien and his host did not meet till dinner-time. The novelist was in his room all day, busy packing, and arranging his papers. He travelled without a valet, and refused all offers of assistance from St Vallier's household. Consumed with rage and agitation, he felt that he could not trust himself in the society of another man's servant. His irritation might break out at any moment and wreak itself upon some rustic wretch who had only offended by sheer stupidity.

Yes, he had wooed his friend's wife. He had found his opportunity in the afternoon solitude of the pleasaunce, screened from the windows of the château by ten-foot hedges of ilex and yew, as secure from observation as in a forest labyrinth. He had brought to bear all those arts and fascinations which he had always found irresistible with duchesses—in his novels—and occasionally triumphant with middle-class matrons in actual life; and his reward had been the scorn of scorn: such scorn as a pure-minded woman who loves her husband must needs feel at the folly of any man who dares to suppose that he can supersede that husband in her affections.

The dinner-table was not so gay as it had been on many another evening. Vivien talked as much as usual; but an angry light in his eyes, and a keener cynicism in his conversation, indicated latent irritation.

Maxime, who had been hysterically vivacious on the evening before his journey to Paris, was now grave and watchful. He and Tolpâche had talked together for half an hour before dinner, walking up and down the terrace on the edge of the moat, in the wintry darkness; and Tolpâche, like his host, was silent and *aux aguets*.

The dinner was long, and the carriage was announced while the men were still lingering over coffee and cigarettes. Madame de St Vallier and her friends had retired to the music-room, whence came the sound of lightest opera-bouffe melodies played by Madame Evremonde, who was passionately fond of the music that lives for a Parisian season, to be as completely forgotten afterwards as the butterflies of last summer.

Vivien began his adieux with a cordial round of hand-shaking, taking the men at random as they happened to be standing. His host was the last to whom he came, with sinister smile, and outstretched hand.

Maxime stood straight and stern in front of him, and did not take the hand.

'You know the old saying, Monsieur, "Speed the parting guest"?' he said grimly. 'I have the utmost pleasure in speeding your departure, which I believe was hastened by the particular request of my wife.'

A quiver of surprise shook Vivien for a moment; but in the next he collected himself, and accepted the situation with all its consequences.

'I am leaving hurriedly, I admit,' he said; 'but although I am in some haste to leave this part of the world, I can spare you an hour tomorrow morning, in the wood on the other side of the railway. I shall spend tonight at the inn in your village, and shall be at your service at whatever hour may suit your convenience, and that of your friends.'

'Tolpâche, you were prepared for this. Loisin, I know I can rely on you?' said Maxime, turning to his two most intimate friends. 'For my own part I have only one desire to express. Let our meeting be at sunset tomorrow: weapons as you please. That delay will give me time to arrange my affairs.'

He turned on his heel, and went to the music-room, leaving Vivien to choose his own seconds, and settle details.

He felt, in his choice of the sunset hour, that he was obeying an old friend's summons, and accepting his fate.

*   *   *   *   *

The next day passed like a peaceful dream. Maxime and his wife were alone together for the greater part of their time, Lucie having excused herself from an excursion to a village race-course in order to be her husband's companion. No cloud upon his brow forewarned her of approaching doom. He wanted that day to be cloudless—that day which he told himself would be his last of love and of life. He parted with her at half-past three o'clock, straining her to his breast, with one long passionate kiss, as he bade her goodbye.

There was despair in that embrace; and for the first time since his return she was startled from her happy security.

'Why goodbye?' she asked. 'How pale you are, Maxime! Is there anything wrong?'

'Wrong? No, dearest. I am only going as far as the village, to settle some farming business with my bailiff.'

'You will be back to dinner?'

'I hope so.'

*   *   *   *   *

When the sun dipped at the bottom of that wooded hollow, where Maxime had seen it sink three days before, the augury of the earnest face and the pointing hand had been fulfilled.

The Ghost's Name

Chapter I
What People Said of the Ghost

THE MOST SINGULAR feature of the Halverdene ghost was that it never appeared twice in the same shape and fashion. The main fact that a certain room at Halverdene was haunted, and a place of horror, had been borne witness to by so many conscientious people as to be placed beyond the regions of doubt. There were records of the ghost nearly a century old; there were histories as it were of yesterday, all vouched for by witnesses most unlikely to lie; but the ghost, though an old-established fact, verified by nearly a hundred years of varied experiences, was by no means a distinct personality of Shadowland. The ghost was a very Proteus of ghosts; now man now woman; now old now young; but mostly horrible, and sometimes deriving its chiefest horror from a hideous indistinctness, a gigantic overpowering presence which weighed on the chilled spectator like a mountain of iron; a shapeless oppression to which he awakened shrieking, with icy water-drops upon his forehead.

Lucilla, Lady Halverdene's younger, lovelier sister, called the cedar-room at Halverdene the room of dreadful dreams. She had insisted on sleeping there once in a skittish Christmas mood, when the house-party at Halverdene overflowed every attic; but vowed afterwards that not to be sure of the best match in the county would she go through that ordeal again.

When pressed with questions as to what she had seen, she answered, 'Caliban, ten times larger than life. He was there all night. I knew of him in my sleep, though I could not open my eyes to look. My eyelids were sealed with lead, and oh, I had such a headache! He gripped me by the throat, he sat upon my chest. Never, no, never again, Beatrice; not for twenty Halverdenes would I endure a night in that room!'

Everybody in Lucilla Wilmot's generation, a generation now mostly dust—for it was in the days when Lord Melbourne was minister, and railroads were a new thing in the land—everybody at Halverdene, in Beatrice Lady Halverdene's time, regretted that the ghost should have chosen so fine a room as the cedar-room for its headquarters, since this cedar-panelled bed-chamber was one of the most spacious, if not one of the best rooms in the house. It was in the oldest part of the house, the Stuart wing, which comprised hall and library, a summer parlour, and this large cedar-room which was known as the garden bedroom.

The old wing was on a level with the most delicious old garden in Yorkshire; or so Beatrice Halverdene called it when she came as a bride with the husband of her choice to the old north-country manor. A garden needs perhaps to be two hundred years old in order to be perfectly beautiful. This was a garden planned in Bacon's time, and with many of the quaint features of that time still remaining, but without the sage's more fantastic and tea-gardenish ornamentation, the mere suggestion of which in the famous essay might convince any reasonable person that if Bacon wrote Shakespeare's plays, Shakespeare did not write Bacon's essays: for he whose lightest line can conjure visions of Arcadian beauty would never have recommended stately arches upon pillars of carpenter's work, crowned with little turrets containing bird-cages, or 'broad plates of round coloured glass, gilt, for the sun to play upon', in his scheme of an English garden.

Beatrice in those early days of happy wedded love called that fair enclosure her garden of Eden; but seven years of childless wedlock had sobered her enthusiasm, and the union between my lord and my lady seemed hardly that of the Miltonic Adam and Eve. There were those in the neighbourhood who said that my lord cared more for the health of his hounds than for the happiness of his wife; and that an outbreak of distemper in the kennel would have distressed him more than a threat of phthisis in the partner of his life.

There are men with whom love is only a transient fever; lovers to whom it comes natural to love and ride away, and who, when riding away is impossible, are apt to become churlish companions by the domestic hearth.

Those were days in which it was counted no disgrace to a man of high station to be a hard drinker. The memory of the Prince Regent, of Fox, of Sheridan, was still fresh in the minds of men. Brougham and other great intellectual lights were carrying on the old tradition. Port, Burgundy, Madeira, and other heady vintages were much more popular than Bordeaux and light wines from the Rhineland. Port was a part of an Englishman's patriotism, almost of his religion. It was a sound orthodox wine which churchmen loved. Rural benevolence found its best expression in port. Your Lady Bountiful no longer brewed unsavoury decoctions of healing herbs and called that charity. She sent strong soup and strong wine to the weak and ailing, and every villager in England smacked his lips at the name of the rich red vintage of Portugal.

Thus, it was counted no shame to Lord Halverdene that after a day in the saddle he recruited himself with a night over the mahogany and a couple of bottles of his famous wine. It was counted no shame if his valet had to help him up the slippery oak staircase now and again, and was occasionally sworn at for his pains. My lord was excused even for occasional rough language to my lady; for, as the village gossips said, 'it was a sad pity she had no children, and it was only human natur' that his lordship should feel disappointed at the non-appearance of an heir.'

Horses, hounds, and wine were my lord's idea of happiness. My lady loved her garden, her books, and her harp, and contrived to preserve an outward semblance of contentment under circumstances which might have driven a woman of lesser nature to open revolt against hard Fate.

My lord had a house in Grosvenor Square and a park in Sussex, besides this manor and park of Halverdene, between York and Beverley. He was fondest of Halverdene, because of its accessibility from York, Doncaster, and Pontefract, where the frequent race-meetings afforded him the amusement his soul loved best. He had a small racing stud at Halverdene, but his best horses were kept at Malton, under the invincible eye of John Scott. The chief ambition of his mind was to win the Leger, or for second best, the Great Ebor.

After three seasons in London, Lady Halverdene withdrew altogether from Metropolitan society, and was to be heard of only in Yorkshire or in Sussex, generally in Yorkshire, where for the first four years of her married life there were large house-parties, and where Lucilla Wilmot found life very enjoyable, attending all the county race-meetings with her sister, and riding to hounds. But for the last two years there had been very few visitors of my lady's choosing at Halverdene. Lucilla was always there, her sister's only companion in the long autumn evenings when his lordship was away at race-meetings; but, of the fashionable world, the dowagers and wives, the young men and maidens, who had once filled all the rooms and corridors with voices and laughter, there was nothing left but the memory of those days when Halverdene House had been hospitable and gay. Visitors there were, it is true, racing men brought home by his lordship without word of warning to wife or housekeeper. Sometimes, after one of the northern meetings, three or four post-chaises would drive up to the door, late at night, and a bevy of half-intoxicated men would come reeling in. Some of these were underbred men whose talk was half made up of turf slang, and from whose society Lady Halverdene and her sister shrank as from a pestilence.

People shrugged their shoulders when they talked of Lord Halverdene.

'There is a mystery of some kind,' said old General Palmer, to a little knot of men at the Rag.

'The mystery is that Halverdene beats his wife,' answered Mr Soaper-Snarle, the famous wit and reviewer. 'We don't call that kind of thing a mystery in St Giles's. There it's only wife-beating; but when an English nobleman turns brute and bully we call it a social mystery.'

'Is that true?' cried an eager voice, strong and stern of accent. 'Is it true that Lord Halverdene ill-treats his wife?'

The inquiry came from a tall broad-shouldered young man, with a sunburnt face and a cavalry moustache, a man just returned from the Punjab, and to whom most English scandals were new.

'I can only answer for what I saw myself when I was at Halverdene two years ago,' answered Snarle, blandly. 'Halverdene was uncommonly disagreeable to his wife then, and she looked as if she was used to it. There was nothing of the snivelling Griselda about her, mind you, but her resistance was quiet and dumb. She met his brutality with an icy scorn; but the house was no longer a comfortable house to stay in. One felt oneself on the crust of a volcano. Since then there have been very few high jinks at Halverdene. I saw her ladyship and her sister at York races last August, and they were both very nice to me, as they always were; only there was no talk of my going to Halverdene, although I was in their neighbourhood.'

'I have heard things,' said General Palmer; 'but one never knows how much to believe. It was a love-match, wasn't it? I was told so when they were married.'

'Yes, it was a love-match. Miss Wilmot was one of the beauties of her year—a belle in her first season—a ward in chancery, with a fortune that came very handy to Halverdene.'

The sunburnt soldier from Kabul had left the group and was looking out of the window. His half-smoked cheroot lay forgotten where it had dropped from his hand, and his thoughts were in a Devonshire orchard, where he was a boy again, fresh from a military school, playing battledore and shuttlecock with two fair-haired girls in white frocks—girls whom, by some right of cousinship, he called by their Christian names. The Wilmots and the Donellys were very distant cousins, but still it was a cousinship, and Oscar Donelly had many privileges in the house of the jovial maiden aunt by whom these orphans were reared. He was a favourite with the elder lady, and the girls were frankly cordial to him. He brought them news of the great world, of which they knew absolutely nothing. Even Beatrice, the elder, would have to wait three or four years before she was to be presented and spend her first season in London, under the wing of a married aunt who had a house in Curzon Street, and was said to know only the best people.

The young cornet sailed for India with his regiment at the beginning of the Afghan war. The campaign had been a long and bitter one, and the subaltern came back to England a captain, but not altogether assured that the hero of Kandahar was more to be envied than the cadet who played battledore and shuttlecock in the orchard between Starcross and Exeter. Home letters had told him of the Wilmots' appearance in society—the sisters had been presented at the same drawing-room, and made their *début* in the great world side by side. There was only a year between them, and Beatrice had begged that they should go through the ordeal together, and had prevailed against her aunt's opinion.

'You will not be thought half so much of,' she said, 'if there are two of you.'

The event proved her mistaken. The fact that there were two girls equally handsome and equally dowered, both bright and spirited and in the first freshness of youthful bloom, impressed people. The two Miss Wilmots were admired and run after wherever they went. No smart party was complete without them. When the two Miss Wilmots took influenza and were laid up together, Mayfair was in mourning.

Each had numerous offers between April and August. Both were difficult, but Lucilla was impossible. She refused some splendid opportunities of doing well for herself and improving the status of her family. Her aunt, Mrs Montressor, who had married three portionless daughters with business-like celerity, was irate at this capriciousness.

'Do you expect to marry the Pope?' she asked.

'I believe a triple crown would tempt me; but then he would be old; they always are,' said Lucilla, who had not been so severely educated as to trouble herself about the arrangement of nominatives in familiar conversation.

Everyone was surprised when Lord Halverdene was announced to the world as Beatrice's successful suitor. His reputation was by no means spotless; his passion for the turf was notorious; but he was handsome, and had that grand open manner and rather haughty bearing which a very young woman is apt to admire; especially when she has seen very little of the world, or of the dark abysses that may lie under that fine candid manner.

No doubt in the beginning of things Halverdene was deeply in love, and a sincere passion gave fire and force to his pursuit of the heiress.

They were married, and for the first year of her wedded life Beatrice was completely happy. Then came the shadow of trouble, and then the cold wind of a husband's indifference blew with deadly breath across the home paradise. Slowly and gradually the wife grew to understand the character of the man she loved. She heard stories of his past; she knew of damning facts in the present. Hymen reversed his taper, and the sacred flame went out for ever.

Beatrice was what is called a woman of spirit. She had made her choice matrimonial, and had stuck to it in the teeth of opposition, disregarding her London aunt's hints and insinuations, her country aunt's prejudices and cautions. Having taken her own course, she was too proud to complain of her disappointment even to her nearest and dearest. The world only knew of her troubles through the gossip of servants and rustic neighbours, and from the cessation of all pleasant hospitalities.

Lucilla, who insisted upon living with her sister, to the hindrance of all matrimonial opportunities for herself, alone knew what that sister had to suffer, and even to her Beatrice never opened her heart.

The affection between the sisters was of the strongest, or Lucilla would hardly have endured life in a house where she was subject to the rough insolence of a host for whom her presence was often an incubus; but Lucilla was not the kind of young woman to be scared by any man's rudeness, and she laughed his lordship's attacks to scorn.

'You don't suppose I stay at Halverdene to please you,' she said, 'or that I care whether you are glad or sorry to have me here?'

Beatrice had urged her sister to find a happier home, even if she did not care to accept any of those offers which would have ensured her a kind husband and a good social position. Any home would have been more congenial to a handsome young woman than Halverdene, where the dullness was only broken by an occasional irruption of noisy racing men. Lucilla was adamant.

'I don't mean to marry till I fall honestly in love,' she told her sister, 'and I don't want to set up a house of my own and establish myself in permanent spinsterhood. As for his lordship, *je m'en fiche*. It amuses me to quarrel with him. I am perfectly happy here. We have the horses and dogs, old servants who are fond of us, and a garden which we both adore. What more can we want for happiness? If you plague me about leaving you I shall order my goods to be taken to the garden bedroom, and establish myself there; and then perhaps I shall see the ghost, and die, as those poor children did.'

This was an allusion to the earliest well-authenticated tradition of the ghost-chamber.

In the days when the garden bedroom had been a night nursery, two children of the first Lord Halverdene, a boy and a girl of nine and seven years old, had been frightened by some ghastly appearance in that fine old room, and had told their nurses vague stories of the something that brooded over their beds. The visions had occurred at longish intervals, and their vagueness had suggested childish dreams; but the death of the two children, which had happened within a year, had given a new aspect to the story in the minds of the superstitious and ignorant. The formless visions childishly depicted were placed on record as ghostly warnings foreshadowing doom, and the reputation of the garden bedroom as a ghost-chamber was firmly established. A century and a half of occasional appearances had maintained the traditions of the house, and to hint a doubt of the ghost in the village of Halverdene, or even in the vicarage drawing-room, was to be assured with gravest head-shakings that this particular case was established by indisputable evidence. Other ghost-stories might be foolishness; but the ghost at Halverdene House was fact.

'And nobody can tell me the nature and appearance of the thing,' cried Lucilla, taking tea in the bosom of the vicar's family, which was not too grand to dine at three o'clock in summer and take tea at six, for the sake of an evening walk after tea. 'That is what worries me about this particular ghost. Nobody seems to know anything about him. When I slept in the room myself——'

The two younger daughters—both in the pinafore period of their existence—crowded upon her at this point, and nearly squeezed her off her chair, interrupting her with breathless interrogation.

'Did you—did you really sleep there, Miss Wilmot? How awful!'

'How lovely!'

'And did you see anything? Oh, did you see *it*?'

'No, Dolly, I didn't see it; but I knew it was there.'

'Oh, tell us, tell us, do tell us!' with growing breathlessness. 'How sweet of you, how brave of you to sleep there! Let me take your cup. Do tell us.'

'There is very little to tell. It was Christmas-time, and we had a big house-party. I had been dancing all the evening, and I was dead beat. I slept like a top for two or three hours; and then I woke suddenly in the pitch darkness, and I felt that there was something—something holding me by the throat and strangling me—something huge and horrible, with red-hot claws that pressed into my chest. I don't know if I fainted, or fell into a dead sleep, or what happened to me; but when the housemaid brought me my tea in the morning, I woke with a splitting headache, and I felt ill, and shivering, and wretched for two or three days after; and then Beatrice insisted on carrying me off to Bridlington to get the ghostly feeling blown out of me by the North Sea.'

'And you don't even know what the ghost was like?' said Dolly, disappointed.

'How could I? The room was pitch dark.'

'How tiresome! There is generally some kind of light,' pursued Dolly, falling back on her knowledge of the stories of Ghostland she had read in gorgeous half-guinea annuals, among the portraits of beautiful peeresses. 'The moon suddenly shines in through an opening in the damask curtains; or the wood fire, which has burnt low, flames up with a last flash, and one sees the ghost's face, and dress, and jewellery.'

'Ah, Dolly, that is the ghost of fiction; a lady in a sacque; a gentleman in a Ramillies wig. The thing that haunts Halverdene is a reality, and the fact that nobody has ever been able to describe the thing goes to prove that it is real.'

Dolly and her sister listened open-mouthed as Lucilla soared into that region of the abstract where their young minds could not follow her.

'The thing that haunts the room may be an unresting conscience burdened with a crime unatoned, or a wicked soul that died and made no sign, and even in the grave is tortured with its lust of sin, hate, jealousy, wicked love—who knows? Oh, my dears, forgive me! I am raving. Don't let me talk of that horrid room any more. When I remember what I suffered there I always get a little mad.'

'It had red-hot claws,' said Dolly, dwelling on the one descriptive touch which appealed to her juvenile ideality.

'Dolly, if you insist upon talking about it, I vow I'll make you sleep in the room,' cried Lucilla, shaking herself free from the two pinafores.

'I should like to sleep there,' said Dolly, opening her eyes very wide.

'Yes, and die like those other children who slept in the garden bedroom when it was a nursery. That room has always been fatal to children. It was not the first Lord Halverdene's children only—there were others who died ninety years afterwards, three children in one family—a younger son's family—three children in one summer.'

'Had they seen the ghost—all of them?' asked Dolly, awe-stricken; while Cecily, the younger pinafore, could only shape the words dumbly with dry lips.

'I don't know; they had been frightened in the room. The old woman at the lodge told me about them. They were nervous, sensitive children—not great bouncing creatures like you and Cis—and they died in one summer. That's all the old woman could tell me about them, and she was nursemaid at Halverdene fifty years ago. But it's very wrong of me to talk to you of such horrors.'

'We like it,' said Dolly; 'we dote upon ghosts.'

'Silly, morbid little things! Why, all sensible people know that ghosts are nonsense. Come and show me your gardens.'

'She has a lettuce in hers,' said Cicely, pointing to the older pinafore. 'It isn't very big yet, but we water it every evening.'

'You'll drown it,' Lucilla told them. 'It will turn into a watercress.'

They took hold of her, one hanging on to each hand, and dragged her out through the French window, and across the lawn to that obscure portion of the vicarage grounds where the children had their allotments. They were two funny little figures in long white pinafores, and plaited pig-tails tied with brown ribbon, and they really were children, which was not so wonderful a fact in the early part of the forties as it might seem now.

Chapter II
How Captain Donelly Heard of the Ghost

Captain Donelly could not banish the thought of the Devonshire orchard and the girls whose bright faces had made the homely scene paradisaic. He was deeply moved at the notion of Beatrice's domestic troubles. That she should be ill-used by a husband, she whose love should have made the meanest of men great and noble, she whom he would have loved kneeling, as devout Romanists love the saints. She was only seventeen in those innocent boyish days, before ever his battle of life began, as fresh and as confiding as a child. He would have deemed it sacrilege to tell her of his love—selfish to ask her to wait for him. What of this world's gear could he ever have worthy to lay at her feet?

They had been boy and girl together, she seventeen, he under twenty, and his love had been but a boy's love. A lad just beginning life in a profession which he thinks the finest in the world, with his future all before him, and the novel delights of uniform, mess, and parade ground, is apt to think just a little more of himself and his own ambitious hopes than of the girl he loves. It was afterwards at a lonely hill-station, where the long evenings hung heavy on his hands, that Oscar Donelly began to discover how fondly he had loved that third or fourth cousin of his. It was afterwards when a letter from his father's Irish vicarage brought him the news of Beatrice's marriage, that he knew how deep he had been in love with her, by the sharpness of his agony at knowing that she was lost to him. His happy-go-lucky Irish temper had made him ignore the probability of her marrying in her first season. He told himself that she would be difficult to please; he flattered himself that he had a corner in her heart which might help to keep out a stranger, and that after a few years of hard fighting he might go home to find her still free, and willing to be won. He knew how daring had been his hopes now that all hope was over.

He had only been in London a few days when he heard his old friend General Palmer and Mr Soaper-Snarle talking about Lady Halverdene. His first duty was to his father and sisters in the south of Ireland, where he spent the second half of July and the beginning of August. That visit finished he set his face towards Yorkshire, a long cross-country journey from Holyhead; but he contrived to arrive at York in time for the summer meting. He had been told that Lord and Lady Halverdene were sure to be at the races.

It was brilliant weather, and the old city was full of gaiety, and overflowing with visitors. Beds, even in the shabbiest lodging-houses, over shabby shops, were at a premium. Happily Oscar had friends at the barracks who were able and willing to put him up for the three nights, and on their drag he went to the Knavesmire.

He did not stop with the party on the drag, but left them in order to look for his friends on the grandstand, after a careful review of the carriages had convinced him that the Halverdenes were not among that giddy and unbusinesslike part of the community to whom a race only means picnicking among a smartly dressed crowd, with all the troublesome accompaniments of gypsies, acrobats, itinerant musicians, and beggars of every description. The nigger minstrel—otherwise Ethiopian Serenader—had not been invented at that period of English history.

The comparative quiet of the grandstand, though it was pretty well filled, was positively soothing after the noise and racket of the course, and Captain Donelly had no trouble in finding the people he wanted. They were in the front seat at one end of the stand, two tall women dressed almost alike in lavender muslin gowns, straw bonnets, and black silk scarves, a style of dress which would seem very dowdy to the modern idea, but which was then graceful and elegant. The reader may refer to *Nicholas Nickleby*, or to the illustrations of Balzac's novels, where he will see a simplicity of drapery which is not unbecoming to a graceful figure.

Captain Donelly thought he had never see a lovelier face than the one which smiled at him in the shadow of a cottage bonnet.

'Beatrice!' he exclaimed, holding out his hands, and seizing both of hers.

'No, Lucilla. Beatrice is so absorbed in the horses that she has not even seen you. How sunburnt you are! When did you come home?'

'Four weeks ago. I need not ask if you are well. Those blooming cheeks answer for themselves.'

'If I were a milkmaid I should curtsy my thanks for your compliment, but blooming cheeks are about the last thing a young woman of *ton* would choose to be accredited with. Pallor and fragility are the essentials of a fashionable belle.'

'I have had a surfeit of pallid beauty in India, and I am charmed to see health and good looks at home. How is Lady Halverdene?'

'You must ask that question for yourself. Beatrice, here is Captain Donelly waiting to be welcomed as a hero after his perils in the Punjab.'

Beatrice rose and came towards them. She was changed from the happy girl he had known in Devonshire. Trouble had set its mark upon her. In the old days Lucilla had been an insignificant chit of sixteen, with hardly the promise of beauty, while Beatrice was radiant in budding loveliness; a rosebud just expanding into a rose. Now Lucilla was the rose, and Beatrice had a faded look, but withal so noble a carriage of head and throat, and so exquisite a smile, that she was to Oscar's eyes even more interesting than in the bloom of her girlhood.

She blushed as she welcomed him, and then sighed. The blush was for an innocent love-story that had long been ended and all but forgotten.

The sigh came with the thought of all she had suffered since they two had parted. Then the woman of society asserted herself.

'Have you seen Halverdene? No! He is in the ring, or in the paddock, I dare say. He has two horses in the next race, both doomed to lose, I fear. Are you not glad to be back in England after that terrible war? What horrors, what suffering! My heart bled—every English heart bled—as I read of that awful tragedy.'

They sat down side by side and talked gravely, frankly, as if they had been brother and sister—talked of himself and of his experiences; but of herself and of what she had done and suffered in the long interval of severance there was very little said.

'You have a place near here, I think?' he said, by-and-by, when the race was over.

One of Lord Halverdene's horses had come in a bad third, the other was nowhere. Beatrice looked distressed at the failure, though it had seemed inevitable before the race began.

'Nineteen miles. I don't know if you call that near.'

'Do you go back tonight?'

'No. Lucilla and I are stopping at the hotel with Halverdene. We shall go back tomorrow evening; but I dare say Halverdene will stay for the last of the racing, and come home on the coach on Saturday.'

Halverdene came up to the stand presently, very angry at the failure of his horses, but flushed with wine, and with a kind of savage mirth which showed itself in his effusive recognition of his wife's kinsman.

'You'll dine with us at the Royal, of course, Captain Donelly, seven sharp, and as good a brand of Moet as you need wish to drink.'

The captain explained that he was staying at the barracks, and could hardly excuse himself from the mess dinner.

'Damn the mess! I know all those fellows, and they know me. Bring as many of them as you like. We'll make a night of it.'

'I'd rather come in for an hour after dinner, if you'll allow me.'

'Do as you like, my dear fellow,' cried his lordship; and then swaggered away and was speedily absorbed into a group of rather disreputable-looking men, and laughing and talking louder than the loudest of them.

His presence had silenced his wife, and Oscar could see that every tone of that loud voice, every peal of reckless laughter, was pain to her. She sat looking across the Knavesmire with eyes that took no delight in the varied crowd, the play of summer light upon the landscape and the people, the movement and the gladness of the scene.

* * * * *

Captain Donelly dined with his friends at the mess, and adjourned to the Royal Hotel at nine o'clock. He found Lady Halverdene and her sister in a dimly lighted drawing-room, while from the adjoining dining-room came the sound of several voices and frequent bursts of laughter.

'Halverdene asked some of his racing friends to dinner,' Beatrice told him; 'so Lucilla and I dined *tête-à-tête*, and have been moping here in the dark ever since. I think there is hardly anything so disheartening as an inn sitting-room for birds of passage, as we are. No belongings, books, work, anything. We have been looking at the engraving of the Queen's marriage as if we had never seen that work of art before.'

'I should have asked the waiter to bring us a pack of cards if I had not been afraid he would laugh at me. We might have played Beggar my Neighbour or Casino,' said Lucilla.

'Will you join Halverdene and his friends in the dining-room?' asked Beatrice.

'What, desert you when you own to being moped! No, Lady Halverdene, I mean to be as amusing—or at least as flippant as a walking gentleman in a five-act comedy. How I wish I were witty for your sakes! Or, a happier idea; you two who have lived in the world, while I have been living out of it, can amuse me with a few of the scandals that have been town-talk while I have been in the Indian hills.'

A waiter brought in an urn and a tea-tray, and Lucilla made tea, and the talk soon drifted out of an artificial channel to the days that were gone, when these three had been happy without fear or even thought of the future. Oscar and Lucilla were the chief talkers, Lady Halverdene sitting in the shadowy region beyond the light of those candles which made so formidable an item in an old-fashioned hotel bill, and yet left a room so dark. Once there came a faint sigh from among the shadows, but there was for the most part silence.

Presently the doors burst open and Lord Halverdene and his boon-companions poured into the room, most of them like the sons of Belial, 'flown with insolence and wine'. The talk became noisy almost to riotous-ness. Halverdene had obviously been drinking, and if his guests seemed less affected by liquor, it was only because they were hardened by longer habit, and that while he had been gradually degenerating into a drunkard, intemperance was with them a second nature.

Tonight he was good-natured in his cups, and he treated Donelly with boisterous friendliness.

'You must come to Halverdene,' he said; 'you can go post with me tomor-row. We'll manage to put you up: the old house will bear a good bit of squeez-ing, though my lady and her sister contrive to absorb a whole wing. Your fine lady is a bird that must have a very roomy cage, nowadays. Let me see,' advancing an uncertain finger and pointing first at one of his companions and then at another; 'there's you, and you, and the major, and Parson Bob,' here the wavering finger indicated a seedy man in a clerical neckcloth, 'and the rest of you,' half a dozen in all, but to Halverdene's blinded vision they may have seemed half a score; 'but we can find a shake-down for her lady-ship's cousin; yes, old file, even if we have to put you in the haunted room.'

He stood in front of the empty fireplace, with his coat-tails under his arms, swaying backwards and forwards, laughing long and loud at what he thought a capital joke. No one noisier than my lord when he took his wine good naturedly.

This was the first that Oscar Donelly had heard of the haunted room.

'What, have you a ghost at Halverdene?' he exclaimed lightly.

'Dozens of 'em. Not that I ever saw anything; but the ghosts have been there time out of mind, and the room they haunt is a plaguey unlucky room. It may be only a coincidence,' said Halverdene, sinking from loud joviality to a solemn whisper; 'but any young people who have slept in that room have come to an untimely end. It used to be a nursery! a nice nursery, by Jove! The children saw something, took it to heart, and died. If Providence—gave me an heir—wou'dn lerr him sleep in that nur-er-y,' concluded Halverdene, becoming suddenly unintelligible.

Captain Donelly thanked him in general terms for his invitation, and declared his intention of profiting by it, not immediately, but at some future time.

'When your house may not be quite so full,' he said; 'though I am not afraid of a night or two in your haunted room. I always carry a pistol-case; and I think your ghost would come off second best.'

'Ah, that's a dangerous dodge, popping at ghosts,' said the seedy parson; 'generally turns out badly. You may shoot the footman who brings you your shaving-water, or a sportsman who has got up at three o'clock for cub-hunting, and happens to look into the wrong room. No use shooting at a ghost! If he is a ghost you can't hurt him, and if he isn't it may mean manslaughter.'

Captain Donelly did not court conversation with the cleric whom his friends addressed as Parson Bob. The old clock on the stairs struck eleven, and Oscar bade his cousins good night, and slipped out of the room while Halverdene's back was turned. His lordship was standing at a card-table with his friends clustered round him, betting on the cut, in that highly intellectual game known as Blind Hookey. The captain's heart ached for the lady whom he remembered so lovely and light-hearted, with life and its chances of happiness all before her.

Yes, he meant to avail himself of Lord Halverdene's invitation. He wanted to see what manner of life his cousin led in her own home, with such a husband as the man he had seen tonight. He had not asked for Beatrice's approval of her husband's invitation, for he divined that she would shrink from admitting even a kinsman to the secrets of her domestic life. His blood burned within him at the thought that such men as those battered *roués*, those second-rate racing men he had seen tonight, were free to enter the house where a refined and beautiful woman was mistress.

* * * * *

Captain Donelly travelled further north, spent a fortnight at a friend's shooting lodge in Argyllshire, shot a good many head of game, tramped over a good many miles of heather, ate a good many bannocks, drank his share of the famous Lochiel whisky, and bored himself stupendously. His heart was not in the business, and his friends found it out.

'You are a deuced good shot,' said one of them, 'but a damned dull companion;' and Donelly owned that he was out of spirits and unhappy about someone whom he—whom he cared for.

He could not get Beatrice Halverdene's face out of his mind, with its wan smile and frequent look of pain. He could not forget Halverdene's brutal manner, the drunken laughter, the thickened utterance, and, worst of all, the raffish dissipated companions, the reprobates who were allowed to sit at meat and drink with this drunken sinner's wife.

To think that she had married this man for love, and that the first year of her wedded life had been an idyll! His home letters had told him, in a young sister's enthusiastic language, of Lady Halverdene's happy marriage, adoring, and adored by, her husband. It was not his coronet that had won her. She had married for love.

That yearning to see more of the woman he had loved in his boyhood grew upon Oscar Donelly in the lonely Scottish hills. His companions of the shooting lodge were sportsmen and nothing more. Their everlasting talk of sport wearied him. He was among them, but not of them; and one morning he pretended that his letters brought him an urgent summons southward, on family business, and a post-chaise took him to Glasgow the following afternoon in time for the coach which left that city at eight in the evening.

It was evening again when he left York in another post-chaise on his way to Halverdene, and it was past ten o'clock when he alighted from the chaise in front of the Queen Anne doorway, with its stone shell-shaped pediment, and tall narrow window on either side; windows within which the light showed dimly, as if the hall of the mansion were but sparely lighted.

'I hope everyone has not gone to bed,' thought Oscar.

He felt that this night attack was rather a desperate style of acting upon a general invitation; but Lord Halverdene was not a man with whom he need be over-ceremonious, and the captain wanted to take his lordship's household by surprise, in order to arrive at the better knowledge of his cousin's domestic life. And yet, alas! what good could come of that knowledge to the lady or to himself? If her husband were unkind, what could he do to help her? If her life were unhappy, what could he do to make it happier?

A sleepy-looking servant opened the door and admitted him into a large and lofty hall, paved with black and white marble, and adorned with the most conventional and uninteresting of family portraits. The weather had been wet and gusty from early morning, when Captain Donelly left Newcastle outside the mail coach, preferring to be wet in the open air than to be dry in a stuffy vehicle with its full complement of passengers. He was chilled to the bone, and he looked almost resentfully at the wide fire-place with its sculptured marble chimney-piece surmounted by a bust of Minerva, forgetting that it was only the first week of September, and that people were still pretending to think it summer.

'Be good enough to bring in my portmanteau, and pay the postilion for me,' said Oscar, counting some money into the sleepy footman's palm.

'Yes, I'll see to that,' the footman answered in rather an off-hand tone. 'You're the person that was sent for, I suppose?'

'The person that was sent for? What do you mean? I am Captain Donelly; her ladyship's cousin.'

'I beg your pardon, sir,' stammered the man, much humbled; 'there was a person expected—from York—and I thought, seeing the portmanteau—and—I beg your pardon, sir.'

'His lordship is at home, I conclude?'

'Yes, sir, but he is not very well, and he went to bed two hours ago. Her ladyship and Miss Wilmot are in the morning-room. If you'll step this way, sir, I'll look to your portmanteau afterwards.'

He led the way to a room at the other end of a long narrow corridor, which looked of older date than the entrance hall, flung open the door with the true London air, and announced:

'Captain Donelly.'

The sisters were seated far apart, Lucilla at the piano, but not playing, Lady Halverdene half hidden in a large armchair by the fireplace, where there was a cheery little fire, which revived Oscar's sinking spirits almost as much as the sight of his cousins.

'Oscar!' they cried simultaneously, and in neither face was there any pleasure mingled with the look of surprise.

It was not a cheering welcome. Captain Donelly could hardly misread the face of his cousin Beatrice, which expressed something akin to fear.

'You didn't expect me,' he said, 'but I hope you are not vexed with me for taking his lordship at his word so completely, and bursting in upon you without notice. You remember he said I might come at any time, there would always be room for me, even if it were only the ghost's room,' he concluded, trying to be jocose.

'Yes, I remember,' answered Beatrice, looking from her visitor to her sister with such obvious embarrassment that Oscar felt he ought not to remain, even although she was his kinswoman, and he had travelled a night and a day for the sole purpose of finding out what her home life was like.

'I see that my unexpected arrival embarrasses you,' he said. 'I have been very inconsiderate. A man's invitation counts for nothing when there is a lady in the case. I ought to have waited for you to ask me here. And I am so atrociously late, too. I thought I should have been here by eight o'clock at the latest, but the Newcastle Lightning is about the slowest coach I ever travelled by. If there is an inn within a walk I'll go there for tonight. I can come back to breakfast with you tomorrow morning; and then you can decide at your leisure whether you would like to have me for a few days or not. If Halverdene is ill you may prefer to be without visitors.'

'Nonsense!' cried Lucilla. 'Of course you must stay; even if we do put you in the ghost-room,' she added, as if answering a look of her sister's. 'Would you mind? It is really one of the best rooms in the house—and as the ghost is so very shifty and intangible nobody need be afraid of him, need they?'

'I would not be afraid if he were the most palpable and clearly defined apparition in England,' said Donelly, trying to infuse some cheerfulness into the situation.

Lucilla rang and ordered the cedar-room to be got ready for Captain Donelly.

'Be sure there is a good fire, and that everything is thoroughly aired,' she said peremptorily; 'and see that Captain Donelly's portmanteau is unpacked for him. And you must have supper,' she said to Oscar, taking the matter into her own hands, while Lady Halverdene sat inert, and apparently uninterested, looking at the fire. 'I dare say you dined early, and perhaps badly into the bargain.'

'Both,' admitted Oscar, and Lucilla gave her orders for a snug little supper to be served in the room where they were sitting.

Her cousin could but admire her grace and brightness, her prompt decided way of settling things. All of energy and vivacity that Beatrice had once possessed—and he recalled the light-hearted shuttlecock player in the Devonshire orchard—seemed to have left her. Tonight she was dull and silent, and it wounded him to think that she was bored and annoyed by his uninvited presence.

'Come and sit by the fire,' said Lucilla. 'Beatrice is out of spirits because of his lordship's illness. You mustn't mind her.'

'But I do mind. I feel very sorry to have intruded at such a time. Is Lord Halverdene really very ill?'

'Yes, he is very bad.'

'What is it?'

'The doctors hardly give it a name. You know how mysterious doctors are. It is some kind of nervous complaint. They say it has been coming on for a long while, and that is about all they say. We have sent to York for a skilled attendant; and in the meantime Halverdene's valet is a very good nurse. There is no use in Beatrice moping. She can do nothing.'

'That is the saddest part of it all,' said Lady Halverdene, and then relapsed into silence.

'What a delightful room!' said Oscar, looking about, and admiring the panelled walls and low ceiling with its carved oak cross-beams.

'Yes, it is one of the old rooms. This wing was built in Charles II's time, when the place was only a hunting-lodge; the Queen Anne front and wings were added fifty years later, so that the principal part of the mansion is only an afterthought! Your quarters are close by. I am very fond of this room, and Beatrice and his lordship are kind enough to let me call it my own, as it is in the unpopular end of the house, and nobody cares about it.'

'I hope the ghost doesn't intrude here.'

'Oh, no; he, she, or it is a conscientious ghost, and never breaks bounds.'

And then Lucilla told him how she had spent one night in the haunted room for her own pleasure, and he questioned her as to what she had seen there.

'I don't believe I saw anything—really,' she said. 'Looking back at my experience in the sober light of common sense, I think the thing which scared me was only a bad dream—a very horrid dream—of the nightmare nature; the sense of some huge indescribable presence squatting on my chest, weighing me down into a bottomless pit of horror and suffocation. I went there prepared to be frightened, and the hideousness—the horrid feeling of the visitation—was quite equal to my darkest imaginings; but after all I believe it was only a dream, and that my own imagination was to blame for all I suffered.'

Oscar moved about the room looking at the books and china, the pictures, which were few but good, and lastly at a row of miniatures mounted upon faded red velvet, which hung upon a panel near the fireplace.

'These are interesting,' he said. 'Family portraits, I conclude?'

'Yes, those two at the top are the boy and girl who used to sleep in the cedar nursery, and who both died. I believe that was what first gave the room its evil repute. And after, when another occupant of the room died young, people talked of it as an unlucky room, and it began to be considered fatal.'

'It was not fatal to you, I am glad to think.'

'No, and it is not going to be fatal to you, unless those servants are careless in the matter of airing things. Perhaps you would like to see the room before you sup?'

'Very much. I should like to make what our neighbours call *un brin de toilette* before I sit down to eat with my esteemed cousins.'

'Then let it be only *un brin*,' said Lucilla; 'don't put yourself into dress clothes at this hour of the night, just because Beatrice and I are in evening gowns.'

'I will do nothing that will deprive me of your society for more than ten minutes,' said Oscar, gallantly; 'but I am dying to see the ghost-room.'

'You shall not be allowed to expire,' Lucilla said gaily, as she rang the bell.

Her life and brightness charmed him. He began to wonder whether he had ever been in love with Beatrice—poor Beatrice, sitting by the fire, dull and despondent, weighed down by anxiety about a sick husband who was reported to have neglected and ill-used her when he was well. Oscar pitied the downtrodden wife with all his heart; but he found it very difficult to associate her with the sparkling young beauty of the Devonian village. The sparkling beauty was here, but her name was no longer Beatrice. She was Lucilla, whose brilliant eyes, sunny curls, and white shoulders shone out in the sombre old panelled parlour, a revelation of unexpected beauty; Lucilla, of whom his earlier memories could only recall pigtails and a pinafore.

He was conducted to a room close by—*the* room, a spacious wainscoted chamber with three windows, one opening to the ground, a noble fire burning in a wide iron grate with old-fashioned hobs and an elaborately floriated back. The bedstead was a fine mahogany four-poster, with slim-fluted columns and handsome green silk curtains, nothing hearselike or gloomy about it. Altogether, the room in the light of that glorious coal and wood fire, and with a pair of candles alight on the dressing-table, had a cheerful and comfortable aspect. The footman had unpacked the portmanteau, had laid out brushes, and combs, and razors on the dressing-table, and placed all things ready for the guest. Oscar made a rapid toilet, and returned to the sitting-room, splendid in a dark brown coat, and a black velvet waistcoat worked with gold thread, and one of those allconquering black satin stocks which are familiar to us in the early portraits of Dickens and D'Orsay. He felt that although he had been forbidden to put on evening dress he was not looking his worst.

A light impromptu supper was laid on a pembroke table near the fire, and the trio sat down together in the friendliest way. Lucilla carved a chicken with skill and *aplomb*—those were the days in which a lady was expected to be able to carve—while Oscar operated upon a ham. The footman opened a champagne bottle and filled the three tall narrow glasses. No butler had appeared on the scene, and Oscar concluded that functionary had gone to bed before his arrival.

Lucilla persuaded her sister to eat a little chicken and drink a little wine.

'You had positively nothing at dinner,' she said; 'you are killing yourself,' at which Lady Halverdene looked at her reproachfully, and then with an evident effort put on an appearance of cheerfulness, and finally, beguiled into self-forgetfulness, joined in the light talk of the other two, and seemed almost happy.

They sat talking till the fire went out, and a loud clock in the distance struck twelve.

'Every stroke sounds a reproach,' said Lucilla. 'Upon my word, Oscar, you have tempted us into most unholy dissipation. Do you know that we usually light our chamber candlesticks and stalk solemnly up to bed at half-past ten?'

'I am ashamed of having made you so late.'

'You have done us a kindness,' said Lady Halverdene. 'The nights are always too long when one is anxious.'

'You ought not to be so anxious,' Oscar said cheerfully; 'with his lordship's fine physique he is sure to pull through, whatever the nature of his illness. He is the kind of man to make a good fight for life.'

The candles were lighted. The footman reappeared, sleepier than ever, to put out the lights in the sitting-room. The little party dispersed, the two ladies to their distant apartments, the captain to his room close by, and silence and darkness came down upon the lonely country house.

Chapter III
How Captain Donelly Met the Ghost

In spite of the fact that he was in a house whose master lay seriously ill—a fact which, no doubt, ought to have saddened him—Oscar Donelly was in excellent spirits as he paced slowly about the spacious cedar bedroom in the cheerful firelight. He had just made a discovery which had gladdened him, which opened up a bright vista of possible happiness. He had found out that his romantic passion for Beatrice Halverdene—the flame which had been fed by absence and fond imaginings—had burnt itself out, and that a newer and brighter flame had risen from the ashes of the old love.

He was in love with Lucilla—Lucilla, with whom he had an indisputable right to be in love if he pleased, and who was free to respond to his passion. Lucilla, who by the brightness of her smiles and the friendly accents of her voice, by all her pretty cares for his comfort, and the unqualified cordiality of her welcome, had shown him that he was by no means disagreeable in her eyes.

He walked up and down in the fireglow, thinking of her looks, her words, her vivacious turns of speech, her arch smiles, her shrewd common sense; and anon meditating ways and means, and wondering whether he were financially worthy. He was neither rich nor poor. A dear old maiden aunt had left him an income which made him independent of his father, who had a small estate in County Limerick which must come to his only son by-and-by. The look-out was by no means desperate. He could afford to sell out and settle in Yorkshire, if Lucilla wanted to be near her sister. He had seen a good deal of hard fighting. He loved his profession, and would leave the army with regret; but Lucilla was worth a sacrifice. He was sure she would want to stay near her sister. She was the stronger spirit, the protector, the guardian angel. One brief hour of Halverdene's society had been enough to show him that some such sustaining influence was needful for Halverdene's wife.

He replenished his fire, heaping up the coals from a big copper scuttle, and looked about the room, admiring the play of light and shadow on the rich brown wainscote, the bright glints on the green silk curtains and pierced brass fender.

He had forgotten all ghostly traditions when he lay down to rest, full of happy fancies about the home that he was to create for Lucilla and himself within a few mile of Halverdene. A smallish house would do, if it were pretty, and picturesque as to situation. There must be a good stable, and some shooting; and no doubt he would have the run of the Halverdene covers.

The bed was of the old-fashioned luxurious order. A delightful bed for a good sleeper, a downy paradise for the first half-hour, but after that half-hour a couch of fever and unrest to the wakeful occupant. Happily, Oscar was tired with many hours of journeying on the top of stage coaches, and, while bodily weary, he had a mind at ease, no carking cares to pluck him from the verge of slumber's comfortable abyss. So for him the bed of downy feathers was the gate of paradise, and he was speedily threading dreamland's fairest labyrinth, albeit Lucilla had christened that very chamber the room of dreadful dreams.

He had laughed at the notion of supernatural manifestations. He had slept the long deep sleep of youth and health and hope.

A wan and sickly daylight was in the room when he woke suddenly to a revelation of horror, which in its spectral hideousness and its grim reality was worse than any vision of dread that Lucilla's stories had suggested to his imagination last night. A figure was kneeling upon the bed, crouching over him, with the strong grip of a burning hand upon his throat. A face, pallid and ghastly, was bending down close against his face, and two fiery eyes were glaring into his eyes.

If this were the ghost, verily it was a vision of fear to bring death or madness upon any young and sensitive creature that looked upon it. He who had never quailed before the Afghan guns, the savage Afghan faces, felt his blood run cold and his heart beat faster.

His first thought between sleeping and waking was, 'No wonder the children died!' Then, as the shadows of sleep were shaken off, reason reasserted herself.

Could a ghost's hand hold him as this hand was holding him? Would a ghost's breath sound thick and laboured like the panting breath he felt upon his face; and was that hideous sound of grinding teeth a sound of any spiritual visitant? No: common sense told him that this was no inexplicable impalpable horror, but a very real and very human assailant— a madman, with one hand clawing him by the throat, and the other hand uplifted and flourishing an open razor.

It was not till he had torn himself free from the clutch of those burning fingers and had leapt to the other side of the wide bedstead, that he recognised his assailant as Lord Halverdene.

In the struggle to free himself he had thrown his enemy from the bed to the floor. He scrambled to his feet immediately, and the two men stood looking at each other with the width of the bed between them, one with a deadly weapon in his hand, the other totally unarmed.

Oscar looked despairingly towards the fireplace, which was on Halverdene's side of the bed. To reach it and get possessed of that useful weapon for emergencies, the poker, he must pass the madman, who stood at the corner of the bedstead ready with his razor, grinning and muttering, his body stooping forward, like an Indian trapper lying in wait for his quarry. He had wounded himself in the scuffle on the bed, and the blood was pouring from a gash on his cheek. He was in his night-shirt, with bare feet.

The bell-rope was on Oscar's side of the bed. He pulled it violently, and in that violence destroyed all chance of communicating his peril by means of the bell, for the hook and loop had both rusted with disuse, and that one sharp tug brought down the bell-rope. No hope there.

Should he try to parley with his foe—try to talk reasonably with a man who was evidently for the time being a homicidal maniac thirsting for his blood? That blood-bedabbled face mopping and mowing at him yonder by the bedpost, that threatening hand with the razor, did not promise much advantage from the force of persuasion.

The faint and sickly light that filtered through the close-drawn blinds told Oscar that it was, at latest, five o'clock. He and the maniac were perhaps the only mortals stirring in the rambling old house. He remembered the long narrow corridor, the isolated position of the room in which he had slept.

'God knows how far off the occupied rooms may be,' he thought. 'I shall be massacred here, and nobody the wiser, till the footman brings my shaving water at eight o'clock.'

He had time to think this while he stood at bay, considering what was his best course. He would give the wretched man a chance, he thought, before encountering violence with violence.

'My dear Halverdene, this is too absurd!' he said, in a loud firm voice, looking fixedly at the gibbering face by the bedpost. 'What have I done to offend you that you should break in upon me in the middle of the night? It's a curious kind of hospitality, after having invited me to take you unawares. By Jove! you have taken *me* unawares!' he added, trying to laugh off the situation, with that blood-stained faced staring at him.

'My wife's lover,' muttered Halverdene—'my wife's lover! Kill him! kill him! kill him! That's what the devil said when he woke me out of my sleep just now—kill him! But Turner had hidden my pistols, and had locked my dressing-case with the razors for every day in the week—Monday, Tuesday, Wednesday. Today's Wednesday, ain't it? I wanted Wednesday's razor, to cut your throat; but the box was locked—curse that man of mine!'

All this was uttered rapidly, and sounded more like a monkey's chattering than human speech. Donelly was looking about him for a weapon, and as Halverdene came towards him with a wild leap, razor uplifted, he snatched up a heavy Chippendale chair, flung it straight at his assailant, knocking him down, and made a rush for the door.

The door was locked, the key gone. The madman had struggled up on to his knees, and was laughing at him, pointing at the door.

'Turner hid the pistols, and I hid the key,' he said. 'We'll have it out! We'll have it out! I can cut your throat with your own razor as well as with mine for Wednesday. We'll have it out!'

He was upon his feet by this time, and bounding across the room like a stag. Donelly remembered that his pistol-case was in a saddlebag that had been left in the hall. Before he could reach the hearth to snatch the poker the madman's clutch was upon him, and the razor would have been at his throat had not the assailant interrupted the business in hand by a violent peal of laughter at the facetiousness of the situation. That laughter gave Oscar time to grapple his foe; and then came a fight for life, reason against unreason, the well-knit limbs and hardened sinews of athletic youth, matched against the hypernatural strength of lunacy in a frame impaired by habitual intemperance.

The razor seemed everywhere. It wounded both men, again and again. They were blinded with each other's blood. Again and again Oscar threw off his foe, and made his despairing rush for door or window, but that foe was always too quick for him. Before he could tear open the casement or batter down the door, the madman had him in his clutch again, and the fight had to be fought again.

The noise, the fury of it, the crashing of chairs, the thud of footsteps, should have waked the seven sleepers, Oscar thought in his despair. Now and again he made a monstrous effort and called aloud for help; but breathless and choking as he was, the cry was not loud enough to reach the end of the corridor, and the grey light was only just beginning to brighten into broader day.

He fought for his life, as a man to whom life was newly and wonderfully dear—and fell at last, aching in every bone, bruised and battered, as if he had been broken on the wheel: fell with Lucilla's name upon his lips, in the last moment of consciousness, which he believed the last moment of life.

'Lucilla!' echoed the savage, glaring down at him. 'That's his hypocrisy.'

His foe lying at his feet senseless, and to all appearances dead, Lord Halverdene looked stupidly at the razor, dripping blood, and then let it fall.

He had forgotten to cut his victim's throat. He had also forgotten where he had hidden the key of the door, which was lying in the ashes under the grate; so he opened a window, and clambered out of it into the dewy garden, in his night raiment and with bare feet.

* * * * *

Before that deadly struggle in the cedar-room was finished, the butler who had been told off to take charge of Lord Halverdene, turn and turn with his lordship's body-servant, had awakened from a nap in his easy-chair, and had missed his patient from the bed where he had lain tossing, and muttering, and groaning, and whimpering all night, a victim to delirium tremens in its worst form.

When the watcher dropped asleep the door was locked, the key artfully hidden behind the candlestick on the mantelpiece; but not so artfully as to prevent Halverdene's finding it and opening the door of his prison. He had seen the man put the key there, with an elaborate pretence of looking for a box of matches; and he had waited his opportunity of getting out of the room.

He had a fixed idea in his mind, engendered of a conversation he had heard overnight from the adjoining dressing-room. The door of communication between the two rooms had been left ajar while the watcher ate his supper, brought to him by a housemaid, who explained that the reason she was so late in bringing the 'tray' was the unexpected arrival of her ladyship's cousin, Captain Donelly, from the north.

'I've had to get his room ready,' said the housemaid; 'they've put him in the cedar-room—because it's furthest from this end of the house. He won't hear his lordship's goings on.'

'Ah,' said the butler, 'he makes a pretty hullabaloo sometimes, I can tell you. I shall be very glad when the nurse comes from York.'

That name of Donelly had been the red rag to the mad bull. In the first year of his marriage, someone had said something about Oscar Donelly which had sown a germ of jealousy in Halverdene's mind.

Civil as he had been to Donelly at York—ostentatiously civil—the embers of angry feeling had been smouldering, and with the drink-madness, they burst into sudden blaze, and the madman had but one thought—how to be revenged on his wife's first sweetheart.

The rest followed in natural sequence. Through the weary night of fever and unrest the patient watched his watcher as he sat in the easy-chair, now attentive to every movement of the restless form upon the bed, now trying to beguile his own weariness by spelling through a county paper. Halverdene had watched his custodian till the man fell asleep, and had seized the opportunity of escape.

*   *   *   *   *

They found him in the gardens, exhausted, and shivering in every limb, blood-stained from head to foot. He had not been in a good plight before, but this morning's work hastened the inevitable end. The wild excitement, the chill of that quarter of an hour in the garden, in the sunless dawn, half naked, barefoot on the wet grass—these experiences were fatal; and within a month of that conflict in the haunted room Lord Halverdene was a dead man, and Lady Halverdene had descended to the minor position of a childless dowager.

She had her own fortune, and she had Lucilla, and the devoted friendship of Oscar Donelly, Lucilla's affianced husband.

The struggle with the madman had left its mark upon the captain in more than one scar, which, although not so deep as a sabre-cut, would be slow to disappear, while the loss of blood from the cuts and gashes inflicted at close quarters had resulted in a serious attack of low fever which detained him at the village inn, where he was removed on the morning of his adventure, until a month after his lordship's funeral.

During that long and wasting illness, and tedious convalescence, Lucilla was his guardian angel. She and her maid went every day to supervise his rustic attendants and his faithful soldier servant, who had followed his master from the north, and who proved himself an admirable nurse.

The captain was just able to accompany his cousins to London when they left Halverdene, which had now passed into the possession of the dead man's uncle, a dry-as-dust county magistrate and scientific farmer, with a stout, homely wife and a prodigious family of children, descending in an unbroken chain from the accomplished eldest daughter of nineteen, to the prattling infant of two and a half.

When this gentleman and his wife came to take possession of Halverdene House, there was a tremendous exploration of rooms, and a tremendous talk of where such and such members of the ruddy-cheeked and healthy band should be bestowed. If there was one point upon which the new Lord Halverdene valued his own intelligence more than another, it was his profound mastery of the laws of health. He was a perambulating book of extracts from Andrew Combe and Southwood Smith.

'Sleep in a ground-floor bedroom! My children!' exclaimed his lordship, contemplating the cedar-room, which the housekeeper informed him had been once a nursery, and which she suggested might again serve for the same purpose, so many of the upstairs bedrooms being wanted for young ladies and gentlemen, tutor, and governess. 'Does the woman think I am mad? A ground-floor room, on a level with the garden, a north-east aspect, and on clay! A murderous room!'

The housekeeper shook her head, gave a deep sigh, and on being interrogated told how that room was a haunted room, and had on more than one occasion proved fatal to the race of Halverdene.

'And yet no one has ever put a name to the ghost, or said what it was like,' concluded the housekeeper.

'Ghost—bosh! fatal—yes, no doubt. This room would be pernicious to infant health, and possibly fatal to infant life. I know what country houses are—cesspools under drawing-rooms, rotten brick drains. None of my family will be allowed to occupy this old wing. Ceilings low, floors too near the earth, windows with only one small casement made to open; picturesque—abominable!'

His lordship the seventh baron was a great improver—a man of energetic temper who could not have endured life without something to build, improve, or spoil. He improved Beatrice Halverdene's old Caroline garden off the face of the earth; he pulled up the floor of the cedar bedroom, and was amply rewarded for his pains by finding an ancient cesspool, and a comparatively modern brick drain, both in the loathsome condition in which neglect and ignorance left half the fine old houses in the land when Queen Victoria's reign was young.

'Shall I tell you the ghost's name?' asked the seventh Lord Halverdene, when people pestered him for the secret of the haunted room. 'The stories of strange apparitions in that room are all nonsense; but there is no doubt the little children had bad dreams, and no doubt their little innocent lives were sacrificed to the criminal ignorance of their parents. The ghost's name was Typhoid Fever.'

The Island of Old Faces

'The mourned, the loved, the lost,
Too many, yet how few!'

I HAVE ALWAYS THOUGHT that there is something mystic and unearthly in the light of a summer dawn—that early light of midsummer, that mysterious day within the night which lights the world while most of its inhabitants are sleeping—a glory and a loveliness of which so few of us are aware; a banquet of colour spread by Nature's lavish hand, while her ungrateful children lie unconscious, or wander in the dark labyrinths of dreamland. It is sad to think how many troubled sleepers lie bound in the thrall of horrible dreams while the meadow-dews sparkle under heaven's canopy of opal and rose, and every forest glade and every stream-let is lighted with the magic of sunrise.

Never had I more keenly felt the beauty of those soft gradations from darkness to dawn—the imperceptibleness of the change which makes the new day always something of a surprise—than I felt it as I stood on the deck of the *Zouave*, waiting while a couple of sailors lowered the dinghy that was to carry me to a tiny island which the dawn had shown me—a cluster of cocoa palms lying on the placid breast of the sea, a tuft of verdure in mid-ocean. It seemed no more than that.

Three months before that summer dawn my doctor had told me that I was overworked, and that my nerves were in a very bad state; so, as I really felt somewhat shaken, I placed myself in the hands of my nearest friend, and let him do what he liked with me.

What my friend liked was to hire a yacht that was to cost me four hundred pounds a month, to engage an intelligent young navy surgeon as my *companion de voyage* and ship doctor, in the event of any one on board wanting medical aid, and to send me off to the South Seas for a half-year's holiday. I was to do nothing and to think of nothing, to forget even that I had lately engaged myself to a beautiful and high-born lady, who had, I believe, fallen in love with my celebrity in the law courts rather than with my very self. Years and years ago someone had loved me—this very me—but when a man has come within measurable distance of the woolsack, he can hardly hope for that kind of love.

The *Zouave* was lying at anchor, and my clever young medico was fast asleep in his berth when I stepped lightly from the accommodation ladder to the dinghy, and bade the men row me as fast as their oars could go, to yonder tufted islet. Did they know the name of it?

No; as far as they knew it had no name. It was a mere speck on the chart, an uninhabited island.

The dinghy crept into a tiny cove under the shadow of an hibiscus tree, whose gold and orange flowers dropped on the luminous green water. I landed, and sent the man back to the yacht.

'You can return for me in the afternoon.'

'At what o'clock, sir?'

'Say three o'clock, and at this place.'

I walked away quickly, leaving the man saying something that was unheard by me.

Oh, the loveliness of that wooded islet in the pearly light and in the depth of shadow, where the tree-ferns spread and mingled their fans and made a canopy above my head, a leafy roof of texture so light that it trembled with every breath of the summer wind, letting in sudden arrowy flashes of morning sunshine and then growing dark again in a moment— a perpetual flicker of lights that came and went, amidst the warm green darkness!

The mosses beneath my feet were so thick and soft that earth seemed to lose its common substance, and to have all the spring and buoyancy of water. The air was filled with the scent of irises, jasmines, and lemon-grass that here grew wild; and the blossoms that leapt from tree to tree, that flashed out in gleams of vivid scarlet, orange, azure, purple, rose, with every flash of sunlight, or deepened into a dark glow of colour with every interval of shadow—how shall poor words of mine depict that splendid loveliness of flowers that were like living creatures, and seemed to flit past me on translucent wings, and flowers that sparkled like jewels and seemed to irradiate light? Among some of that brilliant bloom I saw clusters of purple berries. I tasted some of them, very cautiously, lest they should be poisonous; but they had only a sweet insipid taste that could belong to no deadly juices, and I ate a handful of them slowly as I strolled along.

I thought the island uninhabited, when suddenly a form that I knew sprang into the emerald vista, and drawing nearer each other, Lionel Haverfield and I met face to face, after many years of severance.

Until this moment I had believed him dead. We clasped hands, and he turned and walked beside me.

'My dear old friend, is it really you?'

'Yes, dear Hal.'

That was all we said to each other just at first. There was little need of speech between friends who were in such perfect sympathy as Lionel and I. We had been together at a famous public school, at Oxford, and then again in London, at the beginning of the great life-struggle, the young man's fight for fame and fortune. We had been such close friends, had so thoroughly understood each other. And I had thought him dead. Was it strange that tears rushed to my eyes and blinded me for a moment or two, or that I flung my arm about his neck almost as a woman might have done?

'Lionel, I am so glad, so glad my fancy brought me here. I knew nothing of this island till I saw a tuft of palms on the horizon in the dim early light, and I had the boat off the davits and was on my way here, in a wild haste, to see what it was like. I am so glad.'

'And so am I glad, Hal; for my own sake, very glad.'

'For your own sake, and for my sake. Surely you don't grudge me my happiness?'

'No, no, no. It is your happiness I am considering when I say I am not wholly glad.'

'But I am utterly happy in finding you. What need a man be more than happy?'

'It is of by-and-by I am thinking. When you go back to the world, and may regret——'

'Regret having seen you! Why Lionel, what a thought! Regret! Why, there is hardly anything in the world that could make me gladder than to see your dear old face. Upon my soul, Lionel, I believed you were dead.'

He looked at me gravely, but made no answer. Then, after a pause, he said, 'The world has used you well, I dare say, and you love the world.'

'Oh, I have what you called succeeded. I put on the pace. Ten years of my life, from twenty-five to thirty-five, were years of unmitigated drudgery—and then the reward came in a day, and after labouring in the trough of the sea, I found myself on the crest of the wave, floating along in the sunshine without a single stroke of my own, just tossed like a cork from success to success. But, in spite of it all, I am very tired, and this sleepy hollow of yours is ever so much better than the strife and babble of the law courts, or the row and riot of the bear-pit at Westminster. I should like to stay here with you for ever, on an island which reminds me of the charmed repose that Odysseus and his companions found in the Western sea—an island where it seems always—no, not afternoon, but morning; the still freshness of the new-born day. Whatever I may have done, you have chosen the better part—rest, and for ever rest; no work, no care, only the soft sad lullaby of the sea, and the blue sky, and

'"Flowcrets of a thousand hues...
...the quaint enamell'd eyes,
That on the green turf suck the honied showers."'

I quoted 'Lycidas', remembering how he loved the lines, in those old days when he was a poet, and when we all thought he ought to have won the Newdigate.

'You cannot stay here,' he said, in that serious voice which was so unlike the voice of his youth. 'The world calls you; there are claims you cannot deny. You must live out your life.'

'Yes, there are claims,' I admitted, almost reluctantly.

And then I told him of my recent betrothal to a young and beautiful woman—told him as unreservedly as I used to tell him all my thoughts and feelings, hopes and resolutions, when we were young.

When we were young, did I say? Why, he was young still. I had aged in the strife and turmoil of the great race for wealth and fame, but he, in this island of rest, showed no trace of the passing years. There was only one thoughtful line upon the broad fair brow, the line I remembered when he was a student of the Inner Temple twenty years ago. The face was the face that had looked at me so kindly in the summer dusk the night I started for Scotland. And when I came back from my holiday, somebody told me he was dead. Surely I had been taught to think him dead! I looked back, trying to remember—and I could recall a visit to his empty rooms, and the figure of his sister passing me in the street, six months afterwards, in deep mourning. I had only seen her once before, in the Commemoration week, in my second year at Balliol, and I made no attempt to recall myself to her. She flitted by me, and vanished like a shadow in the busy London street.

I remembered this dimly now, with a vague wonder that he should be here, bright and young, he whom I had mourned for among the dead.

He led me into the heart of the island, a wooded valley, through which there wound a stream of rushing waters, deep and dark in mid-channel, where the strong current swept towards the sea, but with many a reedy inlet and pool, where water-lilies, white and golden, lifted their shallow cups from the level expanse of broad leaves, and where the still water only showed here and there in patches of emerald light amidst the darker green of leaf and flower.

We sat in the shade of a cluster of cocoanut palms, with one of those shallow pools stretching at our feet, between the low grassy bank and the rush of the stream; a level garden of water-lilies, over which birds and butterflies hovered and flitted, creatures of tropical splendour that flashed and sparkled in the light, too swift, too brilliant for human eye to follow them.

We talked of the past, of days that had been happy and gay enough while we lived them, and which when looking back to them seemed a period of unalloyed bliss. We recalled only the brightest hours—we remembered nothing that had been distasteful. Lionel's soft low laugh sounded in the balmy stillness as I lay stretched indolently on the grass at his feet, looking up at the milky blueness of the tropical sky, basking in the slumberous warmth of the tropical noontide.

Presently—I know not how it came there—*her* face was looking down upon me. Lucy Marsden's face—my love, my betrothed of five-and-twenty years ago. Ah, what a lovely face it was!—features delicately chiselled, complexion of an almost alabaster fairness touched with hectic bloom

upon the somewhat wasted cheek, a flush that added depth and bril-
liancy to the large violet eyes. I remembered how those pathetic eyes had
grown brighter and larger day by day, and how I had noted that increasing
brightness with an unspeakable terror, and then one dreary November her
people took her away to Mentone, and I was told to stay in London, and
work and hope, and look forward to her return with the March daffodils;
and then—and then——Well, it was all a dark dream—that which followed upon our sorrowful parting. The letters, the telegrams, for which
I sat and waited in my dismal Temple Chambers, pretending to read law,
with my thoughts far away, following the progress of Lucy's malady. It was
only a dreadful dream, which I recalled shudderingly today, as our hands
clasped again and her eyes looked down at me.

I sprang to my feet, and we sauntered side by side under the palm trees,
and talked and were happy; I with a quiet gladness which asked no questions; she, sweetly, gravely kind; changed greatly, and yet the same. Gentle
as she had ever been, humble as a child in her modest estimate of her own
gifts of mind and person. I felt today an overmastering awe in her presence.
I adored as a good Catholic adores a saint, but hardly dared to love her
with the warm glow of human love—or to question—or to talk lightly of
past and future. She was with me, and that was enough.

My mind was not troubled about my betrothed of the later time, the
girl I was to marry early in the coming year, and who was said to have distinguished me by her regard. She belonged to that far-off world of whose
existence I was scarcely conscious all through that golden day, while those
living flashes of light and colour flitted over the broad white chalices, and
the level leaves rose and fell with the throb of the water, moved with slow
swaying motion by that hurrying tide in the middle of the stream, where a
fleet of hibiscus blossoms marked the swiftness of the current as it moved
towards the sea.

How could I remember the outside world, with its grovelling desires,
its base ambitions, self-consciousness, self-love, envy, hatred, and malice, its
sordid fight for pounds, shillings, and pence! If I thought of it for a moment
in this haven of calm delight, it was only to think with loathing, to hate
myself for the base desires whose gratification I had called happiness—the
gold fever—the hunger for lands and houses, and empty honours, and petty

distinctions, the relentless striving for success, the struggle to be just a little higher placed than this man or that man.

Here I was young again, and all my thoughts had the freshness of young thoughts, before the mind is hardened and the fancy staled by friction with the world of middle age; the cold, calculating period of man's existence, the age in which he thinks he can do without affection if he can but achieve success.

My thoughts were the thoughts of youth; and every picture of those vanished years returned in vivid colouring. I lived again in the unforgotten hours, clasped the unforgotten hands. All I have ever lost of nearest and dearest were gathered together in that nameless island; father, mother, the sister who vanished, ah, so inexplicably, out of the sunshine and the playtime, before I had quite learnt to speak, leaving only the memory of tearful faces and hushed voices in a darkened house. All were there—the familiar faces, the gentle hands, the low, sweet voices of the long ago.

And if I wondered it was only with a child's wonder—easily satisfied. And if I questioned the things I saw, I had my own answer ready for my own question.

I had always known that the black shadow of death which swallows up all we love best in the early years, is but a transient cloud. I had always known that somewhere, somehow, those we love are living yet, and we want but the clue to find them. And to me the clue had been given. That eager instinct which had urged me to come to this enchanting islet was the spirit of love leading me. So my question was answered as easily as it was asked. There is no death. I had always known that it must be so. The God who made us in His own likeness will not obliterate the image He has made.

And so I gave myself up to the unclouded happiness of that golden day. The bright summer noontide melted into the mellow light of summer afternoon. My first day in this happy spot had long passed its meridian.

'"And in the all-golden afternoon / A friend, or happy sister, sung——"' I quoted, from that book which had been as a second gospel for Lucy and me—my first gift to her, the gift of small means and large heart. To my later love I gave diamonds of the first water, but my heart did not go with them as unquestioningly as it went with the little green cloth book.

Alas! The day came, too soon, when I could not read a page of that long lament without blinding tears, when it seemed almost as if I myself had written that elegy for her whom no ship brought home, whose bed of rest had been made on a hill by the historic sea.

'Sing to me, Lucy!' I pleaded; 'one of the old favourites—"I arise from dreams of thee."'

She would not sing; but we talked of the old time—the days before they took her to Mentone.

Something I said of never leaving her again. I had found my anchorage at last, I told her. I renounced ambition—all that the outside world could give. I would have no world beyond this coral reef with its mantle of ferns and flowers, its populace of birds and butterflies, and the friends of other days.

Those others came and went as the day wore on. Sometimes one, some-times another, was at our side; but Lucy was there always, constant and true as she had been from the hour her faltering lips first confessed her love—blessed, unforgettable hour!—in a Warwickshire garden, within sound of the classic Avon. As she had been on that day in the gardens of her father's rectory, so she was today in the shadow of the tufted palms, in the paradise of winged creatures—just as lovely, as guileless, and as young.

But when I talked of never leaving her, she shook her head gravely, and laid her fingers lightly on my lips.

'Dear love, this is no life for you!' she said seriously; 'you will have to go back to the world.'

'Never, Lucy! This shall be my world.'

'It cannot be. You have seen us and lived with us for one golden day; that is all. You will go back to the world, and—oh, my dear, my dear, I am so sorry for you!'

'Dearest, why sorry? I say again that nothing shall part us any more— nothing but death! Death, did I say? No, there is no such thing. We will never part. This island shall be our home for ever.'

'Alas, that cannot be! It is your misfortune to have found us. You will go back, and you will never be happy again. That is the bitterness of it. You have drunk of the fountain of memory, the fatal fountain which makes all that is seem worthless compared with all that has been. The world will be barren and dull and empty; but you must go back to it. Oh, my dearest, yours is so hard a fate! To have seen us, and to remember the days of your youth, and never to know earthly happiness again!'

I would not believe her—would not believe in that stern 'must' which she repeated with sorrowful look and tone. My life was my own, to do what I liked with, I told her, and I meant to spend my life by her side.

And then we talked of lighter things—gaily recalling many a bygone jest, happy as the birds that shot with gleaming wing across the lustrous water. The tropical twilight came down upon us suddenly, like a dim grey veil, and my darling's voice fell on my ear as softly as the murmur of a far-off sea—and then all was blank.

*　*　*　*　*

It was daylight again when I awoke, again the cool pearly light of earliest morning. I sprang to my feet, fearing to find myself in some different place—to have been spirited back to the yacht during that long dreamless sleep.

No, I was on the island still. There were the sleeping water-lilies with their closed cups, and their broad leaves heaving faintly with the slow pulses of that quiet back-water; there was the ripple of the current yonder, where the river ran towards the sea; and now and again, as I looked and listened, came the call of some newly awakened bird; but human presence there was none within my ken, as I stood by the lily pool looking about me. So I walked on hurriedly, searching for the friends of yesterday.

Through open glade and shadowy wood, by hill and hollow, over wide stretches of level greensward, through the moist hot tangle of tropical verdure, I wandered and searched, till the meridian sun made those open spaces intolerable, and till the fervour of my search had to yield to over-mastering fatigue, and I sank down in the shadow of a great plane tree, tired to death, disappointed and almost despairing.

Where were they gone? Why had they left me? How cruel to abandon me thus—to hide themselves from me! It seemed to me that I had searched the island from shore to shore; but there were forest caves, perhaps—secret sanctuaries amidst the wild luxuriance of the wood—which I, as a stranger, must needs be slow to discover. In spite of my utter weariness I meant to continue my search as soon as I was able to walk again. In my present state of exhaustion I could hardly stand.

I lay stretched along the mossy ground at the foot of the tree, staring idly at a vista of light and shadow, where clusters of scarlet lilies flamed like torches as they glanced here and there amid the foliage, shooting up towards the light. Nothing was changed in the aspect of external nature; and yet I felt that I was in another atmosphere, and the change in my own feelings between yesterday and today was a change from hope and gladness to dull despair.

Oh! the silence of all human voices after the familiar voices of yesterday—the sense of utter desolation that had grown and strengthened with every hour of that long weary morning, till now my heart sank within me under the icy sense of fear. I felt the child's fear, who sees itself deserted and solitary in a place where all things are strange—the fear of the unknown.

*   *   *   *   *

Voices—human voices—sounded faint in the distance, grew nearer, louder—near enough to be recognisable—before I could walk half a dozen yards to meet them.

Alas! not the dear voices of yesterday. Coarse common voices these—the strident hail of one of my sailors, and then a loud shrill cooey, piercing this tropical garden; familiar voices, and welcome in my present humour, but bringing little beyond the promise of material comfort, rest for my aching bones, drink for my feverish lips.

The sailors who had brought me from the yacht yesterday came running towards me as I faintly hailed them. They would never have heard that low cry, they told me afterwards. It was the sight of my white clothes gleaming in the sun that guided them to me from the other end of a long glade. They had been looking for me since daylight, having come back to the island in the late evening and camped there, after an ineffectual search for me.

'We waited in the dinghy, in the creek where we landed you, from three o'clock till dark,' the mate explained. 'Then, as you didn't turn up, we went back to the yacht for further orders, and the sailing master sent us back to the island with provisions for the night, and the doctor he came with us, and we've been roaming about all the blessed morning on the look-out for you!'

My young friend and medical adviser came up while the man was talking, and was full of concern about me in his easy pleasant manner, which never made a trouble of anything. I had been more than thirty hours on the island, he said, without food or shelter. He was eager to get me back to the yacht, and in the meantime he wanted to ply me with brandy from a flask which he carried.

'Where are the people,' I asked him—'the people who were with me all yesterday?'

'My dear sir, there are no people—the island is uninhabited.'

I could not argue with him, or tell him of those whom I had seen and mingled with in that long golden day. I was heart-broken at the thought that I should see them no more, that my Lucy had been right, and I must go back to the world—whether I would or no. There are some things too sacred to be talked about except to one's nearest and dearest, and I could not tell this light-hearted young doctor that I had been among the faces of the past, and that the recollections of my youth had been brought nearer to me than the realities of the present.

So I just let them take me back to the yacht, and allowed myself to be nursed through a sharp touch of fever; and I came slowly out of the cloud-land of feverish fancies to remember those dear faces, and to know that they were the faces of those who had crossed the unknown river, and that for me on this hither side life held nothing worth caring about.

The first English ship that we met after my recovery carried home my letter of renunciation to the lady who was to have been my wife. I told her that quiet long hours of meditation in the solitude of my long holiday had convinced me that any bond between beauty and youth, like hers, and a worn-out life like mine would be ill-advised, and must prove an unhappy union, for her at least, and that I therefore declined to take advantage of the girlish enthusiasm which had led her to mistake admiration for the famous advocate for love of the middle-aged man. My betrothed was prompt in sending her reply, which I found waiting for me three days ago at Aden. Only a packet of letters—my own to her—and a diamond half-hoop ring.

The atoms that were once those letters are floating somewhere in space, and the ring lies in a little silver tray on my dressing-table among other unconsidered trumpery; and, in the oppressive heat of the Red Sea, I sit on deck under an awning and meditate on the life that awaits me in the country which I must needs call home.

Oh, how barren and dry-as-dust it all seems! The labour, the success, the troops of friends—the friends of middle-age—picked up in the dust and strife of the arena, too busy to care very much if I were to drop and die in the crowd, like a mustang, newly harnessed, and dragged off his feet in the wild rush of a stagecoach team on the Pampas. What, is the brute down again? Unrope him, and leave him for the crows and the kites; and on with the journey, lashing the rest of the team the harder to keep up the pace.

The Higher Life

THE lights burnt low, and the shadows were deep in the angles of the spacious room, and, though there were people there—doctor, nurse, friends—there was no sound except the sighing of the autumn wind as it rose and fell, now a sigh and then a sob, now a faint shriek at the window, like a spirit asking to be let in, and then a hurrying blast, and a flight of withered leaves brushing against the glass.

Through an open doorway one saw the adjoining room, where the distant fire-place shone like a jewel. A room lined from floor to ceiling with books, bound for the most part in vellum and gold; a room so rich in beautiful forms and splendid colouring that it might have been the show-room in a palace instead of merely the 'book-room' of that well-known member of the Bibliophile Society, old Sir Stephen Stilyard.

He was very old, and he was dying. Even the longest journey must come to an end at last. The inn—that inn we have all heard of, where there are always beds enough for the guests—is waiting with open door for the traveller whose toil is nearly over. Very toilsome that last half-mile, as indicated by the fighting breath, the labouring chest, for which the lightest satin coverlet is too heavy a burden. A very bad bit of road that; but then the rest of the journey has been so easy, the chariot of life has hung on Cee springs, and has travelled along flowery ways through a smiling country.

The man lying there in the solemn stillness of the death-chamber had inherited a large fortune at an age when other lads are trying to make ends meet at the university on a scrimped allowance from head-quarters, and when the glory of life grows pale before the angry face of a dun. He had taken full advantage of the opportunities for evil which money can buy. He had bought his experience of life in the worst markets, and had learnt to despise and hate his fellow-men before he was thirty. He had married early and badly, choosing his evil portion with his eyes wide open, because at that juvenile period he liked bad women better than good women. The former amused him; the latter bored him.

His children had been curses to him; but he had not allowed them to torment him long. As soon as they had shown what was in them, and were old enough to be turned out of doors, he turned them out. One by one they vanished off the stage of his life, and were heard of no more. The turning out of doors was like the coming of age in happier families, inevitable as the progress of years. His children grew up and blossomed in disobedience, and ripened for rebellion before they were full grown. He had divorced his wife a month after the birth of his youngest child—a daughter—whom he considered one too many. She who had been Lady Stilyard was living in Italy—rich with money not of his providing. There was no distracted mother to kneel or tear her hair when another son or daughter was shown out of the hall door, and warned never to cross that threshold again.

At forty Sir Stephen Stilyard began to think he had sat long enough in the courts of folly and vice. There was very little in the way of well-bred iniquity which he had not tried, and enjoyed, so far as that kind of thing may be enjoyable. At forty he felt older than a rural squire feels at sixty; but he looked younger. His mind and morals had been in his own keeping, but his valet and his tailor had taken care of his person.

A disillusion or two, a few crumpled rose-leaves in the bed of vice, had sickened him. He began to seek for other sources of pleasure. The time had come for the cultivation of his intellect. He took to reading the memoirs of men of letters, of great thinkers, of theologians, and students. They seemed to him to have been happy, after a humdrum, unexciting fashion; quite as happy as he could ever hope to be after having snapped every string upon Passion's seven-stringed lyre.

He shut his door upon all his old friends and boon companions. The racecourse, the gambling club, the haunts of marketable beauty, knew him no more. He affected a chronic complaint, which showed itself only in the cessation of all hospitalities in that splendid house which had once been renowned for the best dinners in London. He had done with that foolish crew. He began to cultivate his mind; deeply regretting that he had not lived three hundred years earlier, when he might have dabbled in the Black Art, and tried to discover the Universal Panacea, or even the Elixir of Life.

'All beliefs are dead,' he told himself, 'except a man's belief in his own sensations, his own thoughts. The only world I know is I. Henceforth I devote myself to the improvement and the perfection of that world.'

His life henceforward was a life of contemplation and study. He became a collector of rare books, but they were books which treated of mind only. In all the volumes that walled in his solitude there was no place for the historian. Dreams, not deeds, were the subjects of his study. There was no impostor so shallow, no theorist so crazed, whose visions and hallucinations he did not find an interest in exploring. He fed upon the metaphysics of the past, upon the mysticism of the East and the West. In Buddha, Plato, Zoroaster, he found the familiar spirits whose philosophy filled the void in his mind, wearied with out-worn pleasures. The man he had been—the man of active vices—fell away from his new nature like a ragged garment. Life henceforward meant contemplation. He gave himself up to lofty dreams. He, who in youth had been the loudest reviler among an infidel crew, now turned believer—not in the Christian's creed, but in the Platonic dream of a future life.

'There is some essence here,' he told himself, with pale finger lightly touching the high forehead which he had elevated to a temple of thought, 'there is something here that cannot die. The soul which has fed upon all that is grandest in pure thought will soar upward to a higher life. From sphere to sphere, from phase to phase, the mind that has divorced itself from clay will rise and ripen in the white light of intellect, as the cornfields ripen in the sun.'

The higher life! As the years crept on, and the dreary close of the decades reminded him how near he was to the end of all earthly things, his belief in that progressive existence grew stronger. Not for him the extinction which the Buddhist deems the culminating reward of virtue. No absorption into the universal mind for him, but an extended and an ever-improving individuality—a mind widening with ever new powers, and entering into the mighty throng of exalted spirits in that higher life. Plato, Dante, Galileo, Shakespeare, Descartes, Newton—the poets, the thinkers, the scientific discoverers—would all be sharers in that heaven of exalted intellect.

He was dying on the eve of his ninetieth birthday. For fifty years he had lived only to think and dream. He who, when the century was young, had shared in the wildest revels of the Corinthians, the porter-guzzling, watch-beating profligates of the 'thirties, was dying in the 'nineties, after half a century of life so secluded that only the booksellers and a few of the oldest among the Bibliophiles knew of his existence. Most of the younger Bibliophiles believed that he had long been dead.

For fifty years his house, in one of the older aristocratic squares, had looked on the outside like an uninhabited house, although within there was a sombre luxury, an all-pervading splendour, unsurpassed in any mansion of the great city.

Yet even in this seclusion he could not hide himself from those of his race who thought they had a right to inherit his wealth. The approach of death had opened the door for two of his children, who had pulled up short upon that journey to the dogs on which he started them. A son who had contrived to make his mark at the Bar, a daughter who had married well, were in the room tonight. These, by sheer force of their respectability, arriving at the paternal door in neat one-horse broughams, had got themselves admitted. The miscreants who had failed in life were kept outside the door. Sir Stephen's butler was far too well trained to listen to the pleadings of a son who came to the door on foot, through rain and mud, in a threadbare coat and broken boots, or to a daughter upon whose face and garments appeared the unmistakable brand of a disreputable life.

He who lay there in the shadow of a tall six-leaved screen cared little who came or went in that silent room. Sons or daughters were alike indifferent. He had made his will many years before, leaving all he possessed to a learned society, the income to be devoted to the encouragement of psychological science in England and on the Continent. Not a sixpence was left to his own flesh and blood, or for the corporal wants of his fellowmen.

He heard the footsteps stealing to and fro over the velvet thickness of the Persian carpet, heard the low voices murmuring about him as of one who understood nothing. The end was very near, they told each other; and the doctor assented, with his fingers on the fluttering pulse. Yes, the end was near.

'Do you think he knows me?' asked the bearded man, who had been flung out of that house when the down of adolescence was smooth upon his cheek.

'No. Consciousness has quite gone,' answered the doctor. 'He neither suffers nor understands.'

The passing spirit heard them, and scorned them. Poor worms, clinging to earth, held down by their coarse clay, and by the petty intellect which cares only for sordid things, while his fetterless mind was soaring towards the empyrean—the higher life, the larger consciousness, the world of disembodied intellect—supreme in power to see and understand.

'He has been a cruel father,' said the woman sitting by his pillow; 'I thought he might relent at the last and open his heart to us.'

'I hope he has made us some reparation in his will,' said the son.

Oh, for that loftier world where money does not count! He was going there, leaving these sordid creatures to suffer the pangs of disappointed avarice; while his wealth went to widen the dominions of pure intellect, to feed the lamp of thought.

Darkness closed over that familiar scene, the voices sounded no more. His spirit had left the clay and its surroundings. High in the unfathomable aether the winged soul was soaring towards the paradise of the elect. What power in those broad wings, what rapture in that pure atmosphere. Far and far and farther below him lay the great city. He could see the glimmer of its million lamps, lessening momently as he winged his way through the fields of air. Oh, the rapture of that wild flight, the unutterable sense of freedom, the joy in every feeling of that exalted nature, whose shape and substance he yet knew not. He only knew the power of the wings, the lightness of the whole being.

He is travelling towards the abode of Sublime Intelligences, Plato, Buddha, Confucius. He will be among them. He will see the divine faces, hear the words of riper wisdom, be with them, and like unto them.

But suddenly that glorious light on the outskirts of the soul's paradise fades and darkens, and out of the darkness rush the demon pack, the spectral hounds that hunt the souls of sinful men—the evil spirits of the air, implacable, fierce, inexorable tormentors, who chase unhallowed souls that have escaped from fleshly fetters, and drive them back to the prison-house of clay.

Merciless in pursuit, with hideous howling that only the spirit can hear, they press their agonised quarry. Lower and lower in that pathless waste of air the hunted soul descends. And now it is the radiant bulwark of heaven that vanishes from his straining gaze, while the accursed lights of earth are rising through the deep gulf of darkness. He is going back, driven back to the world he scorns. He must live again, suffer again, sin again, wallow in sensuality, agonise in disease, drink once again the bitter draught of human life.

He struggles against the awful doom; strives with fast-beating wings to escape his hunters. Again he soars in tractless space. He feels the glory of the higher life, the power of the disembodied spirit. Distance and time are as nothing. He sees the earth wheel below him. Those exultant wings are carrying him over the tropical forests, the extinct volcanoes, the great rivers—Amazon, Mississippi, Ganges, Indus, over the roof of the world. Over the desolate places, over the fertile valleys, over the ice-wildernesses of the Arctic and Antarctic seas. All that the earth has of wonder or of beauty rushes past him like a dream-picture; and in the midst of the rapturous sense of limitless space he feels that he is being hunted down, hunted down, hunted back to the life he loathes. His flagging wings, the sound of demoniac voices in his ear, tell him that he is beaten. Those hell-hounds fill the air. They circle him in and bear him down. Vain as the wheeling of the rook under the swoop of the hawk are those last efforts of the tortured soul. The aerial hounds raise their wild yell of triumph. The glory of the universe shrinks and dwindles to a spot where gas-lights gleam redly through a veil of fog. Below in the mists of evening, and under the smoke of the city, he sees one of the most hideous quarters of the town—a slum in the East End, filthy and loathsome, haunt of the sweater's slaves, the Polish Jew, the British thief.

And in one of those courts, reeking with vilest odours, in a garret, poorest where all are poor, a woman lies in the throes of woman's martyrdom—the deserted companion of a felon whom the police are hunting.

'In the offspring of that hapless mother, child of a murderer and thief, born to a heritage of want and shame, thy soul shall recommence the pilgrimage of life, to expiate in long years of suffering among outcasts and criminals thy life of self-worship and isolation from the brotherhood of man. There is no paradise for the soul that has forgotten man's duty to man.'

That was the doom which the sickened soul heard in the darkness, as it shrank and dwindled and grew faint and dim, sinking from the heights of intellectual power to the faint consciousness of the new-born child.

Herself

CHAPTER I.

'And you intend to keep the Orange Grove for your own occupation, Madam,' interrogates the lawyer gravely, with his downward-looking eyes completely hidden under bushy brows.

'Decidedly,' answered my friend. 'Why, the Orange Grove is the very best part of my fortune. It seems almost a special Providence, don't you know, Helen,' pursued Lota, turning to me, 'that my dear old grandfather should have made himself a winter home in the south. There are the doctors always teasing me about my weak chest, and there is a lonely house and gardens and orange groves waiting for me in a climate invented on purpose for weak chests. I shall live there every winter of my life, Mr Dean.'

The eminently respectable solicitor allowed a lapse of silence before he replied.

'It is not a lucky house, Miss Hammond.'

'How not lucky?'

'Your grandfather only lived to spend one winter in it. He was in very good health when he went there in December—a strong, sturdy old man—and when he sent for me in February to prepare the will which made you his sole heiress, I was shocked at the change in him—broken—wasted—nerves shattered—a mere wreck.'

'That was very sad; but surely you would not blame a lovely villa in Italy,' smiling down at a photograph in her lap, the picture of the typical southern villa, French windows, verandah, balconies, tower, terraces, garden, and fountain, 'for the sudden break-up of an elderly constitution. I have heard that old men of very active habits and a hardy way of living, like my dear old grandfather, are apt to grow old suddenly.'

'It was not merely that he was aged—he was mentally changed—nervous, restless, to all appearance unhappy.'

'Well, didn't you ask him why?' demanded Lota, whose impetuous temper was beginning to revolt against the lawyer's solemnity.

'My position hardly warranted my questioning Mr Hammond on a matter so purely personal. I saw the change, and regretted it. Six weeks later he was gone.'

'Poor old gran'pa. We were such friends when I was a little thing. And then they sent me to Germany with a governess—poor little motherless mite—and then they packed me off to Pekin where father was Consul and there he died, and then they sent me home again—and I was taken up by the smartest of all my aunts, and had my little plunge in society, and always exceeded my allowance; was up to my eyes in debt—for a girl. I suppose a man would hardly count such bills as I used to owe. And then Gran'pa took it into his head to be pleased with me; and here I am—residuary legatee. I think that's what you call me?' with an interrogative glance at the lawyer, who nodded a grave assent, 'and I am going to spend the winter months in my villa near Taggia. Only think of that, Helen, Taggia—Tag-gi-a!'

She syllabled the word slowly, ending with a little smack of her pretty lips as if it were something nice to eat, and she looked at me for sympathy.

'I haven't the faintest idea what you mean by Tag-gi-a,' said I. 'It sounds like an African word.'

'Surely you have read Dr Antonio.'

'Surely I have not.'

'Then I have done with you. There is a gulf between us. All that I know of the Liguria comes out of that delightful book. It taught me to pine for the shores of the Mediterranean when I was quite a little thing. And they show you Dr Ruffini's house at Taggia. His actual house, where he actually lived.'

'You ought to consider, Miss Hammond, that the Riviera has changed a good deal since Ruffini's time,' said the lawyer. 'Not that I have anything to say against the Riviera per se. All I would advise is that you should winter in a more convenient locality than a romantic gorge between San Remo and Alassio. I would suggest Nice, for instance.'

'Nice. Why, someone was saying only the other day that Nice is the chosen rendezvous of all the worst characters in Europe and America.'

'Perhaps that's what makes it such an agreeable place,' said the lawyer. 'There are circles and circles in Nice. You need never breathe the same atmosphere as the bad characters.'

'A huge towny place,' exclaimed Lota. 'Gran'pa said it was not better than Brighton.'

'Could anything be better than Brighton?' asked I.

'Helen, you were always a Philistine. It was because of the horridness of Nice and Cannes that gran'pa bought a villa—four times too big for him—in this romantic spot.'

She kissed the white house in the photograph. She gloated over the wildness of the landscape, in which the villa stood out, solitary, majestic. Palms, olives, cypress—a deep gorge cutting through the heart of the picture—mountains romantically remote—one white crest in the furthest distance—a foreground of tumbled crags and threads of running water.

'Is it really real?' she asked suddenly, 'not a photographer's painted background? They have such odious tricks, those photographers. One sits for one's picture in a tidy South Kensington studio, and they send one home smirking out of a primeval forest, or in front of a stormy ocean. Is it real?'

'Absolutely real.'

'Very well, Mr Dean. Then I am going to establish myself there in the first week of December, and if you want to be very careful of me for gran'pa's sake all you have to do is to find me a thoroughly respectable major-domo, who won't drink my wine or run away with my plate. My aunt will engage the rest of my people.'

'My dear young lady, you may command any poor services of mine; but really now, is it not sheer perversity to choose a rambling house in a wild part of the country when your ample means would allow you to hire the prettiest bijou-villa on the Riviera?'

'I hate bijou houses, always too small for anybody except some sour old maid who wants to over-hear all her servants say about her. The spacious rambling house—the wild solitary landscape—those are what I want, Mr Dean. Get me a butler who won't cut my throat, and I ask no more.'

'Then madam, I have done. A wilful woman must have her way, even when it is a foolish way.'

'Everything in life is foolish,' Lota answered, lightly. 'The people who live haphazard come out just as well at the end as your ineffable wiseacres. And now that you know I am fixed as Fate, that nothing you can say will unbend my iron will, do, like a darling old family lawyer whom I have known ever since I began to know one face from another, do tell me why you object to the Orange Grove. Is it the drainage?'

'There is no drainage.'

'Then that's all right,' checking it off on her forefinger. 'Is it the neighbours?"

'Need I say there are no neighbours?' pointing to the photograph.

'Number two satisfactory.'

'Is it the atmosphere? Low the villa is not; damp it can hardly be, perched on the side of a hill.'

'I believe the back rooms are damp. The hill side comes too near the windows. The back rooms are decidedly gloomy, and I believe damp.'

'And how many rooms are there in all?'

'Nearer thirty than twenty. I repeat it is a great rambling house, ever so much too large for you or any sensible young lady.'

'For the sensible young lady, no doubt,' said Lota, nodding impertinently at me. 'She likes a first floor in Regency Square, Brighton, with a little room under the tiles for her maid. I am not sensible, and I like lots of rooms; rooms to roam about in, to furnish and unfurnish, and arrange and rearrange; rooms to see ghosts in. And now, dearest Mr Dean, I am going to pluck out the heart of your mystery. What kind of ghost is it that haunts the Orange Grove? I know there is a ghost.'

'Who told you so?'

'You. You have been telling me so for the last half-hour. It is because of the ghost you don't want me to go to the Orange Grove. You might just as well be candid and tell me the whole story. I am not afraid of ghosts. In fact, I rather like the idea of having a ghost on my property. Wouldn't you, Helen, if you had property?'

'No,' I answered, decisively. 'I hate ghosts. They are always associated with damp houses and bad drainage. I don't believe you would find a ghost in Brighton, not even if you advertised for one.'

'Tell me all about the ghost,' urged Lota.

'There is nothing to tell. Neither the people in the neighbourhood nor the servants of the house went so far as to say the Orange Grove was haunted. The utmost assertion was that time out of mind the master or the mistress of that house had been miserable.'

'Time out of mind. Why, I thought gran'pa built the house twenty years ago.'

'He only added the front which you see in the photograph. The back part of the house, the larger part, is three hundred years ago. The place was a monkish hospital, the infirmary belonging to a Benedictine monastery in the neighbourhood, and to which the sick from other Benedictine houses were sent.'

'Oh, that was ages and ages ago. You don't suppose that the ghosts of all the sick monks, who were so inconsiderate as to die in my house, haunt the rooms at the back?'

'I say again, Miss Hammond, nobody has ever to my knowledge asserted that the house was haunted.'

'Then it can't be haunted. If it were the servants would have seen something. They are champion ghost-seers.'

'I am not a believer in ghosts, Miss Hammond,' said the friendly old lawyer, 'but I own to a grain of superstition on one point. I can't help thinking there is such a thing as "luck." I have seen such marked distinctions between the lucky and unlucky people I have met in my professional career. Now, the Orange Grove has been an unlucky house for the last hundred years. Its bad luck is as old as its history. And why, in the name of all that's reasonable, should a beautiful young lady with all the world to choose from insist upon living at the Orange Grove?'

'First, because it is my own house; next, because I conceived a passion for it the moment I saw this photograph; and thirdly, perhaps because your opposition has given a zest to the whole thing. I shall establish myself there next December, and you must come out to me after Christmas, Helen. Your beloved Brighton is odious in February and March.'

'Brighton is always delightful,' answered I, 'but of course I shall be charmed to go to you.'

CHAPTER II.
AN EARTHLY PARADISE.

I was Lota's dearest friend, and she was mine. I had never seen anyone quite so pretty, or quite so fascinating then: I have never seen anyone as pretty or as fascinating since. She was no Helen, no Cleopatra, no superbly modelled specimen of typical loveliness. She was only herself. Like no one else, and to my mind better than everybody else—a delicately wrought ethereal creature, all spirit and fire and impulse and affection, flinging herself with ardour into every pursuit, living intensely in the present, curiously reckless of the future, curiously forgetful of the past.

When I parted with her at Charing Cross Station on the first of December it was understood that I was to join her about the middle of January. One of my uncles was going to Italy at that time, and was to escort me to Taggia, where I was to be met by my hostess. I was surprised, therefore, when a telegram arrived before Christmas, entreating me to go to her at once.

I telegraphed back: 'Are you ill?'

Answer: 'Not ill; but I want you.'

My reply: 'Impossible. Will go as arranged.'

I would have given much, as I told Lota in the letter that followed my last message, to have done what she wished; but family claims were too strong. A brother was to marry at the beginning of the year, and I should have been thought heartless had I shirked the ceremony. And there was the old idea of Christmas as a time for family gatherings. Had she been ill, or unhappy, I would have cancelled every other claim, and gone to her without one hour's delay, I told her; but I knew her a creature of caprices, and this was doubtless only one caprice among many.

I knew that she was well cared for. She had a maiden aunt with her, the mildest and sweetest of spinsters, who absolutely adored her. She had her old nurse and slave, a West Indian half-caste, who had accompanied her from Pekin, and she had—

'Another, and a dearer one still.'

Captain Holbrook, of the Stonyshere Regiment, was at San Remo. I had seen his name in a travelling note in the *World*, and I smiled as I read the announcement, and thought how few of his acquaintance would know as well as I knew the magnet which attracted him to quit San Remo rather than go to Monte Carlo or Nice. I knew that he loved Violetta Hammond devotedly, and that she had played fast and loose with him, amused at his worship, accepting all his attentions in her light happy manner, and giving no heed to the future.

Yes, my pretty, insouciante Lota was well cared for, ringed round with exceeding love, guarded as faithfully as a god in an Indian temple. I had no uneasiness about her, and I alighted in a very happy frame of mind at the quiet little station at Taggia, beside the tideless sea, in the dusk of a January evening.

Lota was on the platform to welcome me, with Miss Elderson, her maternal aunt, in attendance upon her, the younger lady muffled in seal-skin from head to foot.

'Why Lota,' said I, when we had kissed, and laughed a little with eyes full of tears, 'you are wrapped up as if this were Russia, and to me the air feels balmier than an English April.'

'Oh, when one has a hundred guinea coat one may as well wear it,' she answered carelessly. 'I bought this sealskin among my mourning.'

'Lota is chillier than she used to be,' said Miss Elderson, in her plaintive voice.

There was a landau with a pair of fine strong horses waiting to carry us up to the villa. The road wound gently upward, past orange and lemon groves, and silvery streamlets, and hanging woods, where velvet dark cypresses rose tower-like amidst the silvery grey of the olives, and so to about midway between the valley, where Taggia's antique palaces and church towers gleamed pale in the dusk, and the crest of the hill along which straggled the white houses of a village. The after-glow was rosy in the sky when a turn of the road brought our faces towards the summer-like sea, and in that lovely light every line in Lota's face was but too distinctly visible. Too distinctly, for I saw the cruel change which three months had made in her fresh young beauty. She had left me in all the bloom of girl-hood, gay, careless, brimming over with the joy of life and the new delight of that freedom of choice which wealth gives to a fatherless and motherless girl. To go where she liked, do as she liked, roam the world over, choosing always the companions she loved—that had been Lota's dream of happi-ness, and if there had been some touch of self-love in her idea of bliss there had been also a generous and affectionate heart, and unfailing kindness to those whom Fate had not used so kindly.

I saw her now a haggard, anxious-looking woman, the signs of worry written too plainly on the wan pinched face, the lovely eyes larger but paler than of old, and the markings of nervous depression visible in the droop of the lips that had once been like Cupid's bow.

I remembered Mr Dean's endeavour to dissuade her from occupy-ing her grandfather's villa on this lovely hill, and I began to detest the

Orange Grove before I had seen it. I was prepared to find an abode of gloom—a house where the foul miasma from some neighbouring swamp crept in at every open window, and hung grey and chill in every passage; a house whose too obvious unwholesomeness had conjured up images of terror, the spectral forms engendered of slackened nerves, and sleepless nights. I made up my mind that if it were possible for a bold and energetic woman to influence Lota Hammond I would be that woman, and whisk her off to Nice or Monte Carlo before she had time to consider what I was doing.

There would be a capital pretext in the Carnival. I would declare that I had set my heart upon seeing a Carnival at Nice; and once there I would take care she never returned to the place that was killing her. I looked, with a thrill of anger, at the mild sheep-faced aunt. How could she have been so blind as not to perceive the change in her niece? And Captain Holbrook! What a poor creature, to call himself a lover, and let the girl he loved perish before his eyes.

I had time to think while the horses walked slowly up the hill-road, for neither the aunt nor the niece had much to say. Each in her turn pointed out some feature in the view. Lota told me that she adored Taggia, and doted on her villa and garden; and that was the utmost extent of our conversation in the journey of more than an hour.

At last we drove round a sharpish curve, and on the hill-side above us, looking down at us from a marble terrace, I saw the prettiest house I had ever seen in my life; a fairy palace, with lighted windows, shining against a back-ground of wooded hills. I could not see the colours of the flowers in the thickening gloom of night, but I could smell the scent of the roses and the fragrant-leaved geraniums that filled the vases on the terrace.

Within and without all was alike sparkling and lightsome; and so far as I could see on the night of my arrival there was not a corner which could have accommodated a ghost. Lota told me that one of her first improvements had been to install the electric light.

'I love to think that this house is shining like a star when the people of Taggia look across the valley,' she said.

I told her that I had seen Captain Holbrook's name among the visitors at San Remo.

'He is staying at Taggia now,' she said. 'He grew rather tired of San Remo.'

'The desire to be nearer you had nothing to do with the change?'

'You can ask him if you like,' she answered, with something of her old insouciance. 'He is coming to dinner tonight.'

'Does he spend his days and nights going up and down the hill?' I asked.

'You will be able to see for yourself as to that. There is not much for anyone to do in Taggia.'

*　　*　　*　　*　　*

Captain Holbrook found me alone in the salon when he came; for, in spite of the disadvantages of arrival after a long journey, I was dressed before Lota. He was very friendly, and seemed really glad to see me; indeed, he lost no time in saying as much with a plainness of speech which was more friendly than flattering.

'I am heartily glad you have come,' he said, 'for now I hope we shall be able to get Miss Hammond away from this depressing hole.'

Remembering that the house was perched upon the shoulders of a romantic hill, with an outlook of surpassing loveliness, and looking round at the brilliant colouring of an Italian drawing-room steeped in soft clear light, and redolent of roses and carnations, it seemed rather hard measure to hear of Lota's inheritance talked of as 'a depressing hole'; but the cruel change in Lota herself was enough to justify the most unqualified dislike of the house in which the change had come to pass.

Miss Elderson and her niece appeared before I could reply, and we went to dinner. The dining-room was as bright and gracious of aspect as all the other rooms which I had seen, everything having been altered and improved to suit Lota's somewhat expensive tastes.

'The villa ought to be pretty,' Miss Elderson murmured plaintively, 'for Lota's improvements have cost a fortune.'

'Life is so short. We ought to make the best of it,' said Lota gaily.

We were full of gaiety, and there was the sound of talk and light laughter all through the dinner; but I felt that there was a forced note in our mirth, and my own heart was like lead. We all went back to the drawing-room together.

The windows were open to the moonlight, and the faint sighing of the night wind among the olive woods. Lota and her lover established themselves in front of the blazing pine logs, and Miss Elderson asked me if I would like a stroll on the terrace. There were fleecy white shawls lying about ready for casual excursions of this kind, and the good old lady wrapped one about my shoulders with motherly care. I followed her promptly, foreseeing that she was as anxious to talk confidentially with me as I was to talk with her.

My eagerness anticipated her measured speech. 'You are unhappy about Lota,' I asked.

'Very, very unhappy.'

'But why haven't you taken her away from here? You must see that the place is killing her. Or perhaps the dreadful change in her may not strike you, who have been seeing her every day—?'

'It does strike me; the change is too palpable. I see it every morning, see her looking a little worse, a little worse every day, as if some dreadful disease were eating away her life. And yet our good English doctor from San Remo says there is nothing the matter except a slight lung trouble, and that this air is the very finest, the position of this house faultless, for such a case as hers, high enough to be bracing, yet sheltered from all cold winds. He told me that we could take her no better place between Genoa and Marseilles.'

'But is she to stop here, and fade, and die? There is some evil influence in this house. Mr Dean said as much; something horrible, uncanny, mysterious.'

'My dear, my dear!' ejaculated the amiable invertebrate creature, shaking her head in solemn reproachfullness, 'can you, a good Churchwoman, believe in any nonsense of that sort?'

'I don't know what to believe; but I can see that my dearest friend is perishing bodily and mentally. The three months in which we have been parted have done the work of years of declining health. And she was warned against the house; she was warned.'

'There is nothing the matter with the house,' that weak-brained spinster answered pettishly. 'The sanitary engineer from Cannes has examined everything. The drainage is simply perfect—'

'And your niece is dying!' I said, savagely, and turned my back upon Miss Elderson.

I gazed across the pale grey woods to the sapphire sea, with eyes that scarcely saw the loveliness they looked upon. My heart was swelling with indignation against this feeble affection which would see the thing it loved vanishing off the earth, and yet could not be moved to energetic action.

CHAPTER III.
'SOMETIMES THEY FADE AND DIE.'

I tested the strength of my own influence the next day, and I was inclined to be less severe in my judgement of the meek spinster, after a long morning in the woods with Lota and Captain Holbrook, in which all my arguments and entreaties, backed most fervently by an adoring lover, had proved useless.

'I am assured that no place could suit my health better,' Lota said, decisively, 'and I mean to stay here till my doctor orders me to Varese or home to England. Do you suppose I spent a year's income on the villa with the idea of running away from it? I am tired to death of being teased about the place. First it is auntie, and then it is Captain Holbrook, and now it is young Helen. Villa, gardens, and woods are utterly lovely, and I mean to stay.'

'But if you are not happy here?'

'Who says I am not happy?'

'Your face says it, Lota.'

'I am just as happy here as I should be anywhere else,' she answered, doggedly, 'and I mean to stay.'

She set her teeth as she finished the sentence, and her face had a look of angry resolve that I had never seen in it before. It seemed as if she were fighting against something, defying something. She rose abruptly from the bank upon which she had been sitting, in a sheltered hollow, near the rocky cleft where a ruined oil mill hung mouldering on the brink of a waterfall; and she began to walk up and down very fast, muttering to herself with frowning brows:

'I shall stay! I shall stay!' I heard her repeating, as she passed me.

* * * * *

After that miserable morning—miserable in a climate and a scene of loveliness where bare existence should have been bliss—I had many serious conversations with Captain Holbrook, who was at the villa every day, the most wonderful and devoted of lovers. From him I learnt all that was known of the house in which I was living. He had taken infinite pains to discover any reason, in the house or the neighbourhood, for the lamentable change in Lota, but with the slightest results. No legend of the supernatural was associated with the Orange Grove; but on being questioned searchingly an old Italian physician who had spent his life at Taggia, and who had known Ruffini, confessed that there was a something, a mysterious something, about the villa which seemed to have affected everybody who lived in it, as owner or master, within the memory of the oldest inhabitant.

'People are not happy there. No, they are not happy, and sometimes they fade and die.'

'Invalids who come to the South to die?'

'Not always. The Signorina's grandfather was an elderly man; but he appeared in robust health when he came. However, at that age, a sudden break up is by no means wonderful. There were previous instances of decay and death far more appalling, and in some ways mysterious. I am sorry the pretty young lady has spent so much money on the villa.'

'What does money matter if she would only go elsewhere?'

She would not. That was the difficulty. No argument of her lover's could move her. She would go in April, she told him, at the season for departure; but not even his persuasion, his urgent prayers, would induce her to leave one week or one day sooner than the doctor ordered.

'I should hate myself if I were weak enough to run away from this place,' she said; and it seemed to me that those words were the clue to her conduct, and that she was making a martyr of herself rather than succumb to something of horror which was haunting and killing her.

Her marriage had been fixed for the following June, and George Holbrook was strong in the rights of a future husband; but submissive as she was in all other respects, upon this point she was stubborn, and her lover's fervent pleading moved her no more than the piteous entreaties of her spinster aunt.

I began to understand that the case was hopeless, so far as Lota's wellbeing depended upon her speedy removal from the Orange Grove. We could only wait as hopefully as we could for April, and the time she had fixed for departure. I took the earliest opportunity of confiding my fears to the English physician; but clever and amiable as he was, he laughed all ideas of occult influence to scorn.

'From the moment the sanitary engineer—a really scientific man—certified this house as a healthy house, the last word was said as to its suitableness for Miss Hammond. The situation is perfect, the climate all that one could desire. It would be folly to move her till the spring is advanced enough for Varese or England.'

What could I say against this verdict of local experience? Lota was not one of those interesting and profitable cases which a doctor likes to keep under his own eye. As a patient, her doctor only saw her once in a way; but he dropped in at the villa often as a friend, and he had been useful in bringing nice people about her.

I pressed the question so far as to ask him about the rooms at the back of the house, the old monkish rooms which had served as an infirmary in the seventeenth and eighteenth centuries. 'Surely those rooms must be cold and damp?'

'Damp, no. Cold, yes. All north rooms are cold on the Riviera—and the change from south to north is perilous—but as no one uses the old monkish rooms their aspect can make little difference.'

'Does not Miss Hammond use those rooms sometimes?'

'Never, I believe. Indeed, I understood Miss Elderson to say that the corridor leading to the old part of the house is kept locked, and that she has the key. I take it the good lady thinks that if the rooms are haunted it is her business to keep the ghosts in safe custody—as she does the groceries.'

'Has nobody ever used these rooms since the new villa was built?' I asked.

'Mr Hammond used them, and was rather attached to that part of the house. His library is still there, I believe, in what was once a refectory.'

'I should love to see it.'

'You have only to ask Miss Elderson.'

I did ask Miss Elderson without an hour's delay, the first time I found myself alone with her. She blushed, hesitated, assured me that the rooms contained nothing worth looking at, and fully confessed that the key was not come-atable.

'I have not lost it,' she said. 'It is only mislaid. It is sure to turn up when I am looking for something else. I put it in a safe place.'

Miss Elderson's places of safety had been one of our stock jokes ever since I had known Lota and her aunt; so I was inclined to despair of ever seeing those mysterious rooms in which the monks had lived. Yet after meditating upon the subject in a long ramble on the hill above the villa I was inclined to think that Lota might know more about that key than the good simple soul who had mislaid it. There were hours in every day during which my friend disappeared from the family circle, hours in which she was supposed to be resting inside the mosquito curtains in her own room. I had knocked at her door once or twice during this period of supposed rest; and there had been no answer. I had tried the door softly, and had found it locked, and had gone away believing my friend fast asleep; but now I began to wonder whether Lota might not possess the key of those uninhabited rooms, and for some strange capricious motive spend some of her lonely hours within those walls. I made an investigation at the back of the villa the following day, before the early coffee and the rolls, which we three spinsters generally took in the verandah on warm sunny mornings, and most of our mornings were warm. I found the massive Venetian shutters firmly secured inside, and affording not a glimpse of the rooms within. The windows looked straight upon the precipitous hill, and these northward-facing rooms must needs be dark and chilly at the best of times. My curiosity was completely baffled. Even if I had been disposed to do a little house-breaking there was no possibility of opening those too solid-looking shutters. I tugged at the fastenings savagely, but made no more impression than if I had been a fly.

CHAPTER IV.
SUNSHINE OUTSIDE, BUT ICE AT THE CORE.

For the next four days I watched Lota's movements.

After our morning saunter—she was far too weak now to go further than the terraced paths near the villa, and our sauntering was of the slowest—my poor friend would retire to her room for what she called her afternoon rest, while the carriage, rarely used by herself, conveyed her aunt and me for a drive, which our low spirits made ineffably dreary. Vainly was that panorama of loveliness spread before my eyes—I could enjoy nothing; for between me and that romantic scene there was the image of my perishing friend, dying by inches, and obstinately determined to die.

I questioned Lota's maid about those long afternoons which her mistress spent in her darkened room, and the young woman's answers confirmed my suspicions.

Miss Hammond did not like to be disturbed. She was a very heavy sleeper.

'She likes me to go to her at four o'clock every afternoon to do her hair, and put on her teagown. She is generally fast asleep when I go to her.'

'And her door locked?'

'No, the door is very seldom locked at four. I went an hour earlier once with a telegram, and then the door was locked, and Miss Hammond was so fast asleep that she couldn't hear me knocking. I had to wait till the usual time.'

On the fourth day after my inspection of the shutters, I started for the daily drive at the accustomed hour; but when we had gone a little way down the hill, I pretended to remember an important letter that had to be written, and asked Miss Elderson to stop the carriage, and let me go back to the villa, excusing my desertion for this afternoon. The poor lady, who was as low-spirited as myself, declared she would miss me sadly, and the carriage crept on, while I climbed the hill by those straight steep paths which shortened the journey to a five minutes' walk.

The silence of the villa as I went softly in at the open hall door suggested a general siesta. There was an awning in front of the door, and the hall was wrapped in shadow, the corridor beyond darker still, and at the end of this corridor I saw a flitting figure in pale grey—the pale Indian cashmere of Lota's neat morning frock. I heard a key turn, then the creaking of a heavy door, and the darkness had swallowed that pale grey figure.

I waited a few moments, and then stole softly along the passage. The door was half open, and I peered into the room beyond. It was empty, but an open door facing the fireplace showed me another room—a room lined with bookshelves, and in this room I could hear footsteps pacing slowly to and fro, very slowly, with the feeble tread I knew too well.

Presently she turned, put her hand to her brow as if remembering something, and hurried to the door where I was standing.

'It is I, Lota!' I called out, as she approached me, lest she should be startled by my unexpected presence.

I had been mean enough to steal a march upon her, but I was not mean enough to conceal myself.

'You here!' she exclaimed.

I told her how I had suspected her visits to these deserted rooms, and how I had dreaded the melancholy effect which their dreariness must needs exercise upon her mind and health.

'Do you call them dreary?' she asked, with a curious little laugh. 'I call them charming. They are the only rooms in the house that interest me. And it was just the same with my grandfather. He spent his declining days in these queer old rooms, surrounded by these queer old things.'

She looked round her, with furtive, wandering glances, at the heavy old bookshelves, the black and white cabinets, the dismal old Italian tapestry, and at a Venetian glass which occupied a narrow recess at the end of the inner room, a glass that reached from floor to ceiling, and in a florid carved frame, from which the gilding had mostly worn away.

Her glance lingered on this Venetian glass, which to my uneducated eye looked the oldest piece of furniture in the room. The surface was so clouded and tarnished that although Lota and I were standing opposite it at a little distance, I could see no reflection of ourselves or of the room.

'You cannot find that curious old glass very flattering to your vanity,' I said, trying to be sprightly and careless in my remarks, while my eyes were watching that wasted countenance with its hectic bloom, and those too brilliant eyes.

'No, it doesn't flatter, but I like it,' she said, going a little nearer the glass, and then suddenly drawing a dark velvet curtain across the narrow space between the two projecting bookcases.

I had not noticed the curtain till she touched it, for this end of the long room was in shadow. The heavy shutters which I had seen outside were closed over two of the windows, but the shutters had been pushed back from the third window, and the casements were open to the still, soft air.

There was a sofa opposite the curtained recess. Lota sank down upon it, folded her arms, and looked at me with a defiant smile.

'Well, what do you think of my den?' she asked.

'I think you could not have chosen a worse.'

'And yet my grandfather liked these rooms better than all the rest of the house. He almost lived in them. His old servant told me so.'

'An elderly fancy, which no doubt injured his health.'

'People choose to say so, because he died sooner than they expected. His death would have come at the appointed time. The day and hour were written in the Book of Fate before he came here. The house had nothing to do with it—only in this quiet old room he had time to think of what was coming.'

'He was old, and had lived his life; you are young, and life is all before you.'

'All!' she echoed, with a laugh that chilled my heart.

I tried to be cheerful, matter of fact, practical. I urged her to abandon this dismal library, with its dry old books, airless gloom, and northern aspect. I told her she had been guilty of an unworthy deceit in spending long hours in rooms that had been especially forbidden her. She made an end of my pleading with cruel abruptness.

'You are talking nonsense, Helen. You know that I am doomed to die before the summer is over, and I know that you know it.'

'You were well when you came here; you have been growing worse day by day.'

'My good health was only seeming. The seeds of disease were here,' touching her contracted chest. 'They have only developed. Don't talk to me, Helen; I shall spend my quiet hours in these rooms till the end, like my poor old grandfather. There need be no more concealment or double dealing. This house is mine, and I shall occupy the rooms I like.'

She drew herself up haughtily as she rose from the sofa, but the poor little attempt at dignity was spoilt by a paroxysm of coughing that made her glad to rest in my arms, while I laid her gently down upon the sofa.

The darkness came upon us while she lay there, prostrate, exhausted, and that afternoon in the shadow of the steep hill was the first of many such afternoons.

From that day she allowed me to share her solitude, so long as I did not disturb her reveries, her long silences, or brief snatches of slumber. I sat by the open window and worked or read, while she lay on the sofa, or moved softly about the room, looking at the books on the shelves, or often stopping before that dark Venetian glass to contemplate her own shadowy image.

I wondered exceedingly in those days what pleasure or interest she could find in surveying that blurred shadow of her faded beauty. Was it in bitterness she looked at the altered form, the shrunken features—or only in philosophical wonder such as Marlborough felt, when he pointed to the withered old form in the glass—the poor remains of peerless manhood and exclaimed: 'That was once a man.'

I had no power to withdraw her from that gloomy solitude. I was thankful for the privilege of being with her, able to comfort her in moments of physical misery.

Captain Holbrook left within a few days of my discovery, his leave having so nearly expired that he had only just time enough to get back to Portsmouth, where his regiment was stationed. He went regretfully, full of fear, and his last anxious words were spoken to me at the little station on the sea shore.

'Do all you can to bring her home as soon as the doctor will let her come,' he said. 'I leave her with a heavy heart, but I can do no good by remaining. I shall count every hour between now and April. She has promised to stay at Southsea till we are married, so that we may be near each other. I am to find a pretty villa for her and her aunt. It will be something for me to do.'

My heart ached for him in his forlorness, glad of any little duty that made a link between him and his sweetheart. I knew that he dearly loved his profession, and I knew also that he had offered to leave the army if Lota liked—to alter the whole plan of his life rather than be parted from her, even for a few weeks. She had forbidden such a sacrifice; and she had stubbornly refused to advance the date of her marriage, and marry him at San Remo, as he had entreated her to do, so that he might take her back to England, and establish her at Ventnor, where he believed she would be better than in her Italian paradise.

He was gone, and I felt miserably helpless and lonely without him—lonely even in Lota's company, for between her and me there were shadows and mysteries that filled my heart with dread. Sitting in the same room with her—admitted now to constant companionship—I felt not the less that there were secrets in her life which I knew not. Her eloquent face told some sad story which I could not read; and sometimes it seemed to me that between her and me there was a third presence, and that the name of the third was Death.

She let me share her quiet afternoons in the old rooms, but though her occupation of these rooms was no longer concealed from the household, she kept the privilege of solitude with jealous care. Her aunt still believed in the siesta between lunch and dinner, and went for her solitary drives with a placid submission to Lota's desire that the carriage and horses should be used by somebody. The poor thing was quite as unhappy as I, and quite as fond as Lota; but her feeble spirit had no power to struggle against her niece's strong will. Of these two the younger had always ruled the elder. After Captain Holbrook's departure the doctor took his patient seriously in hand, and I soon perceived a marked change in his manner of questioning her, while the stethoscope came now into frequent use. The casual weekly visits became daily visits; and in answer to my anxious questions I was told that the case had suddenly assumed a serious character.

'We have something to fight against now,' said the doctor; 'until now we have had nothing but nerves and fancies.'

'And now?'

'The lungs are affected.'

This was the beginning of a new sadness. Instead of vague fears, we had now the certainty of evil; and I think in the dreary days and weeks that followed, the poor old aunt and I had not one thought or desire, or fear, which was not centred in the fair young creature whose fading life we watched. Two English nurses, summoned from Cannes, aided in the actual nursing, for which trained skill was needed; but in all the little services which love can perform Miss Elderson and I were Lota's faithful slaves.

I told the doctor of her afternoons spent in her grandfather's library; and I told him also that I doubted my power, or his, to induce her to abandon that room.

'She has a fancy for it, and you know how difficult fancies are to fight with when anyone is out of health.'

'It is a curious fact,' said the doctor, 'that in every bad case I have attended in this house my patient has had an obstinate preference for that dull, cold, room.'

'When you say every bad case, I think you must mean every fatal case,' I said.

'Yes. Unhappily the three or four cases I am thinking of ended fatally; but that fact need not make you unhappy. Feeble, elderly people come to this southern shore to spin out the frail thread of life that is at breaking point when they leave England. In your young friend's case sunshine and balmy air may do much. She ought to live on the sunny side of the house; but her fancy for her grandfather's library may be indulged all the same. She can spend her evenings in that room, which can be made thoroughly warm and comfortable before she enters it. The room is well built and dry. When the shutters are shut and the curtains drawn, and the temperature carefully regulated, it will be as good a room as any other for the lamp-light hours; but for the day let her have all the sunshine she can.'

I repeated this little lecture to Lota, who promised to obey.

'I like the queer, old room,' she said, 'and, Helen, don't think me a bear if I say that I should like to be alone there sometimes, as I used to be before you hunted me down. Society is very nice for people who are well enough to enjoy it, but I'm not up to society, not even your's and auntie's. Yes, I know what you are going to say. You sit like a mouse, and don't speak till you are spoken to; but the very knowledge that you are there, watching me and thinking about me, worries me. And as for the auntie, with her little anxious fidgettings, wanting to settle my footstool, and shake up my pillows, and turn the leaves of my books, and always making me uncomfortable in the kindest way, dear soul—well, I don't mind confessing that she gets on my nerves, and makes me feel as if I should like to scream. Let me have one hour or two of perfect solitude sometimes, Helen. The nurse don't count. She can sit in the room, and you will know that I am not going to die suddenly without anybody to look on at my poor little tragedy.'

She had talked longer and more earnestly than usual, and the talking ended in a fit of coughing which shook the wasted frame. I promised that all should be as she wished. If solitude were more restful than even our quiet companionship, she should be sometimes alone. I would answer for her aunt, as for myself.

The nurses were two bright, capable young women, and were used to the caprices of the sick. I told them exactly what was wanted: a silent unobtrusive presence, a watchful care of the patient's physical comfort by day and night. And henceforth Lota's evenings were spent for the most part in solitude. She had her books, and her drawing-board, on which with light, weak hand she would sketch faint remembrances of the spots that had charmed us most in our drives or rambles. She had her basket overflowing with scraps of fancy work, beginnings of things that were to have no end.

'She doesn't read very long, or work for more than ten minutes at a time,' the nurse told me. 'She just dozes away most of the evening, or walks about the room now and then, and stands to look at herself in that gloomy old glass. It's strange that she should be so fond of looking in the glass, poor dear, when she can scarcely fail to see the change in herself.'

'No, no, she must see, and it is breaking her heart. I wish we could do away with every looking-glass in the house,' said I, remembering how pretty she had been in the fresh bloom of her happy girlhood only six months before that dreary time.

'She is very fond of going over her grandfather's papers,' the nurse told me. 'There is a book I see her reading very often—a manuscript book.'

'His diary, perhaps,' said I.

'It might be that; but it's strange that she should care to pore over an old gentleman's diary.'

Strange, yes; but all her fancies and likings were strange ever since I had entered that unlucky house. In her thought of her lover she was not as other girls. She was angry when I suggested that we should tell him of her illness, in order that he might get leave to come to her, if it were only for a few days.

'No, no, let him never look upon my face again,' she said. 'It is bad enough for him to remember me as I was when we parted at the station. It is ever so much worse now—and it will be—oh, Helen, to think of what must come—at last!'

She hid her face in her hands, and the frail frame was convulsed with the vehemence of her sobbing. It was long before I could soothe her; and this violent grief seemed the more terrible because of the forced cheerfulness of her usual manner.

CHAPTER V.
'SEEK NOT TO KNOW.'

We kept early hours at the villa. We dined at seven, and at eight Lota withdrew to the room which she was pleased to call her den. At ten there was a procession of invalid, nurse, aunt, and friend to Lota's bedroom, where the night nurse, in her neat print gown and pretty white cap, was waiting to receive her. There were many kisses and tender good-nights, and a great show of cheerfulness on all sides, and then Miss Elderson and I crept slowly to our rooms—exchanging a few sad words, a few sympathetic sighs to cry ourselves to sleep, and to awake in the morning with the thought of the doom hanging over us.

I used to drop in upon Lota's solitude a little before bedtime, sometimes with her aunt, sometimes alone. She would look up from her book with a surprised air, or start out of her sleep.

'Bedtime already?'

Sometimes when I found her sleeping, I would seat myself beside her sofa, and wait in silence for her waking. How picturesque, how luxurious, the old room looked in the glaring light of the wood, which brightened even the grim tapestry, and glorified the bowls of red and purple anemones and other scentless flowers, and the long wall of books, and the velvet curtained windows, and shining brown floor. It was a room that I too could have loved were it not for the shadow of fear that hung over all things at the Orange Grove.

I went to the library earlier than usual one evening. The clock had not long struck nine when I left the drawing room. I had seen a change for the worse in Lota at dinner, though she had kept up her pretence of gaiety, and had refused to be treated as an invalid, insisting upon dining as we dined, scarcely touching some things, eating ravenously of other dishes, the least wholesome, laughing to scorn all her doctor's advice about dietary. I endured the interval between eight and nine, stifling my anxieties, and indulging the mild old lady with a game of bezique, which my wretched play allowed her to win easily, Like most old people her sorrow was of a mild and modified quality, and she had, I believe, resigned herself to the inevitable. The careful doctor, the admirable nurses, had set her mind at ease about dear Lota, she told me. She felt that all was being done that love and care could do, and for the rest, well, she had her church services, her prayers, her morning and evening readings in the well-worn New Testament. I believe she was almost happy.

'We must all die, my dear Helen,' she said, plaintively.

Die, yes. Die when one had reached that humdrum stage on the road of life where this poor old thing was plodding, past barren fields and flowerless hedges—the stage of grey hairs, and toothless gums, and failing sight, and dull hearing—and an old-fashioned, one-idead intellect. But to die like Lota, in the pride of youth, with beauty and wealth and love all one's own! To lay all this down in the grave! That seemed hard, too hard for my understanding or my patience.

*   *   *   *   *

I found her asleep on the sofa by the hearth, the nurse sitting quietly on guard in her armchair, knitting the stocking which was never out of her hands unless they were occupied in the patient's service. To-night's sleep was sounder than usual, for the sleeper did not stir at my approach, and I seated myself in the low chair by the foot of the sofa without waking her.

A book had slipped from her hand, and lay on the silken coverlet open. The pages caught my eye, for they were in manuscript, and I remembered what the nurse had said about Lota's fancy for this volume. I stole my hand across the coverlet, and possessed myself of the book, so softly that the sleeper's sensitive frame had no consciousness of my touch.

A manuscript volume of about two hundred pages in a neat firm hand, very small, yet easy to read, so perfectly were the letters formed and so evenly were the lines spaced.

I turned the leaves eagerly. A diary, a business man's diary, recording in commonplace phraseology the transactions of each day, Stock Exchange, Stock Exchange—railways—mines—loans—banks—money, money, money, made or lost. That was all the neat penmanship told me, as I turned leaf after leaf, and ran my eye over page after page.

The social life of the writer was indicated in a few brief sentences. 'Dined with the Parkers: dinner execrable; company stupid; talked to Lendon, who has made half a million in Mexican copper; a dull man.'

'Came to Brighton for Easter; clear turtle at the Ship good; they have given me my old rooms; asked Smith (Suez Smith, not Turkish Smith) to dinner.'

What interest could Lota possibly find in such a journal—a prosy commonplace record of losses and gains, bristling with figures?

This was what I asked myself as I turned leaf after leaf, and saw only the everlasting repetition of financial notes, strange names of loans and mines and railways, with contractions that reduced them to a cypher. Slowly, my hand softly turning the pages of the thick volume, I had gone through about three-fourths of the book when I came to the heading, 'Orange Grove', and the brief entries of the financier gave place to the detailed ideas and experiences of the man of leisure, an exile from familiar scenes and old faces, driven back upon self-commune for the amusement of his lonely hours.

This doubtless was where Lota's interest in the book began, and here I too began to read every word of the diary with closest attention. I did not stop to think whether I was justified in reading the pages which the dead man had penned in his retirement, whether a licence which his granddaughter allowed herself might be taken by me. My one thought was to discover the reason of Lota's interest in the book, and whether its influence upon her mind and spirits was as harmful as I feared.

I slipped from the chair to the rug beside the sofa, and, sitting there on the ground, with the full light of the shaded reading-lamp upon the book, I forgot everything but the pages before me.

The first few pages after the old man's installation in his villa were full of cheerfulness. He wrote of this land of the South, new to his narrow experience, as an earthly paradise. He was almost as sentimental in his enthusiasms as a girl, as if it had not been for the old-fashioned style in which his raptures expressed themselves these pages might have been written by a youthful pen.

He was particularly interested in the old monkish rooms at the back of the villa, but he fully recognised the danger of occupying them.

'I have put my books in the long room which was used as a refectory,' he wrote, 'but as I now rarely look at them there is no fear of my being tempted to spend more than an occasional hour in the room.'

Then after an interval of nearly a month:

'I have arranged my books, as I find the library the most interesting room in the house. My doctor objects to the gloomy aspect, but I find a pleasing melancholy in the shadow of the steep olive-clad hill. I begin to think that this life of retirement, with no companions but my books, suits me better than the pursuit of money making, which has occupied so large a portion of my later years.'

Then followed pages of criticism upon the books he read—history, travels, poetry—books which he had been collecting for many years, but which he was now only beginning to enjoy.

'I see before me a studious old age,' he wrote, 'and I hope I may live as long as the head of my old college, Martin Routh. I have made more than enough money to satisfy myself, and to provide ample wealth for the dear girl who will inherit the greater part of my fortune. I can afford to fold my hands, and enjoy the long quiet years of old age in the companionship of the master spirits who have gone before. How near, how living they seem as I steep myself in their thoughts, dream their dreams, see life as they saw it! Virgil, Dante, Chaucer, Shakespeare, Milton, and all those later lights that have shone upon the dullest lives and made them beautiful—how they live with us, and fill our thoughts, and make up the brightest part of our daily existence.'

I read many pages of comment and reverie in the neat, clear penmanship of a man who wrote for his own pleasure, in the restful solitude of his own fire-side.

Suddenly there came a change—the shadow of the cloud that hung over that house:

'I am living too much alone. I did not think I was of the stuff which is subject to delusions and marbled fancies—but I was wrong. I suppose no man's mind can retain its strength of fibre without the friction of intercourse with other minds of its own calibre. I have been living alone with the minds of the dead, and waited upon by foreign servants, with whom I hardly exchange half a dozen sentences in a day. And the result is what no doubt any brain-doctor would have foretold.

'I have begun to see ghosts.

'The thing I have seen is so evidently an emanation of my own mind—so palpably a materialisation of my own self-consciousness, brooding upon myself and my chances of long life—that it is a weakness even to record the appearance that has haunted me during the last few evenings. No shadow of dying monk has stolen between me and the lamplight; no presence from the vanished years, revisiting places. The thing which I have seen is myself—not myself as I am—but myself as I am to be in the coming years, many or few.

'The vision—purely self-induced as I know it to be—has not the less given a shock to the placid contentment of my mind, and the long hopes which, in spite of the Venusian's warning, I had of late been cherishing.

'Looking up from my book in yesterday's twilight my casual glance rested on the old Venetian mirror in front of my desk; and gradually, out of the blurred darkness, I saw a face looking at me.

'My own face as it might be after the wasting of disease, or the slow decay of advancing years—a face at least ten years older than the face I had seen in my glass a few hours before—hollow cheeks, haggard eyes, the loose underlip drooping weakly—a bent figure in an invalid chair, an aspect of utter helplessness. And it was myself. Of that fact I had no shadow of doubt.

'Hypochondria, of course—a common form of the malady,—perhaps this shaping of the imagination into visions. Yet, the thing was strange—for I had been troubled by no apprehensions of illness or premature old age. I had never even thought of myself as an old man. In the pride bred of long immunity from illness I had considered myself exempt from the ailments that are wont to attend declining years. I had pictured myself living to the extremity of human life, and dropping peacefully into the centenarian's grave.

'I was angry with myself for being affected by the vision, and I locked the door of the library when I went to dress for dinner, determined not to re-enter the room till I had done something—by out-door exercise and change of scene—to restore the balance of my brain. Yet when I had dined there came upon me so feverish a desire to know whether the glass would again show me the same figure and face that I gave the key to my major-domo, and told him to light the lamps and make up the fire in the library.

'Yes, the thing lived in the blotched and blurred old glass. The dusky surface, which was too dull to reflect the realities of life, gave back that vision of age and decay with unalterable fidelity. The face and figure came and went, and the glass was often black—but whenever the thing appeared it was the same—the same in every dismal particular, in all the signs of senility and fading life.

' "This is what I am to be twenty years hence," I told myself, "A man of eighty might look like that."

'Yet I had hoped to escape that bitter lot of gradual decay which I had seen and pitied in other men. I had promised myself that the reward of a temperate life—a life free from all consuming fires of dissipation, all tempestuous passions—would be a vigorous and prolonged old age. So surely as I had toiled to amass fortune so surely also had I striven to lay up for myself long years of health and activity, a life prolonged to the utmost span.'

*   *   *   *   *

There was a break of ten days in the journal, and when the record was resumed the change in the writing shocked me. The neat firm penmanship gave place to weak and straggling characters, which, but for marked peculiarities in the formation of certain letters, I should have taken for the writing of a stranger.

'The thing is always there in the black depths of that damnable glass—and I spend the greater part of my life watching for it. I have struggled in vain against the bitter curiosity to know the worst which the vision of the future can show me. Three days ago I flung the key of this detestable room into the deepest well on the premises; but an hour afterwards I sent to Taggia for a blacksmith, and had the lock picked, and ordered a new key, and a duplicate, lest in some future fit of spleen I should throw away a second key, and suffer agonies before the door could be opened.

' "Tu ne quaesieris, scire nefas—"

'Vainly the poet's warning buzzes and booms in my vexed ear—repeating itself perpetually, like the beating of a pulse in my brain, or like the ticking of a clock that will not let a man sleep.

' "Scire nefas—scire nefas."

'The desire to know more is no stranger than reason.

'Well, I am at least prepared for what is to come. I live no longer in a fool's paradise. The thing which I see daily and hourly is no hallucination, no materialisation of my self-consciousness, as I thought in the beginning. It is a warning and a prophesy. So shalt thou be. Soon, soon, shalt thou resemble this form which it shocks thee now to look upon.

'Since first the shadow of myself looked at me from the darker shadows of the glass I have felt every indication of approaching doom. The doctor tries to laugh away my fears, but he owns that I am below par—meaningless phrase—talks of nervine decay, and suggests my going to St Moritz. He doubts if this place suits me, and confesses that I have changed for the worse since I came here.'

Again an interval, and then in writing that was only just legible.

'It is a month since I wrote in this book—a month which has realised all that the Venetian glass showed me when first I began to read its secret.

'I am a helpless old man, carried about in an invalid chair. Gone my pleasant prospect of long tranquil years; gone my selfish scheme of enjoyment, the fruition of a life of money-getting. The old Eastern fable has been realised once again. My gold has turned to withered leaves, so far as any pleasure that it can buy for me. I hope that my grand-daughter may get some good out of the wealth I have toiled to win.'

Again a break, longer this time, and again the handwriting showed signs of increasing weakness. I had to pore over it closely in order to decipher the broken, crooked lines pencilled casually over the pages.

'The weather is insufferably hot; but too ill to be moved. In library—coolest room—doctor no objection. I have seen the last picture in the glass—Death—corruption—the cavern of Lazarus, and no Redeemer's hand to raise the dead. Horrible! Horrible! Myself as I must be—soon, soon! How soon?'

And then, scrawled in a corner of the page, I found the date—June 24, 1889.

I knew that Mr Hammond died early in the July of that year.

*   *   *   *   *

Seated on the floor, with my head bent over the pages, and reading more by the light of the blazing logs than by the lamp on the table above me, I was unaware that Lota had awoke, and had raised herself from her reclining position on the sofa. I was still absorbed in my study of those last horrible lines when a pale hand came suddenly down upon the open book, and a laugh which was almost a shriek ran through the silent spaces around us. The nurse started up and ran to her patient, who was struggling to her feet and staring wildly into the long narrow glass in the recess opposite her sofa.

'Look, look!' she shrieked. 'It has come—the vision of Death! The dreadful face—the shroud—the coffin. Look, Helen, look!'

My gaze followed the direction of those wild eyes, and I know not whether my excited brain conjured up the image that appalled me. This alone I know, that in the depths of that dark glass, indistinct as a form seen through turbid water, a ghastly face, a shrouded figure, looked out at me——

'As one dead in the bottom of a tomb.'

A sudden cry from the nurse called me from the horror of that vision to stern reality, to see the life-blood ebbing from the lips I had kissed so often with all a sister's love. My poor friend never spoke again. A severe attack of haemorrhage hastened the inevitable end; and before her heart-broken lover could come to clasp the hand and gaze into her fading eyes, Violetta Hammond passed away.

Good Lady Ducayne

I

BELLA ROLLESTON HAD made up her mind that her only chance of earning her bread and helping her mother to an occasional crust was by going out into the great unknown world as companion to a lady. She was willing to go to any lady rich enough to pay her a salary and so eccentric as to wish for a hired companion. Five shillings told off reluctantly from one of those sovereigns which were so rare with the mother and daughter, and which melted away so quickly, five solid shillings, had been handed to a smartly dressed lady in an office in Harbeck Street, W., in the hope that this very Superior Person would find a situation and a salary for Miss Rolleston.

The Superior Person glanced at the two half-crowns as they lay on the table where Bella's hand had placed them, to make sure they were neither of them florins, before she wrote a description of Bella's qualifications and requirements in a formidable-looking ledger.

'Age?' she asked curtly.

'Eighteen, last July.'

'Any accomplishments?'

'No; I am not at all accomplished. If I were I should want to be a governess—a companion seems the lowest stage.'

'We have some highly accomplished ladies on our books as companions, or chaperone companions.'

'Oh, I know!' babbled Bella, loquacious in her youthful candour. 'But that is quite a different thing. Mother hasn't been able to afford a piano since I was twelve years old, so I'm afraid I've forgotten how to play. And I have had to help mother with her needlework, so there hasn't been much time to study.'

'Please don't waste time upon explaining what you can't do, but kindly tell me anything you can do,' said the Superior Person, crushingly, with her pen poised between delicate fingers waiting to write. 'Can you read aloud for two or three hours at a stretch? Are you active and handy, an early riser, a good walker, sweet-tempered, and obliging?'

'I can say yes to all those questions except about the sweetness. I think I have a pretty good temper, and I should be anxious to oblige anybody who paid for my services. I should want them to feel that I was really earning my salary.'

'The kind of ladies who come to me would not care for a talkative companion,' said the Person, severely, having finished writing in her book. 'My connection lies chiefly among the aristocracy, and in that class considerable deference is expected.'

'Oh, of course,' said Bella; 'but it's quite different when I'm talking to you. I want to tell you all about myself once and for ever.'

'I am glad it is to be only once!' said the Person, with the edges of her lips.

The Person was of uncertain age, tightly laced in a black silk gown. She had a powdery complexion and a handsome clump of somebody else's hair on the top of her head. It may be that Bella's girlish freshness and vivacity had an irritating effect upon nerves weakened by an eight hours' day in that over-heated second floor in Harbeck Street. To Bella the official apartment, with its Brussels carpet, velvet curtains and velvet chairs, and French clock, ticking loud on the marble chimney-piece, suggested the luxury of a palace, as compared with another second floor in Walworth where Mrs Rolleston and her daughter had managed to exist for the last six years.

'Do you think you have anything on your books that would suit me?' faltered Bella, after a pause.

'Oh, dear, no; I have nothing in view at present,' answered the Person, who had swept Bella's half-crowns into a drawer, absent-mindedly, with the tips of her fingers. 'You see, you are so very unformed—so much too young to be companion to a lady of position. It is a pity you have not enough education for a nursery governess; that would be more in your line.'

'And do you think it will be very long before you can get me a situation?' asked Bella, doubtfully.

'I really cannot say. Have you any particular reason for being so impatient—not a love affair, I hope?'

'A love affair!' cried Bella, with flaming cheeks. 'What utter nonsense. I want a situation because mother is poor, and I hate being a burden to her. I want a salary that I can share with her.'

'There won't be much margin for sharing in the salary you are likely to get at your age—and with your—very—unformed manners,' said the Person, who found Bella's peony cheeks, bright eyes, and unbridled vivacity more and more oppressive.

'Perhaps if you'd be kind enough to give me back the fee I could take it to an agency where the connection isn't quite so aristocratic,' said Bella, who—as she told her mother in her recital of the interview—was determined not to be sat upon.

'You will find no agency that can do more for you than mine,' replied the Person, whose harpy fingers never relinquished coin. 'You will have to wait for your opportunity. Yours is an exceptional case: but I will bear you in mind, and if anything suitable offers I will write to you. I cannot say more than that.'

The half-contemptuous bend of the stately head, weighted with borrowed hair, indicated the end of the interview. Bella went back to Walworth—tramped sturdily every inch of the way in the September afternoon—and 'took off' the Superior Person for the amusement of her mother and the landlady, who lingered in the shabby little sitting-room after bringing in the tea-tray, to applaud Miss Rolleston's 'taking off'.

'Dear, dear, what a mimic she is!' said the landlady. 'You ought to have let her go on the stage, mum. She might have made her fortune as a h'actress.'

II

Bella waited and hoped, and listened for the postman's knocks which brought such store of letters for the parlours and the first floor, and so few for that humble second floor, where mother and daughter sat sewing with hand and with wheel and treadle, for the greater part of the day. Mrs Rolleston was a lady by birth and education; but it had been her bad fortune to marry a scoundrel; for the last half-dozen years she had been that worst of widows, a wife whose husband had deserted her. Happily, she was courageous, industrious, and a clever needle-woman; and she had been able just to earn a living for herself and her only child, by making mantles and cloaks for a West End house. It was not a luxurious living. Cheap lodgings in a shabby street off the Walworth Road, scanty dinners, homely food, well-worn raiment, had been the portion of mother and daughter; but they loved each other so dearly, and Nature had made them both so light-hearted, that they had contrived somehow to be happy.

But now this idea of going out into the world as companion to some fine lady had rooted itself into Bella's mind, and although she idolised her mother, and although the parting of mother and daughter must needs tear two loving hearts into shreds, the girl longed for enterprise and change and excitement, as the pages of old longed to be knights, and to start for the Holy Land to break a lance with the infidel.

She grew tired of racing downstairs every time the postman knocked, only to be told 'nothing for you, miss,' by the smudgy-faced drudge who picked up the letters from the passage floor. 'Nothing for you, miss,' grinned the lodging-house drudge, till at last Bella took heart of grace and walked up to Harbeck Street, and asked the Superior Person how it was that no situation had been found for her.

'You are too young,' said the Person, 'and you want a salary.'

'Of course I do,' answered Bella; 'don't other people want salaries?'

'Young ladies of your age generally want a comfortable home.'

'I don't,' snapped Bella; 'I want to help mother.'

'You can call again this day week,' said the Person; 'or, if I hear of any-thing in the meantime, I will write to you.'

No letter came from the Person, and in exactly a week Bella put on her neatest hat, the one that had been seldomest caught in the rain, and trudged off to Harbeck Street.

It was a dull October afternoon, and there was a greyness in the air which might turn to fog before night. The Walworth Road shops gleamed brightly through that grey atmosphere, and though to a young lady reared in Mayfair or Belgravia such shop-windows would have been unworthy of a glance, they were a snare and temptation for Bella. There were so many things that she longed for, and would never be able to buy.

Harbeck Street is apt to be empty at this dead season of the year, a long, long street, an endless perspective of eminently respectable houses. The Person's office was at the further end, and Bella looked down that long, grey vista almost despairingly, more tired than usual with the trudge from Walworth. As she looked, a carriage passed her, an old-fashioned, yellow chariot, on Cee springs, drawn by a pair of high grey horses, with the state-liest of coachmen driving them, and a tall footman sitting by his side.

'It looks like the fairy godmother's coach,' thought Bella. 'I shouldn't wonder if it began by being a pumpkin.'

It was a surprise when she reached the Person's door to find the yellow chariot standing before it, and the tall footman waiting near the doorstep. She was almost afraid to go in and meet the owner of that splendid carriage. She had caught only a glimpse of its occupant as the chariot rolled by, a plumed bonnet, a patch of ermine.

The Person's smart page ushered her upstairs and knocked at the official door. 'Miss Rolleston,' he announced, apologetically, while Bella waited outside.

'Show her in,' said the Person, quickly; and then Bella heard her murmuring something in a low voice to her client.

Bella went in fresh, blooming, a living image of youth and hope, and before she looked at the Person her gaze was riveted by the owner of the chariot.

Never had she seen anyone as old as the old lady sitting by the Person's fire: a little old figure, wrapped from chin to feet in an ermine mantle; a withered, old face under a plumed bonnet—a face so wasted by age that it seemed only a pair of eyes and a peaked chin. The nose was peaked, too, but between the sharply pointed chin and the great, shining eyes, the small, aquiline nose was hardly visible.

'This is Miss Rolleston, Lady Ducayne.'

Claw-like fingers, flashing with jewels, lifted a double eyeglass to Lady Ducayne's shining black eyes, and through the glasses Bella saw those unnaturally bright eyes magnified to a gigantic size, and glaring at her awfully.

'Miss Torpinter has told me all about you,' said the old voice that belonged to the eyes. 'Have you good health? Are you strong and active, able to eat well, sleep well, walk well, able to enjoy all that there is good in life?'

'I have never known what is to be ill, or idle,' answered Bella.

'Then I think you will do for me.'

'Of course, in the event of references being perfectly satisfactory,' put in the Person.

'I don't want references. The young woman looks frank and innocent. I'll take her on trust.'

'So like you, dear Lady Ducayne,' murmuring Miss Torpinter.

'I want a strong young woman whose health will give me no trouble.'

'You have been so unfortunate in that respect,' cooed the Person, whose voice and manner were subdued to a melting sweetness by the old woman's presence.

'Yes, I've been rather unlucky,' grunted Lady Ducayne.

'But I am sure Miss Rolleston will not disappoint you, though certainly after your unpleasant experience with Miss Tomson, who looked the picture of health—and Miss Blandy, who said she had never seen a doctor since she was vaccinated——'

'Lies, no doubt,' muttered Lady Ducayne, and then turning to Bella, she asked, curtly, 'You don't mind spending the winter in Italy, I suppose?'

In Italy! The very word was magical. Bella's fair young face flushed crimson.

'It has been the dream of my life to see Italy,' she gasped.

From Walworth to Italy! How far, how impossible such a journey had seemed to that romantic dreamer.

'Well, your dream will be realised. Get yourself ready to leave Charing Cross by the train de luxe this day week at eleven. Be sure you are at the station a quarter before the hour. My people will look after you and your luggage.'

Lady Ducayne rose from her chair, assisted by her crutch-stick, and Miss Torpinter escorted her to the door.

'And with regard to salary?' questioned the Person on the way.

'Salary, oh, the same as usual—and if the young woman wants a quarter's pay in advance you can write to me for a cheque,' Lady Ducayne answered, carelessly.

Miss Torpinter went all the way downstairs with her client, and waited to see her seated in the yellow chariot. When she came upstairs again she was slightly out of breath, and she had resumed that superior manner which Bella had found so crushing.

'You may think yourself uncommonly lucky, Miss Rolleston,' she said. 'I have dozens of young ladies on my books whom I might have recommended for this situation—but I remembered having told you to call this afternoon—and I thought I would give you a chance. Old Lady Ducayne is one of the best people on my books. She gives her companion a hundred a year, and pays all travelling expenses. You will live in the lap of luxury.'

'A hundred a year! How too lovely! Shall I have to dress very grandly? Does Lady Ducayne keep much company?'

'At her age! No, she lives in seclusion—in her own apartments—her French maid, her footman, her medical attendant, her courier.'

'Why did those other companions leave her?' asked Bella.

'Their health broke down!'

'Poor things, and so they had to leave?'

'Yes, they had to leave. I suppose you would like a quarter's salary in advance?'

'Oh, yes, please. I shall have things to buy.'

'Very well, I will write for Lady Ducayne's cheque, and I will send you the balance—after deducting my commission for the year.'

'To be sure, I had forgotten the commission.'

'You don't suppose I keep this office for pleasure.'

'Of course not,' murmured Bella, remembering the five shillings entrance fee; but nobody could expect a hundred a year and a winter in Italy for five shillings.

III

'From Miss Rolleston, at Cap Ferrino, to Mrs Rolleston, in Beresford Street, Walworth.

'How I wish you could see this place, dearest; the blue sky, the olive woods, the orange and lemon orchards between the cliffs and the sea—sheltering in the hollow of the great hills—and with summer waves dancing up to the narrow ridge of pebbles and weeds which is the Italian idea of a beach! Oh, how I wish you could see it all, mother dear, and bask in this sunshine, that makes it so difficult to believe the date at the head of this paper. November! The air is like an English June—the sun is so hot that I can't walk a few yards without an umbrella. And to think of you at Walworth while I am here! I could cry at the thought that perhaps you will never see this lovely coast, this wonderful sea, these summer flowers that bloom in winter. There is a hedge of pink geraniums under my window, mother—a thick, rank hedge, as if the flowers grew wild—and there are Dijon roses climbing over arches and palisades all along the terrace—a rose garden full of bloom in November! Just picture it all! You could never imagine the luxury of this hotel. It is nearly new, and has been built and decorated regardless of expense. Our rooms are upholstered in pale blue satin, which shows up Lady Ducayne's parchment complexion; but as she sits all day in a corner of the balcony basking in the sun, except when she is in her carriage, and all the evening in her armchair close to the fire, and never sees anyone but her own people, her complexion matters very little.

'She has the handsomest suite of rooms in the hotel. My bedroom is inside hers, the sweetest room—all blue satin and white lace—white enamelled furniture, looking-glasses on every wall, till I know my pert little profile as I never knew it before. The room was really meant for Lady Ducayne's dressing-room, but she ordered one of the blue satin couches to be arranged as a bed for me—the prettiest little bed, which I can wheel near the window on sunny mornings, as it is on castors and easily moved about. I feel as if Lady Ducayne were a funny old grandmother, who had suddenly appeared in my life, very, very rich, and very, very kind.

'She is not all exacting. I read aloud to her a good deal, and she dozes and nods while I read. Sometimes I hear her moaning in her sleep—as if she had troublesome dreams. When she is tired of my reading she orders Francine, her maid, to read a French novel to her, and I hear her chuckle and groan now and then, as if she were more interested in those books than in Dickens or Scott. My French is not good enough to follow Francine, who reads very quickly. I have a great deal of liberty, for Lady Ducayne often tells me to run away and amuse myself; I roam about the hills for hours. Everything is so lovely. I lose myself in olive woods, always climbing up and up towards the pine woods above—and above the pines there are the snow mountains that just show their white peaks above the dark hills. Oh, you poor dear, how can I ever make you understand what this place is like—you, whose poor, tired eyes have only the opposite side of Beresford Street? Sometimes I go no farther than the terrace in front of the hotel, which is a favourite lounging-place with everybody. The gardens lie below, and the tennis courts where I sometimes play with a very nice girl, the only person in the hotel with whom I have made friends. She is a year older than I, and has come to Cap Ferrino with her brother, a doctor—or a medical student, who is going to be a doctor. He passed his M.B. exam at Edinburgh just before they left home, Lotta told me. He came to Italy entirely on his sister's account. She had a troublesome chest attack last summer and was ordered to winter abroad. They are orphans, quite alone in the world, and so fond of each other. It is very nice for me to have such a friend as Lotta. She is so thoroughly respectable. I can't help using that word, for some of the girls in this hotel go on in a way that I know you would shudder at. Lotta was brought up by an aunt, deep down in the country, and knows hardly anything about life. Her brother won't allow her to read a novel, French or English, that he has not read and approved.

'"He treats me like a child," she told me, "but I don't mind, for it's nice to know somebody loves me, and cares about what I do, and even about my thoughts."

'Perhaps this is what makes some girls so eager to marry—the want of someone strong and brave and honest and true to care for them and order them about. I want no one, mother darling, for I have you, and you are all the world to me. No husband could ever come between us two. If I ever were to marry he would have only the second place in my heart. But I don't suppose I ever shall marry, or even know what it is like to have an offer of marriage. No young man can afford to marry a penniless girl nowadays. Life is too expensive.

'Mr Stafford, Lotta's brother, is very clever, and very kind. He thinks it is rather hard for me to have to live with such an old woman as Lady Ducayne, but then he does not know how poor we are—you and I—and what a wonderful life this seems to me in this lovely place. I feel a selfish wretch for enjoying all my luxuries, while you, who want them so much more than I, have none of them—hardly know what they are like—do you, dearest?—for my scamp of a father began to go to the dogs soon after you were married, and since then life has been all trouble and care and struggle for you.'

This letter was written when Bella had been less than a month at Cap Ferrino, before the novelty had worn off the landscape, and before the pleasure of luxurious surroundings had begun to cloy. She wrote to her mother every week, such long letters as girls who have lived in closest companionship with a mother alone can write; letters that are like a diary of heart and mind. She wrote gaily always; but when the new year began Mrs Rolleston thought she detected a note of melancholy under all those lively details about the place and the people.

'My poor girl is getting homesick,' she thought. 'Her heart is in Beresford Street.'

It might be that she missed her new friend and companion, Lotta Stafford, who had gone with her brother for a little tour to Genoa and Spezzia, and as far as Pisa. They were to return before February; but in the mean-time Bella might naturally feel very solitary among all those strangers, whose manners and doings she described so well.

The mother's instinct had been true. Bella was not so happy as she had been in that first flush of wonder and delight which followed the change from Walworth to the Riviera. Somehow, she knew not how, lassitude had crept upon her. She no longer loved to climb the hills, no longer flourished her orange stick in sheer gladness of heart as her light feet skipped over the rough ground and the coarse grass on the mountain side. The odour of rosemary and thyme, the fresh breath of the sea, no longer filled her with rapture. She thought of Beresford Street and her mother's face with a sick longing. They were so far—so far away! And then she thought of Lady Ducayne, sitting by the heaped-up olive logs in the over-heated salon—thought of that wizened-nut-cracker profile, and those gleaming eyes, with an invincible horror.

Visitors at the hotel had told her that the air of Cap Ferrino was relaxing—better suited to age than to youth, to sickness than to health. No doubt it was so. She was not so well as she had been at Walworth; but she told herself that she was suffering only from the pain of separa-tion from the dear companion of her girlhood, the mother who had been nurse, sister, friend, flatterer, all things in this world to her. She had shed many tears over that parting, had spent many a melancholy hour on the marble terrace with yearning eyes looking westward, and with her heart's desire a thousand miles away.

She was sitting in her favourite spot, an angle at the eastern end of the terrace, a quiet little nook sheltered by orange trees, when she heard a couple of Riviera habitués talking in the garden below. They were sitting on a bench against the terrace wall.

She had no idea of listening to their talk, till the sound of Lady Ducayne's name attracted her, and then she listened without any thought of wrong-doing. They were talking no secrets—just casually discussing an hotel acquaintance.

They were two elderly people whom Bella only knew by sight. An English clergyman who had wintered abroad for half his lifetime; a stout, comfortable, well-to-do spinster, whose chronic bronchitis obliged her to migrate annually.

'I have met her about Italy for the last ten years,' said the lady; 'but have never found out her real age.'

'I put her down at a hundred—not a year less,' replied the parson. 'Her reminiscences all go back to the Regency. She was evidently then in her zenith; and I have heard her say things that showed she was in Parisian society when the First Empire was at its best—before Josephine was divorced.'

'She doesn't talk much now.'

'No; there's not much life left in her. She is wise in keeping herself secluded. I only wonder that wicked old quack, her Italian doctor, didn't finish her off years ago.'

'I should think it must be the other way, and that he keeps her alive.'

'My dear Miss Manders, do you think foreign quackery ever kept anybody alive?'

'Well, there she is—and she never goes anywhere without him. He certainly has an unpleasant countenance.'

'Unpleasant,' echoed the parson. 'I don't believe the foul fiend himself can beat him in ugliness. I pity that poor young woman who has to live between old Lady Ducayne and Dr Parravicini.'

'But the old lady is very good to her companions.'

'No doubt. She is very free with her cash; the servants call her good Lady Ducayne. She is a withered old female Croesus, and knows she'll never be able to get through her money, and doesn't relish the idea of other people enjoying it when she's in her coffin. People who live to be as old as she is become slavishly attached to life. I daresay she's generous to those poor girls—but she can't make them happy. They die in her service.'

'Don't say they, Mr Carton; I know that one poor girl died at Mentone last spring.'

'Yes, and another poor girl died in Rome three years ago. I was there at the time. Good Lady Ducayne left her there in an English family. The girl had every comfort. The old woman was very liberal to her—but she died. I tell you, Miss Manders, it is not good for any young woman to live with two such horrors as Lady Ducayne and Parravicini.'

They talked of other things—but Bella hardly heard them. She sat motionless, and a cold wind seemed to come down upon her from the mountains and to creep up to her from the sea, till she shivered as she sat there in the sunshine, in the shelter of the orange trees in the midst of all that beauty and brightness.

Yes, they were uncanny, certainly, the pair of them—she so like an aristocratic witch in her withered old age; he of no particular age, with a face that was more like a waxen mask than any human countenance Bella had ever seen. What did it matter? Old age is venerable, and worthy of all reverence; and Lady Ducayne had been very kind to her. Dr Parravicini was a harmless, inoffensive student, who seldom looked up from the book he was reading. He had his private sitting-room, where he made experiments in chemistry and natural science—perhaps in alchemy. What could it matter to Bella? He had always been polite to her, in his far-off way. She could not be more happily placed than she was—in this palatial hotel, with this rich old lady.

No doubt she missed the young English girl who had been so friendly, and it might be that she missed the girl's brother, for Mr Stafford had talked to her a good deal—had interested himself in the books she was reading, and her manner of amusing herself when she was not on duty.

'You must come to our little salon when you are "off", as the hospital nurses call it, and we can have some music. No doubt you play and sing?' upon which Bella had to own with a blush of shame that she had forgotten how to play the piano ages ago.

'Mother and I used to sing duets sometimes between the lights, without accompaniment,' she said, and the tears came into her eyes as she thought of the humble room, the half-hour's respite from work, the sewing-machine standing where a piano ought to have been, and her mother's plaintive voice, so sweet, so true, so dear.

Sometimes she found herself wondering whether she would ever see that beloved mother again. Strange forebodings came into her mind. She was angry with herself for giving way to melancholy thoughts.

One day she questioned Lady Ducayne's French maid about those two companions who had died within three years.

'They were poor, feeble creatures,' Francine told her. 'They looked fresh and bright enough when they came to Miladi; but they ate too much and were lazy. They died of luxury and idleness. Miladi was too kind to them.

They had nothing to do; and so they took to fancying things; fancying the air didn't suit them, that they couldn't sleep.'

'I sleep well enough, but I have had a strange dream several times since I have been in Italy.'

'Ah, you had better not begin to think about dreams, or you will be like those other girls. They were dreamers—and they dreamt themselves into the cemetery.'

The dream troubled her a little, not because it was a ghastly or frightening dream, but on account of sensations which she had never felt before in sleep—a whirring of wheels that went round in her brain, a great noise like a whirlwind, but rhythmical like the ticking of a gigantic clock: and then in the midst of this uproar as of winds and waves she seemed to sink into a gulf of unconsciousness, out of sleep into far deeper sleep—total extinction. And then, after that blank interval, there had come the sound of voices, and then again the whirr of wheels, louder and louder—and again the blank—and then she knew no more till morning, when she awoke, feeling languid and oppressed.

She told Dr Parravicini of her dream one day, on the only occasion when she wanted his professional advice. She had suffered rather severely from the mosquitoes before Christmas—and had been almost frightened at finding a wound upon her arm which she could only attribute to the venomous sting of one of these torturers. Parravicini put on his glasses, and scrutinised the angry mark on the round, white arm, as Bella stood before him and Lady Ducayne with her sleeve rolled up above her elbow.

'Yes, that's rather more than a joke,' he said, 'he has caught you on the top of a vein. What a vampire! But there's no harm done, signorina, nothing that a little dressing of mine won't heal. You must always show me any bite of this nature. It might be dangerous if neglected. These creatures feed on poison and disseminate it.'

'And to think that such tiny creatures can bite like this,' said Bella; 'my arm looks as if it had been cut by a knife.'

'If I were to show you a mosquito's sting under my microscope you wouldn't be surprised at that,' replied Parravicini.

Bella had to put up with the mosquito bites, even when they came on the top of a vein, and produced that ugly wound. The wound recurred now and then at longish intervals, and Bella found Dr Parravicini's dressing a speedy cure. If he were the quack his enemies called him, he had at least a light hand and a delicate touch in performing this small operation.

'Bella Rolleston to Mrs Rolleston—April 14th.

'Ever Dearest: Behold the cheque for my second quarter's salary—five-and-twenty pounds. There is no one to pinch off a whole tenner for a year's commission as there was last time, so it is all for you, mother, dear. I have plenty of pocket-money in hand from the cash I brought away with me, when you insisted on my keeping more than I wanted. It isn't possible to spend money here—except on occasional tips to servants, or sous to beggars and children—unless one had lots to spend, for everything one would like to buy—tortoise-shell, coral, lace—is so ridiculously dear that only a millionaire ought to look at it. Italy is a dream of beauty: but for shopping, give me Newington Causeway.

'You ask me so earnestly if I am quite well that I fear my letters must have been very dull lately. Yes, dear, I am well—but I am not quite so strong as I was when I used to trudge to the West End to buy half a pound of tea— just for a constitutional walk—or to Dulwich to look at the pictures. Italy is relaxing; and I feel what the people here call "slack". But I fancy I can see your dear face looking worried as you read this. Indeed, and indeed, I am not ill. I am only a little tired of this lovely scene—as I suppose one might get tired of looking at one of Turner's pictures if it hung on a wall that was always opposite one. I think of you every hour in every day—think of you and our homely little room—our dear little shabby parlour, with the armchairs from the wreck of your old home, and Dick singing in his cage over the sewing-machine. Dear, shrill, maddening Dick, who, we flattered ourselves, was so passionately fond of us. Do tell me in your next that he is well.

'My friend Lotta and her brother never came back after all. They went from Pisa to Rome. Happy mortals! And they are to be on the Italian lakes in May; which lake was not decided when Lotta last wrote to me. She has been a charming correspondent, and has confided all her little flirtations to me. We are all to go to Bellaggio next week—by Genoa and Milan. Isn't that lovely? Lady Ducayne travels by the easiest stages—except when she is bottled up in the train de luxe. We shall stop two days at Genoa and one at Milan. What a bore I shall be to you with my talk about Italy when I come home.

'Love and love—and ever more love from your adoring, Bella.'

IV

Herbert Stafford and his sister had often talked of the pretty English girl with her fresh complexion, which made such a pleasant touch of rosy colour among all those sallow faces at the Grand Hotel. The young doctor thought of her with a compassionate tenderness—her utter loneliness in that great hotel where there were so many people, her bondage to that old, old woman, where everybody else was free to think of nothing but enjoying life. It was a hard fate; and the poor child was evidently devoted to her mother, and felt the pain of separation—'only two of them, and very poor, and all the world to each other,' he thought.

Lotta told him one morning that they were to meet again at Bellaggio. 'The old thing and her court are to be there before we are,' she said. 'I shall be charmed to have Bella again. She is so bright and gay—in spite of an occasional touch of homesickness. I never took to a girl on a short acquaintance as I did to her.'

'I like her best when she is homesick,' said Herbert; 'for then I am sure she has a heart.'

'What have you to do with hearts, except for dissection? Don't forget that Bella is an absolute pauper. She told me in confidence that her mother makes mantles for a West End shop. You can hardly have a lower depth than that.'

'I shouldn't think any less of her if her mother made match-boxes.'

'Not in the abstract—of course not. Match-boxes are honest labour. But you couldn't marry a girl whose mother makes mantles.'

'We haven't come to the consideration of that question yet,' answered Herbert, who liked to provoke his sister.

In two years' hospital practice he had seen too much of the grim realities of life to retain any prejudices about rank. Cancer, phthisis, gangrene, leave a man with little respect for the outward differences which vary the husk of humanity. The kernel is always the same—fearfully and wonderfully made—a subject for pity and terror.

Mr Stafford and his sister arrived at Bellaggio in a fair May evening. The sun was going down as the steamer approached the pier; and all that glory of purple bloom which curtains every wall at this season of the year flushed and deepened in the glowing light. A group of ladies were standing on the pier watching the arrivals, and among them Herbert saw a pale face that startled him out of his wonted composure.

'There she is,' murmured Lotta, at his elbow, 'but how dreadfully changed. She looks a wreck.'

They were shaking hands with her a few minutes later, and a flush had lighted up her poor pinched face in the pleasure of meeting.

'I thought you might come this evening,' she said. 'We have been here a week.'

She did not add that she had been there every evening to watch the boat in, and a good many times during the day. The Grand Bretagne was close by, and it had been easy for her to creep to the pier when the boat bell rang. She felt a joy in meeting these people again; a sense of being with friends; a confidence which Lady Ducayne's goodness had never inspired in her.

'Oh, you poor darling, how awfully ill you must have been,' exclaimed Lotta, as the two girls embraced.

Bella tried to answer, but her voice was choked with tears.

'What has been the matter, dear? That horrid influenza, I suppose?'

'No, no, I have not been ill—I have only felt a little weaker than I used to be. I don't think the air of Cap Ferrino quite agreed with me.'

'It must have disagreed with you abominably. I never saw such a change in anyone. Do let Herbert doctor you. He is fully qualified, you know. He prescribed for ever so many influenza patients at the Londres. They were glad to get advice from an English doctor in a friendly way.'

'I am sure he must be very clever!' faltered Bella, 'but there is really nothing the matter. I am not ill, and if I were ill, Lady Ducayne's physician——'

'That dreadful man with the yellow face? I would as soon one of the Borgias prescribed for me. I hope you haven't been taking any of his medicines.'

'No, dear, I have taken nothing. I have never complained of being ill.'

This was said while they were all three walking to the hotel. The Staffords' rooms had been secured in advance, pretty ground-floor rooms, opening into the garden. Lady Ducayne's statelier apartments were on the floor above.

'I believe these room are just under ours,' said Bella.

'Then it will be all the easier for you to run down to us,' replied Lotta, which was not really the case, as the grand staircase was in the centre of the hotel.

'Oh, I shall find it easy enough,' said Bella. 'I'm afraid you'll have too much of my society. Lady Ducayne sleeps away half the day in this warm weather, so I have a good deal of idle time; and I get awfully moped thinking of mother and home.'

Her voice broke upon the last word. She could not have thought of that poor lodging which went by the name of home more tenderly had it been the most beautiful that art and wealth ever created. She moped and pined in this lovely garden, with the sunlit lake and the romantic hills spreading out their beauty before her. She was homesick and she had dreams: or, rather, an occasional recurrence of that one bad dream with all its strange sensations—it was more like a hallucination than dreaming—the whirring of wheels; the sinking into an abyss; the struggling back to consciousness. She had the dream shortly before she left Cap Ferrino, but not since she had come to Bellaggio, and she began to hope the air in this lake district suited her better, and that those strange sensations would never return.

Mr Stafford wrote a prescription and had it made up at the chemist's near the hotel. It was a powerful tonic, and after two bottles, and a row or two on the lake, and some rambling over the hills and in the meadows where the spring flowers made earth seem paradise, Bella's spirits and looks improved as if by magic.

'It is a wonderful tonic,' she said, but perhaps in her heart of hearts she knew that the doctor's kind voice and the friendly hand that helped her in and out of the boat, and the watchful care that went with her by land and lake, had something to do with her cure.

'I hope you don't forget that her mother makes mantles,' Lotta said, warningly.

'Or match-boxes: it is just the same thing, so far as I am concerned.'

'You mean that in no circumstances could you think of marrying her?'

'I mean that if ever I love a woman well enough to think of marrying her, riches or rank will count for nothing with me. But I fear—I fear your poor friend may not live to be any man's wife,'

'Do you think her so very ill?'

He sighed, and left the question unanswered.

One day, while they were gathering wild hyacinths in an upland meadow, Bella told Mr Stafford about her bad dream.

'It is curious only because it is hardly like a dream,' she said. 'I daresay you could find some common-sense reason for it. The position of my head on my pillow, or the atmosphere, or something.'

And then she described her sensations; how in the midst of sleep there came a sudden sense of suffocation; and then those whirring wheels, so loud, so terrible; and then a blank, and then a coming back to waking consciousness.

'Have you ever had chloroform given you—by a dentist, for instance?'

'Never—Dr Parravicini asked me that question one day.'

'Lately?'

'No, long ago, when we were in the train de luxe.'

'Has Dr Parravicini prescribed for you since you began to feel weak and ill?'

'Oh, he has given me a tonic from time to time, but I hate medicine, and took very little of the stuff. And then I am not ill, only weaker than I used to be. I was ridiculously strong and well when I lived at Walworth, and used to take long walks every day. Mother made me take those tramps to Dulwich or Norwood, for fear I should suffer from too much sewing-machine; sometimes—but very seldom—she went with me. She was generally toiling at home while I was enjoying fresh air and exercise. And she was very careful about our food—that, however plain it was, it should be always nourishing and ample. I owe it to her care that I grew up such a great, strong creature.'

'You don't look great or strong now, you poor dear,' said Lotta.

'I'm afraid Italy doesn't agree with me.'

'Perhaps it is not Italy, but being cooped up with Lady Ducayne that has made you ill.'

'But I am never cooped up. Lady Ducayne is absurdly kind, and lets me roam about or sit in the balcony all day if I like. I have read more novels since I have been with her than in all the rest of my life.'

'Then she is very different from the average old lady, who is usually a slave-driver,' said Stafford. 'I wonder why she carries a companion about with her if she has so little need of society.'

'Oh, I am only part of her state. She is inordinately rich—and the salary she gives me doesn't count. Apropos of Dr Parravicini, I know he is a clever doctor, for he cures my horrid mosquito bites.'

'A little ammonia would do that, in the early stage of the mischief. But there are no mosquitoes to trouble you now.'

'Oh, yes, there are; I had a bite just before we left Cap Ferrino.'

She pushed up her loose lawn sleeve, and exhibited a scar, which he scrutinised intently, with a surprised and puzzled look.

'This is no mosquito bite,' he said.

'Oh, yes it is—unless there are snakes or adders at Cap Ferrino.'

'It is not a bite at all. You are trifling with me. Miss Rolleston—you have allowed that wretched Italian quack to bleed you. They killed the greatest man in modern Europe that way, remember. How very foolish of you.'

'I was never bled in my life, Mr Stafford.'

'Nonsense! Let me look at your other arm. Are there any more mosquito bites?'

'Yes; Dr Parravicini says I have a bad skin for healing, and that the poison acts more virulently with me than with most people.'

Stafford examined both her arms in the broad sunlight, scars new and old.

'You have been very badly bitten, Miss Rolleston,' he said, 'and if ever I find the mosquito I shall make him smart. But, now tell me, my dear girl, on your word of honour, tell me as you would tell a friend who is sincerely anxious for your health and happiness—as you would tell your mother if she were here to question you—have you no knowledge of any cause for these scars except mosquito bites—no suspicion even?'

'No, indeed! No, upon my honour! I have never seen a mosquito biting my arm. One never does see the horrid little fiends. But I have heard them trumpeting under the curtains, and I know that I have often had one of the pestilent wretches buzzing about me.'

Later in the day Bella and her friends were sitting at tea in the garden, while Lady Ducayne took her afternoon drive with her doctor.

'How long do you mean to stop with Lady Ducayne, Miss Rolleston?' Herbert Stafford asked, after a thoughtful silence, breaking suddenly upon the trivial talk of the two girls.

'As long as she will go on paying me twenty-five pounds a quarter.'

'Even if you feel your health breaking down in her service?'

'It is not the service that has injured my health. You can see that I have really nothing to do—to read aloud for an hour or so once or twice a week; to write a letter once in a way to a London tradesman. I shall never have such an easy time with anybody else. And nobody else would give me a hundred a year.'

'Then you mean to go on till you break down; to die at your post?'

'Like the other two companions? No! If ever I feel seriously ill— really ill—I shall put myself in a train and go back to Walworth without stopping.'

'What about the other two companions?'

'They both died. It was very unlucky for Lady Ducayne. That's why she engaged me; she chose me because I was ruddy and robust. She must feel rather disgusted at my having grown white and weak. By-the-bye, when I told her about the good your tonic had done me, she said she would like to see you and have a little talk with you about her own case.'

'And I should like to see Lady Ducayne. When did she say this?'

'The day before yesterday.'

'Will you ask her if she will see me this evening?'

'With pleasure! I wonder what you will think of her? She looks rather terrible to a stranger, but Dr Parravicini says she was once a famous beauty.'

It was nearly ten o'clock when Mr Stafford was summoned by message from Lady Ducayne, whose courier came to conduct him to her ladyship's salon. Bella was reading aloud when the visitor was admitted; and he noticed the languor in the low, sweet tones, the evident effort.

'Shut up the book,' said the querulous old voice. 'You are beginning to drawl like Miss Blandy.'

Stafford saw a small, bent figure crouching over the piled-up olive logs; a shrunken old figure in a gorgeous garment of black and crimson brocade, a skinny throat emerging from a mass of old Venetian lace, clasped with diamonds that flashed like fire-flies as the trembling old head turned towards him.

The eyes that looked at him out of the face were almost as bright as the diamonds—the only living feature in that narrow parchment mask. He had seen terrible faces in the hospital—faces on which disease had set dreadful marks—but he had never seen a face that impressed him so painfully as this withered countenance, with its indescribable horror of death outlived, a face that should have been hidden under a coffin-lid years and years ago.

The Italian physician was standing on the other side of the fireplace, smoking a cigarette, and looking down at the little old woman brooding over the hearth as if he were proud of her.

'Good evening, Mr Stafford; you can go to your room, Bella, and write your everlasting letter to your mother at Walworth,' said Lady Ducayne. 'I believe she writes a page about every wild flower she discovers in the woods and meadows. I don't know what else she can find to write about,' she added, as Bella quietly withdrew to the pretty little bedroom opening out of Lady Ducayne's spacious apartment. Here, as at Cap Ferrino, she slept in a room adjoining the old lady's.

'You are a medical man, I understand, Mr Stafford.'

'I am a qualified practitioner, but I have not begun to practise.'

'You have begun upon my companion, she tells me.'

'I have prescribed for her, certainly, and I am happy to find my prescription has done her good; but I look upon that improvement as temporary. Her case will require more drastic treatment.'

'Never mind her case. There is nothing the matter with the girl—absolutely nothing—except girlish nonsense; too much liberty and not enough work.'

'I understand that two of your ladyship's previous companions died of the same disease,' said Stafford, looking first at Lady Ducayne, who gave her tremulous old head an impatient jerk, and then at Parravicini, whose yellow complexion had paled a little under Stafford's scrutiny.

'Don't bother me about my companions, sir,' said Lady Ducayne. 'I sent for you to consult you about myself—not about a parcel of anaemic girls. You are young, and medicine is a progressive science, the newspapers tell me. Where have you studied?'

'In Edinburgh—and in Paris.'

'Two good schools. And you know all the new-fangled theories, the modern discoveries—that remind one of the mediaeval witchcraft, of Albertus Magnus, and George Ripley; you have studied hypnotism—electricity?'

'And the transfusion of blood,' said Stafford, very slowly, looking at Parravicini.

'Have you made any discovery that teaches you to prolong human life—any elixir—any mode of treatment? I want my life prolonged, young man. That man there has been my physician for thirty years. He does all he can to keep me alive—after his lights. He studies all the new theories of all the scientists—but he is old; he gets older every day—his brainpower is going—he is bigoted—prejudiced—can't receive new ideas—can't grapple with new systems. He will let me die if I am not on my guard against him.'

'You are of an unbelievable ingratitude, Ecclenza,' said Parravicini.

'Oh, you needn't complain. I have paid you thousands to keep me alive. Every year of my life has swollen your hoards; you know there is nothing to come to you when I am gone. My whole fortune is left to endow a home for indigent women of quality who have reached their ninetieth year. Come, Mr Stafford, I am a rich woman. Give me a few years more in the sunshine, a few years more above ground, and I will give you the price of a fashionable London practice—I will set you up at the West End.'

'How old are you, Lady Ducayne?'

'I was born the day Louis XVI was guillotined.'

'Then I think you have had your share of the sunshine and the pleasures of the earth, and that you should spend your few remaining days in repenting your sins and trying to make atonement for the young lives that have been sacrificed to your love of life.'

'What do you mean by that, sir?'

'Oh, Lady Ducayne, need I put your wickedness and your physician's still greater wickedness in plain words? The poor girl who is now in your employment has been reduced from robust health to a condition of absolute danger by Dr Parravicini's experimental surgery; and I have no doubt those other two young women who broke down in your service were treated by him in the same manner. I could take upon myself to demonstrate—by most convincing evidence, to a jury of medical men— that Dr Parravicini has been bleeding Miss Rolleston, after putting her under chloroform, at intervals, ever since she has been in your service. The deterioration in the girl's health speaks for itself; the lancet marks upon the girl's arms are unmistakable; and her description of a series of sensations, which she calls a dream, points unmistakably to the administration of chloroform while she was sleeping. A practice so nefarious, so murderous, must, if exposed, result in a sentence only less severe than the punishment of murder.'

'I laugh,' said Parravicini, with an airy motion of his skinny fingers; 'I laugh at once at your theories and at your threats. I, Parravicini Leopold, have no fear that the law can question anything I have done.'

'Take the girl away, and let me hear no more of her,' cried Lady Ducayne, in the thin, old voice, which so poorly matched the energy and fire of the wicked old brain that guided its utterances. 'Let her go back to her mother—I want no more girls to die in my service. There are girls enough and to spare in the world, God knows.'

'If you ever engage another companion—or take another English girl into your service, Lady Ducayne, I will make all England ring with the story of your wickedness.'

'I want no more girls. I don't believe in his experiments. They have been full of danger for me as well as for the girl—an air bubble, and I should be gone. I'll have no more of his dangerous quackery. I'll find some new man—a better man than you, sir, a discoverer like Pasteur, or Virchow, a genius—to keep me alive. Take your girl away, young man. Marry her if you like. I'll write her a cheque for a thousand pounds, and let her go and live on beef and beer, and get strong and plump again. I'll have no more such experiments. Do you hear, Parravicini?' she screamed, vindictively, the yellow, wrinkled face distorted with fury, the eyes glaring at him.

*　　*　　*　　*　　*

The Staffords carried Bella Rolleston off to Varese next day, she very loth to leave Lady Ducayne, whose liberal salary afforded such help for her dear mother. Herbert Stafford insisted, however, treating Bella as coolly as if he had been the family physician, and she had been given over wholly to his care.

'Do you suppose your mother would let you stop here to die?' he asked. 'If Mrs Rolleston knew how ill you are, she would come post haste to fetch you.'

'I shall never be well again till I get back to Walworth,' answered Bella, who was low-spirited and inclined to tears this morning, a reaction after her good spirits of yesterday.

'We'll try a week or two at Varese first,' said Stafford. 'When you can walk half-way up Monte Generoso without palpitation of the heart, you shall go back to Walworth.'

'Poor mother, how glad she will be to see me, and how sorry that I've lost such a good place.'

This conversation took place on the boat when they were leaving Bellaggio. Lotta had gone to her friend's room at seven o'clock that morning, long before Lady Ducayne's withered eyelids had opened to the daylight, before even Francine, the French maid, was astir, and had helped to pack a Gladstone bag with essentials, and hustled Bella downstairs and out of doors before she could make any strenuous resistance.

'It's all right,' Lotta assured her. 'Herbert had a good talk with Lady Ducayne last night and it was settled for you to leave this morning. She doesn't like invalids, you see.'

'No,' sighed Bella, 'she doesn't like invalids. It was very unlucky that I should break down, just like Miss Tomson and Miss Blandy.'

'At any rate, you are not dead, like them,' answered Lotta, 'and my brother says you are not going to die.'

It seemed rather a dreadful thing to be dismissed in that off-hand way, without a word of farewell from her employer.

'I wonder what Miss Torpinter will say when I go to her for another situation,' Bella speculated, ruefully, while she and her friends were breakfasting on board the steamer.

'Perhaps you may never want another situation,' said Stafford.

'You mean that I may never be well enough to be useful to anybody?'

'No, I don't mean anything of the kind.'

It was after dinner at Varese, when Bella had been induced to take a whole glass of Chianti, and quite sparkled after that unaccustomed stimulant, that Mr Stafford produced a letter from his pocket.

'I forgot to give you Lady Ducayne's letter of adieu!' he said.

'What, did she write to me? I am so glad—I hated to leave her in such a cool way; for after all she was very kind to me, and if I didn't like her it was only because she was too dreadfully old.'

She tore open the envelope. The letter was short and to the point.

> Goodbye, child. Go and marry your doctor. I enclose a
> farewell gift for your trousseau. Adeline Ducayne.

'A hundred pounds, a whole year's salary—no—why, it's for a——
A cheque for a thousand!' cried Bella. 'What a generous old soul! She
really is the dearest old thing.'

'She just missed being very dear to you, Bella,' said Stafford.

He had dropped into the use of her Christian name while they were on
board the boat. It seemed natural now that she was to be in his charge till
they all three went back to England.

'I shall take upon myself the privileges of an elder brother till we land at
Dover,' he said; 'after that—well, it must be as you please.'

The question of their future relations must have been satisfactorily
settled before they crossed the Channel, for Bella's next letter to her
mother communicated three startling facts.

First, that the enclosed cheque for £1,000 was to be invested in
debenture-stock in Mrs Rolleston's name, and was to be her very own,
income and principal, for the rest of her life.

Next, that Bella was going home to Walworth immediately.

And last, that she was going to be married to Mr Herbert Stafford in
the following autumn.

'And I am sure you will adore him, mother, as much as I do,' wrote Bella.
'It is all good Lady Ducayne's doing. I never could have married if I had not
secured that little nest-egg for you. Herbert says we shall be able to add to
it as the years go by, and that wherever we live there shall be always a room
in our house for you. The word "mother-in-law" has no terrors for him.'

DEAR PARENTS:

The story of Esther has several lessons to teach us. One is that anti-Semitism is as old as the Jewish people. You might use the story as a springboard to discuss this specific prejudice and prejudice in general with the child. Point out that the Jewish people are God's Old Testament people whom He loved—and loves—very much.

Present-day Jews do not accept Jesus as their Savior. But that is no reason to hate and persecute them. Rather we should love them and lovingly share our faith with them. We can learn from them too about the feast of Purim, for example, which recalls Queen Esther's victory and which Jews celebrate every year in late winter.

There's another theme running through Esther's story, the powerful theme of trust that dominates the Old Testament and is fulfilled in the New. Help the child realize ways in which God has been faithful to his trust too.

Finally, there is the theme of thanksgiving. The Jews' celebration of their release from Haman's persecution seemed to be almost a spontaneous thing, a great sense of relief and an outpouring of praise to the God, who delivered them. We too have cause for such relief and praise, for through His Son God has delivered us from the worst persecution of all—that of sin and death. What a reason to celebrate!

THE EDITOR